[*The Sweetness*] is a beautifully crafted portrait of life i
of great unrest...

—**Publishers Weekly**, Amazon Breakthrough Novel Awards

Sande Boritz Berger's impressive debut novel examines the lives of two Jewish girls, cousins, separated by an ocean and connected by brutal world events. Ms. Berger doesn't shrink from the rough history that informs her heroines' lives, but she mitigates its harshness with a deep measure of sympathy and hope.

—**Hilma Wolitzer**, author of *An Available Man*.

Sande Boritz Berger has created a rich novel about survivor guilt and innocence. The guilt is readily understood. The innocence is an original thought. How are people who survived the Nazis supposed to know how to behave in the face of unique evil? The Kanes (Kaninskys) endured the general experience of Jews who got out. But within that experience, they are also a family of complicated individuals, who pursue differentiated goals. It is this – their individuality, not unlike that of the Anne Frank family – that gives Ms. Berger's novel its power as a work of art.

—**Roger Rosenblatt**, author of *The Boy Detective*.

Original characters, against a backdrop of vivid and exact period detail, drive this highly readable saga of two uniquely different Jewish girls and their families during World War II. Warm, rich, and smooth as glass, their stories sweep over you and into your heart. A solid read for devotees of WWII literature, as much for its retelling of the ravages of the Holocaust, as for its insightful vision of a home front population shaken by shock-waves from abroad.

—**Mary Glickman**, author of *Home in the Morning*,
2011 National Jewish Book Award Finalist for *One More River*,
and most recently *Marching to Zion*.

Sande Boritz Berger has written an engrossing family tale filled with promise and hope while paying homage to the undercurrent of survivor's guilt that can coexist beside that joy. The Sweetness explores themes of morality, fate and death while illuminating how grief can effect even a generation removed, and even those thought to be spared. A great read that will touch your heart.

—**Judy L. Mandel**, author of *Replacement Child*

The Sweetness is one of those rare novels that knowingly informs us about not one but two very different worlds. Although we think we are familiar with the horrors of the Holocaust, we can never be. Although we assume we can understand survivor's guilt, we cannot. One of this novel's strengths, perhaps surprisingly, is its restraint. Sande Boritz Berger's skillful juxtaposition of two very different young women, their tenacity, their search, is searing. And memorable.

—**Lou Ann Walker**, Editor of The Southampton Review

Sande Boritz Berger's virtuosity is hard to beat. Her sensitivity to language and the lives of the Holocaust survivors in Europe is perfectly balanced with a deep penetrating vision of what their American lives became. Her book evokes CALL IT SLEEP, the most distinguished work of fiction ever written about immigrant life.

—**Martin Garbus**, author of *Traitors and Heroes*

As with all Ms. Berger's tales of domestic life, her narrative in this compelling debut novel is crisp and eloquent with her hallmark soft hand of familiarity. Though occurring across two continents, THE SWEETNESS is written with sensitivity to time, place, and a subtle eye on the will of humanity, revealing the passions and pains that infiltrate all families.

—**Beth Schorr Jaffe** , author of *Stars of David*

Sande Boritz Berger's novel, *The Sweetness,* engages our senses with its dichotomy of lives in Europe and America during World War II. The vile stench of the holocaust and the survival of a young girl amidst its horrors parallel the lives of American relatives who have escaped the slaughter, yet struggle to elude the guilt that resides with their endurance. The author has introduced a credible array of characters that convincingly carry the narrative forward, as they challenge the reader to decide how to best live with the responsibility of survival.

—**Allan Retzky**, author of *Vanished In The Dunes*

The Sweetness

The Sweetness

A Novel

Sande Boritz Berger

SHE WRITES PRESS

A version of a short story: "Rosha" appeared in The Southampton Review.
A version of the chapter: "Avram Must Choose" appeared in The East Hampton Star.
Cover photo of young girl: Rosha Duchin 1940—provided by author.
Fashion Designs: artist- Manette Duchin 1937—provided by author.

Published 2014
Printed in the United States of America
ISBN: 978-1-63152-907-8
Library of Congress Control Number: 2014934832

For information, address:
She Writes Press
1563 Solano Ave #546
Berkeley, CA 94707

This book is dedicated to
Murphy, Jack, Carly, and Zach
who taught me the true meaning of love
&
my beloved grandparents
forever in my heart

Hope is the thing with feathers that perches in the soul—
and sings
the tunes without the words—and never stops at all.

—Emily Dickinson

Part One

Rosha
Vilna 1941

Like most Friday nights, I wait for Poppa by the parlor window. Leaning against the pane where someone recently threw a fistful of stones, I run my fingers along the spidery break. Bubbe looks up from her crocheting (she is making a wool cap for me in this heat) and scolds. She warns me to move away from the window. There is such fright in her voice that all the hairs on my arms stand straight up. Yet still I don't budge.

"They might see you," Bubbe says, "no matter what Rosha, you must not let them see you."

But because I am not certain who it is that may be watching me, and Bubbe's words create even more curiosity, I take one more peek.

"I am watching for Poppa . . . what is the harm?"

Without speaking, my grandmother raises herself from the creaky, wooden rocking chair and marches straight across the room. The floor appears to sink a bit under each of her steps. My hand is twisted around a panel of lacy white curtain, one finger poking through a circular hole. It is a tiny hole, the center of a floral pattern, maybe roses, and quite convenient to peek from. Beside me now, Bubbe peels my bent fingers, one by one, from the curtains.

"Ouch," I complain, though the truth is Bubbe is not really hurting me.

"Never mind *mein kind*," she says. Bubbe takes my hands in hers and kisses the top of my forehead. Her breath smells from pickled herring and onions, and I allow her to kiss me, mostly because she has not yet smacked me. She smacked me just the other day, for the very first time, after she caught me scooping all the melted wax from a *Yahrtseit* candle. Bubbe had lit the fat white candle for her husband, my Grandpa Yussel, who died last year of something called *the pneumonia*. She slapped my hands until they stung, and told me I might have put the entire house on fire, and that an eight-year-old should stay away from matches, flames, and anything hot. But it was so much fun to pour the melted wax into the palm of my hand. As the warmth oozed between my fingers, I rolled the soft glob into many shapes, working quickly before the wax became too brittle like candy. I made a little bear like the ones Poppa says live inside Ponary, a deep, dark forest only a few miles out of town. Another time, when I didn't get caught, I made a giraffe from the warm wax of our *shabbos* candles.

"Come, sit with your Bubbe and let me hear you read." She licks her fingers to smooth my braids, and all I can think is now I, too, will smell of pickled herring and onions. Yet I smile at my grandmother as though I am really happy, and for a minute that's exactly the way I feel. Bubbe leans in and quietly examines my new front teeth that take up much too much space in my mouth.

So my question about what harm can come from standing by the window goes unanswered. Like most of the questions I ask, this one is also ignored. Instead, like always, someone stands up or moves around and says something that has nothing to do with my question, until I become very confused, sometimes a little bit frightened.

Still, most of the time, I try to do what I am told. Especially because of all the tears and sadness since Grandpa Yussel was buried, and Bubbe and Poppa threw shovels of red dirt on the long pine box that carried his body to the cemetery. Since then, Bubbe spends a lot of time with us up here on the third floor, although she still has her own place downstairs at 118 Sadowa Street. She and Grandpa Yussel have owned this building for years, since the family moved here, from so many different places—places like Riga, which is in Latvia, and Prague, in a country really hard to say, and some from as far as Budapest, which Poppa says is in Hungary but has nothing to do with hunger.

Bubbe is Poppa's mother, and so he often teases her that she spends too much of her time worrying about things that aren't real like me burning down the house and putting us out on the street. Once I almost said, *Poppa, now I see why you are so careful to always do or say the right thing, so not to make a mistake, but isn't that a little bit like worrying?* Still I kept my thought inside. Besides, I love to watch when Poppa thinks long and hard about a problem. I laugh when the pointy V appears between his bushy, dark eyebrows, and his tongue pokes in and out like bait teasing for an answer. And no matter how hard the question, Poppa always finds an answer.

In the past few weeks there are so many people asking questions, and lots of talking, talking that sounds mostly like worry. Whenever we go to the grocer, the butcher, or to the open market before each weekend, all we hear are deep sighs and the dry clacking sounds of people's tongues. When they whisper, their heads shake and their smiling eyes turn dark. All of this makes me think I am not paying good enough attention. That I am indeed "a dreamer" as Bubbe likes to remind me time and time again.

Wearing her Friday evening dress-up apron, Mama comes from the kitchen and heads straight for the scrunched up curtains. She pretends to be fluffing them out, but I know she is looking for Poppa. I know because of what she says next. What she has never said before.

"It is nearly sundown, and Mordecai is late. Could he have forgotten today is Friday?" She asks Bubbe. "No one in our *shtetl* is to be out after dark. Everywhere they have patrols." Mama stops talking as soon as she realizes that I am listening to her every word.

Here I am, split into pieces: one piece thinking about Poppa's whereabouts; the second, trying to understand the meaning behind Mama's words; and the third, wanting to go sit in Bubbe's mushy lap, to forget everything and help her roll a skein of the pretty pink yarn.

While Mama circles the table arranging the dinner plates, I squeeze my eyes shut and think of us all together before everything became so mysterious and confusing. Before I had to stay at home and learn my lessons, while some of my friends still go to our neighborhood school. Before the soldiers with those horribly mean faces stood guard on every corner and forced people to show their papers and empty their pockets for no reason at all.

I do miss running and playing outdoors with my friends, especially now in the warmer weather. It was only a few weeks ago when Mama and I went about our day preparing for *shabbos*. I remember how the heat from the sun settled on the cobblestones baking them dry after they were scrubbed clean by the shopkeepers. Mama and I counted the rainbows that danced upon the rocks slippery surfaces, brightening the dusty blues and silvery grays until the colors seemed to blend and disappear into the hot air.

If Mama hadn't seen the rainbows as well, Poppa might not have believed me. He might have asked if I was "stretching the truth" like, I'll admit, I do to get his attention. But because he wears his widest grin when he asks, I know a bit of truth-stretching is far from a terrible thing.

An orangey sun trailed behind us as we made our way down the aisles of the open market in the square, a few steps from the old synagogue. Though now we can no longer pray there in the evening. I miss watching the hundreds of candles flickering behind the *bimah* near the carved doors that hold the Torah and all the ancient scrolls. Everyone stands whenever they take out the Torah. They unroll it tenderly as if they are handling a newborn baby, and people, once even my very own Poppa, was called to read a story in special Hebrew words. When the rabbi shook his hand afterward, my face began to burn. I felt so proud.

That morning Mama bought two whole chickens from Mr. Gursky—one for Bubbe, which she says will last the week since Bubbe eats like a little birdie now with Yussel gone, and one for us. Although I don't swallow one bite since I looked up at the exact moment that Mr. Gursky chopped off the chicken's droopy head. All I can think about is the blood squirting like soda pop on Mr. Gursky's white jacket, and the red speck that landed on his nose. Yes, I am done with chicken. I will agree to some spoonfuls of potato soup, a slice of Mama's stringy flanken, but not one bite of chicken.

We made our very last stop to Mrs. Juraska, the candle maker. Mama likes to keep a supply of candles in the drawer next to the silverware, and so she stopped to chat with Mrs. Juraska, who sometimes invited me to watch her make her candles when she wasn't too busy.

That day, she took me in the back of her tented space and showed me hundreds of little tin molds and large blocks of paraffin. She had a box of glass vials filled with food coloring and dried wildflowers that she sometimes presses into the wax molds.

Although she's only a few years older than Mama, the candle maker looks as old as Bubbe. I wonder if that's because she has more children, and Mama has only me. I once heard her telling Mama that children can often rob the life out of you. Still, I wish Mama would have another. It would be real nice to have a baby sister, someone to cuddle and play with especially indoors. It gets very lonely here on Sadowa Street.

"Rosha, you are getting so tall," Mrs. Juraska said, her eyes widening with surprise. She was wrapping four long white candles in dark brown paper, reminding us they might melt if we didn't go straight home.

"She is much too skinny, my precious Rosha. Not *so* tall," Mama said, paying the smiling candle maker, "she eats like her grandmother. Food grows mold in her plate." Mama brushed my hair back with her fingers. I grabbed her pinky and held it tightly in my hand.

"Well, you never know Mrs. Kaninsky, one day she may be as big as a house or like the monument on the square, a real hausfrau like me. I, too, was once a scrawny child. Thank goodness my husband likes some flesh on his women."

Mama was trying to be polite when she laughed. Impossible, I thought. Me? A big girl? I gazed down the street to the bronze statue of a heavy peasant woman carrying a basket of fruit on her head. Pigeons have made it a favorite nesting spot, and there is always thick white pigeon poop dripping down the poor woman's face.

Just as we were about to leave, Mrs. Juraska held up two long tapered candles. They were peach-colored and wavy like hair ribbons. I had never seen such beautiful candles, but Mama shook her head no. "Nothing fancy for *shabbos*," she said. "Only pure white." Then she added, "perhaps another time," and I felt happy picturing the wavy candles glowing brightly on our dinner table. As soon as we walked away, Mama leaned in and whispered what I never knew.

"Mrs. Juraska is Catholic, and her husband is just like us—Jewish."

"Really?" I said, and then Mama said she'd forgotten something.

"Wait here, darling." Mama dug deep into her satchel then handed Mrs. Juraska a white envelope. I thought maybe she had forgotten to pay her for the candles, but then I remembered seeing a few *sheckels* pass between their fingers.

"What was that, Mama?" I asked when she grabbed my hand again and started walking toward home.

"What was what, Rosha?"

"Never mind, I answered." I was too hot, too tired and still nauseous thinking about that poor dead chicken.

But then a few minutes later, I asked Mama if the candle maker ever got the chance to light and enjoy the beautiful candles she made. Did she celebrate the Sabbath? Did she watch the candles glow against the walls and ceilings of her home through long summer evenings until their flames flickered and the wax disintegrated into nothing? But Mama just sighed loudly and said: "Enough Rosha, it's late, time to go home."

"Thank you God!" Bubbe and Mama sing out at the exact same moment. Poppa's footsteps sound like thunder. I imagine him climbing the stairs two at a time, each step stamped like an exclamation mark at the end of a sentence. When he enters the room, he is out of breath and sweating, carrying his suit jacket over his arm.

Bubbe stays glued to her chair, but she is rocking back and forth so hard I am afraid she may go flying across the room. Mama runs to Poppa, her eyes searching every single inch of him, her hands touching his face.

"I waited to light the candles, Mordecai. Is everything all right?" Mama glances in my direction; she remembers I'm in the room. "Never mind, we'll talk later. Go now, wash up."

I am standing next to the buffet table getting ready to do my special job, the one I do every Friday night. Carefully, I fit the tall candles into their shiny silver holders so they will not tip over onto the lace doily when Mama says the blessing into her hands before lighting them.

"Ester, I'm going to change out of my wet shirt," Poppa says, moving quickly past the women in this room. *His women*, he calls us. He places a kiss on the back of Mama's neck, nods to Bubbe who stalls in her chair. And just when I am certain he has forgotten me, he sticks his fingers into my ribs for a surprise tickle making me giggle and buckle at the knees.

"Please hurry Morde," Mama says, stealing away my fun with Poppa. He tosses his jacket across the arm of a dining room chair. Mama picks it up, shakes it out, then stares.

"What's that, Mama?" But like so many questions—the too many I'm told I ask, this one does not need an answer. What I see is as clear as the glass that used to shine brightly in our parlor window. Wrapped around the sleeve of Poppa's jacket is a cuff made of a gauzy gray cloth. Sewn into the middle and as large as a melting sun is a six-pointed yellow star. In the middle are the letters: J-U-D-E.

Mira
Brooklyn 1941

~

In stocking feet Mira Kane leaned against the gilded vanity to apply the final touches of her make-up. She was already on her third coat of mascara, mumbling aloud: *apply wet brush to cake, again and again, until your long black lashes look as though they are about to take flight.* And wasn't that exactly how Betty's looked, and Joan's, and Jean's? Over and over, the starstruck teenager studied the glossy pages of *Modern Screen Magazine* as if it were a medical journal describing an intricate life-saving procedure. Mira believed in the magical powers of make-up and how easily it camouflaged a myriad of imperfections. Like most of her movie star idols, she was intent on getting *this* right.

Though she'd already learned there was much she could not control, still, she kept on trying. It puzzled Mira that while most days she awakened incredibly hopeful, most of her family seemed perpetually braced for doom. She tried not to think of the *whys* and instead focused on her daily escape. Once dressed, her most skillful trick was to sneak from the house before her parents arose from their warm, cushiony beds. More than once they had made it a point to tell Mira they hated when she looked "painted."

"We don't understand dear daughter. Why is it you wish to look thirty when you're barely eighteen?" her mother had asked only last week after halting Mira at the top of the landing. Without commentary, her father had grabbed her wrist and ushered her into the bathroom. There he tossed her a blue washcloth and stood, arms folded, tapping his foot, while Mira scrubbed her entire face, until it was free of all pancake make-up, lipstick, and mascara, including the black beauty mark she had so meticulously penciled onto her cheek.

A rare fury began churning inside her, but Mira bit her tongue in an attempt to be respectful. Satisfied, but perhaps also guilty, having witnessed her daughter's obvious disappointment, Mira's mother cast her one small, pitying gaze. As if to say she'd truly liked the face Mira had created—the face that magically altered her into the glamorous young woman standing before her, concealing the more ordinary, very tall, and gawky teenager.

Today, though, luck seemed to be on Mira's side. As she tip-toed down the long hallway to the staircase, she heard her parents' loud harmonious snoring, rising and falling in perfect sync with Big Ben—the mahogany clock that stood like a staunch and dependable watch-man on the landing. The time was 7:05 AM, and in just minutes Mira would be flying out the door on her way to what she believed was the most exciting place in the world—New York City. There, and only there, she could pretend to be whomever she pleased. For a few short hours each day, Mira could block out all concerns about her parents' approval, a myriad of worrisome thoughts that draped her body like an invisible shawl.

Mira's eyes scanned the hallway, settling on the cut-glass knob attached to the door that gave entry into Aunt Jeanette and Aunt Rena's room, her father's two unmarried younger sisters. Next door, slept Roy—Mira's older and only brother, who reluctantly shared a room with the elder family bachelor, Uncle Louie. Everyone who resided in the house on Avenue T was employed by Kane Knitting, all but Mira's mother, Ina, who managed to keep herself occupied by chairing various charity benefits and luncheons attended by well-dressed, be-jeweled, buxom women, not to mention planning elabo-rate brunches and dinners for her own extended family.

Mira's aunts, Jeanette and Rena, worked in the sewing plant super-vising the finishing process of the knitwear, while Roy and Louie haggled with buyers from the company's plush midtown showroom. That is, when nephew and uncle weren't screaming their lungs out at their suppliers, or blaming each other for each and every faux pas, which lately seemed to be many.

Now though, during the early morning hours, before the familiar clatter of breakfast dishes, and the windstorm of hurled resentments, the atmosphere was blissfully tranquil, void of the dreaded commotion that was capable of sending Mira out frazzled, unnerved, and jittery—making it difficult for her to catch her breath. Today, alone in the home she had grown to love so much, she felt nearly royal and pretended she was roaming her own lavish, medieval castle. She knew she was privileged to enjoy such privacy, which was certainly a rarity for the only daughter of Ina and Charles Kane.

Mira's leg grazed a rough spot on the wooden banister. She could feel it snag one of her brand new stockings. "Ouch!" she said, "damn!" She leaned over and straightened her crooked seams, wondering if royalty ever cursed, and she tried to imagine what punishment might befall them if caught in the act. When she approached the vestibule, she was startled by Hattie, the housekeeper, who was spitting saliva into a dust rag while buffing a cherry wood table.

"Well, would you look at you," Hattie said, a hand pressed to her chipmunk cheeks.

"Shh!" Mira brushed past her and reached for her black portfolio that she'd kept on the floor of the hall closet. "Not one word, Hattie, please."

"But those stockings . . . Mr. K. will have himself a conniption . . ."

" . . . I promise they'll be off by the time he gets home for dinner. Besides, all the girls in the city wear nylon stockings. They're so much sleeker than my bobby sox, don't you agree?"

"Well, all right, but what about that ridiculous black speck growing out of your cheek?" Hattie pressed her damp fingers to Mira's skin. She stood so close that Mira smelled the Nescafe layered on her breath. She smiled noticing her own reflection in Hattie's toasty, brown eyes. Leaning in, Mira puckered her lips in place of a kiss before flying out the front door and knocking over the Borden's milk box and making a racket. As usual, Mira Kane was running late.

Today, Friday, Mira's favorite day, she wore a tailored knit gabardine suit with a peplum jacket—one of Kane Knitting's most successful and sell-out styles. She'd placed a pink sleeveless sweater underneath to compliment her nearly alabaster skin, and her face was framed by lush black hair, tied in a snood at the nape of her long pale neck. On this dewy summer morning, the lilac bushes and honeysuckle burst with fragrance while wasps and bees buzzed past her, frenzied. She stopped to pick a twig of honeysuckle and taste the sweet nectar. *Nature, better than breakfast,* she thought. She felt lucky to feel this unbound and free of cares, but then, almost instantly, she reminded herself it was best to never, ever, take anything for granted. To do so would be terribly irresponsible. Under her breath, Mira began her secret ritual of thanking God. If she forgot to thank Him, she was convinced something dreadful might happen, to either her or someone in the family. She didn't really mind the potent power of this fear or how it adhered to her like an extra layer of skin; she was certain she needed it to keep herself in check.

Only recently, Mira had come to the realization that her prayers could do little to alter the multitude of problems spreading rapidly through-out the world. A champion eavesdropper, she had heard clips of the radio broadcasts her father listened to most nights when he thought she was upstairs fast asleep. Often, and as she had done since childhood, she pressed her ear to her parents' door and recognized the desperate tones of fear resonating from their nightly pillow talk. The talk was always the same: why hadn't anyone heard from Mira's uncle, wife, and young child who were still abroad living in Vilna? For years, her Uncle Mordecai had written lengthy letters and sent photos of his little daughter's progress. It had been weeks now without any word. Whenever she'd asked questions, she felt as though she made everyone's fretting worse. So today, this especially beautiful day, Mira did her best to push these thoughts away.

Her long thin legs carried her down the terracotta steps of her parents' three-story brick and stucco home, and as she did most mornings, Mira paused to glance back at the house bursting with pride. She thought she saw the curtains moving from the second floor window, which was her parents' bedroom. Just in case, and because she felt especially jubilant, she lifted her hand and blew a kiss in their direction. She imagined them beaming, poking each other gently while whispering: *There goes our lovely young daughter. Look, isn't she something?* Again she was struck by a guilty thought: If they only knew how often she had dreamed of running away from that most opulent home, they would be shocked, perhaps heartbroken. She doubted they would ever understand how difficult it was for her to live in that house with her two unmarried aunts, a bachelor uncle, a girl-crazy brother, and parents who tracked her every move.

Lately, she could barely catch her breath. Yet, of course, she wished them all to remain healthy, regretting every single negative thought. For now all she could do was to work really hard and maybe one day, if she were lucky, her talents might be discovered. Then she might finally be out on her own, though living *completely* alone was something she could hardly imagine.

The Kane residence on Avenue T was the grandest of three Spanish style homes on a densely tree-lined block in the part of Brooklyn that intersected the highly trafficked Ocean Parkway. Over the years the area had become an integral part of the affluent neighborhood, home to mostly Syrian and Eastern European Jews, a place where many strolled, pushed prams, or relaxed on redwood benches while playing endless games of chess or catching up on the latest neighborhood gossip. It was not unusual to see a police officer in shiny black boots sitting astride a stately horse trotting up and down the designated center aisle, where bicycle racks sat parallel to manicured lawns, emerald and lush with the shrubbery of fuchsia and white azaleas.

As she reached the corner of Ocean and Avenue T, Mira spotted her bus heading west about a quarter of a mile away. To catch it she'd have to make a mad dash across two local lanes, the grassy rest area, and the double lane parkway. And, as she did most mornings, not waiting for the light, Mira raised up her large black portfolio as a shield from the oncoming traffic. She surprised herself that she could sometimes be so fearless, for someone possessing at least a million fears, or as her brother Roy preferred to label her—so incredibly idiotic.

"Thank you, thank you," Mira yelled, as cars came to a dead halt, short of a pile-up, allowing her to cross and reach the bus stop. Today her bus driver was Jackie, (she made it her business to know their names), and he shook his head having witnessed Mira's brazen routine many times before.

"Come on, Mira, move it, girl. Aren't you a little young to be sporting those stilettos? And hey, why's there a black bug crawling on your cheek?"

Her heart soaring underneath the sheer sweater, Mira tossed a nickel in the metal box and plopped down on the seat behind him. Out of breath, she loved the feeling of momentary exhaustion, as if she had just won a race. It was not unusual for Jackie to comment on her looks. She expected a remark or two and had no intention of answering him. Mira placed the portfolio horizontally on her lap, apologizing to the tiny woman sitting in the seat beside her whom she accidentally bumped. The woman smiled, mumbled something in a thick accent. The only words Mira deciphered were *shana maidele*, which was the Yiddish phrase for pretty girl. Though she'd heard the compliment many times before, she never truly believed it.

"Oh, thank you," Mira said, fiddling with a hairpin that had loosened. The woman reminded her of a munchkin from her favorite movie—*The Wizard of Oz*. Her feet didn't even come close to touching the floor. She wore her peppered gray hair short, and her eyes sparkled with flecks of green and gold. Mira detected the familiar smell of mothballs, most likely, from clothing stored away the entire winter. With a slight nudge of her elbow, the woman motioned toward Mira's portfolio.

"Vat is dat shana?"

"Oh, I'm studying fashion design." The woman stared at her blankly, so Mira referred to her outfit, sweeping her delicate fingers along the buttons, then gesturing to her own trim waistline. Still no response, so Mira unzipped her portfolio and the woman shimmied in closer. Their heads touched slightly as they looked through the several sketches in Mira's book. The woman reached out and ran her pinky over one of the drawings. Most were of attractive young women all wearing Mira's designs. Some actually resembled Mira, especially those wearing beauty marks placed precisely on the left cheek. The fashions themselves were upscale and elegant, not what anyone would expect emanating from an eighteen-year-old's imagination. Mira had used her palette of paints to simulate fabrics like shiny satins and textured velvets. Her brush strokes were so fine that she managed to create the illusion of fur trim along a sweeping dolman sleeve. She used sparkles of silver and gold glitter to indicate beading. Her teachers had constantly showered her with praise, and some of their notes were written in the far corners of the sketches: "Spectacular, Mira!" or "Mira, no doubt you have a future in couture."

Without hesitation the woman leaned over and planted a slightly moist kiss on Mira's cheek. The gesture felt so genuine that Mira was immediately overwhelmed with pride. Again, the woman spoke, and although Mira didn't understand a single word of what she was saying, she could tell by her exuberance that the woman was impressed, and so, to be respectful she nodded her appreciation enthusiastically.

As they neared her stop, Mira tucked several loose sketches into a folder and began gathering up her things. Though tempted, she decided not to share her very latest design, mostly because she wasn't quite sure the work was finished, and until she had given the creation every last drop of her scrutiny, it would remain under wraps.

The woman reached into her purse and pulled out a small photograph, its edges frayed and worn. She tugged at Mira's suit sleeve, coaxing her to have a look. It was of a young man in his early twenties. Leaning against the side of a brick building, though it was hard to tell, he looked quite tall and slender. His hair was dark, glossy, and parted down the middle. He wore an expression that was a mix of seriousness and impatience, as if slightly annoyed at being photographed. Mira instantly liked that. She could see he was handsome but without an air of vanity or arrogance like too many of the boys from her neighborhood. Boys from well-to-do families, boys like her brother, Roy, spoiled American boys, passively parented by their hard-working European folks. Perhaps all that giving was some compensation for the difficult adjustment they had when leaving their homeland, finally settling in a place where they learned to absorb the true meaning of freedom. Yet, *something was always lost or traded away...* Mira had heard her own mother say, using a tone that rang melancholy, as if she were perpetually homesick.

"Ah, so is this your son?" Mira asked, holding the photo close to her eyes and staring hard. She had the fleeting thought to keep it for herself.

"*Mein boychick*," the woman beamed. Her face became nearly angelic while she stared at the picture, as if also viewing it for the very first time.

"Well he looks like a very nice young man," Mira said, reluctantly handing back the photo. "And I can tell that you're very proud of him."

Just then Jackie called out to her, "hey glamour girl, now!" Mira turned to wave goodbye before stepping down from the bus. She didn't notice the woman standing, her arm outstretched, offering Mira the photo. The doors closed, and as Mira watched the bus pull away, a peculiar wave of melancholy swept over her, piercing all the vivacity she'd felt only moments before. She stood on the sidewalk routinely checking her portfolio and supplies. But as hard as she tried, she could not shake the awful tugging sensation—a sense that she had been terribly careless by leaving something of value behind.

Once more a surge of urgency took over as Mira mumbled a quick prayer to her ever-present God. Taking a deep breath, she fought the desire to glance over her shoulder. She counted slowly to three. Then finally, giving in to the ever nagging compulsion, she allowed herself one more look but saw nothing.

Rosha
Swept Away

~

All night long they whisper. Once I thought I heard Mama weeping, so I leaned against their bedroom door and tried to listen. I had to lie on the floor and make my body as flat as a soup noodle, but the only sound I heard was the squeaky squeak of their saggy old bed. Just like when I was four and used to jump up and down on it until they awakened, rubbed their eyes, and smiled. Someone, usually Poppa, would say, "Okay, Rosha, we see you, darling, you can get down now. But the bed was much too high, and Poppa had to slide out from under his warm covers and place me back on the floor. Somehow I always managed to climb up one more time.

Bubbe returned to her apartment soon after we ate our usual Friday night dessert: sponge cake sprinkled with powdered sugar and honeyed tea. She said she had things to do like gathering all her "important" papers. Though she invited me to come keep her company, tonight I wanted to stay here and watch what I call *the dance of the magic candles*. I like to have my own special race with them to see who shuts their eyes first, me or the two golden flames.

It is quiet now, the middle of the night, and the candles flicker wildly, their shadows climbing up the peeling walls. A tall flame bends like a ballet dancer reaching over to touch her toes. I slip from my bed to try and copy the movement of the flame. Twirling around the glowing room, I chop at the air with fluttering hands. Moving slowly about the parlor, I pretend to be a blind girl, and soon I feel it—a cool breeze, pushing from behind the curtains, finding its way through the crack in the window. I slip into a fold of fabric twisting around once, twice, covering my head, shoulders, and knees making myself the scariest of evening ghosts.

A glaring light bounces up and down from the street below. Though my eyes are shut and I am wrapped inside the curtains, its whiteness captures me. I am stuck. There is no place to go, nothing I can do. When I try to open my eyes, the light is so bright I feel like I am entering daylight right after a picture show. Bubbe's warning haunts me: "You must not let them see you," and my heart, this heart that has seen a scary ghost, begins to beat faster and louder. How do you stop a heart from beating this loud? *Okay, Rosha*, I say, taking a deep breath and calming myself like Poppa once taught me. I unwind in the opposite direction, and slide to the floor with a loud bump. I shimmy backward feeling the burn of the lumpy rug beneath my thighs. I will never look out that stupid window again. Never! From this day on, I will do what I am told.

Because I am very wide awake and the candles are still glowing, I think this time I will win the race. Hot wax drips and gathers on a glass plate. It is piled up like a snowcapped peak. I reach in to touch the warm, milky heap. With the end of a soup spoon I scrape the softened wax and roll it gently between my fingers. Working fast, yet not knowing what to do, I let my fingers move as if only they have the answer. I make a small head and place it on a long skinny body; it is a ballet dancer reaching for her toes. I run out of wax, and my dancer has just one leg. Though I am shaking from all the excitement I have already had tonight, I scoop wax from a pool settled around the flame. Before long the dancer has both legs and two pointy slippers. And then, on my last dip into the wax, both candles go out making the room pitch black. I hope Mama won't notice they burned out too soon. Once I heard her say that if you blow them out before shabbos has officially ended, it is a sin . . . and very bad luck. When I find my way into bed, I pull my blanket over my head. I say a little prayer and wish for sleep.

Sirens whine in the distance like hungry babies. When I open my eyes I find Poppa and Mama scurrying about the parlor. They remind me of a story I read about little pink mice running from a fat black cat in the night. They open and close drawers leaving things hanging out, and now they are like another story: pirates looking for hidden treasures. The clock on the mantle chimes six times. I sit up and rub my eyes. From my bed way in the corner of the room, I watch them move and mumble, move and mumble; they are hardly speaking to one another. I am about to shout: "Cat got your tongue, Poppa?" But I am supposed to be sleeping.

Mama stuffs some of my summer frocks in a cloth sack: a pair of shoes, some sweaters, and my books from the tall oak bookcase beside the buffet. She puts the bag on her shoulder, testing its weight, then returns two books to a shelf. I slide under the covers just as Mama lifts my match box from the dresser. Her jaw gets stiff, and when she looks over at me, I squeeze my eyes tight. After I count to ten, I open them to find her holding my wax figure in her hand. From here I can't tell if she is cradling my bear, the giraffe, or the brand new dancer.

"Oh Morde, look," she whispers, "this is what our Rosha does with the wax." Mama's voice sounds like there are bubbles stuck inside her throat.

"Put them with the rest of her things," Poppa says, and I wonder why they are packing up while the room is barely lit, why they are packing at all. An instant later, he is sitting on my bed shaking my shoulders. He leans in and pecks my nose too hard. He is unshaven.

"Ouch, Poppa, stop."

"Up, up Rosha. We have a busy day ahead."

"Why must we go to synagogue so early?"

"Rosha, Rosha, always with the questions. Okay, first you know I like to get a good seat up front to hear the wisdom of our Rebbe Lefkowitz. And second, after services a surprise trip. We are taking the train to visit Mama's cousins in Dolginov. You will like that my shana. It is a bit cooler there.

"What about Bubbe? Isn't she coming?" I can't imagine leaving Bubbe behind. We are all the family my grandmother has right now.

"Yes, of course, I will go down to make sure she is ready."

Rushing through the kitchen door, Mama hands me a green glass plate. On it she has placed a piece of challah covered with raspberry jam. I love the surprise and sweetness of the jam, the seeds crunching against my teeth, but it is too early, even for something as delicious as jam. Still, with both legs flopping over the sides of the bed, and Mama brushing my hair and hurting my scalp, I force myself to take a bite. I will be what Poppa calls *cooperative* and make him proud.

"I have to pee, Mama." It is better than saying she is making my scalp bleed.

"In a minute, *ess ess*." Mama knows me so well. It is difficult to get away with anything. It was so much easier last year when I was only seven.

"No time for braids today, Rosha, only a pretty ponytail and a big red ribbon. Ah, look at you, like a little Swedish doll with eyes like big blue saucers. Here, put this romper on, but first go finish your bread and jam."

"Mama, I..."

"Rosha, it will be long day. You must have some food."

Below us, on the street, I hear a commotion, what Poppa says happens when a lot of confused people gather together and everyone has something they want to say.

"We will leave right now," Poppa says to the air, the walls, the ceiling, the loud ticking clock on the mantle. "You have to carry this, Rosha." The bag is heavy but I am happy knowing my match box is inside. And the silver candlesticks—Mama wraps them in a cloth napkin and places both deep inside.

"Do we really have to go?" My stomach is turning over in my belly, and I want to put my fingers down my throat and make it stop.

"It will be fine," Mama says, but I see her glance at Poppa. There are tiny crystal tears in her eyes. She takes one last look around the room. The embroidered cloth from last night's dinner is spread across the table. Mama empties some ripened fruit into the cloth and places it inside her overstuffed satchel. Within seconds we are out the door heading for the stairs.

Out in the darkened hallway the air is thick with the odors of many different people. Old men. Young men. Ladies wearing too much face powder, some sprinkled with the sweet fragrance of rosewater. I breathe in the clean smell of babies. Everyone is clutching someone or something. No one looks happy. I am the only one with a big smile on my face, though my sack begins to feel heavier with every single step. But I am going on a trip today and should not complain. Mrs. Friedlich, who lives upstairs, is holding onto two sacks the size of bed pillows, while her husband carries their sleepy twins, one over each shoulder. Seeing me, one of the twins stretches his curved hand to touch mine. I am still clutching my piece of bread and jam. But I know not to give a small child food without checking first with their mother.

"Pay attention, Rosha or you'll tumble down the steps," Bubbe says, startling me. She joins us in line with one more flight to go. Bubbe is wearing a white, rose-patterned housedress, and her hair is tied in the red babushka she usually wears on weekends. I notice sweat pouring down her neck, almost the color of her dress.

"Where are your things for our trip Bubbe?" All my grandmother is carrying is a glass jug filled with ice and lots of sliced lemons.

"This is all I need my Rosha. Something to remind me of sweetness," she says, walking right beside me now.

"What?" If I could I would scratch my head. "But aren't lemons sour, Bubbe?"

"True, true, mein kind, but only by tasting lemons are you sure to remember sweetness."

I think I understand—how things can be different yet nearly the same. How everything has an opposite, like the colors black and white, feelings of joy and sadness, the tastes of sweet and sour.

We pass an old bearded man who we nearly trip over. He is sitting on a step, not moving, wiping his eyes with a handkerchief. All he is carrying is a prayer shawl, his *tallis* in a blue velvet pouch. On the back of his jacket someone has pinned that same big yellow star.

"Poppa, Poppa, do you have your star?" I make many heads turn around but I am worried that he has forgotten, and we will have to go all the way back upstairs.

"It's okay, Rosha," he tells me. "Not today, but it's okay."

Someone has propped open the doors to our building. Outside, the light is blinding, and I can't help but squint. There is a trail of people walking from every curve and corner. They are pushed together in one long line like a sash made of many different colors. I stop to pick up a stone, and Poppa yanks my arm. He scolds me to stay in line. He sounds terribly stern, really mad at me, and I begin to cry. I look back for Bubbe, but she has fallen way behind.

"God Morde, oh God," Mama cries. Her face is pale like the color of the early morning sky, and her lips are trembling. Mama has one arm hooked through Poppa's, and she looks straight ahead straining her neck above the crowd. I am crying louder now mostly because of the terrible shouting. There are so many mean looking soldiers walking among us, pushing some of the people with the ends of their guns. I don't know what they are saying, though it is something in German, and all I make out is the counting. And pointing. So much pointing, and I can tell they are angry. But I don't know why. What have we done? All we are doing is what we do every Saturday, going to synagogue, and later taking a trip to the country. Why are they pulling people aside and shouting, knocking some to the ground? Why is Poppa not saying anything? It is as if he's gone blind. I am straining to see Bubbe and her rose-colored housedress. So badly, do I want a taste of her ice water and lemons, so I can remember something good. And as if she had read my thoughts, Bubbe's hand flies up, like a butterfly, white and floating above the heads of so many people.

We are ordered to halt in front of the square, near the open market. Many of the merchants have already set up their stalls to sell their wares. I take a deep breath, feeling better that there are a few familiar faces, and knowing that our synagogue is so close by—steps from the marketplace. Today, I promise to listen to the wise words of the Rebbe. I will not let my mind wander. I will pray for forgiveness that I ruined our shabbos candles by stealing the wax.

"Mama, look, there's Mrs. Juraska!"

"Shhh!" A cry from Poppa.

The candle maker stands outside her stall watching all of us, the colorful parade of people moving through the town. The sun is heating the stones beneath my feet, and I think of all the lovely candles wrapped between waxed sheets waiting to be sold. But we will not buy anything today, never on the Sabbath.

"Morde, what is that smell?" Mama asks. Something is burning, like grease in a frying pan. Poppa looks around him and I follow his eyes. Our line is dividing like a snake that sheds its skin then leaves it behind.

"You, Ponary," one soldier shouts.

"You, Gogol, moch schnell!" The veins pop from the sides of the soldier's neck. He spits yellow water on the ground. There is more counting, and as we approach the front of the line my head is dizzy with the strange sound of numbers.

"That smell, Morde, tell me what it is, please!"

I am crying again, mostly because I can no longer find Bubbe's dress in the crowd, or her hand waving like a butterfly.

Poppa moves us into the line where they are shouting . . . Ponary! I remember that place now. It is a dense pine forest with the tallest of trees—trees that can touch the bellies of clouds.

"Come here my darling girl," Poppa says, scooping me up into his arms, holding me, his duffel bag, and mine. Mama presses her fingers into my cheeks and kisses me on my lips. Hers taste like salt, another opposite of sweetness. Then Poppa takes off weaving in and out between people. Just like the little baby, Friedlich, I stretch out my arms toward Mama, and stop my crying. I will go anywhere with Poppa, anywhere he wants to take me.

The soldiers do not see Poppa who starts running in the direction of the marketplace toward Mrs. Juraska. All the time he is reciting a prayer, and in between the words:

Baruch Atoi Adonai, he whispers my name, as if it were something really good, something sweet and sacred.

Mrs. Juraska holds a crumpled sheet in front of her as if she were about to hang it out to dry. "Please, please," are the last words I hear my father say. He places me in the candle maker's damp fleshy arms, turns, and is gone.

Mira
New York City

~

After a short ride in a stifling subway car, she began walking cautiously up Fifth Avenue. Mira hadn't yet adjusted to the height of her three-inch stilettos and was hoping to avoid lodging a heel into a crack on the sidewalk. Only days before, she had stepped out of her shoe, and while passers-by gazed in amusement, she hopped backward on one foot, inventing her own version of the Irish Jig.

She was aware of a strange, frenetic buzzing on the street. People seemed a lot more aggressive today, some actually shoving, as they headed toward their destinations, but maybe it had always been like that, and she just hadn't noticed. She passed a newspaper boy dressed in a leather cap and jodhpurs. He was waving a paper like a flag, shouting: "Extra, Extra, read all about it!"

Nazis Attack Soviet Union...breaking pact of 1939

Mira's eyes skimmed the headline, half taking it in. She thought about buying a paper then changed her mind. There was a weird churning in her belly; it was that fear again, bubbling up and ready to take over. No, she thought, as she lifted her chin and faced forward. She strode along the busy street imagining herself in a film—the star—Carole Lombard. Yes, that's who she would be this morning, even though Carole was much older and had bleached her hair platinum blonde.

Mira glanced at the gold *Bulova* encircling her tiny wrist. She hoped there'd be time for coffee with her one true friend at school, a lively, never boring redhead named Faye.

Located in the basement of the towering, green brick building of The Rockefeller Institute of Design was a small café, one flight down from the main entrance. It was the perfect place for a cup of coffee, a sandwich, or chatter and a smoke before class. Mira had resisted that nasty habit, and instead used her time at the popular 'slop shop' to scrutinize her latest design, and in this case, her assignment. Most days she was too nervous to have the other students snacking around her work, and for that reason she usually sat alone, trying to ignore their rude snickering and curious glances. At times, she worked hard to stifle her hurt feelings. She knew she couldn't cry. To do so might cause a mud slide of thick, black mascara, and wouldn't her classmates just love that?

Though Mira's unique look gave her an air of sophistication, it also isolated her from many of the other students. While most were in their own right eccentric and arty, she had taken her creativity to a higher dimension. In many ways she had become the living, breathing replica of her own designs and smiled smugly whenever she heard the expression: "Life Imitating Art." Yes, she'd thought, I can not only create my art, I can *be* the art. Her parents, she realized, might agree that often she had taken this concept a bit too far.

Thankfully, she was not completely alone, as Faye often surpassed her in the race for outlandishness. Faye adorned her petite body in long, flowing skirts and wore scarves in dark mournful colors, accessorizing each outfit with a floppy beret pulled over her flaming red hair. Both girls were attracted to each other from the first day of classes, and over the last year had become good friends. Without the burden of envy, common among most design students, they complimented one another, showing their generosity with astute suggestions on their respective designs.

On this particular Friday, Faye, dressed in a shredded chiffon boa worn over a strapless summery frock, entered the coffee shop ignoring the bold stares and took a seat behind Mira at a separate table. She slurped her coffee noisily, alternately humming *Tara's* theme just inches from Mira's ear, a reminder of her year-long obsession with *Gone with the Wind*. Most of Faye's latest designs were reminiscent of the Civil War era—gowns with thick velvet bodices and layers and layers of white petticoats. Mira was grateful for the warmer weather and her friend's recent switch to more conventional clothing.

"Faye, stop, you're driving me crazy. I'm trying to concentrate."

"Oh, Rhett, please, give me another chance. I know I can change," Faye recited, alternating between both Brooklyn and Southern dialects.

"You really are strange," Mira said, stifling a laugh.

"Oh yes, my dear, and you Mira *Kaninsky*, later changed to *Kane*, are *so* normal—just look at that get-up you've created. What exactly do you call that?"

"Obviously Scarlett, my dear, you forgot our assignment. We were to design a ball gown appropriate for the Fourth of July. This, my friend, is my own original *Americana* design. See? When my model here wears my gown and lifts her arms up, like this, the sleeves become a cluster of red, blue, and gold stars. The long tunic has stripes in red and gold, and I've designed open-toe pumps, trimmed with metallic stars."

"I like this. Actually I love it, but do you think someone might actually wear this?" Faye asked, blowing the feathers on her boa as she carefully studied Mira's artwork.

"Well, you're one to talk. Come on, let's see what you've got in that big fat book of yours." Mira turned around and pried Faye's hands off her design book.

"Oh, this is great!" Mira beamed. "You've designed a swimsuit, a two-piece, no, three-piece swimsuit!"

In lieu of one of her usual flowing gowns, Faye had created a simple two-piece swimsuit: Big red stars to cover each bosom and a full cut blue- and white-striped matching bloomer below. The costume was topped with a white sailor hat, a gold star stamped on the crown. Very Fourth of July, indeed, but her face seemed to ask Mira: was it practical?

"Okay, now tell me, who might wear this?" Mira asked, staring right into Faye's deep green anticipatory eyes.

After some seconds of heavy silence, then breaking out in laughter, they cried in unison, "us!" But Mira knew that their teachers, Mrs. Blanchard and Mr. Forte would not think Faye's design funny. Not because they didn't admire her creativity or raw talent, but because they were sticklers for discipline. And, an assignment was an assignment. But also, and for the very first time, there was a huge extra bonus: the winning design would be showcased in the school lobby, and press releases would be sent out to all the city's fashion trade papers and magazines, giving any young designer a head start in pursuing a career.

They risked being late for class, but Mira had an idea to salvage Faye's unique work. She truly cared for Faye, who, unlike the others, didn't exhibit an iota of envy. Using a soft grey pencil Mira quickly sketched a filmy tent dress over the swimwear. The suggestion was a sheer gown of organdy under which you could still see the stars and bloomers. Mira reminded Faye that they didn't actually need a customer, only a unique design.

Satisfied and eager, the friends ran down the long hallway, their precious portfolios pressed to their chests like shields. The commotion they made on approach caused Mr. Forte to open the classroom door. Faye was safe from being scolded with Mira by her side. As always, they took the two seats closest to the teacher's desk. While Mira sharpened her pencils for sketching, Faye stared back unflinchingly as another student whispered loudly enough for the whole class to hear, "well, get a look at Miss Brown Nose and Company."

Mr. Forte cleared his throat, and everyone's attention shifted to the front of the classroom. Today's lecture was on the methods of pleating used in formal wear. Front pleats, side pleats, soft pleats. Faye yawned loudly. She was already an expert in ball gowns, but since fashion seemed to be in a constant state of flux and feather, both girls had to keep up with the trends. Faye hummed ever so softly, enough so that Mira shot her fierce dagger looks while taking down pages of copious notes.

After the lecture, the students were allotted extra time to finish their assignment. Mr. Forte announced that he and three other staff members including a fashion editor from *Women's Wear Daily* would judge the work over the weekend. Mira peeked once more under the tissue paper at her "Flag Woman"—the name she gave her creation based on Faye's initial response. Her own instincts told her to leave the thing alone. But she had to force herself to stop fussing before she ruined her entire design. In order to have a shot at winning the contest, Mira knew the work needed to be extraordinary, its execution perfect. While sitting on both her hands, she allowed herself a final look. Her throat felt parched, and her heart performed tiny cartwheels inside her chest. This was it, she was nearly certain, the one good thing that might be her ticket to freedom.

The Women of Ave T

~

On Fridays, The Rockefeller School ended classes early so as to accommodate students like Mira who needed to be home before sundown for the Sabbath. The Kane family was ritualistic, though not religious, and so these rituals became the rules of the house—the stability of their large tumultuous family, some of whom had shared the same roof for over twenty years.

By late afternoon, Mira had licked off all of her lipstick. Her face appeared softer—flushed by the exhilaration of her day. She felt proud of herself for working so hard on her assignment, but then her mood shifted as she felt twinges of guilt for wanting something solely for herself—especially now, with more significant problems pressing on everyone's mind. A part of her believed a fashion design award commemorating Independence Day seemed trivial. Yet, just the word *independence* and its allure sent chills up her spine.

The instant Mira turned the big brass knob and walked through the front door, she was anointed in the fragrances of holiday cooking. From the kitchen, down the foyer in the back of the house, she smelled onions she imagined burnt to a crisp and wading in a pool of grease. She could distinguish the mingling aromas of roasted chicken, brisket, and the sweetness of two freshly baked challahs—their tops crisp, glazed, and bubbly. As she snuck up the stairs to change in order to prevent any commentary on her nylons, an entire culinary orchestra welcomed her. She heard the clipped questions like: so, are we out of chicken fat? Did you add more water to the broth? And cabinets opened and closed above the noisiness made of pots hitting against the porcelain sink, where water gushed like rapids through open spigots. The finale was the distinct sound made by seltzer as it squirted from blue glass containers with the force of a hydrant—seltzer, the quick reward for thirsty cooks.

After putting away her portfolio, and checking herself in the mirror, Mira dashed downstairs through the swinging doors that led into the steamy kitchen. Without saying a word, not even hello, she plopped herself onto her mother's wide lap. In turn, Ina clasped both arms around Mira's waist rocking back and forth as she'd done from the time Mira was a child. But now Mira's long legs flopped in opposite directions resting on the linoleum. Her mother's skin felt clammy, and the faded housedress she wore looked as if it was glued to her ample breasts.

"So, are you hungry, darling?" Ina asked, pushing stray hairs behind Mira's ear.

"Hmm, I have to think about it," Mira said, peering up at her mother's perspiring face.

"Nu? So this is something that takes a lot of thought?" shot Aunt Rena, who stood stirring the soup with a wooden ladle. Mira knew by the sarcastic tone that her aunt was in one of her crabby moods. Aunt Jeanette, who Mira affectionately called JJ, busy at the pastry board, looked up and smiled. It was strange, Mira thought, that no one ever asked about the events of her day, her classes, or to see any of her work. JJ was the only family member who had shown a genuine interest, sitting with Mira sometimes late at night, while the others played Gin Rummy or listened to the radio. As far as everyone was concerned, Mira was out all day, "killing time." Even her mother, who she was certain loved her deeply, could only muster up phrases like "Oh, that's so lovely, dear," whenever Mira shared enthusiastically about the goings-on at school. She had gotten used to their indifference and had learned to keep this segment of her life almost private.

Mira thought the women seemed more subdued than usual. No high-pitched chit chat to ring in the weekend. They were all work, no talk. She watched them move about the stifling kitchen like surgeons performing a delicate operation, except instead of sterile hospital garb, they wore their old reliable floral housecoats, each steadfast at their individual food station. JJ was the older of the sisters, supposedly thirty-three (though no one knew for sure, since her papers had been changed prior to coming to America in the 1920s). Her features were surprisingly Aryan: a full rosy face, perfect ski slope nose, steel blue eyes, and a deep cleft in her chin—the most notable Kane family feature, which Mira felt grateful to also have inherited.

JJ's round tortoise spectacles were covered in white flour. She stood in her fluffy slippers meticulously cutting strips of dough and placing them on a dampened towel. Soon Mira would assist spooning dollops of apricot preserves and chopped nuts onto the raw dough. Together they would roll the strips into perfect crescents, brush the tops with egg whites, and bake them until golden in the oven. The result was always prize-winning *Rugelach*—a hit with male suitors, who seemed fewer and fewer as JJ and Rena became older. Although she was still in her teens without a boyfriend or any thoughts of marriage, Mira was sometimes fearful of being stuck in the quick sand of the clan. She wondered if one day soon, she, too, might be preparing pastries for some unknown fellow, though she felt troubled by that fantasy, not, at all, enthralled.

Except for the notable Kane family cleft, Rena looked nothing like her older sister. Her face was so gaunt and angular that she appeared undernourished, and her thin lips stretched over a turned-down mouth of crowded teeth, perhaps one of the reasons she rarely smiled. Leaning over a huge porcelain pot, Rena slurped a spoonful of chicken soup.

"Mira, fetch me the batter from the icebox." Rena appeared uncomfortable with her sister-in-law's open display of affection toward Mira. Evidence of some deep-rooted jealousy often leapt from Rena, uncontrollably, stinging Mira when she least expected it.

"Come, make yourself useful," Rena said, acting more like a nagging older sister. Mira had to remind herself that Rena worked hard; most likely it was her fierce pride pushing her to earn her keep. She had come to this country clinging to her sister's hand at the constant beckoning of Mira's father, leaving behind her mother and father, who owned a successful haberdashery in their childhood home of Riga, a port city in Latvia. The youngest of five, Rena had been spoiled by her father's doting attention. Attention that could never be duplicated in America—especially here, now, in her brother's home.

Mira stood and washed her hands before moving to the stove. Rena then showed her how to roll neat little balls from the matzo batter before dropping them, one by one, into the steaming soup. It took mere seconds for them to rise to the top and triple in size like baseballs. Mira imagined hitting one over the fence at Ebbets Field. Beside her, Rena worked furiously scooping out the piping hot *kneidlach* and placing them in a striped bowl. When Mira tasted a misshapen one, it was so scalding she had to juggle it in her mouth.

"Careful!" Rena yelled, moving her own mouth as Mira chewed.

Across the room, Ina, looking flushed and exhausted, let out a long, deflating sigh. She was having difficulty attaching a metal grinder to the table where a large bowl was filled to the brim with boiled chicken livers, eggs, onions, and melted fat. By the handful, she began loading the top of the grinder, pushing the livers through while turning the crank in a circular motion. The result was a steady stream of grayish paste that had always reminded Mira of earthworms and kept her from going anywhere near the traditional dish. But everyone knew chopped chicken liver was Poppa's favorite dish, what he had labeled 'the tie that binds.'

As her mother began chopping the ingredients in a rounded wooden bowl, Mira noticed that she seemed especially troubled—lost in a mire of deep thoughts. She appeared decades older than her forty-six years, and her head shook uncontrollably, as if it were attached by a coiled spring. The shaking usually became worse whenever Momma worried too much. Though, it was rare for Ina Kane not to worry. Maybe she believed if she worried enough, really bad things might never happen or, at least, never again. Mira watched her mother quietly for a few minutes until she saw that she appeared almost frenzied by the need to please, the compulsion to make things better—as if preparing the perfect dish might alter the state of the world.

"Momma, dinner will be fine," Mira placed a hand on her mother's shoulder, but Ina appeared startled, like she'd journeyed to a foreign land and after embarking on a hot, crowded train had to strain in order to find her bearings. Then she stood and shuffled over to the sink where she began scrubbing an oval pan crusted with brown gravy.

*

For years, Mira had tried to forget, but her memory persisted like a swarm of mosquitoes hovering above stagnant water. Momma's shaking began one beautiful late spring day, much like today, right before sundown. Mira had recently turned nine, and her mother had promised that she could help bathe her baby sister, Sarah. For months, Mira had prayed for a sister. She already had a brother. A truly annoying one that she called: *Roy, Oh Boy.* One brother like Roy was enough.

She'd raced home from school that afternoon, and when she reached the front door she was surprised to find it locked. Standing on tip toes, Mira banged on the door using the hefty brass knocker. Although there was no answer, she heard muffled sounds and a piercing cry, like the cats she often heard late at night—an eerie sound that prevented her from falling back to sleep. Her heart began heaving in her chest, and she tried prying the metal mail drop open with her fingers. Layered underneath shrieks and howls, she could hear the shattered voice of her mother. Aunt JJ and Aunt Rena were sobbing, all the while trying to console her. They never heard Mira begging to be let inside the house, crouched and shivering on the doorstep, or sometimes she wonders, maybe they had? It was Mrs. Shein, the woman they'd labeled the *yenta* neighbor, who came running across the street to fetch Mira, to give her shelter from the sudden chilly air.

Later, after they had had a cup of tea, Mira and Mrs. Shein went searching the entire neighborhood for Roy. It took quite a while, but he was found playing stickball in a deserted field with some friends, something totally forbidden on Fridays. It was late, almost bedtime, before JJ finally came to take Mira and Roy back home. But first, she sat them down in Mrs. Shein's dingy foyer and told them what had happened. Mira recalled covering her ears, sure that she was about to hear something dreadful. She began to sing loudly and stomp her feet on the floor. *Take me out to the ball game, take me out to the crowd ...* so as not to hear the sting of her aunt JJ's words.

What would change Momma forever had occurred in this same jade and white tiled kitchen. In the amber glow of fading daylight, she had nursed her baby girl like she had done so many times before. She had been humming a quaint Yiddish lullaby and waiting for the exact time of sundown, waiting to cover her head with a circle of white lace before lighting the candles to recite the solemn prayer.

While steam erupted from the clattering pots, Momma sat watching JJ and Rena rush about, a blur of floral housecoats. Then, her baby, pressed into the folds of her warm, milky breast suddenly stopped nursing. Ina had lifted the child up so that the two were face to face. But baby Sarah barely made a sound, only the faintest whimper before she opened and shut her eyes.

There had been concerns just days before, though Sarah had not shown any significant symptoms of illness—the slightest fever, nothing more. The doctor assured the Kane family everything was fine. But the same day the baby died, her blood test came back revealing she had contracted a rare Staph infection. At first the family blamed the doctor, saying he was unkempt and his methods unsanitary. They thought he might have infected the baby during a routine check-up two weeks earlier, but it would be sacrilege to pursue the matter further since Dr. Liss was the most well-respected pediatrician in all of Brooklyn.

There were hours and hours of conversations that spun around the rooms like a toy top. Mira had hated when they talked on and on about Sarah. They could not change anything. No matter how hard she prayed for this to be some frightful malaise they would soon recover from, Mira understood, too well, that her baby sister was gone forever.

Immobilized by grief, Momma took to her bed where she was waited on day and night by JJ and Rena. Mira watched helplessly as they scurried about carrying tray after tray up the winding steps through the mahogany doors that led to the Kane's bedroom. The women glided in and out of their sister-in-law's room wringing their hands and fighting back tears. Sometimes Momma sipped from a glass of tea, nibbled on a biscuit, then slept for hours. Mira sat on the edge of her mother's bed waiting for her to open her eyes, but when finally she did, her glance was frozen, as if something she'd seen in Mira's face prompted a terrible memory. Momma refused to have the drapes drawn open or mirrors stripped of the white sheets placed over them during the week-long *Shiva*.

Throughout this solemn period Charlie Kane slept in the guest room on the third floor. He barely spoke to a soul, including his wife and daughter. If he were harboring his own grief, he carried it to his place of business, where, each day, he stayed later and later into the evening. He seemed oblivious to Mira's needs, almost tripping over her as she knelt outside the master bedroom night after night, waiting for glimpses of her mother, to hear her voice or some small assurance that she was all right and that life as Mira once knew it might begin again soon. The dreariness was evident in each and every household sound. Strained, muffled laughter and voices, once boisterous, rang apologetic in tone.

Then out of the grim bleakness, one warm June morning, Mira's father announced he was anxious to resume the ritual of Friday night dinner, followed by the customary game of gin rummy. And on Sunday he expected the usual feast for brunch. Everyone knew how proud Charlie Kane was of his grandiose home; how he longed to welcome business associates and their wives, cousins, and neighbors to partake in the sumptuous meals prepared by his wife and sisters. And, as if sensing his desires, after exactly four weeks of mourning, Momma rose like a ghostly spirit from her bed, put on her dressiest of housedresses and took her place opposite Poppa at the breakfast table. On that ebullient morning of her return, Poppa didn't make much of a fuss when Momma forgot to place his copy of the *Brooklyn Eagle* alongside his plate. He did mention, however, pausing his frenzied eating, that the fried butterfish she had prepared was especially delicious.

Mira would never forget the pure happiness she had felt that morning. How the sun's rays poked through the blinds covering the curved bay window in the breakfast room, making her squint when her mother appeared in the doorway. It was evident something had changed. Her mother's face lacked its milk and honey richness; her cheeks had thinned as if pleated, and then, there was the shaking. What was that strange tremor in Momma's head and shoulders? Hadn't anyone else noticed? From then on, Mira was reluctant to leave Ina's side. Though, at nine, she was hardly aware of how this silent vow of dedication might become an arduous burden—denying her the fulfillment of so many wishes and dreams.

My Name is Rosha

~

"Please child, don't cry. Don't you remember me? Marta Juraska, the candle maker," she said over and over again, while she carried me in her arms. She had wrapped me in a pile of damp sheets that felt rough and scratchy against my face. My body was pressed tightly against her big bosom. So tight, I could smell the salty sweat as it poured from her neck, and the stinky odor from her armpits that reminded me of soured milk.

She moved quickly though, like a zebra running through the jungles of Africa. I remember that above all the loud commands and sirens that would not stop, all I heard was the sound of the candle maker's heart. It beat faster and faster as she ran, pulsing through her big bones and soaked skin, drumming into my ears and muffling everything. Even the really loud scream I did not know was possible to scream. That was when Mrs. Juraska pushed her fist into my mouth. Surprised, I bit her fingers. I bit her so hard I could taste her blood.

I awakened later after what felt like an entire week's sleep. Mrs. Juraska's daughter, a blonde and skinny girl like me placed a basket on the floor beside the cot. Inside were some clothing, blankets, and a doll. At first, my hands reached out, but I quickly folded them behind my back. I noticed the doll's long braids, like a child from Norway or Switzerland. My teacher had once brought a doll like that to school and passed it around for all of us to hold. She told us to be careful because it was delicate and could easily break.

41

"She looks a lot like you, Rosha pretty and petite—the doll," Mrs. Juraska said. "We can fix your hair like hers if you want. *Sophie* has lots of ribbons to share with you, don't you, Sophie?"

Sophie nodded yes and lifted the doll from the pile and placed it beside me on the cot. She stepped back, looking as if she was about to curtsy to me. I glanced up at her face and could tell that the doll was very special to her. That she had decided to give her to me and was now saying a final goodbye.

Say thank you, say thank you, Rosha—Mama's voice rang in my head as loud as a school bell, telling me to be *gracious* and kind. But it was much too soon. I can't Mama. I can't. If I'd spoken, I would have shattered into a hundred pieces like Mama's crystal decanter that she used to pour the sweet wine for Poppa. The wine he sometimes placed on his pinky for me to taste when I'd begged enough times that he had to give in.

I reached for the doll, and though I wanted to hug her and keep her for my own, I knew I could not. I jumped from the cot and stared at Sophie's surprised face.

"Here, take her back, she's yours," I said. I hardly recognized the sound of my own voice. It sounded older, like ten or eleven. I pressed the doll to her chest though it rolled right off onto her rounded belly. Sophie caught the doll before it landed on the floor. She kissed the doll's head, rocking her back and forth, like, I guess, any mother would do with a child she thought she had lost.

Mrs. Juraska whispered something to her son, the boy she called Victor, who stood by staring at me, and not uttering a sound. She waited a bit and then nudged him forward. Finally, when some time passed, he put out his right hand and I shook it until, after a few seconds, he let mine drop away. Both children glanced over their shoulders at me as they turned to go upstairs. They looked a bit confused, as though they were afraid to leave and afraid to stay. Who was I? I wondered then. What was it about me that made me so different now, so strange, like the monkeys people study at the zoo? Mama had taught me never, ever, to stare at people, because it was rude.

"Come on, Ma," the big boy finally said, pulling at Mrs. Juraska's apron. "You said you would take us berry picking today." How I wanted to go with them, but I already knew I could not leave this chilly dark room that smelled like onions and wet leaves. I was the mysterious new stranger to them and *they*, not me, were a family.

Poppa's Doldrums

~

No one could predict how Charlie Kane might walk through the front door, even though his gruffness was part of his old world charm. Bad as his demeanor might be, Mira knew her father would never miss a meal, especially on a Friday night.

"Mira, I have something to tell you." Ina Kane stood rinsing her greasy hands under the faucet. "You should know, my love, your Poppa's got his doldrums again."

"Oh, I'm not surprised really. He's been acting very strange lately, disappearing downstairs after dinner each night. He stays there for hours. But thanks for the warning, Momma. I'll try my best not to aggravate him."

Just then Mira caught JJ and Rena glance at one another before quickly turning away. Hattie, who had been setting the table in the dining room, dropped what sounded like a complete set of silverware. In truth, Poppa's doldrums were certainly nothing new. They came and went as rapidly as the seasons, leaving in their wake a houseful of mostly exhausted people.

These somber moods, usually spurred on by a failing business deal, manifested themselves in strange midnight stalks. Clad in only his silk pajama top, which barely covered his pale pink thighs, Charlie Kane would spend the early morning hours surveying his possessions, floor by floor, taking stock, as if everything in the house were on loan. He started downstairs at the foundation including the ballroom, a huge rectangular room with a large crystal chandelier, where some of the walls were lined with images of relatives waving from ships, or worn sepia pictures of people who looked too bashful for the intrusive lens of the camera.

An entire wall was dedicated to Kane Knitting Mills fashion awards and recognitions in the form of framed letters from dedicated customers. Centered among all this adornment were several photos of past Knitting Associations Conferences spanning over two decades. Mira enjoyed gazing at these the most, because, through the years, her father had been diligent in drawing bold red X's over the faces of the deceased. One particular picture dated 1929, was a huge red blur except for Charlie and a few other survivors standing on the top row. Poppa often smirked while he scanned the Association's yearly group shot searching out the latest fatality after reading the obits, his other favorite pastime. If she happened to follow him downstairs, Mira usually heard him talking aloud:

"Bye, bye Max, you dirty bastard!" and "So, Sammy, screw you too, no more last minute returns now, ha!" Then he traveled upstairs to the dining room where he'd make himself a snack of salami on a slice of rye. Within minutes, his hiccupping began echoing throughout the house. Mira watched, concealing her laughter. After his snack, he'd push through the carved French doors that lead into the living room. Here he examined the baby grand piano, painted gold with dancing baby cherubs; he ran his hand over the Italian marble fireplace and kneeled on one of the many intricately patterned Persian rugs. Sometimes he chanted something reminiscent of a cantor's prayer, though Charlie Kane rarely attended synagogue. The chanting usually dragged JJ out of her bed, and as she passed Mira on the staircase, she gestured for her to return to bed. She would take over from here.

Then, while the others slept, JJ sat with her brother on the tapestry loveseat in the downstairs foyer. Sometimes their voices traveled, and Mira, curious and still dallying on the staircase, absorbed tidbits of their conversation.

"Charl, maybe you want a cup of tea?" JJ asked.

"Nah, nah" he'd say, waving his hand as if nothing could make things better.

"Charl, we are all doing fine, there are other accounts, please don't make yourself sick," JJ pleaded, while the clock ticked loudly. When they talked about the past, Poppa always expressed the same regret, "I never should have brought you and Rena here."

"Charl," JJ answered, "it's fifteen years already. We're all together, that's what matters most."

"Is that so? Fifteen years!" he'd answer, startled. He stared at his sister while she continued her efforts to pump him up.

"Look at what you've accomplished, see what you've built, this home, a family, the business." On and on, JJ chattered into the night, expending much affection and energy on her older brother. Finally, they climbed the stairs, JJ holding his hand, not noticing as Mira flattened herself against the side of the statuesque Big Ben, wide awake and eavesdropping.

*

By the time Charlie, Louie, and Roy returned cranky, tired, and overheated from their long day in the city, the women had changed into loose-fitting, simple dresses. Mira decided to slip back into the skirt and pale pink sweater she had worn to school, heeding her mother's warning, and hoping to cheer her father from his dreaded moods. He was constantly amazed by his "beautiful merchandise." Mira could have been wearing a brown bag over her head, but Poppa would definitely notice the sweater, stroke the sleeve, test the resilience in the ribbing, and check the label to validate what always made him the proudest: *Knitwear by Kane*. But tonight her father seemed especially distracted. He let his newspaper drop to the floor and struggled to stand from his chair. He took a very long time to clear his throat, and while the others watched, Charlie Kane said what he said every Friday night:

"We are grateful for this bounty God has put before us. May he continue to bless each and every one of us! Dinner is served." This time, Mira noticed, Poppa's head remained bowed much longer than usual, as if he were engaged in prayer. He then lifted his head and glanced at her for only a split-second.

"What?" Mira said, staring back, but he sat down, opened his napkin, and tucked it under his dimpled chin.

She waited, patiently, but there was not one exalting remark about the best-selling bouclé she had worn to dinner hoping to lasso his attention. Eyes fixed to his plate, he looked a bit dazed, off somewhere on Jupiter or Mars. Not that this kind of behavior was rare and unexpected. He consumed his meal greedily, ripping drumsticks off the roasted chicken, licking each of his pudgy fingers. Mira watched as the perspiration beaded on her father's forehead. Pausing for barely a second, he tugged at his high-starched collar before gesturing for seconds of everything, which he piled high onto his plate.

"Charl, slow down, where's the fire?" Rena asked.

You could usually count on Aunt Rena to break the tension but more often cause it. Unlike her brother, Rena would rather pick at her food than eat it.

"Look my sister, it's growing on your plate." Charlie replied.

Everyone knew what was coming next. His banter was so predictable.

"Think of all the *kindele* starving in Europe, those who do not have this smorgasbord laid out before them?"

"Shah, everyone . . . let's not talk about this now," Momma chimed in.

JJ squirmed in her seat. She loathed all references to poverty, to war, especially war. She had begged Charlie to send for Mordecai, their youngest brother still living in Vilna. Roy appeared oblivious, busy mimicking his father's zest for eating, while Uncle Louie didn't have to guess where JJ's mind had already wandered.

"Don't fret, sister," Louie said, rubbing JJ's shoulder, "I'm certain our Mordecai is fine. Remember that letter we received, what was it Charlie a month ago? He sounded quite pleased with his job. Shell Oil has remained strong in the European market, and our brother has carved out a nice position within the company. And that little one, Rosha, did you see how big she's gotten? Morde said he wants her to know her father's relatives, and so they plan to come soon, bringing the family to New York, maybe in September for the holidays."

A deep silence filled the room, like the calm at the end of a torrential downpour. Yet, nobody asked the question. How could he possibly come now?

Charlie nodded at Louie's response, but he kept his eyes fixed on his greasy plate.

"Yes, Louie, I know, I know," JJ said, "but I'd rest easier with him here."

"You must realize that Bubbe is much older now. Who but Morde can care for her now, especially with our Yussel gone?" Louie added.

Though he had put forth a great effort, JJ didn't appear one bit consoled by her brother's gentle words. Picking up on her mood, everyone at the table ceased chewing and became silent; eyes closed and fluttered opened as in a séance. The vibration and swishing of the brass ceiling fan circulating the air above them sounded intrusively loud, like a helicopter about to land.

Month after month, for more than a year, their fears had been intensifying, especially when they'd read about the incident referred to in the Jewish papers as *Kristallnacht*—"the night of the broken glass." It was an event spurred on by one determined teenage boy, who went about seeking revenge for his parents. They were Polish Jews who had been living in Germany when they were deported and sent back across the border to Poland only to be refused entry into their homeland. Hearing of the fate of his parents, the enraged son set out to shoot a Nazi official at the German embassy. Then, within hours, the Germans retaliated. Hundreds of synagogues were burned to the ground, their centuries old sacred Torahs destroyed. Jewish businesses were set on fire, their owners arrested and sent to labor camps, some to the first concentration camps, which were built originally for those political opponents of the Nazis. Gradually, Jews, homosexuals, gypsies, and other known dissents would be transported to these camps which were rumored to have brutal living conditions.

Although Charlie and Louie were cautious when discussing anything relating to the war around the women, they were constantly gathering information. Lately, what they heard made them doubt Mordecai would be visiting America any time soon. News, mostly terrifying news, had filtered through to them from business associates with connections to the Jewish Council overseas. Appointed by the Nazis, the council provided names and lists of Jewish scholars and businessman living in every town and village throughout all of Lithuania. These men bore witness to incidents and had first-hand information of the Jewish ghettos, labeled *shtetels*, which had become the newly restricted way of life for Jews like Mordecai, who against his brothers' warnings had decided to remain in their homeland. Both brothers had written to Mordecai urging him to begin the process of applying for visas for their Bubbe, him, his wife, and child.

He had written back insisting they were fine and that his employers at Shell promised they would do everything they could to have the family transferred to the States. But within weeks, fewer and fewer visas were being issued, and to make matters worse, the United States had in turn tightened up immigration. Just at the time so many Jews were trying to leave.

"Damn, son-of-a-bitch Roosevelt," Charlie had raged two years before, bile rising in his throat, after watching a newsreel that showed nearly one thousand German Jewish refugees on the *SS. St. Louis* being turned away from Cuba, and then suffering the same fate in Miami as the Coast Guard followed strict orders prohibiting those who tried to jump to freedom. Many were taken in by France, Belgium, and England. But hundreds of telegrams to the U.S. President seeking refuge for these lost souls had gone unanswered. How the hell was that possible? No matter how hard he tried, Charlie could not comprehend the injustice.

For the first time since he arrived on Ellis Island more than twenty years prior, he questioned those principles, once revered, that symbolized America as the one place on earth promising freedom. How could he not feel responsible for Mordecai's difficulties in relocating to the states? More than ever now he wished he had known the right people, sent money to *the source*—the really rich and powerful who had all the connections.

Rosha
Alone In the Darkness

~

Every day when they come down the creaky stairs, Sophie and Victor stare at me, saying nothing while they shuffle their feet against the wooden planks of flooring. They make little squeaks as they make circles with their toes, and I wish they would stop.

Go away. Please, leave me alone. Their mother, Mrs. Juraska, moves quickly past them holding a piece of old lumber that she uses as a tray. On it today she has placed my breakfast. I think it is breakfast, though I am not certain. I have not eaten anything in a very long time. I don't remember when I tasted food last. Was it that last Friday night, *shabbos* meal with Mama, Poppa, and Bubbe? Was it jam and bread on the morning we left Sadowa Street, or was it here, in this cot, the candle maker begging me to try to eat something, anything?

The room is dark but not so dark that I can't tell it is morning. There are small rectangular windows high on the wall near the ceiling. They are unreachable unless you have a ladder, but through a fan of cracked wooden slats, I can see the sunlight. Bold lines of yellow light fall across the sheet on my bed. I place my hand over the light, and it wraps itself around my fingers. I don't look up at any of them though I know they are all staring at me. These are the small things that I busy myself with to pass the time, since the day in the marketplace when I last saw my mother and father.

I can hear *their* father. He is in the corner of the room packing up bags and bags of rhubarb and potatoes. He glances over at me quickly as if he doesn't want me to know. He looks like he is about to talk but then mumbles something to himself and then changes his mind.

"Here's some nice hot soup for you, child," the candle maker says. Maybe it is lunchtime if she is offering me soup. I look down and notice there is something green and strange floating in the middle of the bowl. It looks like a frog's leg or maybe a twig of parsley. I shake my head no, though I am afraid that "*no*" might sound impolite or rude. Mama would want me to say *no thank you* or *maybe later*, but it is hard for me to speak. I have tried many times, but all that comes out of my mouth is a cool puff of air. My words are stuck somewhere far inside my throat, down way below my heart in the hollow part of my belly.

"Is there something wrong with her?" The big brother, Victor, asks, and his sister, Sophie, whispers for him to hush his *big mouth*.

"Rosha will eat when she is hungry, won't you dear?" When I nod, Mrs. Juraska smiles, then she places the tray on the crate next to my cot.

"But it's a waste, because her soup will grow cold," the boy says. He is much bigger than me, maybe eleven or twelve years old. His face is perfectly round with a thicket of ringlets like a crown circling his head. His eyes are the color of the sky on a summer afternoon after all the clouds have blown away, and someone looks up and says, *what a perfect day!* It is hard for me to look at him now. He scares me, and I can tell he doesn't like me, not one bit. His face is much too bright and filled with mischief.

So instead of looking at Victor, I stare down at my feet. Today I am wearing my white socks with the eyelet cuffs that Mama packed in my duffel with three other pairs of socks, one pair of shoes, two sweaters, two dresses, a wool hat made by Bubbe, my wax figurines, and our silver candlesticks. This is all I own, everything I have here in the candle maker's house—because this is all that is left. I have no smiles to share with these children. No words. Not even tears.

Letters and Lies

Charlie Kane sat at the head of the dinner table among those he cherished most concealing a hideous truth. He wondered how he was able to swallow down his food, to joke lightheartedly with his sisters. Had he always expected this outcome, or was he still in a state of complete denial? The letter, in its terse delivery, forced the reality he had failed to imagine.

He thanked God that Louie and Roy had been out to lunch when the letter was delivered to the office. Only Margaret, his seventy-year-old bookkeeper, had watched him collapse into his chair after he read it. Every muscle felt weak, as if his body were made of rubber. At least Margaret had shown the decency to turn away until he was able to rise to his feet, his face drained of color. He methodically tucked the letter inside his suit pocket and walked over to the water fountain. It was an easy place to cry, the cold water moving over his lips and mouth, then his eyes, nearly numbing the sockets. But nothing could deaden the images conjured up by the letter's cruel message.

Less than half a page, the letter was handwritten by a man named Isaac Shultz. He was a member of the Jewish Council and a former business associate of Charlie's with strong ties abroad, yet not strong enough to have helped him obtain the necessary visas. While this information came from someone he knew, its delivery lacked all traces of empathy and sentiment. Instead, the words pulsed like Morse code, reporting that Charlie's brother, Mordecai, along with his mother, wife, and child had been among those murdered by Nazi soldiers in Vilna during the first round up, just days after the German occupation. Witnesses reported their entire ghetto had been first sought out by a squad of Lithuanian and Polish youths, as ordered by the Gestapo to bring Jews out of their homes and onto the streets. Sometime later, Mordecai Kaninsky and his family were marched into the Ponary Forest where, along with over three hundred members of their shtetel, they were executed. Others had perished that day in one of the two synagogues that were set on fire. However, it would be impossible to determine if that had indeed been their fate.

Charlie had read the letter over and over again in the stall of the men's room, hoping to find an error, some mistake or loophole to negate the horrible truth. Tears fell onto his blue-striped shirt and golden tie as he rubbed his eyes desperately needing to remember the last time he saw his brother. Then what followed was the stabbing realization that his mother was also gone. He was catapulted to the time of his own brief youth and remembered how fair and patient she had been with the daily ruckus of raising three sons and two daughters. How her wry sense of humor had always kept them close and filled the days with laughter. What a cruel end, he thought, to such an arduous and loving life. Images of when he had last seen them bombarded him as if to say: remember this, please, do not forget us!

It was the summer of '36, when Charlie and Ina had traveled through Europe to celebrate their anniversary. They had first spent a joyful week in Paris visiting the Eiffel Tower, walking the Champs Elysée, and antiquing on the left bank. Ina had fallen in love with a teal and gold Limoges tea service. And, as was his nature, Charlie balked at the price, but eventually gave in especially when the antiquarian noted the prestige attached to such a rare item from a French courtesan. Not until they brought the item back to the states did they notice the so-called antique was made in Hong Kong.

On the last leg of their journey, they took a long tedious train ride to meet Mordecai in the gloriously thriving city of Vilna, what was called the Jerusalem of Lithuania. They had spent a week with him and his wife, Ester, and their little girl, Rosha. Charlie had tried to entice his brother with pictures of the house on Avenue T, the nearby beach at Coney Island, and summer trips to the Catskills. But Mordecai only glanced at the images amused, solidly stating his position.

"Look around you, *bruder*," he'd said wearing his proud smile. "How could any place on earth be more beautiful than here? Smell the air rich with the fragrance of wild flowers, and always, in every village square, people gather daily to listen to the most magnificent music. These are our roots, Charles. Someone has to stay and cultivate the soil. I must remain here to carry on the family name."

Mordecai's argument was indeed convincing, but Charlie believed the real truth was that Ester's parents resided in a nearby village. It was obvious neither of them had a glimmer of thought about leaving Vilna. Charlie, however, could not hold his tongue. He reminded Mordecai that Riga had been the *real* place of their family's roots— where their parents had owned a successful haberdashery for over forty years, and that his two sisters and two brothers were living in America, all waiting for him. By the time he and Ina were ready to return home, there was noticeable tension pulsing between the two brothers, but Charlie's pride and stubbornness kept him from attempting an apology.

It had been exactly a month since anyone had heard from Mordecai and now there was deep concern. Charlie had taken it upon himself to call the New York office of Shell Oil to see if any contact could be made through other executives employed overseas and was assured someone would follow up on the matter as soon as possible. He thought it likely that the oil conglomerate's top executives had been notified immediately of what had recently occurred in Vilna's ghettos and did not want to be the bearer of such tragic news. He guessed, as a thriving corporation, they wished to keep their distance of all things political, especially when it pertained to slaughter.

Tonight though, the burden fell upon him and only him to tell his sisters and brother that their worst fears had materialized. The atrocities that seemed to be part of another world had indeed penetrated theirs, and they, too, would never be the same. He knew the women of his house well and imagined they would grieve interminably. He believed the best thing for all of them now was to stick together. It would be his job to keep everyone close and involved at home. He had no choice.

The letter pressed inside his breast pocket like a piece of jagged steel, its message piercing all hope. Charlie could barely breathe. He needed to tell them, but his first business at hand was to deal with the problem of his daughter. He would forbid Mira to run off to California, especially now, all to chase some half-assed, crazy dream.

As if on cue, the tea kettle Hattie put up to boil sent its shrill sound throughout the room. Ina motioned Mira to help clear the table for dessert. She chided the men, begging that there be no more talk about Europe, the war, or any situation about which they seemed to have only bits and pieces of information. But Mira, especially, wanted to learn what was really going on; she couldn't comprehend why JJ was so fearful, and why she had not been given any concrete answers to the rumors she heard mushrooming throughout her school. Almost every day there was graphic talk about trains transporting Jews, both young and old, to special camps where many were being gassed to death. People rounded up and arrested just because they were Jewish? All these rumors were beyond her comprehension. Mira tried to block them from her mind. How else could she enjoy her life, which on good days was spread before her like a borderless picnic blanket set on a lush and rolling hill?

Charlie ended all his meals with a shot of his favorite schnapps. He pushed himself away from the table, walked to the mirrored bar and poured himself a drink from the cut crystal decanter. The honey-colored liquid went down in one swift gulp followed by the habitual, "Ahhh!" Dinner was officially over. Tonight, however, Charlie took a second swig. He asked Mira to stop clearing the table and summoned her into the grand dining room. She looked over to her mother for some sign or explanation, but Ina looked oblivious as she bent over to slip into a pair of comfortable shoes.

Mira felt her mouth go dry the moment her father slid the huge panel doors shut. She was aware of a strain, the rarity of the two of them being alone together. They took opposite ends of the cherry wood table. Poppa cleared his throat, averted his daughter's curious stare, and began to speak. Mira watched his mouth move, but the words did not register.

"Poppa? What, what did you just say?"

He seemed annoyed at having to repeat himself.

"I said I am not intending to continue your enrollment at that Rockefeller school come the fall."

His words pummeled her like a shower of hail. She rubbed at her temples. Still he would not look at her.

"But why?" she asked, swallowing hard.

"Because dear daughter, I am not Mr. Rockefeller!" His voice rose as he stared at her, noticing for the first time all night the pink bouclé knit she was wearing.

"What do you mean, Mr. Rockefeller!" Mira screamed back.

"Business is not good, Mira. We are having a very bad season. The orders are down 50 percent from last year. His hands began to tremble, but he pushed forward, perhaps afraid of jinxing his business.

Mira mustered up all her courage. "But Poppa, I gave up that scholarship to go to Pomona in California. Remember, you didn't want me so far away from Momma? You said this was the better choice, because I'd be home for a while. Here the tuition is only three hundred and fifty dollars. I have coats that cost more." She was whimpering like a wet puppy, her nose dripping, and the corners of her mouth drooped hopelessly down.

"Next year, daughter, you won't have such fancy coats, trust me." He rose from his chair without expressing remorse, without touching Mira's shoulder as he passed through the majestic dining room doors.

As soon as she heard the doors click closed, Mira lay her head down on the table and began to sob. It felt as though she were crying for all that had gone wrong her entire life. She cried remembering her baby sister, Sarah, and for her mother's perpetual sadness, for all the lost and frightened Jews ousted from their homes, and for herself, stripped of the chance to do the one thing she did best. Eyes blurry, she looked into the pools made of her own tears. They clung to the surface of the highly polished veneer like tiny crystal balls forecasting her dim future.

*

Charlie hid in the ballroom the entire weekend trying desperately to avoid everyone's prodding. Downstairs, he counted his red X's over the faces of his dead colleagues stopping at fifty. Sooner than later he expected he would join them, wherever they'd landed: whether up there, or down here, where it seemed to him like hell. He felt like an ogre, mean and unfeeling. All questions about his sudden decision to yank Mira out of designing school went unanswered. Almost immediately, everyone became Mira's advocate, and although he had warned the women that he was planning on ceasing his daughter's fashion education, most likely they took it as bravado, just another complaint about the recent sales slump in Kane knitwear.

But by Sunday brunch time, he could no longer contain his knowledge or prolong the agony. He sat down and stared into the platter of smoked fish. Mira entered the room with a deep sigh avoiding everyone's eyes. Hers were visibly swollen. Charlie took a nibble of rye toast then used the crust to push around the poached egg floating in his plate. Ina's steel grey eyes burned into him. He looked up once, gave her a quick smile, but knew he was not convincing. Putting down his knife and fork, he began speaking faster than he had ever spoken in his lifetime. At times, he broke into Yiddish and saw Mira and Roy straining to understand.

The aromas of food became repugnant, and already chewed food dripped upon the tablecloth. Spittle was folded into napkins. Louie, appearing ghostly, slurped water from his goblet. Jeanette and Rena clung to one another, hands clasped, while Charlie answered questions. The questions sounded as though they came from the shallow voices of terrified children. As he spoke, there were gasps, the stifling of a scream, as if stuffing something peculiarly rancid down the throat.

Roy yelled, "How the hell did you hear about this?" Others whispered, afraid that speaking loudly would render the news true. Are you sure this is not some horrible mistake? Dinner plates were left half full as everyone followed Charlie through the living room into the cool den. Hattie, whimpering softly, a nervous wreck by now, needed to busy herself, and brought tea on a large tray. The clatter made everyone look up as it exaggerated the impenetrable silence. Their devoted housekeeper stood there staring at them all, her eyes brimming with tears.

It had been years since the Kanes had endured the pain and suffering partnered with loss, the loss of their own little girl. Charlie knew that Ina, above all, never took the peacefulness of their lives for granted. He and the others watched in amazement as his wife was forced to draw on some powerful inner strength none had ever before witnessed. It seemed as if this terrible news had released every imaginable fear within her. Ina was always waiting for tragedy; but this time she was braced and ready. She walked around the den, touching shoulders, whispering consolations to everyone in a voice that sounded strong and full of compassion. Who else, but her, could comfort them now? It had fallen upon her shoulders to help those she loved prepare for their mourning. Ina did not shake, not once.

That is how Charlie left her on Monday morning, taking charge, practically forcing food down her sisters-in-law's mouths as they sat in the kitchen, noses and eyes red-rimmed and swollen from tears. Ina begged Charlie not to go to work that day, to remain home with Rena and Jeanette, but he and Louie had appointments with important buyers they could not afford to cancel. Both adamantly refused Roy when he suggested he take their place.

Outside the building at 1400 Broadway, Charlie nodded to his colleagues who shouted out their usual warm greetings. It was obvious that the Kane's bad news had not yet traveled to the street. Charlie was struck with the thought that last September during Yom Kippur, the holiest of holidays, he had complained, uncomfortable with the incessant growling in his stomach. He had been fasting with the hopes God would forgive him for his myriad of sins. Nothing too terrible, but they were listed right there in the italics of the prayer book, and he realized that he had committed his fair share of transgressions. He had nearly fainted when he was called up to the pulpit in order to recite the solemn mourner's prayer then for his dead father. He was relieved that he was not the only one called because, in truth, he had forgotten most of the sacred words.

And today, as if he had read the story as another bold headline in his daily newspaper, Charlie knew, without a doubt, that he and his family were no longer special. It was as though enemy bombs had exploded right in the middle of the Kane's majestic home—a lush and comfortable place filled with fancy Persian rugs, Baccarat crystal, and the finest of china—a place where all the Tiffany glass in the world could not soften the glare of such horror.

The war, once distant with all its underlying hate, had swept across the Atlantic snatching everything they held precious away.

Avram on Sadowa Street

~

Walking the eerily barren streets, Avram wondered why he was so foolish to believe that things might stay the same—that all his special privileges might continue even though there were fewer and fewer of them. *Them*. Wasn't he one of them? Still a Jew, or had he, in order to survive, adopted the demeanor of the SS soldiers involved in the daily actions of the special council, controlling and manipulating lies? He had heard of incidents whereby committee members were ordered to execute other Jews as a way to gain favors for their own family, but he had not yet seen this first hand.

Avram refused to believe rumors borne out of fear or speculation. Certain he was still being used, he knew that pride could not co-exist with the desperation for survival. He had been coached by others in his position: *You do what you have to do. You keep your eyes straight ahead and cold, as icy as theirs.* Yet, everywhere he went, Avram heard the enemy's bold pronouncements of ongoing slaughter. Who would be next? Whose kin was divided and sent away to die? The agonies would only be prolonged if sent to one of the death camps, where the fumes from the gas chambers filled the lungs of those left, all skeletal beings barely clinging to life. The SS patrolled everywhere. He saw them: standing, slouching, staggering in gutters, intoxicated from the liquor they had confiscated from the musty rooms of what had become an abandoned city.

His first time on Sadowa Street, the evening following the round

61

up, Avram realized he was about to take his privileges to another level when climbing the three flights to the Kaninsky's abandoned apartment. His heart thumped so hard, he wondered if it might explode. If caught, red-handed, he was prepared to say he had noticed lights being switched on and off behind the lace curtains and thought he better investigate. He found himself skulking through the narrow streets of the largely populated Vilna ghetto, feeling nauseated and guilt-ridden. His position on the newly formed counsel would not allow him to perform miracles. Many of the people who he and his father had known for decades had already mysteriously vanished and were presumed dead—their swift migration, never imagined. Mementos of those full lives, once lived in freedom, lay in the gutters like refuse. Everything had been ransacked by the soldiers and hoarded depending on its value. He left the ghetto quickly that first night fearful of being halted and delayed for questioning. Yet he knew he would have to go back. He had given her his word.

All this, and more, he had done and would still do for her—his Marta. He had never known another human being with a more gracious soul than his pleasingly round, soft-hearted wife. Avram had never been as good with people. Fifteen years later, he still questioned why Marta had accepted his proposal for marriage. She came from a family of hardworking dairy farmers, who had had little time to practice the stringent rituals of most Polish Catholics, unlike Avram, born into an observant Jewish family and three generations of cabinet makers. To be good with one's hands to his late father-in-law meant to be able to fix the bent blades of a till or the treads on a tractor while maintaining all your fingers.

Who would have guessed that the biggest gift Marta would give Avram, besides his children, was that she had been born Christian? Although he was a well-respected cabinet maker whose merchandise adorned the homes of many wealthy families, it was because of his wife that the children were not labeled: *Judeans*. To feel good about that often filled him with guilt and dismay.

His family had stopped speaking to him when he had announced his plans for marriage. He was the first in the history of Juraskas to marry out of his faith. But it was Marta who eventually went to his parents' home in Belarus to make peace and mend her husband's family. On her third try, the stern couple finally asked her to stay for dinner. Slowly they warmed to her, and then after Victor's birth, and her promise to have the boy circumcised, Marta was welcomed but always with cautious affection.

Now on his return to Sadowa Street, nearly two weeks later, Avram noticed a pair of broken eyeglasses, coins, a soiled scarf, a child's shoe, and the eerie head of a doll as he entered the swastika-signed building where the Kaninsky's once resided. He was struck by the deadly silence, unlike any silence he had ever known. It was as though the same sad collective record played on each and every *Victrola*, when suddenly the needle became stuck in its groove, spinning indefinitely while waiting for someone's hand to lift that needle—someone who had loved beautiful music.

Once inside the Kaninsky's finely decorated apartment, Avram found himself struggling to breathe. Lingering in the thick humid air was the pungent smell of the family's last Sabbath dinner, the tablecloths mussed and stained, a rotting pear lost in an over-sized silver bowl. Feeling like a thief, he slid open the buffet drawers and found the flatware and linens still intact. Everything was organized in a way that promised an immeasurable future of Sabbaths and celebrations. And then there were candles, melted, but not indistinguishable. They were ivory colored, pure and thick. His Marta's candles, of course. And now he was standing here, looking for what exactly? It felt as if he were looking at a mirror image of his life. *There, but for the grace of God*...go Marta and our precious children.

When he tried to open another drawer, it jammed. Avram's curiosity took over, and when he yanked the drawer open, a slew of sepia photographs toppled to the floor. He bent and reached for them noticing the shots of men and women, some wearing large brimmed hats and posed alongside a fancy automobile, the make of which he could not identify. In the background, reminding him of a small castle stood a beautiful brick and stucco home with windows of interesting shapes and trims. He grabbed a handful of the photos and carefully placed them under his shirt, against where his heart beat furiously.

In the corner of the room was a child's bed, what he realized must have been where Rosha had slept. The bed was unmade and two square satin pillows lay scattered on the floor. He sat down on the bed immediately aware of the thickness of the mattress. Not one complaint from the girl who slept now on an old sled, converted into a cot. He must figure a way to provide more comfort lest he ruin the child's frail bones.

The envelope from Mr. Kaninsky had said to look inside the pantry where there was a large bag of flour. He wondered if Mrs. Kaninsky had known the contents of the letter she squeezed into Marta's hand on that day in the marketplace.

"Here is your payment for the candles and for the lovely new table your husband crafted for us, thank you for everything," she'd said to Marta. If he were Rosha's father, he, too, could never have told his wife of his plans. She would have kicked and screamed before parting with her child, any of the children—even Victor, the most difficult— the angriest of souls. Victor shook his head and whined "no" before he could sit unassisted.

Avram found a paring knife in a drawer and slit open the only bag of flour. He purposely knocked down a few cans and boxed food to draw attention away from the heavy sack in case someone suddenly barged in. As soon as he split open the bag, he became immersed in flour, his pants a dead giveaway of some strange treasure hunt. Then just as he was about to bolt out the door, nerves gripping the muscles in his chest, Avram's fingers bent into a hard papery lump. He slid a folded envelope from the sack and shoved it deep inside his pants. Now, he thought, *even my balls are covered in flour.* On the cupboard door someone had thumb-tacked colorful postcards from America. He glanced at them, noting the return address: a fish market in Brooklyn, one from Paris, then shoved them in his back pocket along with an address book he grabbed next to an open jar of apricot jam sitting near the sink.

His stomach churned with nervous indigestion. On his way out the door, he shamefully took an apple that must have rolled underneath the dining room table. A small but beautiful table, he thought, admiring the quality of his own workmanship. It had taken him months to complete the French-inspired furniture for the Kaninsky's.

This was a table he and Marta could never have afforded. He was a carpenter who owned little carpentry, crafting wood for whoever was willing to pay for his artistry.

From the street below he heard voices bellowing in the night air. Avram peeked through a crack in the living room window and saw three soldiers directly across the street hoisting the body of an elderly person into a horse-drawn wagon. He guessed that the person, male or female with hair pure white, had stayed behind when the orders came to evacuate the ghetto. Perhaps, they had chosen suicide, deciding to control their own fate rather than to die at the hands of Hitler's beasts. Reality struck him like a fallen beam. If caught and interrogated, he'd better have a solid story, or his body might find its way into a wagon or maybe a shallow ditch.

Furious now, he grabbed two tiny vases and stuffed them in a small velvet cushion. Before leaving, he glanced back at Rosha's bed. A yellow crocheted blanket swept the floor. Maybe he'd come back for the blanket, and inspect the grandmother's place as well, though he guessed that would be nearly impossible. He was aware of the quiet, which at another time might have felt peaceful.

Once outside, he had taken no more than twenty steps when, out of a narrow alley, someone shoved him hard from behind. He gathered himself quickly trying to stand as straight as he could. The commandant, a young fellow not more than eighteen, with a fresh air face splattered with russet freckles demanded that Avram show his papers. As he handed them over, he felt the envelope left by Mordecai Kaninsky shift inside his underwear and slice painfully into his groin. When he tried to adjust his pants, the postcards and address book fell to the ground, but he dared not reach for them.

"What is that smell?" the officer asked, "and that white powder?" The commandant licked one finger and placed it on Avram's pant leg, then tasted it again. "Baking goods? Have you been cooking Mr. Juraska?" He let out a squeal of laughter, though not for a second did Avram let down his guard, especially when he eyed the Lugar hanging from the young man's belt.

"Ah, looks like we have a full moon," he taunted. Avram nodded in agreement, afraid to breathe. He imagined the children back home asleep in their beds, Rosha, the girl filled with terror, the smell of potatoes, rhubarb, and celery root nauseating her tiny stomach. Sophie making presents for Rosha, Victor, dreaming of pranks to try on the young boarder all alone in the chill downstairs.

Avram folded his papers and stuffed them back in his pants pocket.

"Not so fast. . . tell us what are you doing with these items?"

"I found them in the street sir, right over there." Hands trembling, Avram got mixed up and pointed in the wrong direction.

"Put down that pillow and empty your pockets, at once!"

So this is the young German youth, Avram thought. How easy they had learned the art of intimidation. He watched, knees shaking, as the soldier held up the vases, both *Limoge*. Though the style was probably lost on this mere child, he wanted the stash anyway.

"Thank you for the gift," he said smirking, and Avram noticed how his left eyelid drooped, lazily, as if half of him was falling asleep. He thought of killing him then, slitting his throat and watching the blood saturate the stiff collar of his uniform.

Only a sliver of him still believed that his special appointment mattered, which had given him a false sense of hope that his family would be spared. Within weeks of his joining the council, Marta had surprised him with an eight-year-old pale little girl, wrapped in soaking sheets, who was to be hidden away in their root cellar. A child appearing so shaken, she remained mute for nearly a week.

Some days he thought of himself as sewage. Wasn't that what you call someone who was about to steal from a child? An orphan? Mordecai Kaninsky had left more than a decent sum of money for his only child's care. The envelope Avram would hand over to Marta spoke of special needs, things like Rosha's terrible fear of the dark— oh, and when she learned that, how Marta would make sure to bring the girl candles every night Friday night, to remind her of the Sabbath.

Finally, they allowed Avram to leave. He knew not to look back or stoop for the postcards and address book laying in the gutter. He could only remember the one postcard with a picture of the Eiffel Tower but nothing else.

Once he returned home, Avram counted out half the money from the powdery envelope and stowed it away in his tool shed. He placed it in a rusty metal can that he filled to the brim with heavy nails and screws. On top he placed a silver mallet. The rest he stuffed inside a pouch. This money he would use for household expenses, especially when all the supplies dwindled to nothing. He convinced himself that all of his actions fell into the realm of self-preservation. He could not let his own go hungry. After all, by hiding the child, hadn't he and Marta risked their own lives? And so for the first time in his life, Avram felt shamelessly entitled.

Jeanette
Two Sisters Longing

~

From the day she had arrived at her brother's home, dizzy from the long and nauseating voyage, Jeanette Kane was intent on earning her keep. On a particularly warm Saturday afternoon, she orchestrated the summer transformation of the house on Avenue T, frenetically, as though the tempo of "Flight of the Bumble Bee" whirled inside her head.

Heavy velvet drapes were hand beaten by her lithe figure and stored away for winter. In their place, Jeanette arranged sheer organdy panels that beckoned the ochre glow of a summer sun. This busy work seemed to sooth her, kept her steady, but more than that, stalled her incessant weeping over her mother, brother, and little niece, Rosha—the child she had dreamed of loving after her brother arrived in America, the child whose birth announcement, a one line telegram, she had kept in her wallet for the past eight years.

She didn't remember covering the mirrors or placing wooden crates for seating in preparation for her family to mourn. She had trouble remembering anything these days—especially the tiny blue pills that she was supposed to take for her insomnia. She lay awake, night after night, trying not to think, but the loss was still so fresh, so raw.

On a rain-soaked afternoon, three days after Charlie had gathered everyone into the den to share the news about Mordecai, Rabbi Kirchenbaum of the Midwood Chapel had led the family into his study, prayer book in hand. The words to honor the dead had cut through the air with such force that the doors in the shul flew open with not a soul entering. Reality didn't sink in until the rabbi mumbled the most solemn of prayers, *Yiscah*, while he tore the black grosgrain ribbons pinned above her breast pocket, next to the heart.

Jeanette had glanced down at the polished marble floor expecting to see a puddle of blood. She thought she'd been stabbed with a small knife; the pain had felt that sharp. To make the pain worse, there was not a cemetery to visit or graveside service or place to mark with the stones of their sorrow. Eventually, her family would erect a monument in their brother's and mother's memory. All agreed it was time to invest in a family plot, though this was something that could never be discussed in front of Ina. She had made it clear many years before that she wished to be buried beside her baby, Sarah, in the old Jewish cemetery near the Belt Parkway, a place she often visited.

They drove home huddled together in a long black limo provided by the chapel. The family followed the rules of *shiva* for two days only: Tuesday and Wednesday. By Thursday morning, everyone returned to work, to the one place that remained the constant in their lives, promising the illusion of safety.

Today, desperately trying to keep her mind busy, Jeanette removed the dark, damask slipcovers from the dining room chairs. Over them, she slid covers of bright floral cotton, perfect for summertime. Her lips were pinched together holding onto pins. Rena and Hattie assisted, looking to her for cues; she pointed and they understood by her gestures what went where and when. The metamorphosis was nearly complete when the den's leather furniture was stored and white wicker pieces switched in its place. Finally, the big front porch that looked out on Avenue T was transformed to look like a French Manor house. Jeanette cranked open the bold green and white-striped awnings that surrounded the porch. She silently prayed that soon everyone would once again sit together on warm summer nights, relax on rockers, and wave to neighbors as they strolled down the tree-lined street. She pictured helping Hattie as she served iced tea in tall, frosted glasses, and Charlie, pacing the porch smoking one of his Cuban cigars, while

Mira returned breathless, chattering over some new movie she'd seen with her new friend Faye. Jeanette easily envisioned Ina, rocking quietly, perhaps with a needlepoint in her lap, her head shaking as she thought and thought about all that had happened, and what might still happen to each and every one of them.

Though she never talked about it, Jeanette secretly dreamed of a tall handsome gentleman to one day climb the terracotta steps and stop to visit. Someone new and outside the Kane's tight knit clan to break up the monotony—to keep talk about family business at bay. Perhaps, the caller might be one of the wealthy Syrian brothers from next door. Though Charlie had made it clear he vehemently disapproved of such "foreigners." He had gone as far as to impose certain physical boundaries like: his sisters and "those boys" could talk on the driveway, the sidewalk, but never on the front porch. Both Jeanette and Rena, more than once, had scolded him for his rude, prejudicial behavior but to no avail.

"Charl" they'd argued, "are you forgetting that we, sitting here on this very porch, are also foreigners?"

"It is different," he had answered, dangling the mangled mouthpiece of his cigar in front of their faces. "Those men are not from our village."

"So what," Rena reminded him, "neither are the Bleckers from Belarus or the Fegelmans from Lodz. With them, you like to talk plenty, no?"

But it was useless. Even though Charlie had no retort, he knew and she knew it was because they were from a part of the world he knew nothing about. Though they were Jews, they did not share the same customs or rituals that had brought the Kaninskys and their *landsmen* together in America.

The only way to cease the tiresome bickering was by taking a long walk, which the sisters did most evenings. More than ever they needed to escape as the sadness in the house beat like crows wings against their chests. Work was often helpful, but walking was reminiscent of their childhoods, growing up in Riga by the sea. But then, they might recall how much Mordecai loved to carve model ships from pieces of balsa, which would make them cry until their skin stung from the heat of lingering tears. They kept hankies stuffed in the shallow pockets of their cardigans, mementoes of their perpetual grief.

Tonight, while Hattie and Ina cleared the dinner table, Jeanette and Rena slipped out the door and headed to Ocean Parkway. The sky above them resembled a paper fan, folded into layers of indigo and gray. They hooked arms, walking and sharing complaints about their overbearing brother. Rena reached out and cupped a glowing firefly in her fist.

"Careful, not too tight, you'll kill him," Jeanette said.

"I'd certainly like too," Rena answered.

"I meant the firefly, sister."

"I didn't!"

Since the day they arrived in America the two were inseparable, but each suffered a private loneliness within the walls of their brother's home. Jeanette's came to her late at night when she tossed and turned in the confines of her twin bed. Sometimes, she wondered what it would be like to reach out and feel the warmth of a man's body lying next to her, to understand the real meaning of passion. She imagined herself with a lover, allowing him to touch her where she secretly ached to be touched. She longed to be held, to depend on the strengths of someone other than herself. As they strolled along, she saw benches filled with young men and women all gazing at each other, melded together in a heated embrace. A few seemed so intense that just the sight of them took her breath away.

But who was she trying to fool? Jeanette knew she'd push away any real chance of love or romance. She'd done it many times before. How could she ever really trust a man? Didn't they all want to... take ... then take some more...only to drop her as if she were yesterday's paper tossed in the gutter? Still she was drawn to all the faces; they appeared so in love. Busy hands moved onto shoulders, stroked long curvy necks, cupped flushed cheeks.

"Look at those two. They are absolutely disgusting!" Rena said, suddenly startling her. "Why don't they just find a hotel room?"

Jeanette could no longer avert her eyes from the sailor who began unbuttoning the top button of a beautiful older woman's blouse. Rena, although grunting in disapproval, seemed reluctantly transfixed. It was times like this that Jeanette wished she could tell her younger sister, but she knew it would serve no purpose. It might even distance the two, and they needed each other, at work, at home, and especially during long, desolate evenings. Maybe Rena would have blamed herself if she knew.

The sailor kissed the woman's neck and a carload of young men began to hoot and whistle. It reminded Jeanette of them: Two young soldiers. German. More and more of them occupying Lithuania, but they did nothing more than patrol the streets and buildings. Most of the time, they lolled around, always stinking drunk. It was the year before Charlie sent for them. Jeanette, then seventeen, had been riding her bike to the nearby village to buy flour and eggs for her special *Bundt* cake. Cooking was what she had loved best. She enjoyed a rare sense of control whenever she cooked. Riding back from the village she heard the distinct sound of galloping coming from behind. In the distance she could see two young men in uniforms approaching her rapidly. Scared, she lost control and the bike swerved suddenly, forcing her to lose her balance. She fell over on her side feeling her ribs bounce on the gravelly road. Her cotton frock caught in the spokes of the wheel, and she had to tear it free, leaving a gaping hole up to her scraped thighs. The soldiers brought their horses to a dead halt, dismounting instantly.

"Fraulein, are you hurt?" the pale one had asked.

"No, no, I'm fine," she said, gathering the few saved eggs in her apron, afraid to look up into their eyes.

"Here, let us help you," the darker one said, and then they began tossing an egg between them, laughing.

What could she do but join in? It was a game. She was nervous. They were soldiers.

"Jump, Fraulein," one shouted. "Higher, higher," he screamed, while the other lay down on the ground looking up Jeanette's torn dress and cheering. His hand shot up to grab her panties yanking them down to her ankles.

She couldn't remember how long the game continued, but she knew that she got cold, so cold that her teeth began to chatter. She thought she must have bitten her tongue. Her mouth filled with the taste of her own blood. She recalled the rough feel of their uniforms, her small, but strong hands as they tore at the stiff tan fabric. And the laughing. The disgusting grunts they made as they rolled over her body, one licking her ears, the other moving down her stomach pushing his tongue into every part of her.

They left her swollen and bleeding on the dirt road. Broken eggshells lay strewn on the ground and a thin line of blood mixed with the dirt. Only the familiar sound of galloping, loud at first shaking the earth, then fading softly in the distance, convinced her she was still alive.

This buried memory catapulted her to thoughts of Mordecai—her handsome brother, his wife and poor, sweet Rosha. She prayed that they did not suffer. That whatever happened to them happened fast. A gun shot, rapid fire, to put them out of their fear and misery, quickly sealing their fate. So many years had passed since she tasted the pebbles of hate stuffed in her mouth then shoved between her thighs with unrelenting bulbous hands.

What had changed? There was still so much poverty, war, and the senseless slaughtering of young mothers and innocent children. She understood all about this new America with its flag waving songs and promises of golden opportunities. But who, among them, was not tangled up in some intricate netting of unfinished business? Was anyone really free, not taunted by some dark and complicated past?

"Look, you're shivering, sister. Let's go back," Rena said, rubbing her hands briskly against Jeanette's arm.

"Sure, but I'm really okay. You'd think I'd be smart enough to take a sweater." Jeanette quickly turned off the switch that had led her back to childhood and began focusing on the endless responsibilities at work that saved her each and every day. She realized she sounded a lot like Charlie, but once she started, she could not stop.

"Oh, and speaking of sweaters, our customers are complaining that the new Woolon blends have a tendency to fall apart after a single washing. Macy's is threatening to cancel. If that should happen, I'm afraid our brother might drop dead," Jeanette said, as if she, herself, were a machine primed for perfection.

Rena, also, leaped to her place of family duty. "I've told him a hundred times to switch yarn houses. The difference is pennies to us yet he wants to pass the increases along to Macy's and Ohrbachs. The stores are holding tight and won't blink. So, I said, Charl, these are solid accounts, why not shut up and absorb the costs? But our brother is a stubborn ox. You know what I think," she went on, "I think Roy is nuts over Fleigelman's daughter, and that's why he continues to buy all that crappy yarn. I heard him on the phone with her just last week. He makes his calls from the factory so Charlie won't hear him. The little *schmo* ordered so much extra this month we should start manufacturing matching hats and gloves."

"Rena, shame on you. That's our nephew you're talking about." Jeanette knew Rena was right, but she was too busy overseeing that all orders were cut on time. She could not be involved in purchasing. If a machine broke down, it was Jeanette who had to find one of the imported German engineers to fix it immediately or production would be down for an entire day. The finishing was done by hand, workers paid for the total amount of piece goods sewn. All of the workers were immigrants, many mothers and daughters, and they were grateful to be earning a living. Miraculously, ten years before, during the Depression, Charlie had kept the plant intact, firing not a single one.

So many friends had gone down for the count. One successful coat manufacturer had locked himself in his garage and run the motor while his wife and three children slept, unaware. Charlie had paid for the burial and gave the oldest son a job in outside sales. Others fought their pride and came to Charlie for a cash loan. Here Charlie Kane had gloated just a bit, keeping a little black book of some of the prestigious family men he had helped out.

"I'll talk to him," Jeanette said. "Maybe he'll listen to me although I got nowhere pleading for Mira's return to school this fall. They haven't spoken a word in two weeks. It's killing Ina."

"He'd never let us loan her the money," Rena said, "Not with that foolish pride.

If he wants Mira by Ina's side, then that's where she'll be. Don't even waste your breath. He's nervous and wants us together, especially now. Who knows what will happen next?"

As they reached the corner of Avenue T and Ocean Parkway, two police officers on black horses tipped their hats. Tugging at Rena, Jeanette quickened her pace.

"Come on, sis," she said, "It's getting late. Our brother will lock us out, or you know we'll get the third degree on where we went, who we saw, and so on and so on."

"Well, what if I said we met two handsome men on horses?" Rena asked, but Jeanette had begun shivering again, watching the police officers as they grabbed the horses' reins and finally galloped away.

They returned to find the porch light still on, yet everyone had gone inside, everyone, except Mira. She was sitting on the green chaise, holding one of her *Screen Idol* magazines close to her face. Dressed in a short pleated skirt and high socks, her hair pulled up in a barrette, she looked like a Catholic schoolgirl, sweet and hardly sophisticated. As her aunts climbed the last step, approaching the porch, Mira jumped up and dropped her magazine.

"It's only us," JJ said, "why aren't you inside with the others?"

"They gave me some whopper of a headache tonight," Mira said. "First, Poppa screamed at Roy, then Roy screamed at Uncle Louie, and Hattie brought out tea to calm everyone, but a huge beetle flew into her ear and started buzzing so loud, she lost her balance, dropped the tray and all the glasses went flying. Momma and I tried to help her, of course, but Poppa went downstairs, in one of his lousy moods. I hope he stays there forever."

"Looks like we missed a really good show," Rena said. "Did Hattie get the beetle out of her ear?"

"Oh yes, it flew out as soon as the tray crashed to the ground. You should have seen the size of the thing. It's amazing Hattie didn't go completely deaf."

The sisters squeezed in on each side of their niece. Cold now, they each took part of her oversized cardigan and draped it over their shoulders. Mira described the beetle incident to them once more in full detail. Miming Hattie, she leaped up hopping on one leg, her head sideways. She smacked her ear while JJ and Rena howled, tears running down their faces. Just then, Hattie appeared at the front door, pressing a hot water bottle to the side of her face.

"Hush you girls, it's getting late," Hattie scolded. She was oblivious to Mira's imitation, intent as she was on locking up.

The three filed past her clamping a hand over their mouths. They rushed across the living room to the steps. As they tried to get up the stairs, a rare giddiness took over. Resting on the landing, Mira yelled, "Oh no!" This only made JJ and Rena laugh harder. Since she was a child, Mira was known to have a ridiculously weak bladder, especially when under stress. Hattie could tell by Mira's unique pretzel like position, she better quickly find a rag. Her boss would definitely notice the carpet stain and think that someone, maybe even his vengeful daughter, had sent him a hardly subtle, acidic message.

Later that night, as she lay in the darkness listening to the noisiness made by Rena's nasal breathing, Jeanette thought how in some ways they were all alike. That no matter their ages, she, her sister, and even her niece had learned to stow away their dreams and unfulfilled longings.

For hours, she tossed and turned imagining the lusty laughter of the dark, evocative Syrian brothers next door. Finally, she jumped out of bed and moved to the window where she lifted the curtain. Forcing herself to stare beyond the eerie blackness, Jeanette was overcome by an all too familiar sinking feeling. *I am the most different*, she thought, *the one carrying the ugliest of secrets.*

Mira
A Dose of Humiliation

~

Morning and night, imaginary words ricocheted between Mira and her father like a tennis match played with an invisible ball. Both were stubborn opponents waiting for the weaker to fold. One morning, as Mira neared the front door, she heard a sound coming from the kitchen that distracted her. She guessed it was Hattie, and thought she should stop and ask whether she'd regained all her hearing.

Mira pushed through the swinging doors leading to the kitchen and dropped her portfolio. Her father turned from the sink, meeting her eye to eye. It looked as though he had just poured himself a glass of something brown, what she guessed was prune juice. She froze, caught in her Veronica Lake look, her dark wavy hair cascading over one eye. Today she had on her favorite floral halter dress and open-toed red pumps; her rouge and lipstick perfectly matched the scarlet in the dress's rosebud pattern. Mira's hand flew up and rested on her cheek, her pinky spread out intentionally to shield her beauty mark. Her father stood still, clad only in a striped pajama top. Mira kept her eyes above his waist. Modesty, she knew, had never been one of her father's traits.

Without his glasses, he squinted, studying her as she breathed a long sigh of relief. Mira could tell that he had not slept. He had the Kane's trademark "valises under the eyes," as Rena had labeled them. The sun streamed through the window shades, a bright band of gold as if holding him at bay. Mira wrestled with the thought of whether to turn and leave the room or not. This was the last week of school at Rockefeller Design. Part of her wanted to stay home; it was so painful to have to go and sit through classes, though she savored every last minute. She felt the anger stirring inside her like thick pudding bubbling on the stove. Her father sank slowly into a chair, rays of sunlight grazing his bald head. He looked tiny and insignificant. But she had already given up the fight—the conflict that needled her daily.

He spoke first, a beat before her, "Well, good morning, daughter."

"Good morning." Arms folded, Mira tapped her toe against the tiled floor.

Her father sipped his juice, sip and "Ahh," sip and "Ahh." What was he waiting for? Maybe just another useless plea from her, or perhaps he expected another round of begging?

Mira understood that "no" meant "no." Charlie Kane rarely, if ever, reversed his decisions about anything. She also knew there were usually two reasons for every decision. The spoken one, which never seemed to ring true, the one that any normal person would question, and the unspoken, the *God forbid* you should push and probe, going into forbidden territory, reason. Here it was seamlessly clear: Poppa's bad season was the "spoken," and his desire to have Mira keeping company at home with Momma, the "unspoken." Yet, deciphering any of this craziness was far from easy. What Uncle Louie might toss his hands up to God and call: *Mesugah*!

Only recently she had felt a kind of explosion inside her brain. It was as if her childhood had blown up into fragments overnight, pieces impossible to put together. Had she been wrong for taking so much for granted? And then there was the stark realization that her father's actions might have nothing to do with her at all. The news of Mordecai's family had turned everything upside down. Life in this house was different now. Poppa was different. Her aunts and uncle were different. Though she tried thinking of other things, like school and boys, she knew that this newest loss had ripped open all the healing of the last terrible thing, her baby sister's death, leaving a deep cavern filled to the brim with misery and regret. So it helped, but only a little, to think it wasn't really all about her.

Without looking up, he said, "you look very pretty, daughter."

Surprised, she breathed in and hesitated. "But aren't those shoes a little high?" He couldn't even see them, he was just judging from her height, she guessed.

"They're quite comfortable, Poppa, they have what is called a stacked heel." Mira took one off, waved it in the air, and balanced herself against the wall. "Listen, I've got to run or I'll be late."

"Daughter," he said, attempting to catch her before she left, "maybe, soon you'll make the beautiful designs for Kane Knitting. Sweaters, suits, you think you can do?"

Mira wasn't sure she'd heard him correctly and made him repeat twice what he'd said. She didn't know whether to laugh or cry or throw the shoe straight at his head, but she thought by the softness in his eyes that he meant what he was asking. She would like very much to forgive him, to return to the way everything was, to run over and plant a kiss on the top of his glistening scalp, but instead what came sliding out of her mouth was her own question.

"Hmm, Poppa, are you certain you can afford me? You know, what with your financial problems and all." Then, not waiting for his response, she flew out the door, rushing as usual to the corner to catch her bus. She felt breathless from the splatter of words she'd muttered to her own father, guilty at having shown him such disrespect, but needing to, so she wouldn't crumble into a hundred little pieces.

Of all days for him to show some interest, she thought, while staring out the bus's dirty windows. Today she would have to tell her teachers she will not be coming back. She had ignored the last two notices about fall's tuition. It was also the day she planned to tell Faye. For weeks, she had played a charade with Faye, sharing her enthusiasm about their future as fashion designers.

"Hollywood, here we come," Faye loved to shout as they ran, always late, to the next class.

Pride tinted with embarrassment had kept Mira from telling her friend earlier. She doubted Faye would understand her father's surprising demands on her future. Their families were very different. Faye's father drove a taxi, and her mother worked long hours in a neighborhood bakery. They had a son attending Lincoln High School who delivered newspapers for extra cash. Unlike Mira, they lived in a small, two-family house on Bedford Avenue, just the four of them, renting the top floor from the owners. But Mira had noticed that they'd seemed happy, happy with so much less than her family on Avenue T.

Faye once shared with Mira how her parents bragged about their daughter's talent to everyone they met, and how it often embarrassed her. Mira imagined Faye's father driving his yellow cab and beaming while telling a customer about his soon-to-be famous fashion designer daughter. She pictured Faye's family sitting around their blue Formica table after dinner, drinking tea and marveling at Faye's latest creation. She could see Faye's mother, pudgy from eating too many pastries, howling at her daughter's outlandish swimsuit creation. All of these images were capable of making Mira sick with envy and then, because she liked Faye so much, consumed with guilt.

Mira grabbed Faye's arm before she opened the door to Mr. Forte's classroom.

"Listen, I've got to tell you. I'm not coming back next year," Mira blurted out surprising herself.

"What? Come on, you're kidding me, right?"

Mira bit the inside of her cheeks so hard, she tasted blood. "Nope, I wish I were, but there's important stuff happening at home. You know how miserable everyone has been since we heard about my uncle and his family, and now, on top of that, there are some major business issues. My father said he needs me, and so, he's asked me to design."

"That sounds amazing, Mira! You'll have a real head start. Maybe your Pop has some connections. You know, for us both when I finish next year. We'll still be a team, right?" Mira could feel Faye's growing disappointment. She saw her friend's brown eyes blinking, digging in deep, looking for much more than Mira was capable of giving her right now.

"Oh, you mean, Hollywood? Well, maybe we'll have to settle for Broadway."

"No, not me," said Faye. She sounded indignant now, her hurt feelings punching through a veil of pride. Faye lifted her chin, "I'll be designing for Vivien's next movie." She said this like a threat.

Just then, Mr. Forte opened the door, "Ladies, care to join us?"

They filed past him to their seats in rows parallel to one another. Mira, aware of Faye's eyes fixed upon her, forced a strained smile in her direction.

Mr. Forte waited until he had the full attention of the class. He cleared his throat.

"First, some announcements." He glanced down at the letter he held in his hands and then directly at Mira. More throat clearing.

"I'm terribly sorry to report the news that Mira Kane will not be continuing at The Rockefeller School in the fall due to personal matters." There was a burst of snickering from the back of the room. Faye turned to give everyone daggers. Mira leaned back stunned, as if she'd been shot with an arrow.

"Shh!" continued Mr. Forte. "Let us all wish Miss Kane luck and success in whatever avenues she explores!" He clapped his hands while few joined in, then he turned in a clumsy pirouette to face the blackboard.

Mira felt that the blood in her body had settled in her feet. She suddenly wished she was dead. Mr. Forte began sketching collars on the board and all that was heard were pencils being sharpened.

Faye leaned over and touched her shoulder. "Mira, are you all right?" No answer. "He's an idiot," she whispered. "He didn't have to make it public."

"Personal matters, personal matters," Mira mumbled aloud.

The impact of Mr. Forte's words confirmed her dilemma as a reality. At the end of the summer semester, she would never sit in these classes again. There'd be no reason to spend hours in her bedroom, late at night, with her sable brushes spread out on oil cloth, a fresh white board beckoning her to begin a new assignment. Here in this small design room with walls covered with sketches and swatches of coordinating fabrics, Mira had always felt more than just someone's teenage daughter. Here, she was noticed, respected, sometimes silently envied for her talent. This was the one place for her to feel separate, peaceful, in contrast to the invasive and calamitous atmosphere of home.

Minutes passed and she was unconsciously moving her left hand, finishing a neat Peter Pan collar and about to attempt the more challenging, Mandarin. She had not looked up from the sketchbook, not once. She glanced over to Mr. Forte's desk and noticed that the beige and brown stationery he'd read from was Kane Knitting's letterhead.

Oh yes. Poppa must have layered the schmaltz real thick, Mira thought. Momma called his blaming things on business: "putting on a poor mouth." The underlying reason filled with some insane ancestral superstition. *You must never tell people if you were doing well.* Never! Yet, Poppa was quite selective in this process. Mira wondered if her father was sparing her from some future disappointment. But she quickly dismissed that idea. He was taking control as usual. Just being himself. Mira pressed down on the pencil so hard, it snapped in half.

By lunch time, rumors began buzzing through the student lounge. One speculated that Mira Kane was five months pregnant. Everywhere she turned, someone gestured in her direction. Faye suggested turning the pregnancy rumor into a joke, telling Mira to wear a full empire dress the next day, but Mira's veil of humiliation prevailed. So much so that it marred the joy in having her design showcased in the school's lobby, her name appearing in six-inch red, white, and blue lettering. Now she thought her work looked bizarre. If only she could recede into the mustard-colored hallways instead of being sorted out for her special talents. What good was there in being talented, anyway?

On the bus ride home, she pictured the beige stationery as it lay opened on her teacher's desk. She tried imagining her father's, full-of-baloney, words:

> *Dear Mr. Forte:*
> *Let me take this opportunity to thank you for your kind inter-*
> *est in our daughter, Mira. We are pleased with the quality of*
> *education at the Rockefeller School of Design. As you know, our*
> *family is also in the fashion business. So it is with deep regret*
> *that I must inform you of Mira's withdrawal from your school*
> *due to the serious illness of Mira's mother. Unfortunately, our*
> *daughter is needed to care for her at home.*
>
> *Sincerely yours,*
> *Charles Kane*

Mira wondered if her father would go so far as to use Momma as the excuse for her having to withdraw from classes. She felt a cold rush of adrenaline and fear. Maybe her mother was sicker than she thought, what if...she were... dying of some mysterious disease? But no! Look how busy Momma was; everyday, except of course, Fridays, Momma got dressed up in one of her beautiful suits, under which she usually wore a silk blouse with a big starched bow. And always a jeweled stick pin placed in her lapel. Her auburn hair was always neat, pulled tightly off her face into a round chignon that she wrapped in sheer netting. She spent most days with friends, usually the wives of Poppa's business associates or involved with the wives of members of an organization trying to help the homeless Jews in Germany and Poland, of which there were now a huge population. Momma gathered merchandise for bazaars. She became the president of a fund-raising committee for the Brooklyn Woman's Hospital. Before each and every weekend, Momma spent the morning with Hattie going over the entire week's menu and preparing shopping lists. Sometimes she was withdrawn and distant, but not sick, Mira was certain she'd be the first to know if that were true.

As she walked down the tree-lined avenue, heading home, even the smell of the lilac bushes couldn't buffer the rage she felt toward her father. She thought of other possible fabrications in Poppa's, full of malarkey, note:

Dear Mr. Forte:

Due to extreme financial difficulties, unfortunately, I am forced to discontinue Mira's studies at the Rockefeller School this coming fall. Please accept my gratitude for the high quality of learning you have bestowed upon her. Hopefully, she will use these tools in the future.

Sincerely yours,
Charles Kane

Mira understood that her father had always been a very selective boaster. He made it a practice to play down his wealth with those in lesser positions. That, coupled with his generosity, insured his ongoing popularity. With his wealthier acquaintances, he had always been a fierce competitor. Never would they have a clue about his business troubles or failings. "Knock on wood. Thank God, couldn't be better," were his pet phrases whenever speaking to his business cronies or their bejeweled wives.

Mira landed home that afternoon feeling as if she'd been dropped like Dorothy and Toto from the whirl of a tornado. She didn't remember getting on the subway or the bus, but miraculously found herself on her doorstep. She'd endured a dreadful day, a day of deprivation followed by a sudden unexpected reward. Her shock was slowly percolating, then roasting, into anger. How was she to manage getting through dinner? On Mondays, the family usually partook in a meal of dairy— leftovers from Sunday's sumptuous brunch. Mira stayed in her room until she was beckoned several times by JJ.

During dinner everyone seemed more tired and cranky than usual. Aunt Rena commented on Poppa's "valises." Momma and JJ clucked their tongues in sympathy. Out of the corner of her eye, Mira watched her father dissect a small, fried kippered herring. He sat there intent on the chore, stiff as a fence in his starched collar and suit. The circle pattern in his tie was making her dizzy, almost queasy. She picked at her cheese blintz while watching Roy make love to a mound of potato salad, shoveling forkfuls into his mouth. He took a pause, hit his chest and belched loudly. He was quickly berated by Uncle Louie and Momma in unison.

Mira sat there, but her appetite was gone. She was struck by the thought that her life would be nothing more than a series of meals in this Wedgwood blue dining room, with foods served on delicate floral plates. Her existence would be as sterile as the starched white tablecloth, and the satin ecru napkins; if she were a color on a palette she thought for sure she'd be: Beige.

Daydreaming, Mira dropped a heavy sterling fork instantly shattering her porcelain teacup. All eyes turned toward her; even Roy looked up, his fork locked between full cheeks. They were paused, waiting for something. Come on, Mira. She could almost hear Faye, her built-in cheerleader, goading her to speak.

Mira cleared her throat. "Sorry about the teacup, Momma. Maybe it can be glued. I guess I'm a little excited. You see today I had quite a few surprises." She looked toward JJ, her reliable safety

net. "Remember, Aunt JJ when I was working on that design assignment, the one for Independence Day?" JJ, having bitten off a piece of
pumpernickel, nodded, her eyes widening. "Well, I wanted you all to
know that the school has selected this design, which I've named "Flag
Woman," for the once-a-year student showcase."

Mumbles of warm recognition were heard from the entire clan,
but Mira was not at all finished. "However, the best news is that the
Fairchild Garment Newsletter will be publishing my design on the
front page. A reporter came to school at the end of the day and inter-
viewed me. Oh, and Poppa. . . ." He looked up from his fish, his face
as red as the borscht and cream floating in his glass. "They wanted
to know my name, my parents' name, what my father did, and how I
saw my future. So I told them, Poppa, what we both know—I have no
future! No future, no plans, not anymore!"

Come on, Mira, you can do it. Faye's words rallied in her head like
a football cheer.

"For your information, I told them, Poppa, what you apparently
had already told my teachers. That my father, Charles Kane, president
of Kane Knitting, was having a terrible season!"

Mira left the table as quickly as she could, but through the reflection of the china closet, she could see everyone gaping at her father,
who, trying to appear innocent, simply shrugged his shoulders and
continued eating.

Roy called after her. "Hey, Sarah Bernhardt, wait up," but she just
kept walking, even though she was hungry as hell.

Ina began shaking soon after Mira exited the room. Rena
demanded an explanation from Charlie. "Why is she so upset? Who
did you tell you were having a bad season, Charl?" She was standing beside his chair waiting for his response. JJ sat, arms folded; her
expression did not fit her quiet demeanor. She looked as though she
wanted to strangle him. Louie turned his chair toward the ever raven-
ous Roy. He didn't like watching his brother squirm.

"What's the big deal? I wrote a little note to the school to explain
the circumstances. To tell them Mira would not be back. I thought
I'd save her the trouble." Charlie stood up; he was ready for his shot
glass.

"But Charl," Jeanette said, "maybe you should have told her before, that this was your plan. And what's this "bad season" business? This you discuss with strangers?"

"No, no, no" Charles waved his hand like a maestro trying to soften the many chords of concern. "I merely said there were some financial difficulties which would keep her from returning."

"So now the entire world knows about our personal matters."

JJ jumped in, "Charl, business is not so terrible. What is your real reason for this decision?"

"Enough, everyone! This is best for Mira and the entire family. Trust me."

He turned his back to the table and poured himself a Scotch from the buffet.

The others watched, but all they saw was the back of his balding head as it tilted in one quick deliberate motion.

Upstairs, Mira leaned against her bedroom door, her body quaking, her mouth parched. She half-expected someone, maybe her mother or Aunt JJ to follow her, to soothe her, but no one did. Something felt different, but she couldn't quite describe it. Was it all anger or some new confidence blossoming inside of her? Reminding herself that she had won the competition fair and square, she tried focusing on that recognition to fight the tears that usually followed whenever she stood up for herself, or fought for what was especially important to her. Why, she wondered, did everything have to be so hard?

Rosha
The Root Cellar

Each night I scratch a number onto the wall behind my cot. I use the tip of a fork that Mrs. Juraska left one night when she brought dinner. Today is the 18th day of the month and though I know the number is *Chai* and is supposed to be lucky, I don't feel lucky at all. Every day I awaken thinking: today is the day Poppa will come for me, but by evening when I can no longer see the slats of light, and all I hear is one lonely cricket far in the distance, my hopes disappear like the dust on a dandelion.

This room they call *Rosha's Room* has an odor that is quite familiar—a smell that sometimes makes me happy and other times sad. It reminds me of parsley, the fresh green sprigs that Bubbe always let me drop, one by one, into her special soup. The soup was special because she said she never, ever used a recipe, only the vision of her own mother chopping up all the ingredients, then tossing chicken thighs, necks, and vegetables into the simmering broth. The brew was quite unique Bubbe had said, after I asked my allotted amount of questions, because it could cure any ailment: a cold, the croup, even a bad bellyache.

Bubbe told me that her family had a root cellar in Riga, where they lived before her family moved south to Vilna. I wonder if it was cold like it is here, with only two small windows. In Riga, Poppa and his brothers and sisters could run free through fields and fields of beautiful wildflowers trying to catch butterflies with nets. They rode their bicycles and had to walk nearly three miles to a schoolhouse every day. But the best part was they lived close to the water, Bubbe said, her face turning rosy while she spoke. In summertime the family enjoyed picnics by the shore so they could watch beautiful sailboats as they pulled in and out of the busy ports. Then, one day, everything changed. Bubbe snapped her fingers. "Like that," she said, "in a blink of an eye."

When she spoke again, Bubbe's face looked like it had turned to stone. Something terrible had happened to Jeanette, her oldest daughter, though no one knew for sure what it was. On the way to the market she had fallen off her bicycle is what she told the family. When I questioned Poppa, he said he thought perhaps she had banged her head badly because she'd forgotten almost everything. Poppa said his sister had become extremely quiet after that time, keeping to herself after what he called "the incident." She was scared to leave the house, but managed to help with many household duties, because, as Poppa told me many times, Bubbe and his Zedde, did not believe in raising spoiled brat children—and I should never forget that neither did he.

Soon after this, one day, Poppa's two brothers announced they were going to live in America. Only in America, they would not have to worry about war ever again on their own soil, or the "Ruskies" patrolling their quiet streets and spitting on you if you looked at them with curiosity.

Before long the remainder of the family moved to Vilna. They hoped Vilna would be a much safer place to live. But that was so long ago; Poppa was a very young man, a rascal, he'd said. He felt he had to stay behind and take care of his parents and make sure his two sisters stayed safe. But then the brothers in America sent for their sisters, and still Poppa decided to stay in Vilna. I will never forget the way his eyes lit up when he said he was a "rascal." They glowed like sparks flying from a wooden matchstick—bright, green, and bursting.

I can tell that the father is home. But it is *their* father, not mine. Though it hurts my belly to hear the laughter above my head, upstairs, I like the sound of Mr. Juraska's deep voice. He sounds a tiny bit like Poppa. In the weeks since I have been here, waiting for news of Mama and Poppa, Mr. Juraska is hardly around. He comes home late, very late, after the house is very still. Some nights I think I hear a mouse scratching inside the wall next to my cot. But the walls are thick, made of wood and plaster and stones. The air is so tight that nothing could live inside these walls, not a mouse, a spider, not even an ant.

The voices are coming closer, which means soon I will have some company. I hope it is Sophie. But no, it is much too late for Sophie. Sometimes watching how carefully she studies me, I smile, then I stop quickly. When I smile though, it always feels like I have committed a sin. When Grandpa Yussel died and we sat in the parlor and guests came to visit our family, I felt the same exact way. I was afraid to laugh or be happy, even for a second. It was very difficult, especially when Bubbe's friend, Mrs. Boristofsky, missed the rocking chair and landed smack on her *tuches*. Lying here now thinking of Mrs. Boristofsky makes me think of Bubbe, how she laughed so hard we had to bring her a glass of water so she wouldn't choke.

I lift my face off the pillow to find Mr. Juraska standing below the narrow stairway leading to the cellar. Mrs. Juraska is crouched behind him, her head peering at me from over his broad shoulders. Her lips form one thin horizontal line. I think they are about to tell me I must leave. I begin gathering my things: everything Momma had packed for our special trip to my *tante* who lived close to the water.

"Please, sit down, Rosha. Marta and I wish to speak with you. Do you hear me, dear?"

"Rosha, there's no need to take your bag, no need at all," Mrs. Juraska adds. Her eyes are pointing downward as if searching for words between the boards of the scratched wooden floor.

"Avram," she whispers, "perhaps we should wait." But he begins, and then she interrupts him, immediately. "But nothing is certain, Rosha, there is always hope, always," she says, rubbing her forehead like she has a bad headache. But it is my head that begins to pound like a drum. While Mr. Juraska speaks, a strange sound escapes from my mouth— something like a loud yawn. Words travel through my ears as fast as shooting stars: He says: *Ponary, Fire, Camps.* I watch Mr. Juraska's lips because soon there is nothing, no sound at all.

And I think, please go away. I want to be left alone, to sleep for a very long time.

Nathan
Somebody to Love

~

"Wait until you see this place, Mira. There are photographs of all our favorite movie stars plastered all over the walls," Faye said, buttoning her sweater, one of Kane's not so terrific Woolon cardigans the company had dropped from the line.

"Great, but they better have something decent to eat. I hardly ate a thing tonight. I can't sit at the dinner table in my own house without feeling nauseous."

"I know, sweetie, and I am so sorry." Faye took Mira's arm as they walked out of the movie show onto the noisy street. It was already a little past nine. "Well, I don't know about you, but I loved that movie. Absolutely perfect performances."

"Faye, you do realize you say that every time we see that film? This makes four or five times for me, but it must be at least twenty for you. To tell you the truth, I'm starting to get a bit annoyed at Scarlett and her cocky attitude."

"Yes Ma'am, you are so right. I must agree."

"Faye, quit it. I'm not in the mood. So where's this place you've been raving about?"

"Two blocks up. Hmmm, I can taste that hot fudge now, and wait till you get a load of the cutie-pie guys that work there!" Faye took out a small square mirror to freshen her lipstick. Mira followed suit, then paused to give her dark eyelashes a quick curl. They walked, arms hooked, both dressed in flowing rayon dresses worn off the shoulder.

Mira towered over Faye, even in her low espadrille pumps. It was a good thing she'd worn them, since they had walked from the Canarsie Theatre all the way down on Avenue L. It was the only movie house where the film, in Technicolor, was still playing.

A couple of badly dressed skinny guys passed by them, then made an about face and began tailing them. Faye turned to sneer at them, hoping to lose them. Finally ahead, Mira spotted a well-lit marquis that flashed the name *Pearly's*.

"I've never seen this before," Mira said, "When did it open?"

"Just a few months ago. It used to be the old shoeshine place. Two of the shoeshine chairs are still inside. Kids love to sit in them while eating their ice cream."

"Hey, look, they're still following us," Mira said, glancing over her shoulder.

She and Faye purposely stalled and the guys filed past them to enter Pearly's where they took seats at the counter. Ignoring them, Mira and Faye chose a round chrome table closer to the entrance. Mira looked up to see an entire wall covered with silver framed photos of movie stars. Some actually had autographs with warm salutations written personally to Pearly. The black and white checkered floor was mopped clean. Mira, tickled by the lingering aroma of bleach, rubbed her nose and sneezed. Behind the long black Formica counter were two soda jerks and Pearly herself.

Mira was surprised that Pearly was what most might describe as unhealthily obese, yet with a beautiful glowing complexion. But Pearly's size didn't appear to slow her down one bit as she busily filled orders and carried a large banana split and two ice cream sodas to one of the tables. She moved about carrying the tray of orders with one hand; in the other, she gracefully held a long cigarette holder. After she served her customers, Pearly stood back and smiled, her bright eyes and high cheekbones nearly luminescent.

"She was once a Ziegfield girl," Faye whispered.

"I can tell she must have been really something, what do you think happened?"

"I'm not certain, but I think it had something to do with her not being able to swim. You have to know how to swim for most of the

Ziegfield's extravaganzas. Anyway, she saved her money, and she and her boyfriend decided to open this place."

"Shh! here she comes," Mira said.

"Hi ya! Look at you two gorgeous girls, so what'll it be?" Pearly took a drag on her cigarette and blew a perfect O of white smoke into the air. Mira and Faye watched, their lips unconsciously mimicking the dramatic movement.

"Ah, I'll have a chocolate hot fudge sundae," Mira said.

"Ditto," from Faye.

"Oh, but no nuts please," said Mira, hoping Pearly heard her as she sauntered over to the counter, giving the order to one of the soda jerks.

"That's not a real autograph from Katherine Hepburn, Faye," Mira said. "I have the exact same one. You can send away for it from *Modern Screen* for a nickel."

"No, are you sure?" Faye sounded terribly disappointed. She slumped back, perusing the walls for other possible phonies.

Mira studied the two soda jerks who were supposedly adorable, but the two real jerks who had followed them kept turning around and waving. She would not wave back, afraid of giving them the wrong idea. She knew the slightest recognition and a guy might assume you were interested in him. Especially cute guys like Donny Blau, the boy who lived around the corner. He was tall, very tall, and that made him appealing, especially to Mira. Donny drove a blue and white Cadillac convertible, his father's car, and he only dated the most stunning buxom blondes. Mira once saw four girls around her age pile into his back seat when he stopped at a traffic light. Sometimes, he would drive a bevy of young hopefuls up and down Ocean Parkway, drop them off and pick up four more. He never once looked in Mira's direction, but nevertheless she remained one of the many who worshipped Donny from afar.

"Two chocolate hot fudge sundaes, as ordered."

Mira watched the huge glass bowl as it was placed in front of her. Six goldfish could easily have made the bowl their home.

"Is anything wrong?" Her eyes followed the masculine hand all the way up to where the voice came from. Whoever he was, soda jerk, waiter, she could not turn from his gaze. He had the steely good looks of Tyrone Power, a younger version, of course, with thick wavy hair. She felt her heart leap as she stammered to answer his question.

"No, not really." What harm could a few crushed walnuts do to her digestive system? Though lately, thanks to her family, she had been going to sleep each night with a hot water bottle pressed to her belly.

"Are you sure?" he persisted.

His eyes were the deepest brown, the color of the syrup that dripped over the bowl. His uniform consisted of a blue-striped shirt with a black bow tie. Over that, he wore an apron that had some rather colorful smudges on it. Ah, must be Pistachio, she guessed. She noticed the apron was embroidered with his name: *Nathan*.

"No, this looks perfect, really." Mira could hardly keep the spoon in her hand from shaking. She wished he would leave so she could regain her composure. Was he actually waiting for her to taste the ice cream? She felt too shy to open her mouth in front of him.

"Well then, enjoy," he said as if it were an instruction. He tucked the tray under his arm, nodded to Faye and Mira, and returned to his post behind the counter.

"Didn't I tell you," said Faye, leaning in toward her friend. "Wait till you see Freddy!"

"I don't want to see Freddy," Mira said, nervously popping walnuts into her mouth, "I think I have just fallen in love."

"You can have him, he's the tall one. I'll take Freddy," Faye said, rocking her chair back and forth until she nearly toppled backward.

Before they knew it, the guys who had followed them pulled over chairs, joining Faye and Mira at their too small table. They introduced themselves as brothers: Joey and Frank Ferrara.

"Nice to meet you," Mira said, as she leaned to her right to catch a glimpse of Nathan, who was serving a tray of vanilla malteds to a group in the back. She straightened up quickly, realizing that she had practically put her head on Frank Ferrara's dandruff-covered shoulder.

"So, you girls come here often?" asked Joey, the shorter and plumper of the two. It sounded as though he'd been rehearsing that pick-up line for years.

"Aw, gee, no, couldn't you-all tell? Me and my sweet cousin here,

Mary Belle, are visiting from Atlanta," Faye recited in a most impressive drawl. Mira kept shoveling ice cream in her mouth to keep her composure. At one point she inhaled whip cream through her nostrils.

"Ya kiddin'me right?" Frank asked. "I thought for sure you were a couple girls from Coney."

"Thought wrong, honey chil'. You see, that be our cousin Rory, over there, working that counter. He'll be driving us home shortly."

Listening to Faye, Mira's eyes nearly popped out of her head. Faye was getting in deeper and deeper. Mira thought of telling her she ought to look into acting the second she got to Hollywood. She hoped these guys would get up and leave, but they didn't budge.

"Two southern belles. Well, hey, ain't that somethin' Frankie?"

God, save me, thought Mira. And just then Nathan came toward them with the check. There was something extremely sexy about him, a subtle kind of sexy, not flashy in the least. Mira loved the way he pulled the pencil from behind his ear, the way he cocked his head to the side while he tallied the numbers. He appeared so serious. She watched his thick eyebrows scrunch together in a knot. His face was as familiar as her favorite dream—the one when she wakes up feeling rested and completely safe.

Nathan plopped down the girls' check and stared hard at Joey and Frank. Without a word, the two nodded to Mira and Faye, pushed their chairs out of the way, and backed out of Pearly's, nearly tripping over one another as they ran out the door and onto the street.

"Were those two bothering you?" Nathan asked Faye. Mira wondered why he was ignoring her. Maybe he didn't like brunettes. She studied his face while he spoke to Faye. It was a nice face. He looked kind, she thought. She noticed how his dark brown hair glistened and wondered if he used pomade. No, probably not. Nathan didn't look like the vain type, not at all like Donny Blau.

Mira realized she hadn't heard a word Faye and Nathan were saying. She was in her own wonderful, though slightly painful, trance. Was this what they meant by *love at first sight*? Her face felt hot, and she hoped she wasn't blushing.

Finally he spoke to her. "You can pay me now because we're closing up in a few minutes."

Mira reached into her dress pocket and peered nervously under the table.

"Oh no, my change purse, it's gone. I think I must've dropped it in the movie theatre," she said, "what am I going to do?"

Nathan tilted his head back and squinted a half smile at her. He waited patiently while Faye and Mira discussed their limited finances.

"I can't loan you, Mira. I won't have enough for the bus."

Mira felt some loose change jiggling around in her pocket, but then, something made her keep from pulling it out.

A second later, Nathan said, "Listen, if you two can wait about fifteen minutes, I'll drop you. You don't live in Jersey, right?" he laughed.

Mira liked the way his eyes crinkled up in the corners and how that laugh changed his demeanor so quickly.

"Don't worry about the money, you'll give it to me next time." Nathan said, and he ran back to the counter to talk to Pearly. She glanced over at Mira and Faye and winked. They could see her busy at the register. A minute later, Pearly was greeted by a heavy-set bald man sporting a waxed, pointy mustache. He kissed her on the forehead, and they left in a flash through the back door.

Outside, at the curb, Faye practically jumped in the back seat, leaving Mira and Nathan up front.

"Would you like me to drive past the movie to see if they found your purse?" Nathan asked Mira.

"No thanks, I'll call them tomorrow," she said nervously.

"Okay then, tell me who's first."

In unison both Mira and Faye yelled, "Me!"

"Well, I live closer to Ocean Parkway," he said, turning to Faye, who was hunched down in the back seat. "So I guess you win."

Mira's stomach jumped into her mouth. Instantly, she realized this meant they'd be absolutely alone, driving together on this perfect summer night, she and this sweet, handsome guy, who concocted the most delicious sundaes.

On the short ride to her apartment house Faye yakked so profusely that Mira thought she might scream. But instead, she became mute, anticipating the glorious moment when Faye would exit the car.

Mira listened, intently, while Faye pumped Nathan for information regarding the "adorable Freddy." From the way he spoke, Nathan seemed to admire Freddy a great deal. They were both enrolled in courses at Columbia and working at night to support widowed mothers. Freddy, Nathan said, worked two jobs, one at Pearly's, the other at Klein's Department Store where he sold men's hats and gloves.

Mira couldn't believe her ears when Faye blurted out, "So Nathan, how exactly did your father die?"

"Faye!" Mira turned toward the back seat giving her a warning look.

"No, no, it's okay," Nathan said. "I'm asked all the time. He was hit by a truck as he crossed the street on his way to pick up milk. I was five."

Mira mumbled a *so sorry*, but nothing more.

"What kind of truck?" Faye pressed on.

Mira wished this conversation would end. She couldn't believe her friend's boldness. Maybe Faye should not be a designer, or actress... maybe she should rethink her career and try journalism.

"A bread truck hit him. The kind you smell about a mile away."

"Yeah, and what about Freddy, how did his Dad kick the bucket?"

"Actually, Freddy's father died a couple of years ago," Nathan answered. "He was old, about sixty. Freddy is the youngest of four."

"That's awful," Faye said, leaning over the seat.

Sixty? Mira realized her father would be fifty-four soon. The thought of him dying sent a chill to the top of her head. She couldn't imagine what it would be like not to have both parents. Who would take care of her?

"Next stop," said Nathan looking through the rear view mirror at Mira.

Faye jumped from the car so fast Mira couldn't say good-bye. By the third traffic light while approaching Ocean Parkway, the silence became as loud as fireworks on the Fourth of July. Nathan lit a cigarette and turned on the radio. The Inkspots were singing: "If I Didn't Care..." and Nathan began whistling along with the song. Mira never heard anyone whistle so well. It wasn't a loud annoying tea kettle sound, the high-pitched tone that made you want to clamp your ears. Nathan's whistle was more like a small wind instrument, a recorder or a flute.

But the whistling stopped abruptly as the car's engine began to putt, putt, and stall out just in time for Nathan to pull over to the curb.

"What's wrong?" Mira was surprised by the high-pitched sound of terror emanating from her voice.

"Don't worry this happens all the time with this heap. Hey, will you do me a favor?"

"Of course." Just the idea of helping him thrilled her.

"I need you to hold the flashlight." He reached over Mira into the glove compartment. Mira smelled the musky oils from his hair. His right arm slipped momentarily on her lap. The hairs on her neck stood up and waited for a cue.

"Really sorry," he whispered, while continuing to look through the messy glove compartment. He glanced up at Mira for a split-second and grinned. She wondered if he could hear the loud uneven sound of her heart. But worse, her stomach had started to groan like a squeaky door from her consumption of nuts. She was mortified he would think something was wrong with her. She started to cough in sync with every stomach cramp, but Nathan remained focused on his car.

"Got it," he said, and he ran around the front of the car to open Mira's door and help her. Nathan took her hand lightly, and she tried not to bump her head as she stepped onto the street. It had started to drizzle, and Nathan's curls glistened in the reflection of a street lamp.

"Lean in a bit more," he said, gently directing her.

The flashlight was beginning to feel heavy. She glanced at her watch; the time read 10:55.

Mira remembered that Hattie was off tonight, which meant her father would be the one locking up.

Nathan tugged at a mass of color coded wires.

"That should do it," he said. "Hop back in."

Nathan pumped the car three or four times until the ignition caught. He winked at Mira, looking extremely proud.

"See, that wasn't so bad. So, do you drive?"

"Actually no," she said shyly. "My brother Roy was supposed to teach me, but he's never home or when he is, we're usually fighting."

Nathan laughed. "Well, I wouldn't mind teaching you. I've taught a lot of the teenagers in my neighborhood."

"I'm not really a teenager. I'm close to twenty," Mira said.

"Oh, I could tell that. I was only offering."

Mira was afraid that her nerves had caused her snap at Nathan's suggestion. "I'd love to have you teach me. I could pay you," she said.

"Hmm, that won't be necessary," Nathan answered. For the rest of the ride silence enveloped the car. Mira sensed his pride and hoped she hadn't offended him.

It was exactly 11:10 when they reached the driveway at 611 Avenue T. Nathan pulled in a little too quickly, coming to a dead halt within inches behind Mira's father's turquoise and cream Cadillac.

Unlike some of the other young men that Mira had brought to her home, Nathan made no mention of the opulence surrounding them as he walked Mira to the front door. The porch light was still on and there was a yellow glow coming through the shade in her parents' upstairs bedroom.

When they reached the last of the terracotta steps the front door opened slowly. Mira leaned in and nearly bumped heads with her father who peeked from the other side of the door. Nathan stood rigid beside Mira taking her lead. She silently thanked God that Poppa was dressed in his terrycloth robe tonight and not his famous polka dot silky shorts.

"You do realize, daughter, it is now after eleven? Your mother was very worried. We did not get a phone call to tell us you'd be late. For all we know you might have been kidnapped."

"Excuse me, sir," Nathan cleared his throat.

Mira saw that he was nervous. He pulled his hands from his pockets and stood tall.

"Hello sir, I'm Nathan Berk, a friend of Mira's. It's completely my fault that your daughter is late. You see, my auto stalled about a mile from here. I was taking Faye, you know, sir, Mira's friend, and your daughter home. Neither of the girls had bus fare."

"How do you leave the house without money? This, you did not learn from me or your mother." He stared at Mira wearing his number one stern expression.

"I dropped my change purse in the movies. It's not the end of the world."

Nathan shifted his weight one foot to the other. He looked anxious to leave.

"Well, sir, again let me say I'm terribly sorry. I hope you understand my intentions were good. Goodnight now, sir. Goodnight Mira, it was very nice meeting you."

Charlie Kane stepped out onto the porch; he studied the car in the driveway parked much too close to his prized Caddy.

"Young man?"

"Yes," Nathan said, halting before getting back into his car.

"May I ask what you do for a living?"

If Mira had a hook she'd have lifted her father by the collar and dropped him in the next door neighbor's prickly bushes.

Nathan looked up, first at Mira standing below the porch light and then at Poppa planted like a Buddha, dwarfed by his tall beautiful daughter. "Me, sir?" he said, smiling more than Mira had seen him smile that night. "Oh, I'm in the food business." With that Nathan waved a hand and then slowly began backing out of the driveway.

Though Poppa walked down the porch steps and tried directing him to cut his wheel more to the right in order to avoid a privet branch. Mira could no longer watch. She ran inside and galloped up the twenty-two steps to her mother's room.

Lying atop her gigantic mattress, Ina Kane was propped up on several satin pillows flipping through a copy of the *Ladies Home Journal*. When she looked up and noticed Mira, she sighed deeply, bringing both hands to her chest.

"You're home, well thank God!"

"I'm sorry if I made you worry. But I was with Faye and we, I mean I met this boy named Nathan," she said, out of breath.

"Anyway, he drove us home, and then the car had problems, and it was raining and Momma. . . ." Mira spun around, losing her balance, falling dramatically on Poppa's side of the bed.

"Momma."

"What, angel? Tell me."

"I think I've fallen in love."

"Really? How nice, darling. And this took what? Ten, twenty minutes?"

"Oh, Momma."

"Nathan, hmm, this is a Jewish Nathan, of course?"

"Of course," Mira said. His name is Nathan Berk and he lives with his mother on Avenue U."

"Oh, so, the family is poor?"

"I don't think so, Momma. He attends Columbia during the day, and ah, he's ah, working for a food company part time."

"Food? Lovely. What kind of food may I ask, darling?"

Mira closed her eyes and pictured Nathan's warm caramel eyes.

"Syrups, Momma. The company produces several kinds of syrups."

Mira felt pleased with her ad-lib byline of Nathan. She knew it would have to suffice for now. Her mother would, of course, discuss every word of this with her father. At least, the two stories would match. She heard Poppa clicking off the lights downstairs. Mira kissed Ina on the cheek and waltzed out of the room into the adjourning bathroom, which led to the hallway. She noticed that JJ and Rena's light was still on. Not thinking, she burst into their bedroom, stumbling over a pile of books on the floor adjacent to JJ's bed. Rena was fast asleep on her back, mouth wide open. JJ jumped from under her covers, startled. She tried to shuffle the books under the bed, but it was too late. Mira kneeled down beside her and began studying each book's cover, then looked curiously at her aunt.

"What are all these JJ?"

"You really should have knocked, Mira. You frightened me plowing in like this."

"I'm sorry, but I had something I needed to tell you. I didn't think JJ, please forgive me."

"Well, all right... I guess so," her aunt exhaled.

"So, where did all these books come from? *The American Poet, Leaves of Grass, The Works of Emily Dickinson.*" Mira lifted the organdy dust ruffle to peek under the bed. There were at least twenty more books stacked in big white hat boxes. "Tell me, you know me, my lips are sealed."

"Shh! They'll hear us," JJ said. "Okay, but you can't breathe one word. Your father would have a fit if he knew how I spend my spare time."

"I promise, please."

"You remember that I've been volunteering at the Ladies Auxiliary Club on Tuesday and Thursday evenings since last summer?"

"Yes," Mira said, "you were learning to make patchwork quilts, preserving jams and. . . ."

"Right, well, that's not what I was doing. I was doing this... something for me, something I have always wanted to do." JJ held up some blue books of tests she'd taken. The first thing Mira noticed on the cover was the letter A, circled in red ink. "I went back to school so I could be with interesting people, to have more in my life than just factory work, aggravation, and housekeeping." JJ raised her voice then glanced in her sister's direction. Rena snored loudly and Mira stifled a laugh.

"I understand because that's exactly how I feel too. JJ, you know that."

"Yes, honey, I do." She lifted a hair from Mira's cheek. "I feel terrible that your father won't allow you to continue school, but you're still so young. I'm a whole lot older and it felt like my entire life was slipping through a sieve, one boring week after another. So, a few months ago, I decided to get my degree... a college degree in English. It may take me a hundred years, but this is what I want."

"Does Rena know?"

"Of course, she's my sister. Rena wants me to be happy."

Mira was aware of a hard lump forming in the back of her throat. This was her home, and yet she felt like a stranger. And now she had intruded on her aunt's private life, a life that she shared intimately with one special person, her sister. How Mira wished for that same closeness with someone or something. She was desperate to find a place where she could connect, afraid without that connection she might fade away. All the elation she'd felt over meeting the kind, sweet-looking Nathan had swiftly disappeared, like melted snow. How confusing life could be. One minute, she felt high and jubilant, the next an icy splash of reality...and bam! It seemed everywhere she turned there were reminders of her own captivity, and her father's unyielding dominance over her life. She rested her head upon a worn copy of *Great Expectations* while JJ: cook, decorator, now scholar, and constant mender of the Kane family's inner squabbles, understood her desperation and the need to cry.

Rosha
Across the Sea

Mr. Juraska stands back from what he calls his *handiwork* and asks me if everything looks good. I nod my head, yes, though I am worried that I have nothing to put on the two wooden shelves he has nailed above my bed. Both he and Marta are smiling at me with soft eyes like those of a cocker spaniel.

Since they sat me down and told me the news about Mama, Poppa, and Bubbe, they are up and down the cellar steps ten times a day. Marta comes each and every morning to touch my head, to see whether I'm running a fever. Then she checks me for rashes, and always, always tries to get me to eat. I wish they wouldn't visit quite so much, because then maybe my tears would have a chance to move out of my chest, into my head, and out my eyes. I think all my tears are stuck. I felt them swishing around just once when Mrs. Juraska, Marta, brought me a plate of boiled beef and sauerkraut. The food burnt my tongue and turned my eyes into faucets.

The new book shelves are made of white pine, and Mr. Juraska has carved tiny butterflies in the corners, which he's painted yellow and red. These are the brightest colors in the root cellar other than the faded blue quilt thrown across my cot. I miss my bright yellow crocheted blanket that Bubbe made me for my sixth birthday.

The children must be at school, because there are no sounds above us, but then Marta says, no one is allowed to wear shoes inside the house anymore. "This way, they won't disturb you," she says. I don't tell Marta that I like listening to everybody's footsteps. It is one of the games I play each day trying to guess whose feet are scampering around above my head. There is the flat, hard, drum-like sound of Avram's feet. The quick, yet heavy move of Marta's feet when she is busy in the kitchen. The children are easy. The boy runs all the time. He never stands still. Sophie, the girl like me, walks delicately as if on tippy-toe.

"Rosha? Do you need my help reaching the shelves?" Marta asks. I stand upon my cot, on top of the sack stuffed with rags for my pillow, and reach up with my arms.

"This will be fine," I say. "Thank you. Here is where I will put the pictures of my family. That way I won't forget what they look like."

"Use these stones to prop them up," Avram says, clearing his throat. He shakes his head then lays a few colorful rocks across the bottom shelf for me to arrange when I am ready. When will I be ready?

That night, the night Poppa woke me from the sleep he thought I was in, Mama had already placed some photos in the bottom of my duffle. When I got here I didn't find them at first, and because I wanted there to be more things in the bag, I turned it upside down and shook it with all my might. Just one thing please, and I promised myself I would be satisfied. Of course, I lied. I will never be satisfied. But the day Marta and Avram came to my room to tell me about all those poor people that were marched into the forest, I knew that one day I would have to go and search for Mama and Poppa and Bubbe. Maybe they were not among the people the soldiers had taken in the woods to be shot. Maybe they were hiding somewhere and waiting for *me* to find them. And then I remembered that Avram said "he" had to be extremely careful, and I had to promise to stay very quiet. If I made even one little peep, and it traveled up the wall and through the one little window with the stripes of light, Avram, Marta, and their children might also be taken to the forest, lined up, and shot . . . or worse. What was worse I wanted to know, then didn't want to know, and then wanted to know again?

I promised Mr. Juraska that I would obey all the rules of his home. But I hoped that soon I would have the chance to search for my own family. If Mama and Poppa taught me one thing, it was to listen to my elders. That didn't mean I couldn't ask a question or two, but they always said I had too many.

Before they go back upstairs for the evening, Mr. Juraska says he has a surprise for me. I have not heard those words in such a long time—maybe since my birthday last March when I received that special package from America. Wrapped in white tissue paper were two beautiful sweaters: one pink, the other one yellow, with tiny pearl buttons sewn over a satin ribbon. Poppa had said the sweaters were a present from his relatives who lived far away. Taped to the inside of the parcel was a birthday card, a card designed with dried flowers and signed from my Aunt Jeanette and Aunt Rena, and there was a photograph of a very pretty, dark-haired girl. On the back she had written her name with a tiny heart over the "i". Her name was Mira. There was another picture that Mama hadn't noticed when throwing out the wrapping. Bubbe discovered it inside the trash. Thank goodness Bubbe always checked the trash, looking for coins, stamps, or anything she said might remind her of what she called "much better times."

"What's wrong, Bubbe?" I had asked.

All she said was, "Never mind."

Tears slid down Bubbe's face like skiers, resting in the dimple of her chin. The picture Bubbe found in the trash was of her two daughters, two other sons, her granddaughter, Mira, and a grandson named Roy, posed like statues on the steps of a huge front porch. I wondered if all houses were this big in America, and if so, was there room for all the relatives thinking of, one day, moving there?

"Where did you find these?" I am looking up at Mr. Juraska, but he doesn't answer me. He hands me a few new photos. Some are of people I don't even know, but then there a few of my favorite faces: my aunts and cousins living somewhere in America.

Avram and Marta leave quietly, although I hear them as the folding stairs collapse with the annoying snap reminding me that I got my wish, that I am once again alone. I spread all the photos across the quilt and study them one by one. The first one is of Bubbe lying inside a hammock on a beach; her eyes are shut tight yet she's smiling. Behind her there are boats, both big and small, appearing in the far distance floating on top of the inky sea.

Here's one I remember, though I wasn't there—the wedding day. Mama has a wreath of tiny flowers around her head. Poppa looks uncomfortable in his high-collared shirt, but he has his arm around Mama's tiny waist. Oh, this is one of me: baby Rosha, my eyes and ears poking out like an owl. It looks as if I am trying to hear everything—not wanting to miss a thing.

I place the photos on the bookshelf with my wax bear, ballet dancer, and broken giraffe, along with my favorite book of animals. All the people I don't recognize go back inside my duffel. Standing against the hidden staircase, I look at the beautiful butterfly shelves built especially for me. I wish I could just run up the stairs and see all the other pretty things inside this house. Maybe I could sit in the kitchen and sip a cup of honeyed tea, or play a game with Sophie, or fall asleep in her big warm bed.

Later, when the light dims, all that shines is one fat candle floating inside a round metal tray that Mrs. Juraska has filled with water. *For safety, Rosha, and remember always, always roll up your sleeves.* I check to see if my duffel bag is still here. I keep it hidden behind a sack of potatoes, ready for that special day when I will finally go home.

Mira and Nathan
A Day at the Fair

⌒

Balancing herself on a rickety stepladder, on a cloudy Saturday, Mira buried her portfolio on the highest shelf of the linen closet under a box of hot water bottles. If her designs were too accessible, she might be tempted to look through them only to become terribly melancholy.

Once Aunt JJ shared the secret that she was taking college courses, Mira was determined to become a woman of significance too—someone who possessed a special knowledge fueled by passion. Although she feared her designs were her only real passion and true expression of herself.

Trying to avoid self-pity during the last weeks of summer, she dedicated herself to raising money for some very needy local charities, including the Red Cross, which had already made pleas for donations on the radio. With her aunts' help, Mira gathered a huge amount of the seconds merchandise from the factory downtown and began selling them at weekend bazaars run by Ina's committee at The Brooklyn Women's Hospital. In just two weeks, she alone raised over $3,000. While she began to feel better, even proud, her father lamented about all the merchandise that might have put some more bread on his table had there not been so many screw-ups and damages to these goods in the first place. He was spending more and more time sulking in the room downstairs, and Mira, for one, did not long for his presence.

Then, on an unusually hot August day, her father came home from the city drenched with perspiration. It was only two in the afternoon, a really bad sign. All he wanted was to take a bath and sit in the cool, dark den reading his paper. Momma, who usually stayed dressed for the evening, had wrapped her apron over her bodice like a slip, allowing her fleshy chest and upper arms an airing. She sat in the kitchen pressed to the cold chrome chairs, letting the fan blow in her face while she listened to her favorite radio show: *The Shadow*. Mira's mother knew not to ask her husband what was the latest disaster in the factory. She guessed this had to be something to do with their son.

Roy had become completely girl crazy over the summer, flirting with every model that came strutting into the showroom. If they were in dire need of work, the young Kane jumped right in promising jobs and what he could not possibly deliver since business had slowed considerably. Perhaps this was because Flegelman's daughter had already dropped him, especially after Roy attempted to return his huge Flegelman yarn order, saying that the gauge was much thicker than he was used to receiving.

"The only thing thick Roy is your goddamn head!" Flegelman had supposedly screamed when he'd barged into the Kane's showroom just as two showroom models, auditioning for work clad in only brassieres and panties, dove for cover under Roy's desk. Flegelman stormed out fuming, adamantly refusing to take back any surplus yarn. He warned Roy that he had better learn to order more carefully or go find another supplier. It was a good thing that Margaret was on vacation that week.

Their building on Broadway had buzzed with this story, and putting on a good face, Charlie laughed along with all those on the street making jabs. But when he first learned that his son had been caught in the act by Flegelman, he had turned crimson and refused to comment. Mira had noticed that the tip of his nose twitched every time the subject came up. Even though the Flegelman dilemma would eventually put her and her father back on speaking terms. That, and the fact that he allowed her to go with Nathan to tour some of the original displays from last year's World's Fair, most of which had been moved to Coney Island after the fairgrounds closed.

Mira was shocked when her father granted her request for a midnight curfew. Was this his way of making up to her? She guessed he had his reasons, as every decision he made was based on some careful well thought out plan. Only the year before, she had begged to go to the Fair with a sweet and rather short boy she had known from high school, the son of one of Charlie's competitors. When the young man had called the house to invite Mira, her father had yelled in the background:

"You'll go out with that little shrimp over my dead body!" The thought had made Mira shake, because for the first time she had actually allowed herself to imagine him dead. But this time his behavior was totally different. Sometimes, it seemed as if her father was pushing her right into Nathan's arms. This was so unlike him, but then, who could really predict the incongruous ways of Charlie Kane?

*

When Nathan said he was taking the day off from Pearly's to enable them to visit the exhibits, Mira felt like she'd been given an early birthday present. After breakfast he showed up at her door, dressed casually in a pair of loose grey trousers and a white shirt, while Mira was outfitted in ladies luncheon attire: a crisp navy and white polka dot, short-sleeved dress with a matching white straw hat that fit around the crown of her head like a halo. On her feet she wore white stilettos. Once down the front steps, Nathan came around to help Mira into his Packard, which was difficult to enter since the car was without its running board.

"Uh, oh," Nathan said, as her left leg entered the car. "You look terrific, but I don't think you'll be happy for long . . . not in those Mira, we've got a lot of walking to do."

She looked at Nathan, her face glowing in appreciation, while mischief danced in her eyes. While he helped her from the car, and without taking her eyes off of him, she rummaged through her straw bag and pulled out a pair of red ballet slippers. Seeing his surprised look, she kissed him softly on the cheek.

"Thanks for thinking about me, Nathan. Where'd you learn to be so sweet?"

Nathan grinned, "I guess I'm my mother's lifetime project."

"Well, I hope I get to meet her soon so I can thank her myself."

"She wants to meet you too. Maybe tonight before I take you home?"

"I'd like that." Mira felt a chill spread through her belly. He must really like me, she thought. None of her other dates had ever brought her home to meet the parents, and this had always hurt her feelings.

There were many more exhibits than they'd both expected, and the two strolled hand in hand for hours. Hot, Nathan had rolled his white shirt sleeves to his elbows. He said he was tempted to take it off, but that would leave him in his undershirt, and he would hardly be a match for Mira's fresh summery look. Nathan sweated profusely, while Mira remained powder puff perfect and unruffled throughout the day.

Fascinated particularly by the Asian Emporium, they both tried on bright red satin kimonos, and then sat on straw mats watching a troop of Kabuki dancers perform. But the food displays were the best part of their visit. They sampled raw fish wrapped in seaweed from the Japanese and crispy fried noodles served in greasy cellophane bags from the Chinese. There were spicy tortillas from Mexico, and grape leaves and baklava pastries from Greece. The couple rested on the damp and dusty lawn and sipped Pepsi-Cola from the same tall green bottle, while the enormous *Perisphere* sculpture became their cinematic backdrop.

For dessert they fed each other profiteroles, gently wiping stray crumbs from the other's chin. The day seemed to fly by with Nathan cataloging every exhibit and display with his beaten up Kodak camera. Mira loved the way he took his time to pose her in front of a Chinese twelve-foot dragon, a pyramid, a simulated Eiffel tower. "Okay kiddo, this is my last shot," he shouted, and Mira lifted her skirt to her knees imitating a can-can girl at the Follies Bergère. Some passersby applauded, which egged her on more.

"Merci, merci," she said, curtsying. Mira was buoyant from the attention, but Nathan appeared beside her and pulled her away. He was clearly protective of her or maybe just more private and reserved. Sometimes his pensive side confused her, and she thought it was anger. She hoped she hadn't ruined their perfect day. Nathan remained silent for several minutes, which began to worry her. Her first thought was that perhaps he had tired of her already. The silence became overbearing; what was she to do, what could she do? Feeling she might burst, she cleared her throat.

"Nathan, are you mad at me?" she asked, about to cry. Still silence. God, what was he thinking? "Nathan, did you hear me?"

His face was like a slab of granite. But suddenly, with his camera slung at his side, he lifted Mira off her feet, spinning her around, two, three, four times. All the time his lips pressed at the nape of her neck. She squealed, feeling so relieved, light-headed, and then slightly nauseous from the concoction of food she had eaten.

"Mad at you, mad at you?" he whispered in her ear, while his hot breath sent chills down her spine. "I'm mad about you." Nathan put Mira down, but he didn't let her go. His arms formed a tight ring around her body while he tilted her chin kissing her hard, like she had never been kissed before. Like the kisses she and Faye had swooned over in the movies. She looked into his always serious face, a face she could cherish forever.

They parked for the first time in a dark sandy lot right off the Belt Parkway. Several cars had already lined up on the half-mile strip that faced the water. In the far distance they could see the Steeplechase ride at Coney Island where lights flickered in shades of gold and red. It was hot, very hot, and Nathan opened his window then leaned over Mira to open hers. There were no sounds coming from the cars parked on either side of them, but one car gyrated in place, its windows tinted grey with fog.

Suddenly they were alone, really alone, without the safety net of hundreds of people strolling past them, without the intrusion of whiny children, or anxious groups pushing and asking for directions. Nathan fiddled with the car radio, but there was too much static. He reached over to touch Mira's cheek with the back of his hand. She felt the roughness of his knuckles. She guided his hand as he slowly stroked her neck, shoulder, and arms. His grip became firmer, and she dropped her hand allowing him to stretch his torso across her body. She wrapped her arms tightly around his neck just as she'd seen Katherine Hepburn do with Jimmy Stewart in *The Philadelphia*

Story. His hands moved up and down her sides, his thumbs grazing the bottom of her breasts, then moving on to her nipples.

She could not believe it, the timing, but she was getting an awful cramp in her calf muscle, her legs stretched rigidly in front of her. Mira took Nathan's hands from her and pushed him gently back toward the driver's seat. She rolled her window down all the way and fanned herself with her hand. Without a word, Nathan jumped out of the car and was soon leaning against the hood. From inside the car, Mira saw his shoulders rising and falling as he took in several deep breaths. He reached into his pocket for a cigarette and lit it, took two drags, and tossed it away. Mira watched from the car, her eyes following his every move.

She wondered what he might be thinking, and if this time he had finally lost his patience with her. She couldn't really blame him, but chose to wait in the car to catch her breath. When she pulled down the visor to look at herself, she gasped. Her lipstick was smudged clear up to her nostrils. She spit on her hankie and rubbed her face clean. She was mesmerized by her own image. Was this what happiness was supposed to look like? Her eyes sparkled back at her, and there was a dewy softness to her skin. Oh, she thought, she had it—the glow! What she'd read about in all her movie magazines.

The car parked next to theirs revved up its engine startling her. All Mira could see was someone's hand rubbing the inside windows. Small delicate fingers drew a heart across the window while the car backed out of its spot onto the nearly deserted road.

"Well, I guess we scared them away," Nathan said, climbing into the front seat. He stared at Mira with an intensity she had not yet seen. Beads of sweat clung to his forehead, and his chin was speckled with her Wildberry lipstick. She wanted to giggle, but suppressed it, using her hankie to dab his cheeks. He seemed momentarily hypnotized.

"Is everything okay, Nathan?"

"Yep, fine. It got, well, a little warm," he said, then abruptly changed the subject. "So, do you think you're up to meeting Mom?"

Another wave of relief blew through the window and across her face. "Are you sure it's not too late?"

"Don't worry. On warm nights like this, Mom usually sits in the back of our building talking to her cronies late, until the neighbors shout from their windows threatening to pour water on them."

"This I have to see," Mira said, "but only if you promise to come over to my house tomorrow night straight after work." She tried inching closer to him, but still it wasn't close enough.

"It's a deal," he said, and as the tension between them faded, they headed back on the Belt Parkway to the Berk's apartment building on Avenue U.

Unlike the quiet, tree-lined Avenue T, Avenue U was action packed, even after ten on a Monday night. Some young boys were playing stick ball guided by street lamps and lighted store signs of Gross's Delicatessen and Passano's Fish Market. At the end of the block stood a dark, red brick building, almost completely covered in ivy. In front near the curb was a long bicycle rack, and further back sat a swing set with a long, metal slide. A bushy pathway led to the rear of the building. Laundry lines were hung between windows, and white wooden chairs were strewn randomly about the crab-grassy lawn. The only real light emanated from the windows above or from the ends of cigarettes being smoked below.

Nathan took Mira's hand to help her along the narrow path. She had insisted on putting on her heels to meet his mother. She now regretted that decision as her shoes sank into the damp earth below. Perhaps this visit was not such a terrific idea after all. The effects of a very long day were beginning to get to her. How was she supposed to meet Mrs. Berk, anyway? It was pitch black out here. And then, within seconds, she heard a chorus of gravelly voices, lyrical sounds of Irish brogues, Yiddish, Italian, blended together and underscored with jovial laughter.

As they approached, a small shadow of a woman seemed to anticipate Nathan's arrival and sprung to her feet. Mira squinted trying to focus on the woman and her female friend. Ignoring Mira, momentarily, they greeted Nathan with tiny kisses. Mira stood a step behind, one hand on his back for support. Both women were short, that Mira could see. They wore house dresses, and although it was way past dinnertime, they still had their aprons on.

"Mom, Mrs. O'Hara, this is . . . ah . . . my friend . . . Mira . . . Mira Kane. Mira, meet my Mom, Gertie Berk and her good friend, Mary O'Hara."

"Pleased to meet you both," Mira nearly curtsied. She could only see an outline of bodies, not complete faces, not even teeth or hopefully their smiling lips.

When Nathan's mother tried whispering in his ear, he bent over, nearly knocking her to the ground. Soon Mrs. O'Hara said her goodnights and hobbled into one entranceway, while Mira, Nathan, and his mother entered a green metal doorway several feet away. Mrs. Berk's buxom figure led the way down a dank, narrow hallway that was cluttered with crates holding empty milk bottles. Mira inhaled the aroma of pungent chicken soup that wafted down the long corridor, but she was much more tired than hungry.

"I'll get the door, Mom," Nathan said. Mira waited while he turned the knob on the unlocked door and flipped the hall switch, illuminating a small crystal globe. The three entered Mrs. Berk's foyer, adjusting to the light, all squinty and smiley. Mira looked down and met Mrs. Berk's face straight on. There was a moment of vacuous silence followed by a few high-pitched squeals that flew simultaneously from both women's mouths. Their hands alternated from covering their eyes in disbelief to clutching one another tightly.

"*Gut en Himmel,*" Gertie Berk squealed once more.

"You're that sweet lady from the bus!" Mira said wrapping her fingers around Mrs. Berk's.

The neighbor next door banged on the wall, and Mrs. Berk instantly banged back using only her foot. Mira noticed Mrs. Berk's stockings, rolled liked cookie dough at the top of her ankles.

"It's you!" Mira said as she jabbed her finger into Nathan's chest. "I knew I'd seen that face before. It was driving me crazy, I thought maybe I dreamed it."

"What do you mean, what's going on?" Nathan asked. Mira realized it was the first time he'd spoken since they walked through the door.

"Nathan, your mother and I rode the bus together a couple of months ago. Right, Mrs. Berk?" Mrs. Berk nodded, her hand petting the soft down of Mira's arm.

"And," Mira continued, "I showed your Mom all my drawings, and, just as I was leaving, she handed me a photograph of this really handsome young man! It was you, Nathan. You're the man in the photo!"

"Oh, Mom, were you bragging about me again?" Nathan stooped and gave his mother a full body hug practically lifting her off the floor.

Mrs. Berk pointed to Mira's shoes. Understanding the gesture and not the words, Mira slipped out of her muddy heels and left them on the rubber mat in the doorway. Smiling, the woman took Mira's hand and led her to a small living room with two overstuffed chairs and a curved burgundy loveseat. She motioned for the couple to sit on the loveseat, and then plopped herself down opposite them and folded her arms.

After a few minutes, when she finally stopped grinning, Mrs. Berk offered glasses of seltzer and hard candies from a crystal dish that appeared much too heavy for her to lift. She stood and opened and closed the windows several times apologizing for the heat. Mira guessed that all this busyness compensated for her inability to communicate in English.

As the minutes passed into an hour, Mira felt as though she was on a giant Ferris wheel looking down at the rest of the world. Although it was late, she was rejuvenated by a rush of pure joy as she observed Nathan talking to his mother: How he tried to engage her, allowing the woman to feel his genuine pride in her, and now Mira as well, who, for the very first time, he had finally called—*his girl.*

An Act of Denial

~

For Charlie Kane, especially, the fall was a time of renewal. There were the high holidays, the admittance of sin and the cleansing of the soul, and always, the promise to forgive those who had asked for forgiveness. There were crisper days and cooler nights, and, most important, the hustle and bustle of new business, when buyers from all over the country visited showrooms. Charlie would have to push himself to get through the busy weeks ahead. It was his and Louie's job to entertain these buyers taking them out for expensive dinners and often providing, as an extra bonus, a personal wardrobe of Kane Knitting's finest ensembles.

This was also the time when both brothers were happy to have Rena and Jeanette working downtown at the factory. They would never approve of how openly Charlie and Louie gushed over every young and attractive out of town buyer. Julia Crane was a buyer for Dillard's, a rapidly growing chain of retail stores in Virginia. She was a divorcée, thirty-five, with two small children. Julia was known as an extremely cautious buyer, selecting merchandise that she was nearly certain would fly out of the stores. She often sat back smugly watching Charlie trying to hard sell her on items they both knew she had no intention of buying. But he pitched with such an energetic enthusiasm that he always managed to charm her. He could be fatherly, even a bit brash, and his thick European accent gave him an air of authority.

Charlie had promised Julia dinner tonight at the Stork Club. He felt very guilty to be staying out late, but Louie said he'd go home and cover for him. Charlie and Louie told the women that the buyer's name was "Mr. J. Crane—the royal pain." This amused Ina, and of course no further questions were asked, even if Charlie came home reeking of Shalimar. He'd tell her the restaurant was filled with rich, overly done up wives.

Charlie suggested that Julia meet him at the restaurant in case he was running late. The moment he walked in and laid eyes on her, he was taken aback. Julia was dressed elegantly in a shapely black bouclé knit suit. Her platinum blonde hair was pulled back neatly in a gold lamé ribbon showing off her nearly perfect smooth white skin, not a blemish or a freckle. When she smiled at Charlie, her blue eyes sparkled, reflecting the small crystal chandelier hanging above their table in the corner of the restaurant. Charlie felt weak in the legs as he pulled out his chair and sat down. He cleared his throat, then stood back to take her in, his hands folded in front of him like a Buddha's. Yes, he thought, Julia Crane was indeed the epitome of *shiksa*, the forbidden fruit, but he was totally enraptured. Yet, in truth it was that black bouclé suit she wore so elegantly that made his heart heave inside his chest. He could not wait to get both his hands on the merchandise. Who in hell's garment was it? He had to know.

After she had had her second martini to Charlie's first scotch on the rocks, Julia finally removed her jacket, commenting on the stuffiness of the overcrowded room. Charlie, being the quintessential professional, hoped that Julia wouldn't get the wrong idea as he leaned in closer to peek at the large satin label stitched into her suit jacket. It read: *Chanel* in bold, golden letters.

He was embarrassed when Julia spurted out, "Oh, the suit. I got it last year on a buying trip to Paris. Let me tell you this rag was a small fortune, Charles. Wish I could find somebody to knock it off here in the states, but it would probably be too costly." She licked the stirrer and then popped the olive into her delicate sensuous mouth, but Charlie was already twirling the soft bouclé fibers between his chubby fingers. His mind was already replacing the beautiful wool fabric with some of the new synthetic blends, rayon being one of them. His head began tabulating the costs for production, when Rudy, the robust

122

waiter, brought over the steaks they'd ordered. The volcanic sizzling from the huge pewter serving plates brought Charlie out of his trance. There was nothing better than a thick, juicy steak, even if it was, like Julia, forbidden because it was *trayf*. Kosher meat was too lean, salty, and lacked the flavor of butter that was often brushed on the meat before the final grilling. Ina knew Charlie ate trayf on the outside; she just refused to hear his praises over such culinary delights.

Julia, an expert in the dinner banter of Southern men and women, tried to keep up the conversation. "So how were your holidays, Charles?"

Charlie just nodded while looking down at a piece of charcoaled meat. He was uncomfortable with references to his Judaism, especially whenever it emanated from Christians. He always felt a strange blend of paranoia and embarrassment. Among his own, he was the proudest of Jews, but his past and now present told him the world did not hold his people in high esteem. So, in business, he chose to downplay his faith while this always left him feeling shamefully guilty.

Julia's question immediately transported him to thoughts of Mordecai. Suddenly, in this woman's presence, hearing Rudy's guttural German accent vibrating throughout the restaurant, Charlie began sweating profusely. He took a napkin and dabbed at his brow, while Julia chattered on about the new private school she had found for her children.

"Charles, my goodness, are you okay?"

"Yes, dear, I'm fine. Perhaps, a little too much scotch."

He patted her hand to reassure them both, but Julia's arm flew up to beckon Rudy. The waiter was not accustomed to being summoned by a woman, so he purposely took his time. When he finally arrived at the table, he was stiff and formal.

"Sorry, madam, but Eddie Cantor just walked in with a party of eight, and we're short-staffed tonight."

"I don't give a goddamn if that old geezer, Franklin D., is being wheeled in here, my host is not feeling well!"

Charlie squirmed in his seat when several people in nearby banquettes looked over at them. He smiled wanly at a man he knew from his building; the man was flanked by two buxom blondes, probably showroom models. In his dizziness, he felt a twinge of envy. Maybe, he really was a son-of-a-bitch and should drop dead now.

"Mr. Kane, forgive me, sir, is there anything I can get you, perhaps a bromide might help?" Rudy asked, avoiding Julia's fiery glare. Everyone knew that Charlie Kane was a good tipper. Tipping was another way of competing with his peers.

"Just some ice water, Rudy. It's been a tough few months on the old man," Charlie said, winking at Julia. He tried focusing on the bouclé and said, "If I were to send you some samples of this magnificent garment in the mode of Kane Knitting, you might be interested?"

"But of course, Charles. I'll drop the suit off to you tomorrow when I check out the line," Julia said enthusiastically.

He was already feeling better.

"You mean you're going to buy from us, Julia?"

"Yes, Charles," Julia said coyly, playing along, sounding more Southern than she had all evening.

"Well, then, not only are you my most beautiful customer," he said, taking her delicate porcelain hand in his, "but you are also, by far, the smartest."

Charlie went home that night feeling guiltier than he had ever felt in his life. He walked into the house and was instantly struck by the changes he noticed in his two sisters and brother. How was it that it still surprised him to come through that door and see the shadings of grief etched into their faces? For a few days, he might actually forget that things were no longer as they'd been. He would forget that no amount of new business or money could erase the pain that had seeped into their souls and mixed with their blood. That was the truth he had failed to swallow with his watery scotches, and overly salty, sinful steak.

Business as Usual

~

"No, no, no, Poppa. I told you, no more rush jobs." Mira stood behind the design table Kane Knitting had purchased for her. Before she agreed to work part-time for the company, she had set down a list of rules a mile long. Her work hours would be decided by her, so that lunches with Nathan and Faye would be possible. Also, she demanded a flat salary of thirty dollars per week. This way she could put away some money and possibly return to Rockefeller Design if things did not work out. Poppa reluctantly agreed, but only if Mira allowed him to put the money into a special savings account. She yielded when he bribed her with a beautiful oak design table. But the table was not enough. Mira needed new lighting installed in her workroom, and she asked for her own fit model, and lastly, her own design assistant. The assistant would be paid fifteen dollars per week. And so in the middle of September, Mira hired Faye. Yet, before too long, this began to place a terrible burden on their relationship. No matter how careful Mira was not to patronize Faye in the workplace, she could sense Faye's resentment, something born perhaps out of feeling as though she was walking in Mira's shadow.

Every day while working on the new fashion line penned: *Designs By Mira*, Faye had become more and more reticent. It had been much too long, Faye told Mira, since she had one creative idea of her own. One day, over lunch, Faye burst out crying. This was not the Faye she knew, and Mira felt immediately guilty for hiring her in the first place. "How could I have been so blind and selfish, Faye. My, God, I think I've become a true Kane after all."

"Mira, please, don't think like that. I jumped at the opportunity." She sipped her chocolate shake loudly. "You know I've always respected your work. Truthfully, I think you taught me a great deal more than I ever learned in school." Faye took her friend's hand in hers. "Mira, you have to believe that you're a natural at this. I swear it bubbles in your blood."

"I couldn't have existed here without you," Mira said. For the first time, she noticed the contrast in their hands. Hers were soft, her long fingers delicate and pale, nails perfectly groomed, while Faye's hands were covered in cuts and calluses. There were scratches from all the fitting pins that left her fingers red and raw. Faye had worked so hard these past months never once asking for a raise.

"What if I were to go to my father and tell him it's time we hire you as a full-fledged designer?" Mira asked.

"But this is your family's business, Mir, it wouldn't really change much, would it?"

Mira sunk back in the booth. "No, I guess not, but what will you do? It's not so easy to get a job right now."

"I've thought about this a great deal. I know you're right, but I feel like my life is going nowhere fast."

"But, what about you and Freddy? Nathan said he really thought Freddy was crazy about you."

"I think he is the most adorable and lovable guy I've ever met, but the fact remains that Freddy doesn't have a pot to pee in."

"So, you're both young, why not give him some time."

Faye frowned. "Mira, you can't possibly understand what it means not to have the simplest things. Even if they make him manager of men's hats, what kind of a future is that? What happens, God forbid, if one day men stop wearing fedoras? We'd starve."

Mira giggled at her friend's logic. When she smiled, it made Faye less defensive and the tension between the two vanished instantly.

"Okay," Mira said, "so I'll ask you again: what will you do?"

Faye took a long noisy slurp through her straw and drained her malted. Mira watched her wide-eyed. "I'm going out West . . . to

Hollywood," Faye said, in the same tone she had used earlier to order her tuna fish sandwich.

"What!" Mira said, leaning completely over the table, inches from Faye's face.

"I've saved every single cent of my money, and I'm going. I'll bang on every single door if I have to. I'll drop my sketches into the convertibles of each and every star."

"And how, pray tell, will you get onto the studio lots?" There was more than a hint of jealousy in Mira's voice. She tried to conceal it, but it was as evident as the foam on her root beer flowing over the top of her glass onto the tablecloth.

"I believe there is always a way, and I am ready to do whatever it takes. I only wish you'd come with me. I know we'd make a great design team, no, not great, the best. The Academy Awards' costume design goes to Mira Kane and Faye for *Return To Tara*.

Faye bowed her head side to side to an imaginary audience. Mira felt a stab of pain so deep in her chest that she could not finish her lunch. How could someone be so certain, as Faye seemed certain of her future and destiny? What had happened to all of her own dreams? Listening to Faye, it seemed as though she had none, not one dream at all. And then she remembered. Sure, she sighed, relieved, there was Nathan. She could not imagine her future without him. With Nathan she had a chance at a life charted by them and not by her father. That would be so very different, so freeing. Nathan was independent, and she admired and respected that quality more than any other he possessed. She wanted to learn to be more like him so that no one would ever control her again.

Nathan had finished his courses and just landed a job at a small company—Global Fabrics. One of the partners, a jolly little man named Harry Simon, had also taken business courses at Columbia. They were in the same class, and Nathan nudged him constantly for a job, especially after Harry let it leak out that he was a business owner and already established. Nathan told Mira that he didn't mind that he'd be starting out work in the stock room. He was smart enough to know that an opportunity like this did not come along every day. This had to be a more promising future than he had at Pearly's. This was an opportunity that allowed the couple to talk about their future. About this, Mira was very private, not even sharing details with JJ. She had begun spending more and more time with Nathan, and although the apartment was overstuffed and hot all the time, she slept over constantly on Mrs. Berk's loveseat, waking up each morning twisted like a pretzel.

"So, what do you think?" Faye said waving a blue napkin in Mira's face. "You can take some of the dough you've stashed away, and we'll get a small place to start. Before you're twenty-one honeychil', you'll own a Beverly Hills address. Come on, just think how proud your Poppa will be."

"I'm in love with Nathan, Faye. I can't think of leaving him, not ever."

"But maybe he'll come along, why not ask him?"

"Enough Faye, you know that's impossible, he's waited forever for his job. This one has a real future."

"What about you, Mira, and your future?"

Mira felt claustrophobic, she waved to the waitress and asked for the check. Faye thumbed through her wallet. "Forget it, this one's on me," Mira said.

"No, no, I insist. Please let me pay."

Faye counted out the eighty-three cents for their lunch, and then left ten pennies for the tip. Mira replaced them with a dime and handed back the loose change with a wry smile.

"So, what do your folks say about all this?" Mira asked.

"Um, they're thrilled. Mom has a first cousin in West Hollywood who's offered me a room until I'm settled. You know I'm not shy. I'd wait tables if necessary."

"You? Not shy? That's an understatement."

On the way back to the office both girls were unusually silent. But in a surprising gesture, Mira looped her arm through Faye's and kissed her on the cheek leaving a perfect outline of cherry lipstick. Faye put her head on Mira's shoulder. Neither of them cared about the looks they got as they walked up Broadway. In the short time the two had been friends, they had shown enormous kindness toward one another, always there to boost each other's morale and moods. That, indeed, was the understatement.

Back in the showroom, Mira tried to imagine what it would be like without Faye. Faye served as a buffer. Poppa, Uncle Louie, and even, the pain in the ass, Roy seemed more subdued with an outsider working there. It was so much quieter. Mostly, because they were more cautious discussing business dealings with a stranger in their midst, and if your last name wasn't Kane, you were indeed a stranger.

Mira dreaded the search for a new assistant. Especially now, when the demands from the stores seemed greater than ever to get the goods shipped out in time. The pressure was enormous, and at home, everything was gloomy. She realized that she had not allowed herself to feel what the others were feeling. Was it fear or just her selfishness? No, she told herself, that was not the case. She could not get the photo of her uncle's family out of her mind. She had studied Rosha's sweet, heart-shaped face, her angular cheeks, the tiny dimple etched in her chin, so distinct and familial. The child looked like she was brimming with untapped energy. Her expression hinted of impatience, as if she could not wait for the photo session to end so she could run outside and play.

The next morning, Charlie arrived at the office very early and placed the bouclé suit across Mira's design table. His scribble merely said: *So this, you can do better?*

Mira cornered him outside the bathroom.

"Poppa, so let me get this straight. You want me to copy Coco Chanel? Have you completely lost your mind?"

"Copy, schloppy. This, they do all the time, why shouldn't we be first for a change? If we had waited for an original idea to come along, we would have gone broke years ago. Plop! All of us in the toilet."

"Look at this yarn!" Mira squealed. "Do you have any idea how expensive this will be to try and reproduce?"

"We will try it with some blends: a *bissel* rayon, some cotton, maybe just 30 percent we actually will use wool."

"I see," Mira said, "and the buttons, Poppa, where do you suppose we find buttons like these?"

"Mira, darling, don't worry your pretty little head. You will find buttons, maybe not with a C. Yes, I agree we need something else." He was thinking out loud, watching the smoke rings from his cigar disappearing in the air. "Maybe a simple round button would do."

Mira examined the garment inside and out, marveling at how beautifully it was crafted. She had always admired expensive clothing and had some in her closet as well, but Chanel was definitely what her teacher, Mr. Forte, had meant when he mentioned couture.

"Poppa, I know you," she said. "You did not buy this sample, where did it come from?"

"Julia Crane."

"Julia Crane, the buyer? Poppa, you took her suit."

"What took?" he answered annoyed. "She gave to me."

Mira looked at Charlie Kane suspiciously. She was the only one privy to the truth that the J in J. Crane was indeed feminine. She wondered if her father realized their last name rhymed with his favorite buyer's.

"The woman practically begged me to copy this. If we do a decent job, I know she will buy for all her stores. And she will want an exclusive."

"Poppa, I don't think giving Miss Julia an exclusive is a wise idea. Won't it upset some of your customers, especially when they see such quality goods? Charlie squinted at her through a dense cloud of smoke. She could swear she saw a slight grin, maybe even a look of pride, but then he cleared his throat.

"Daughter, let me worry about the customers. You worry about the design."

Soon after Faye was gone, Mira was struck with the realization that she had officially joined them—the clan of the Kanes. She was connected to these people she called family on a 24 hour basis, 7 days a week, 365 days a year. They were beginning to invade her dreams, which were now frequently nightmares. She worried about getting her work completed, especially since she could not find anyone to replace Faye. There had been one or two young hopefuls from Parsons, but none of them lasted more than two weeks. One quit after Roy had pinched her behind at the water cooler. Although she immersed herself in work, Mira continued to join her mother at the Brooklyn Women's Hospital for several bazaars and fund-raisers. Even though most of the women were older, she enjoyed the compliments and sense of pride on Ina's face. She noticed that since the loss of Mordecai's family, Momma continued to be strong for everyone. This was so completely out of character for Momma, and it seemed strange that it took such an awful event to have her revitalized. Or was it that there had never been room for Ina to express herself through the zigzag maze of bickering and all the explosive egos caged under that one enormous sloping terracotta roof?

Of all of them, JJ had taken the deaths the hardest. Over time, she became more and more withdrawn and void of energy. She rarely spoke to anyone at dinnertime, hardly ate, and was rapidly losing weight. Rena tried harder than ever to be pleasant, to keep from upsetting her sister. Mira, too, worried about JJ a great deal.

One night, when Charlie and Ina were with clients out to dinner, Rena found JJ burning all her books in a steel garbage bin in the backyard. The flames had risen so high that Rena got frightened and screamed for Mira to help. Mira ran outside and grabbed the garden hose attached to the garage and helped Rena put out the fire. JJ glanced up at the sky and watched the orange embers falling to the ground. JJ trampled some in her bare feet.

Later, looking through the bin, Mira found the seared pages of Whitman's *Leaves of Grass* and a skinny book of Dickinson's poems. Mira pulled them from the charcoaled mess. She noticed how JJ had scribbled her initials all over the Dickinson poem, "Pain Has an Element of Blank." Mira read the poem over and over again trying to decipher its meaning:

> *Pain has an element of blank,*
> *It cannot recollect*
> *When it began, if there were*
> *A day when it was not.*
> *It has no future but itself,*
> *Its infinite realms contain*
> *Its past, enlightened to perceive*
> *New periods of pain.*

When Mira showed Rena the poem, her aunt's eyes brimmed with tears. They were the only ones who knew about the secret classes at

New York University, though JJ had not gone to class in recent weeks. The medication the doctor had prescribed to help JJ sleep made her much too groggy. Not yet confident in her English, Rena had asked Mira to go speak to the bursar's office to see if they would return her sister's money. But since it was already weeks into the semester, the best they could offer was a small credit whenever she returned. Mira was amazed that while clearly depressed, JJ had never once missed a day at the factory.

A week after the book incident, JJ was downtown filling in for a sewing operator who had called in sick. There was a particularly heavy order of goods to get out, and everyone began pushing real hard. Mira planned to work in the factory as well, and Poppa was expected to arrive at the close of the workday to check on the progress. This had everyone nervous as hell. Piece goods flew through the air like swarms of bees. Khaki, colored cardigans—1500 to be shipped out immediately to the number one client: J.C. Penney.

The sewing operators sat hunched at their stations ready to begin. To be sewn in the middle of each breast pocket was a small fleur-de-lis crest. Rena walked through the plant supervising and checking over the items as they were thrown into large bins. Some would require refinishing if not within Kane's standards. Across the large loft space, Mira noticed Rena lingering at JJ's table and whispering in her ear. Rena looked worried and whispered again. The frenetic buzzing and whirring coming from the machinery made it impossible to hear anything. Suddenly, JJ leaped up and covered her ears. There was a look of intense fear on her face, an expression Mira had never seen on her before. Rena took JJ by the shoulders and shook her, while most of the others stopped working, stealing long, curious glances. Mira pushed through bins and bins of sweaters, her feet getting caught in scraps of discarded knitting. JJ was sobbing, her head resting in Rena's lap.

Rena yelled out a warning for the women to continue working if they cared about their jobs. She had never yelled at them before. She had always reserved her anger for the house. Mira helped to drag JJ out a large floor to ceiling window onto the sooty fire escape. JJ's body slumped limply like an oversized rag doll. But the brisk fall air and blinding sunlight began to calm her. She took several deep gasping breaths until she was able to speak. Mira and Rena held her hands while she described what had happened as she'd sat at her station sewing her allotted garments.

In a soft faltering voice, almost childlike, JJ told how she had stared and stared at the crests while centering them on each of the pockets. Her eyes were blurry, most likely, from lack of sleep, and the swirls of green and gold from the fleur-de-lis began to take on their own distinct shape. No longer were they sweeping or delicately edged like the beautiful corners of a leaf. In her eyes and mind, the shape had transformed into an eerie monster, so that her focus saw only the menacing edges resembling a Swastika, the hideous symbol of the Nazis. The rough, khaki fabric slipped through JJ's shaky fingers, while the sounds of incessant buzzing returned her to a dark, furtive place in her memory. She was on the ground again. Glass and pebbles stuffed up her dress, someone pushing deep inside her—a shard of hot flesh tearing her in two.

By the time Charlie arrived, things seemed back to normal, and the orders all on schedule. That night, at dinner, Charlie was more jubilant than he had been for months. He barely noticed his sister slouched and rolling a single pea around the edge of her plate. Mira and Rena watched JJ while holding one long, collective breath. All at once they understood the power and paralysis rendered by grief. How it so rapidly transforms a person's life.

Bubbe Sends Some
Unexpected Warmth

Marta sets the tray on the crate beside my cot. I glance behind her to see if Sophie is tagging along with her this morning, but no she is not.

"What's the matter Rosha, you look a little tired today?" Marta asks. "Did you have some of those scary dreams again?"

"Only one," I lie.

"Perhaps you might feel better if you tell me about it. If you like I will sit here while you drink your tea and talk. Oh, and I saved this piece of the special cornbread you like, although I'm afraid it is a bit hard. We are running low on supplies, so I had to bake it with fewer eggs."

"Thank you, yes, I would like to tell you, but I must think for a second." I take a sip of the warm tea and close my eyes to help me remember.

"Okay," I say, as things become clearer, "what I dreamed was that Momma, Poppa, and Bubbe have been waiting for me at our place on Sadowa Street. I could tell they are very angry with me for leaving them, for going away to live with you and Mr. Juraska. In my dream, Poppa keeps telling Momma: "But I told her we would be home in only a few days. Why hasn't Rosha returned?""

Marta's eyes stare at the floor. Her lips move a little but there are no words. I think I must have upset her. To make her feel better, I reach for the piece of cornbread and lift it to my mouth. It feels as heavy as one of the potatoes stuffed in the many sacks in the corner. I take a big bite aware of Marta's eyes now studying my face. I try chewing a piece of the cornbread. The flavor is delicious, but it is so hard I worry that I may lose a tooth. I haven't lost one since I'm here, but I guess I will sooner or later. "This is very good," I say, "thank you."

Marta takes a deep breath. "Rosha, do you remember what Avram told you about your family soon after you came to live here?"

"Yes, but no one knows where they've gone for sure, right? And Poppa always told me to never draw conclusions until I had all the facts."

"Dear, dear, child. Do you also remember when you asked where Avram found the pictures of your family living in America? Well, the truth is he came upon those pictures when he went back to your home. As he said, almost everything else was gone, because the German soldiers had taken all the valuable objects. The pictures were scattered over the floor. Most likely they had fallen out of a drawer."

"How was Mr. Juraska able to go into our building? I don't understand."

Marta takes another deep breath, and for a second I fear she is annoyed with me, that I am not grateful enough that she has taken me in to her home. Me, someone she hardly knows. She brings me food three, four times a day, and checks to see if I am cold. Her children come to visit me, though her son, Victor, doesn't like me at all. He kicks things around and walks with one foot, lifting up then falling, as if over an imaginary rock. Victor has never once spoken to me. He stands in front of my cot and stares, his mouth in an upside down *U*, his blue eyes, grey and cold, as cold as the draft pushing through the window sill.

"Avram has special privileges, Rosha. I thought we'd told you."

"I must have forgotten. There was so much to think about when I first arrived."

Marta pats my head and pours me more tea. She measures some honey in and stirs it in the cup, then leans in so I can lick the spoon. Oh, I think to myself, just like Bubbe did whenever I got the croup.

"You see, Avram belongs to a group of people who can go about their business as long as they carry their special papers and follow all the rules."

"But aren't those young soldiers and the German officers cruel? Especially to anyone who is Jewish and wearing the star? I saw them, I really did, out in the square. They were kicking an old man as if he were a bad dog. I watched them spit in the face of our neighbor who was carrying her twin babies."

"Yes, I know, and that is terrible and why Avram must keep his important job to help get answers for families like yours who have been separated. Although no one must *ever* know you are with us. You are safer here than anywhere in all of Vilna."

I remember our home, the dining room table, the fruit bowl centered in the middle. Mama dropping an apple or perhaps it was a pear.

"Avram risked a great deal when he went back to your place. One never knows how the Germans might react. Even though because of me my children are considered Christian, since their father is a Jew, they are no longer safe to wander about freely. When someone hears the name Juraska, right away they ask: Polish? Polish Jew? As if any of this matters. I am sorry to tell you anything to worry you, but these are very bad times."

Marta stands and walks to the small cellar window. She checks making sure all the slats are tightly closed. She raises her hand to feel for drafts. I watch as she stuffs a small crack with her hankie. "Oh, I almost forgot! I have something that will keep you warmer," she says. "I'll be back in a few moments." Warm sounds very good to me. Lately, I sleep with all the extra clothes Mama had packed for our trip, the trip to the shore—the trip never taken. Every day I wear both sweaters from my family in America. My family. Surely, they must be thinking about us now, wondering how their relatives in Vilna are getting along. I wonder if Avram will search for them, let them know that Poppa left me with the candle maker and him—a man who makes furniture and is special only because he is married to a Christian.

Marta climbs down the steps carefully. I think the staircase is much too narrow for her hips. Over one arm, she carries something dark and furry. She has a big smile pasted on her face. For a moment, I think she has brought me a pet—a little puppy to keep me company, but puppies bark, and then what would happen if I were discovered? What would happen to all of us?

As Marta comes closer, I see the ragged fur of a dead animal. It is black and very curly. Marta gently tosses the thing near the foot of my bed. I have seen this before, I know it. But where? There are deep pockets inside this animal. I reach inside one and pull out a white embroidered lace handkerchief. The initials are LK. Yes, now I remember. This once belonged to Bubbe, whose real name is Lena Kaninsky. This is Bubbe's black Persian jacket that she refused to wear because she had said it felt heavy on her shoulders. But she once whispered to me so Grandpa Yussel wouldn't hear, "shush, mein kind, but it is also very, very ugly." She had called it her *sacrificial* lamb making Poppa laugh till tears fell all over his evening paper.

"Where did you find this?" I ask. I am happier and sadder than I've been for months.

"It was hidden underneath your grandmother's mattress. This will keep you very toasty, you'll see." I lay the curly black animal across my cot and pet the matted fur. Now my Bubbe's ugly jacket and me are together, here in a freezing cellar, where I spend every moment of every day hoping my family will come, one day soon, to take me home.

Mira

Intentions Please

~

How surprised she was, then frantic, when her mother announced that both she and Mira's father thought it time they invited Nathan and his mother to brunch. After all, hadn't their children been seeing one another steadily since July? The Kanes agreed that perhaps Nathan needed the collective push of not one, but two, mothers to clarify his intentions when it came to their only daughter. Brunch would be quick, informal, and much less intimidating than dinner. Hopefully the tensions initiated by work could be placed on hold until Monday.

Mira felt certain her mother was on to her when, a few weeks before, she began asking some very intimate questions: "So, daughter, do you really think you love him? Is he the man you want to spend the rest of your life with? Do you ache when you're away from him?"

Mira was shocked at this uncharacteristic interrogation. As far back as she could remember, her mother had never once meddled into her private life with those of the opposite sex. When Mira tried to answer, Momma, seeing how flustered she became, simply kissed her on top of the head.

"It's okay, sweetheart," she'd said, "just some things to think about. It's been nearly half a year now, hasn't it?"

Until her mother provoked her, Mira had been caught up in the whirlwind of work and too immersed in the present to ponder her future. The future once meant: dreams of designing for Hollywood, coupled with glamour, perhaps even fame. Now it was a different kind of responsibility that shielded her from the lingering twinges of regret and self-pity from being taken out of school.

Marriage had not permeated her thoughts until she met Nathan and simultaneously began worrying about losing him. Maybe it was time for something to change, or she might easily become a fixture in her own house, like one of the Italian paintings of old women baking bread or sweeping streets adorning the living room walls.

It took just a few days to throw the plan together, and so on a brisk Sunday at precisely high noon, The Berks arrived at the Kanes for brunch. In addition to JJ's signature Rugelah, which she'd insisted on making, the house was filled with the aroma of the cinnamon beignets Ina had ordered from the fancy C'est La Vie bakery on Avenue U. She said she had read somewhere that cinnamon was a type of aphrodisiac and mood enhancer, and she wanted the atmosphere as pleasant as possible.

After changing her outfit three times, Mira looked out her bedroom window just as Nathan was helping Mrs. Berk out of his car. From her perch on her window seat, she could tell Nathan was a bit nervous. He kept tugging at his coat collar like a turtle wanting to hide. She felt an instant rush of love for him and wanted to protect him from the onslaught of her hungry family waiting behind the front door. She practically slid down the banister to tell her mother they had arrived.

"Please, Momma, you must come out immediately to meet her. Poppa and Uncle Louie are in the foyer arguing about some new business deal. I don't think this is the time for that, don't you agree? It's embarrassing!"

"Okay, okay, let me wipe the fish oil from my hands. You wouldn't want me meeting your future mother-in-law smelling like a herring? Would you?"

"Momma, shush or they'll hear you. Nathan hasn't even asked me yet. He's only recently started his new job and besides where would we live?" Mira asked, nervously popping a cube of sweet Muenster into her mouth.

"You know darling you could always live here. Think of all the money you'd save." Mira understood that her mother had meant what she said quite seriously. But this was not the right time to admit that she would prefer death from typhoid fever. Instead, Mira squirted herself a tall glass of seltzer to drown out any other ideas her mother had conjured up for her future.

Then, as promised, Ina rushed to the front door at the sound of the first chime. Mira not wanting to miss any of this first meeting, stood a few feet behind her, like she had when she was little. She had already sent the men to the den urging them to stop their banter. After removing his coat, Nathan kissed Mira lightly on the lips then introduced his mother to Ina Kane. Taking her hand in hers, Ina welcomed the woman into her home. Mira loved this version of her mother. Here was Ina Kane in charge, strong, but mostly warm-hearted.

"Nu? No kiss for me?" Ina said leaning in to kiss Nathan. "And what is this?" She asked.

Nathan handed Mira a Pyrex dish containing the crispiest potato kugel she had ever seen. But it was Mrs. Berk's cherubic face that revealed the most pride. "From one mother to another," she said, and then she opened the clasp of her bag and removed a small package wrapped in white tissue paper. "And for you *shana Mira...das.*"

Mira immediately ripped open the paper revealing a tiny glass picture frame. She blinked once and then again. The second time tears spilled down her cheeks. "Ah," the mothers said in unison.

"It's that picture!" Mira said, the one you showed me that day on the bus; it's Nathan. I almost took it from you then. I wanted to, you know."

"Yes, that's me all right," Nathan laughed. He lifted his arm over Mira's shoulder and pulled her closer to him. His nervousness had already faded. Then together they walked through the hallway into the sunny breakfast room where everyone else waited, though not so patiently, to dive into many of their favorite foods.

During the meal everyone appeared to be on their best behavior. The Kanes, of course, were all talking at once while Mrs. Berk sat quietly listening, wearing an ebullient smile. Soon after they ate, the men and women separated, moving to different parts of the house. While the women carried the soiled dishes to the kitchen, the men, sucking on toothpicks, marched off to the den.

Within seconds Charlie attempted to engage Nathan. When he offered one of his Cuban cigars, Nathan smiled but refused. Previously warned by Mira of her father's habit of interrogation, he was already an expert at avoiding any questions about his previous work. Besides Mira, Roy was the only one who knew that Nathan had worked at Pearly's. He had stumbled upon this information when taking a date to the popular sweet shoppe after a movie. Thereafter, each time Nathan visited, Roy did not miss an opportunity to mention his craving for an ice cream soda or frappe. But today, even Roy behaved. He kept his mouth shut when his father and uncle began pummeling him with criticism over a decision that had cost their company a great deal of money.

Although he knew his involvement would infuriate Mira, Nathan was suddenly fascinated by the mechanics of her fiery family. So not to appear disinterested, he would attempt something new. Nathan listened to all sides of the story and acted like a natural mediator, when indeed he was to become the family's buffer. He saw this as an opportunity to put his business courses to good use and involve himself in what would be a future of heated discussions about management and inventory control.

Later, when Nathan confided to Mira that he was planning to use Kane Knitting as a case study for his last course at Columbia, she asked if it were a case about: When things go badly . . . what to do. The truth was Nathan had been the first outsider in which the Kanes had placed their trust. Whether or not that was a good thing only time would tell.

*

All day long Mira's lips stung from the marathon kissing she and Nathan had enjoyed the night before, especially after they dropped Mrs. Berk off at her building. Now, while taking a quiet walk around the corner, she reached into the pocket of her cardigan for a hard candy (one from Mrs. Berk's crystal dish) when something rough grazed her finger. It was the gold *Perisphere* pin Nathan had bought for her as a souvenir commemorating the World's Fair. It was round and about the size of a nickel. She went to pin it on her sweater when the thought occurred to her that it would make a really nice button—a button for perhaps a sweater, or, if not a sweater, then a vest. Yes, a sweater vest with three buttons. Mira envisioned the vest clearly in her head; she pictured women, even men, wearing it with a pair of casual slacks. It had been too long since she'd had a creative thought.

Later that night, alone in her room, she sketched several designs using the Perisphere button. First, she drew a vest with two side pockets, which she thought would work for menswear, and then a simple three-button style with a V-neck front for women. She signed her initials in the lower right hand corner of the boards. On the top she lettered, "World's Fair Vestquette."

The vest would be constructed of washable Orlon and very affordable. It was nearly 4 A.M. when Mira turned off her lamp and collapsed on her pillows. Only when she was finally satisfied with her sketches would she allow her body to drift into sleep. Even in her mind, she was adding a detail here and there until she visualized the perfect design.

When JJ and Rena dragged in exhausted from work the next evening, Mira stopped them before they had the chance to go upstairs to change. Mira excitedly escorted her aunts by their elbows into the den with the haughty confidence of a French maître d, but instead of menus, she shoved a batch of sketches in front of their faces. She talked quickly, gasping for air. She rushed before the men would storm the Bastille, signaling the women they were needed in the kitchen.

JJ and Rena passed the drawings back and forth between them. They put on their spectacles to get a better look. Rena pointed, tapping on one of the designs twice with her finger. Then she broke the silence.

"The stores will never go for this," Rena said.

Mira's heart sank. "But why?"

"First of all, by the time we pitch them this item and they make a decision and we ship, the World's Fair will have entirely lost its appeal. You know that it's been a year since the fairgrounds have closed down."

Mira felt a jab of true disappointment. She was certain she had come up with a winner.

"Besides," Rena continued, "the stores are not so crazy about us right now, we'd have to promise them the world—let alone a World's Fair sweater."

"I've got an idea," JJ said. "What about pitching this to catalogues?"

"Catalogues?" Mira asked.

"Their buyers are always looking for novelty items, and customers are told four to six weeks delivery, which gives us the time we need," JJ said. "Also, they handle all advertising and photography, so we will net more on each item."

"This sounds good, really good," Mira beamed. She was happy to see a smile on JJ's face.

"Sis, you have a point there. Also, it might be a way to dump some of Flegelman's yarn. Let's bring it up tonight after dinner. Is that okay with you, Mira?" This, from Aunt Rena? Mira could not believe her aunt was actually asking her permission.

"Yes, of course, that's fine."

"We need to work fast," JJ said.

"We could have samples made by next week," Rena joined in.

"What about the buttons?" Mira asked. "I imagine them looking like this." She showed them the pin that Nathan had given her.

"We can have a small white button done. I have a supplier," Rena said, "Nice work, Mira, nice work. Looks like your Nathan might be your lucky charm."

That night after a fairly uneventful dinner, Aunt Rena told her brother Charlie she had a surprise for him. She asked him to come into the grand dining room where Mira and JJ were already waiting with the sketches laid out across the long stretch of table. For a second, Mira recalled the last time she and her father had been in this room together and the awful news he had bestowed on her. But the mood here tonight was different. Her aunts did all the presenting while she sat hands folded at the end of the table. Poppa's ears perked up when Rena suggested using all the excess yarn that Roy had ordered. Also, he loved the idea of seeing his merchandise in the Spiegels' or Montgomery Ward's catalogue. Even though he realized that the companies would deduct that advertising fee from his profits. People would always want mementos of their travels, especially the World's Fair, with its promise of hope and a better future. Why not an article of clothing, something long-lasting?

"Heh, heh, heh." Charlie lit a fresh cigar as his sisters chattered on and on. He glanced up at Mira and she stared back at him, a grin stenciled on her face. He wore his signature look. She had seen it before, many times when things were better. Poppa was already counting the cash.

Snow

There is a sudden change in the morning light, like a milky curtain falling upon the earth. Outside the cellar window I hear voices and the sounds of children's laughter. Just imagining children having fun puts a smile on my face. But I was warned never to prop myself up and look out the window because someone might see me. So I am startled when someone starts banging hard on the glass as if trying to break through. Scared, I peek my head out from under my pillow, and there he is—Victor. He is pressing his face against the window, his nose all red, squashed and drippy like a hog. Victor is wearing a knit hat pulled over his ears. He holds a huge snowball in his gloved hand that he is trying to show me. I stare, not moving an inch, as he takes a bite out of the snowball. Next, Sophie pops her head in next to him and begins dragging him away by his jacket collar.

"Get away, Victor!" I hear Sophie shout. "Pa told us to never go near any of the cellar windows."

"Oh, Rosha," Victor chants, ignoring his younger sister, "this is what is called snow remember? Victor laughs, and then his laugh is cut off in the middle as if a large tree branch has snapped in half. Next to Victor's head, where Sophie stood, now are two long legs covered to the knees in black rubber boots. A huge bare hand swoops down and swats Victor on top of his head. He spits out a mouthful of snow onto the glass window. I recognize Avram's voice, but not this, what must be his most furious tone.

"This is the last time I will tell you, Victor Juraska. It is no time for taunts and nasty games. Get away from there and stay away!"

All I can see are the father's and son's feet slowly disappearing. Then a large hand returns and places a pile of vanilla snow against the window blocking my view completely. The cellar darkens as if it is already evening. I sit on the crate below the window. This way I get to listen to the children playing outside in the snow. I pretend I'm with them, riding on a big red wooden sled, being pulled along by my tall and handsome older brother who is very kind to me, who has promised to always protect me from bullies like Victor Juraska.

An icy breeze dances past my face giving me a sneezing fit. I cover my mouth afraid that someone can hear me. If I can hear Sophie and Victor outside near the barn, then can't they hear me? Or maybe all these sounds have something to do with wanting and wishing. On my sixth sneeze, my knee jiggles the crate. The only candle in the room blows out. A pool of wax sits in the tray like Bubbe's leftover batter when she used to make me her delicious sugar cookies. I scrape the wax up with my fingernails and roll it into three little balls. I wonder how many candles Marta would allow me to have; time would pass so much faster if I could once again make my wax figurines. I work quickly now and make three separate parts, a head, a belly and a base for my snowman. I will find shavings of wood for his hands and eyes and mouth. Maybe one day Marta will teach me how to be a candle maker just like her. Then I will make candles in the shapes of animals, dancers, and little children that she can sell at the marketplace, well maybe not now, but soon, after things are better again. After all the fear stops and the windows are thrown wide open and nobody ever has to hide.

What We Ask For

All issues of the *Fairchild Daily* had sold out by noon. The daily tattler for the garment trade referred to him as the "King of the Bouclé Knit." Charlie Kane was indeed a star, especially in front of 1400 Broadway. Men with hunched shoulders and husky voices stood huddled together as they puffed on cigars and read of Kane Knitting's latest success. The mumblings among these men was reminiscent of the chanting of voices during the High Holy Days at The Midwood Chapel. Charlie wondered what they were truly wishing for him. He knew, too well, that one man's joy was another man's misery, especially in the garment business.

At the corner newsstand, the *Fairchild* sold better than the *Times* that day, even though most of the headlines told of Germany's increasing victories throughout Europe. Charlie seemed to be the only one not impressed with the article about Kane Knitting. Since the fall the business had seen several small successes, starting with its entry into the catalogue business. The World's Fair sweater vest had already sold out twice and was now back-ordered. Then at his daughter's urging, Charlie began experimenting with new lighter yarns. They were perfect for skirt sets and knit dresses. The stores couldn't keep these items in stock, and Charlie bent over backward to fill orders and keep his accounts satisfied. But nothing wowed the buyers more than Mira's knock-off of Julia Crane's prized Chanel fringed jacket. After Dillard's placed an order for a thousand pieces, Best and Company quickly doubled theirs. And then the catalogues called to see if it could be made less costly for their mass market customers.

It had never occurred to Charlie that he would be working harder than he ever worked, staying at the office until all hours, making trips several times a day downtown to the factory to check on production. He and Ina had not been away for over a year. He longed for a relaxing week in the Catskills, sumptuous Saturday night dinners, variety shows followed by a smorgasbord of rich desserts, but that all seemed impossible now.

As was his habit, Charlie rationalized that Julia Crane would hardly care if he had not followed through on his promise to give Dillard's an exclusive; after all, wasn't the garment just another *schmata*, like all the other *schmatas* Kane had been producing for years? Though Mira, the best designer, the only designer he'd ever employed, had reminded him of his promise over and over again.

*

This was the coldest December Mira could remember, and the mood in the house had remained somber and bleak since JJ's recent breakdown. But now, since the Japanese surprise attack on Pearl Harbor, more and more neighborhood boys were converted from their warm woolen overcoats to the earthen colors of the United States Army. The country was at war.

Women stood huddled in grocery stores and fish markets consoling one another about their young sons either being drafted or joining up against family wishes. Mira felt sorry for the very pregnant women who looked visibly shocked, sending their husbands off to war, not knowing when or if they might ever return home. The thought sent chills up her spine. Then, a few days before Christmas, Nathan showed up at Avenue T wearing a double-breasted deep blue wool jacket, topped with a crisp white sailor hat. Earlier that morning he had joined the U.S. Navy. Mira burst into tears. But through her tears, she realized she had never seen him looking so handsome, so determined and proud. He wore a perpetual smirk that made it hard for her not to smile when she looked at him. Nathan said he chose the

Navy because ever since he was a small boy, he'd dreamed of being on a big ship somewhere in the middle of the sea. For the time being that sea would have to be the Atlantic Ocean, as his orders were for the east coast of Florida. But first he was to be sent up to Elmira, in upstate New York, for six weeks of boot training. He looked forward to thawing out in sunny southern Florida. He'd be leaving in only two weeks.

On Christmas Eve they told their families they were attending a big office party at Nathan's boss's home in Ramsey, New Jersey. Mira packed a small overnight bag with a satin nightgown, several pairs of panties, her toothbrush, and makeup bag. Her hands were shaking as she tucked the bag under her flared wool coat and walked downstairs to meet Nathan who chatted with Roy in the foyer. Roy had received his draft notice that same morning, which sent Ina straight to bed with a splitting headache. Mira offered to stay home, but her mother urged her to go be with Nathan, especially in their last days together.

Roy nervously stuttered on about some plan he had to get out of the draft. Although they were around the same age, Nathan seemed so much more mature than her brother. "So where the hell are you lovebirds off to now?" Roy probed, curiously looking at the bulge under Mira's coat. Mira became edgy and tried switching the subject.

"Just a party and why are you home this evening brother dear?"

"I didn't want to leave Momma, not until Pop gets back from the factory. He's closing down for two weeks, until after New Year's. That's a first in the history of Kane Knitting," Roy said.

"Yes, but that doesn't mean he won't go down to the office. You know Poppa."

"Well, I guess he'll just be shuffling papers, 'cause there's not much else to do with everyone else on vacation." Roy looked in the hall mirror and rubbed his unshaven cheeks. Mira guessed he was really staying in or she would have smelled his strong citrus cologne that often made her sneeze.

Nathan glanced at his watch. "Mira, let's go, we're going to be late."

"Don't drink too much of that eggnog crap," Roy said, following them to the door.

"You can certainly bet on that, brother."

151

As Nathan pulled his car slowly out of the driveway, Mira could see the familiar amber glow of her mother's night lamp. She had the urge to rush back in to see her again, to check if she was all right, but she fought off these feelings, moving closer to Nathan, putting her head on his shoulder as they began their long snowy drive to Virginia. This was the bravest thing she had ever done in her entire life.

She had not asked permission. This was her choice and her choice alone. She was about to marry Nathan Berk. This would be their secret and something for her to cherish while he was away. It would give them hope and something to look forward to once things settled down.

By ten o'clock, as they reached D.C., the snow began tapering off. Nathan had the name of a justice of the peace near Alexandria, who, for a small fee, agreed to waive the legalities of the required blood test. He had told Nathan that he had at least five couples wanting to be married on this Christmas Eve, and there might be a little wait.

They found the house, a small colonial, which was overly decorated with Santa and all of his reindeer. Bright lights were hung around all the windows and doors on the front porch. Two cars were already parked in the driveway—one had attached tin cans and a "just married" sign to the back bumper.

Nathan and Mira looked at each other and grinned. "You sure you want to get hitched now? Last chance to get away," Nathan said, and he took Mira in his arms and kissed her tenderly on the lips.

"I intend to stay right here," she said. "But I really do have to pee, honey, so let's go get married."

Nathan reached in the back seat for a brown grocery bag. "I'm not going to pee in that. Are you crazy?"

Laughing, Nathan pulled a large, slightly wilted orchid out of the bag. As he fumbled, trying to pin the thing on Mira, she began to cry, leaving a stream of mascara cascading down both cheeks. She knew this was a moment she'd never forget. It was easy to memorize: "Mairzy Doats" by the Merry Macs, was playing on the radio, Nathan smelled like Old Spice, and her notoriously weak bladder felt as though it was about to push up through her throat.

"I now pronounce you man and wife. You may kiss the bride." And it was done.

Thirty minutes later they were checking into the Dorian Hotel, a popular spot for tired and anxious elopers. The ad offered a free champagne breakfast. Mira's alibi for Christmas Day was a party at Faye's parents' apartment. Faye would be flying in later that day, so that gave the newlyweds time to enjoy their brief, but hopefully romantic honeymoon.

The hotel clerk, an old man as bent over as the pipe he was smoking, had them sign the register. The smell of cherry tobacco filled Mira's nostrils as she meticulously wrote for the first time the words: *Mr. and Mrs. Nathan Berk, Brooklyn, New York.*

Nathan took the room key attached to a rolling pin, and the two headed up the long, creaky staircase that led to the bedrooms. Nathan shushed Mira lovingly as she began to giggle from nerves. Coming from inside the rooms, they heard the muffled sounds of lovemaking, sighs, rhythmic knocking, a box spring creaking, someone sobbing. They struggled to keep silent as they reached the threshold. There Nathan swept Mira up into his arms, her legs hitting the doorjamb as he rushed in and tossed her on the overstuffed double bed.

Exhausted, they lay side by side breathing heavily, clutching hands until Nathan, propped on one elbow, began unbuttoning Mira's coat. He pulled her up out of her coat sleeves. His cool hands slid up the front of her sweater, warming against the dependable heat of her breasts. Mira felt her nipples turn hard as Nathan's tongue circled them gently. There was no time for the nightgown that she had wrapped neatly in pink tissue paper, no time for the matching feathered slippers. Within seconds the bed became a laundry heap of clothing flying in every direction. Clumsily, yet lovingly, Nathan's fingers curled over the elastic of Mira's satin panties. His hands swept up her belly to her breasts and down again where they rested on the tops of her inner thighs. She wanted to scream, but she remembered the sounds they'd heard earlier in the hallway. Instead she pushed her head deeper into his chest hiding her face, which she was certain had transformed into a much older woman.

The long silver chain and dog tag Nathan wore grazed her cheek as he climbed carefully upon her. She knew he could see her face entirely now, and feeling shy, she shut her eyes. She had felt his hardness before on hot summer nights when they had walked the boardwalk and taken a blanket out of the car, seeking a secret place to be alone. But they had always stayed fully clothed, Nathan usually quiet and moody afterward. Slightly embarrassed, he'd pull his long shirt over his pants to conceal his bulging erection. Mira pretended not to notice. It was something you knew existed but of course didn't mention. But tonight there was no coyness, no pretending. Mira ached with passion for him. She surprised herself as she guided his fingers over the soft down of her pelvic bone moving him inside her ever so slowly. She gasped as the strange new pain startled her. Nathan began kissing the crook of her neck lost in his own desire. When he entered her he stopped momentarily, trying to slow down, but by now she did not want him to stop. She never wanted him to stop. She wondered why the heck they had waited so long. Mira wrapped her long legs around his, and they rocked, rhythmically, to the incessant hiss and beat of the steaming radiator, the only witness, hiding behind the striped satin curtains.

The next morning, Mira awakened before Nathan. There were no sounds coming from the hallway. For several minutes she lay on her side watching her new husband sleep. His beard was heavier than she had ever seen it, and his dark curly hair fell over his forehead reminding her of a sweet teenage boy. He didn't stir when she lightly kissed his cheek. She was hungry, really hungry. The noises emanating from her stomach competed with the radiator.

Naked and shivering, she tiptoed into the bathroom, taking her small overnight bag. The toilet seat was freezing, and she realized that if she flushed, she'd awaken Nathan. So first, she put on her new cream-colored satin nightgown. She washed her face, cleaned the mascara from under her eyes, and tied her hair in a gold ribbon she had saved when she bought the nightgown.

She peeked out of the bathroom, and saw Nathan rubbing his eyes squinting to see her.

"Sorry if I woke you, Mr. Berk," Mira said, tip-toeing into the room.

"Come here," Nathan said, as he propped himself up on the pillows, arms outstretched.

Within seconds the nightgown was on the floor, along with Mira and Nathan as they shimmied their bodies over the slippery fabric. This time their lovemaking felt freer, more furious, both of them recharged from a good night's sleep. For a brief second she thought of her parents, imagined their dismay, but quickly pushed them out of her mind. I am married, she reminded herself. I'm doing nothing wrong.

When they finished, Mira stood up, first pulling a piece of the bedspread around her. Nathan kept tugging at it, and she began to feel annoyed. Maybe they were about to have their first real fight.

"So where is this champagne breakfast we're supposed to be getting with this honeymoon suite?" Mira said, looking at the peeling paint on the ceiling.

Nathan looked at his watch on the night stand. "It's only seven o'clock. Everyone's still sleeping or. . . ."

"Well, since we've already done . . . *or*, can we please get some breakfast?"

Nathan laughed. "Sure you don't want to wait for the champagne?"

"I think I might fade away."

Nathan jumped into his clothes, and they were packed and in the car in five minutes. Mira thought perhaps she should have straightened the bed, hidden the lusty evidence of Christmas Eve.

Little icy snowflakes had formed on the windshield, and Nathan tried scraping them off with his nails. He wore no gloves. Mira handed him a small metal nail file from her purse. The car started up reluctantly, and they gave each other a sidelong glance. They drove through the quiet neighborhood, and watched night posts being turned off, and shades being pulled up. Mira imagined young children eagerly tumbling out of bed running down the stairs in little red pajamas to see what Santa had left them. Santa and Christmas. "Oh, No!" Mira said, causing Nathan to come to a quick stop. "What did you forget?" he asked.

"Nathan, it's Christmas. Nothing is open today, I'm sure."

"Don't worry," he said, "there's got to be a diner or something." But they could already see that the little town they drove through looked boarded up. Mira moaned in hunger; she guessed it was from all the sex. Nathan spotted a Texaco sign in the distance. He needed gas and would ask for a recommendation for a good, hearty breakfast. But only a young pubescent boy was working the pumps. By now most of the men had already been shipped off to duty.

Mira rolled down the window and instantly smelled coffee. She jumped out of the car and followed the seductive aroma into the little shack that adjoined the gas stop. There in the middle of the counter she saw what she hoped was a freshly brewed pot of coffee. Next to it sat a basket of Christmas tree cookies decorated with colorful sprinkles. Nathan came in to pay and saw his new bride stuffing both her pockets. "And how do you propose to drink the coffee," he asked, appearing amused.

Mira's eyes searched the counter and dusty shelves, resting on a bright plaid thermos. She reached into her purse and found a five dollar bill. Then, while the boy watched, his eyes gaping, she emptied the contents of the coffee pot. She dropped four sugar cubes into the thermos, and handed the boy the money. "Merry Christmas," she said, and ran quickly back to the warming car, Nathan following.

As they pulled away, Mira told her new husband she hoped the nice young boy would never have to go fight for his country. And then she said a silent prayer, wishing the war would end so families could be together again celebrating holidays, celebrating life. From the rearview mirror, she continued to watch the boy, the five bucks she'd handed him waving like a small flag in his hand.

When they got to Faye's parents' apartment, a little after five, they pushed through a boisterous crowd of unfamiliar people and parked themselves in front of a tray of sliced cold cuts. They had each downed three mini-sandwiches when they were accosted by Faye. Mira tried chewing quickly, so she could talk, but all she could do was embrace her friend, a hand around her shoulder, that hand grasping pastrami. Mira stepped back to examine Faye as she had once studied patterns on a mannequin.

"My god, Faye, is this really you?"

"Who'd ya think, honey?" Having most likely bored enough people with her rendition of Scarlett, Faye now tried a pretty convincing Mae West routine.

Nathan dabbed at his mouth with a cocktail napkin and kissed Faye on the cheek. "It's good to see you Faye. So how's the Wild West treating you?"

"Fabulous, really fabulous, didn't you hear? I've been asked to do some sketches for Loretta Young. Her agent loved all my ball gowns. Mira, I even showed them my Fourth of July number from school. Wow, did you ever save my *tushie* on that one."

Mira had a sinking feeling that she tried to push away, but it just would not leave. She should be feeling high, on top of the world, but listening to Faye and seeing her sparkle like the tinsel adorning the windows of the crowded room made her sullen and painfully envious.

"Faye, we're both so happy for you, aren't we, Nathan? Now, we have a surprise for you. Can you keep a huge secret?" Mira spoke trying to regain her composure. "We've just eloped."

"Fabulous!" Faye bellowed. Mira leaned in and shushed her. "But when?"

"Last night. We drove down to Virginia. It was truly wonderful. We wanted to do it before Nathan goes off to boot camp. He'll be down south for God knows how long."

"And your parents, how do you think they'll react to this news?"

"We plan to keep it a secret for as long as we possibly can. Of course, we'd like a wedding, but we'll have to wait until the war is over and who knows when that will be?"

Mira clutched Nathan's arm as if he was the prize she had always wanted that had just been delivered. She looked around the room and all she could see was uniforms. Most of these men had only just signed up, and many were on a short leave for the holidays. The atmosphere in the room felt tentative. It was as if people wanted to rejoice, but their voices grew loud more from a stifled nervousness than joy. The newlyweds reluctantly toasted Faye with a strange Borsht version of eggnog before slipping out the door. Mira guessed it would be a long time before she saw her old friend again.

"Hey, are you all right?" Nathan asked. They were in the car heading for Mira's house.

"Yes, I'm fine, a little tired, that's all. Isn't that great news about Faye? I knew she was going to do fine out there."

"Mira, are you sorry now that you didn't go with her?"

"Nathan, how could you ask me that? You know how much I love you. You're all that matters to me, don't ever forget that." Mira brushed the side of his face with her gloved hand. He, too, looked tired, and his beard was shadowy. He smiled back and reached for her hand. Mira removed her gloves as they pulled into her driveway. She slipped off her thin gold wedding ring and placed it into her purse. She stared at Nathan, taking him all in.

"Goodnight, Mr. Berk," she said, sliding out of the front seat.

"Good night, Mrs. Berk," he answered back. She ran up the porch steps to the front door, which was already propped open.

"So, nu? daughter, where have you been for the last twenty-four hours. I was thinking maybe I should rent out your room, maybe make a little extra cash." As expected, Poppa was in rare form. She tried not to laugh at his sarcasm.

"Merry Christmas, Poppa, how's Momma feeling?"

"Funny that you should ask. Maybe a phone call would have made her worry a little less?"

"But I told her that Nathan and I had parties to go to last night and today, and that I'd be sleeping over at Nathan's. Mrs. Berk invited me."

"So, there's no telephone at Mrs. Berk's?"

"Okay, okay, you're right. I'm sorry. Where's Momma?"

"In the kitchen," he replied, triumphantly.

"And Rena and JJ?" she asked.

"They went up to Grossingers in the Catskills and are probably eating up a storm."

"You and Momma should have gone away with them. You know how you love that place. I heard that Georgie Jessel, your favorite, was performing this weekend."

"Nah, your mother's not in the mood, she's worried sick about Roy. I've got to do something next week after the holiday," he said, thinking out loud.

"What do you mean you've got to do something?"

"Never mind. Go, go to Momma."

Mira's mother sat at the kitchen table stirring her tea. She didn't notice Mira until she pulled out the kitchen chair to sit next to her. Ina's face looked as white as the Frigidaire doors. She wore a thick coat of night cream that made her face stick to Mira's when they kissed. Mira rubbed the cream into her own face, a habit she had adopted from the time she was little.

"Hmm, always loved your Jergen's," Mira said. "Momma, I thought I'd told you I had parties to attend. Sorry if I made you worry."

Ina waved her hand, "I remembered something about parties. I guess I didn't listen that well. So, tell me. Did you have a good time with Nathan?" she asked, looking up from the tea and staring directly into Mira's eyes.

Mira felt her skin flush as scenes from her wedding night flashed before her eyes. Before she could answer, her mother raised both of her hands to her cheeks.

"You are married, aren't you?" she asked, leaning forward into her daughter's face.

Mira was speechless. Her mother had to be some kind of a witch, like those they'd burned in Salem. Mira ran to shut the swinging doors that led into the kitchen.

"Promise you won't tell Poppa, please," she begged.

"Oh, my goodness, you're not pregnant?"

"No, of course not, how could you ask such a thing?"

"Darling, it happens, in the nicest of families. It wouldn't be such a tragedy. War, Hitler, his senseless murdering. That? That is a tragedy." Tears sprinkled down Ina's cheeks.

"You *are* happy for me Momma, right?"

"Yes, yes, of course." She kissed her daughter on both cheeks. This time Mira didn't mind the stickiness. She loved the way Ina smelled, and she knew she would always remember this moment with just the two of them alone in the nest of their safe warm kitchen on Avenue T.

Later that night, Ina had difficulty sleeping, so she turned on the night lamp to read an old cookbook. Charlie lay there squinting at her through one eye. He could see she was not concentrating.

"So," he said, "what was such a big secret that you had to close the kitchen doors?"

"Oh, you're up too," Ina said. She continued flipping through the pages, dodging his question.

"Ina, I asked you a question. Never mind, I think I know," he said.

"What Charl, what do you think you know?" She tried to hide her smirk, but her husband's undaunted curiosity always amused her.

Charlie propped himself up on one elbow, leaned over and whispered, "Ina, sweetheart, our daughter, the one with those big sparkling blue eyes, and burning cheeks . . . you want I should continue?" Ina nodded for him to go on. "That girl, our little girl, I think is now officially a married woman."

He didn't wait for any reaction from her. That was never his way. He merely rolled over, and in mere seconds was fast asleep. He snored like a contented lion, leaving Ina staring at the back of his sun-spotted head.

So Much for Secrets

~

Tossing and turning among her fluffy pillows, Mira slept until noon the next day. From downstairs, wafted the familiar aroma of fried eggs and onions, and her stomach began its annoying rumbling. She heard a car pull up to the curb and when she peeked from her window, she saw her aunts stepping cautiously out of their cab into the snow. The family always used the same dependable driver to take them back and forth from Grossingers; he was a sweet man they had nicknamed, *Maxie the Taxi*, and who was now schlepping two blue suitcases up the front steps. Would she ever be able to keep her secret from them? She knew Momma would never tell Poppa, but Aunt Rena was like a hound dog, always a pro when it came to sniffing out information.

She heard the front door open and shut, and the habitual stomping of feet to remove any snow. Within seconds there was the usual kitchen clatter and chattering. Mira had memorized these sounds, the melodies of the home she had always loved. They touched the part of her that had never really grown up. She squatted down on the upstairs landing just to listen. She measured the lilting voices and their tones like a musical conductor, eyes closed, her head swaying. Even Poppa sounded especially jubilant today. Something he said made JJ respond as if surprised. She actually squealed. It had been a long time since Mira had heard anyone sound this exhilarated.

She hurried downstairs, but then caught herself and tried walking

161

nonchalantly into the kitchen. After all, she was a woman now, a real woman. All eyes turned toward her. Poppa rose from the table quickly, his orange juice swaying in the glass. Momma sat by the window beating eggs with a long wire whisk; she froze and looked at Mira with a nervous smile. Aunt Rena stared at Mira biting her lip. Mira couldn't tell if she looked angry or concerned. But JJ could not control herself.

"Mira, I'm so very happy for you." She ran to Mira and hugged her tightly while dabbing her eyes with a corner of her apron. Gently pushing JJ away, Mira sank down into one of the cold metal chairs. She clutched the chair's arms as if she was about to ride the steeplechase at Coney Island.

"Momma, I just can't believe you told them!"

"Mira, sweetheart," Ina said as she pried her daughter's hand off the chair. "Poppa knew, he just knew, and so of course he told everybody."

"Poppa? But how?"

"Shah now," he said, in an attempt to calm her down. "It was not difficult to know, daughter. All I had to do is look at your face, and I knew that you were not telling me the truth. So I figured there was a special reason for this. Then I notice your Momma is very flushed after her little chat with you in the kitchen. Doors are opened, doors are closed, so I guessed out loud, and your Momma's lovely *punim* told me . . . like always, I guessed right."

Mira's mouth had dropped wide open while listening to her father's explanation. For a second she pictured him as Sherlock Holmes, his fat cigar magically turning into a curled meerschaum. She shook her head and came back to reality. It suddenly occurred to her that her father didn't seem particularly upset by the prospect of his only daughter having secretly married, or was he, too, caught up in his game of having guessed right? Mira knew how he loved to let everyone know they couldn't put one over on Charlie Kane. She hoped she wasn't going to have to pay for this deception sometime further down the road.

Mira stood up straight and regained her composure. "So I gather Poppa, that Nathan and I have your blessings?"

Charlie took a long drag on his cigar. The other women looked first at Mira, then Poppa. "You'll need a lot more than my blessings.

What you'll need is a lot of mazel. Daughter, may I remind you that our country is at war?" He cleared his throat. "So, I guess your Nathan figured I would support you while he was away?"

Rena shot her brother an angry look.

"No Poppa, you don't have to support me. I can always get another job, certainly one that pays a lot more than you're paying me. And it's because of the war Poppa we decided not to wait. We wanted something to look forward to when Nathan returned. He'll be stationed in Miami after training, waiting for his orders to ship out." Mira stood, her arms folded, strong and stubborn although her eyes brimmed with tears.

"Yes, I know all about this," Charlie said. "I have friends on the boards, people I gave work to after the Depression. You were a baby still."

"You mean the draft boards?" Mira asked.

"And the recruiting offices as well. Nathan and your brother will not be leaving this country so fast."

"I don't understand."

There's nothing to understand, except that as long as I live and breathe, Nathan and your brother Roy will be safe, unless, of course, they cut off their arms peeling potatoes."

The women began to clean-up the kitchen. Hattie was down south for the holidays visiting her sister. My God, Mira thought, all conversations in this house ended in suspense, like the radio programs she and Mama once listened to when she was younger. Tune in next week to see who is saved.

Charlie sat down and opened up the morning paper to his favorite section, the obits. He was already tsk-tsk-ing somebody's recent demise, mumbling as he read about those less fortunate than him. He seemed oblivious to Mira's curious glances.

Aunt Rena was the first to break the silence. "So, when does Nathan leave, Mira?"

"In nine days, unless Poppa knows differently," Mira answered, turning her head in her father's direction.

Charlie put down the paper, stood up, and placed his arm around Ina's shoulder. "Now it is cold, winter time, so God willing, in the spring, we shall host a beautiful wedding for our daughter. It is only right. This way our friends are not hurt, and nobody whispers. There are no rumors. People will know what a wedding should be," he said proudly.

"But how can there be a wedding with my husband away?"

"Perhaps Nathan will come home on a long furlough. It happens all the time. Don't worry, just leave everything up to me," Charlie said.

"We discussed this many times. I really don't think Nathan wants a big wedding. It is too extravagant a thing to do especially in times like these."

"You both deserve a big send off, not to mention a little nest egg that a wedding would give you. Momma and I have gone to a lot of weddings over the years, we know about such things. Isn't that so, Ina?" Ina nodded sheepishly.

Mira knew how much her mother wanted this. They had talked about the day Mira would become a bride when Mira was a young child. How could she even think of depriving her mother of not planning a wedding for her only daughter?

"Okay, okay, but I'll have to talk to Nathan, and please don't say anything to any of your friends. Mrs. Berk doesn't know yet."

"Not a word, we promise, right Charl?" Ina said.

Although Aunt Rena seemed genuinely happy, Mira felt uncomfortable, struck with the thought that she was now married and her aunts were not. Funny, but she had never even pictured them married. Yes, they had men stop by the house, and they'd often act giddy, even a bit silly at times. But the fact remained that neither of the women had enjoyed a serious relationship. At least, none that Mira had observed, but she wondered about JJ a lot. Mira remembered her aunt's obsession with a few of the love poems written by Dickinson and Browning. How JJ had memorized and quoted passages to Mira whenever they took walks after dinner. Maybe JJ had fantasized more than she ever let on about having love in her life.

More than ever, Mira realized that the war was not the only motivation for her elopement. The real issue was to spare Nathan the task of undergoing Poppa's version of the Spanish Inquisition. Poppa had been curious why he had left the food business—the food business being Pearly's Place, of course.

Nathan explained that he'd been wooed by Mr. Simon for months, and that Global had offered him what seemed like a real solid future. Poppa liked the idea that Nathan would be involved in the fabric industry. Although he moved out of the stockroom after only a month, Nathan hadn't made any real substantial sales. But he had a fistful of very good prospects. He had always been a saver and had stashed away enough money to pay off the Packard his friend sold him after his old heap-a-hearse made by Lincoln finally died. He bought Mira's platinum wedding band and a lamb jacket for his mother. He told Mira that one day soon he would ask his mother for the small emerald cut diamond ring that his father had given his mother over forty years ago.

Mira truly believed her father approved of Nathan. Why shouldn't he? He was a good listener and had a great deal of common sense. Many times, Charlie asked Nathan's advice, sometimes talking to him for hours after Mira had gone to bed. Seeing them talking together eased some of her own conflicts with her father, but you could never bet on how Poppa would react to something, especially marriage. She simply never wanted to be in the position of asking his permission for anything, anymore. He loved the control, and Mira hated giving it to him with a vengeance.

She hoped that someday she would no longer be an employee of Kane Knitting although there was a great deal of status and recognition that went along with being the head designer, albeit the only designer. It would be wonderful to be out on her own, designing her own fashions, haute couture with trimmings and fabrics beyond her father's imagination, and most certainly, budget. Mira had not looked at her sketches in over six months. Seeing them could only make her resentful all over again. Her mind might wander, and she'd be back at Pearly's talking to Faye about their shared dreams. Faye had shown no desire for marriage. Changing her life as Faye had was much too courageous for Mira. But those nagging jealous pangs remained. Loving and being loved by Nathan had eased many of those feelings, yet some still lingered. She wondered when and if they'd ever go away.

*

Mira broke the news to Nathan over the phone. The jig was up. She was surprised that he sounded relieved. He was glad that Mira's family knew they were married. He didn't like keeping that big a secret, especially from Charlie Kane. He said now he could finally tell his mother and propose to Mira in an appropriate way.

"But we're already married, silly," Mira said.

"I know, I know, but you'll see, it will be very romantic," Nathan answered.

"And you're okay with a big wedding?" she asked.

"I can't wait to see you as a beautiful and blushing bride. Maybe we'll even get a few days away for a real honeymoon. That's if I can get a long enough leave. Late March, hmm, that's only three months away. Gosh Mira, what if I've shipped out by then?"

"Nathan, I have this lucky feeling that everything will work out," Mira answered. How could she tell him that his new father-in-law was already pulling strings? It might make Nathan furious at her. No, it was better that he didn't know. After all, maybe Poppa hadn't done anything. Maybe he just liked you to believe that he was like a magician capable of altering everyone's lives, turning dusty pigeons into lovely flower bouquets.

A few days before Nathan left for boot camp, he joined his new family for a sumptuous dinner of brisket, potato pirogues, and baked apples for dessert. Mira felt all eyes on her and Nathan, as if they were now altered—a different Mira, a different Nathan. She looked up from her plate and saw Roy staring at them. He had this strange grin on his face that made Mira squirm. She felt herself blushing. She knew what he was thinking. Sex . . . sex! It was probably all Roy ever thought about. Aunt Rena poked Roy, and he went back to slurping the juice from his baked apple. Mira had found the silence unbearable. All she heard were the familiar sounds of eating. Lips clacking together, tongues sucking and clucking on teeth, and the occasional ping from someone's ring hitting a crystal goblet. She felt like she was at the Bronx Zoo visiting among orangutans. All at once, she began laughing out loud. This caused JJ to join her, then Rena and Momma. Hattie emitted a howl from the kitchen, which only made the women laugh harder, tears streaming down their faces. The men stared at each other, shrugging their shoulders and looking for clues. Finally, Poppa took his spoon and tapped on his glass like a judge regaining order in his courtroom. He asked Hattie to quickly refill everyone's wine glass, which she did, scurrying around the table so fast that she caused Mira to squeal all over again.

Charlie cleared his throat. "Okay, okay, I want you should all raise your glasses and join me in a toast to the new couple, of course, it is not yet official in God's eyes, but that will happen soon. To our Mira and her Nathan . . . may you both have a lot of *naches* and give us many healthy grandchildren and soon. *L'Chaim*."

Everyone chanted l'chaim. Hattie's came out "lay-hay-men" a beat later, causing Mira to spit drops of red wine on to the white tablecloth. Hattie grabbed some seltzer to rub out the spots, and everyone followed Poppa into the den.

The women immediately clustered together and ogled over the ring Nathan had given Mira the night before. He had looped the one carat emerald cut gem through a cherry stem inside the drinks they were having while out for a special steak dinner. It took Mira three sips of her Manhattan before she looked inside the glass and noticed the ring floating below the brim.

"I know this seems a little backward," Nathan had said, slipping the ring on her finger, "but will you marry me . . . again?"

"Hmm, can I think about this? Maybe I should ask my husband."

"I think he'd definitely say give the guy a shot." Nathan grinned.

"Well, then, I guess the answer's YES!" Mira threw both arms around his neck, hating to have him go home that night without her.

"Soon, honey, you'll see, we'll be together," he had said while she buried her face in his chest; her tears dampening his shirt.

Mira told this story to the women as they sat huddled together in the den, the afghans they'd crocheted tossed over shoulders or tucked around legs. Through the den windows they could see a light dusting of snow encircling the street lamps.

The men stood gathered around Nathan each telling some version of a problem they'd had with a worker. Roy was insistent about firing the man. Uncle Louie wasn't sure, and Poppa was afraid because the guy had rough relatives, *trombeniks,* who could cause real trouble among the workers. Momma wanted to distract them from this annoying chatter. She motioned to Mira to help her open the card table and then took four fresh decks of Bicycle cards from a carved mahogany box. Nathan had not officially played in any of the Kane's gin rummy or poker games, mostly because no one had asked him. Mira winked at him and motioned for him to sit down. Tonight would be the night. They would play gin rummy with two teams, Mira, Momma, and Aunt Rena against Roy, Uncle Louie, and Nathan. Poppa had no patience for cards. He preferred standing over everyone's shoulder, *kibitzing,* or he'd take one of his strolls through the house, rearranging figurines or other collectibles.

JJ begged off and nobody pushed. It was hard for her to concentrate. JJ, still quite fragile, seemed a bit more focused on the day to day goings on at work and at home. Rena continually kept a close watch on her and had insisted that they both go away to the Catskills over the holiday. JJ was still under the care of a doctor and back on medication that made her seem much more relaxed. She served some of her delicious Linzer tarts, placing a sterling tray in the center of the table. Then she excused herself saying she needed to make a phone call. She became flustered when Mira asked her who she was calling. JJ mumbled something about an old friend. Rena seemed just as surprised, but they were already arranging their cards with Mira having dealt the first hand. Nathan looked more than a little bit nervous, Mira thought, but so adorable. She winked at him across the round card table hoping to instill a little confidence.

Since it was already late, they agreed to play to 200 points. Nathan, used to the quiet card games on a slow day at Pearly's shoppe, was not prepared for the outright malice suddenly erupting like Vesuvius from these people who were now his family. Mira played against Roy, who acted like he would rather die than give away a card she needed. "But Roy, you don't need that card," she said.

"Ha, but you do," he answered smugly. Roy said he'd rather break up his hand, giving up his own chance to get gin than to give his sister the card she needed. Louie and Ina played a nice congenial game, sister-in-law against brother-in-law, not out for blood or so it seemed. Nathan was surprised by Louie's card sense and grasp of the game, since he spoke so little English. But Rena was the real card player in the family, taking no prisoners. Mira begged her aloud to please be kind to Nathan. She almost let the words slip out that she didn't want to be an "old maid." Instead, she said she didn't want Nathan running out on her. Rena didn't attempt to apologize when she *double-schnei-ded* an unsuspecting Nathan, putting the women way into the lead.

Ina took a second and covered her eyes. She looked as though she'd realized that a game of gin rummy with the competitive Kaninsky clan might not have been the most affable way to welcome the new-comer Nathan Berk into the family.

Just Sophie and Me

~

It is finally Saturday, my favorite day of the week, when Sophie brings my breakfast and stays for most of the afternoon. After I eat a few bites of bread, we begin our game. Today we pretend we are taking our make-believe sisters (our rag dolls) on a very long trip to America.

Because I am older, it is my job to tell the story. I remind Sophie that we are on a very big ship in the middle of the ocean with lots of other people aboard.

"We must keep quiet," I say, "it is early and people are still asleep."

"Okay," Sophie says, but I know she likes when we become the characters. It makes the game feel almost real. So this morning, while looking out at the rolling sea with Sophie close beside me, I begin. First it is very peaceful and quiet, and then we see a very scary man coming toward us. He has a long, pointy mustache and is dressed in a uniform with high black leather boots.

"Oh no, he has a gun. Quick Sophie, run!"

"You! Kinder!" he yells, and starts chasing us around the slippery deck. We fall and get up, then fall again. Every time we think the scary man is gone, he appears again, standing right in front of us. Sophie and I duck around a corner to lose him. He follows us and slips, falling flat on his big scary face. That long pointy mustache of his is stuck like nails to the deck.

Sophie turns to me and asks if we should help him.

"No, no, we mustn't. He will hurt us and then we will never get to America." I tell Sophie he looks like one of the soldiers I saw on Sadowa Street. "He was mean to an old man and a mother carrying her babies."

We grab our pretend sisters and move to the upper deck. I'm afraid I've made Sophie scared. "Don't worry. He will have to stay on the ship forever," I say. "He will never, ever see America."

"That's too bad," she says. Sophie only likes happy endings.

The next character is a big old lady who eats so many corn muffins that when it is time to leave, she has trouble getting out of her cabin. This story makes Sophie laugh and laugh.

"Shh! Listen, Sophie," I say. There is an announcement by *me* pretending to be the captain: "ALL STRONG MEN PLEASE REPORT IMMEDIATELY TO THE CAPTAIN'S QUARTERS."

Most of the people in my stories are stuck somewhere, wanting to be somewhere else.

After a while, I tell Sophie it is time for us to wave. "Why?" she asks, holding her pretend sister closer.

"See that green statue way over there? That is America!"

I show her the pictures of my aunts, uncles, and cousins I keep on the shelf above my cot. She says she likes the one where everybody is wearing fancy hats, and standing in front of a big house with two lions sitting on the front step. Sophie asks if they are real lions. I shrug my shoulders; they look like statues to me, but I really can't say since there's no longer anyone to ask.

When our make-believe ship arrives in America, Sophie and I take our sisters by the hand and start walking until we find the house that looks like the one in the picture. We are awfully tired and hungry, but we keep on walking because we can't go back now. We don't want to go back. We've come too far.

"Here we are," I shout, "we've found it!" And we take turns knocking on the big brass door. Sometimes, it's my pretty cousin, Mira, who answers, and she is always happy to see me, her eyes filled with tears. Or sometimes, it's my Aunt Jeanette and Aunt Rena, Bubbe's two daughters, who she missed so much after they left to live in America. My aunts will have crispy pastries baking in the oven and give us beautiful new dresses and shiny black shoes that Sophie and I try on. Of course, everything fits perfectly.

We are both happy and begin dancing around the room. I get dizzy and fall down on my cot with a loud bang. Lying there, I can smell the candle wax, or something stronger reminding me of when Bubbe ironed Poppa's shirts. I sit up and see that the shabbos candle has fallen off the crate and on to my cot. Puffs of grey smoke rise up from my pillow, the pillow Marta had stuffed with rags.

"Hurry!" I cry.

Sophie flies up the stairs. I want to follow her, but know that, no matter what, I must stay down here.

Pinching the pillow between two fingers, I bring it to the corner of the cellar where a big vat sits half-filled with my old pee and water. I stuff the pillow deep inside the vat, pushing and pushing until there is no more smoke, only the sound of a steamy sizzle.

Within seconds Marta rushes down the stairs with Sophie close behind. Marta takes a wooden bucket filled with water and empties it over the vat until it overflows onto the floor stopping only a few feet from all the bags filled with supplies.

Marta's breathing is so loud, I doubt she can speak. But then she says: "let me see your hands Rosha. Turn them around."

I'm crying because I'm glad she is not yelling at me or telling me to leave.

She moves over to my cot and pounds the mattress with her fists. Finally Marta takes a long, deep breath and sits down. She calls Sophie and me to her side and snuggles us with all her warmth.

After she sends Sophie upstairs to finish her chores, Marta looks at me for a very long time. Her eyes move around the room as if searching for her missing words.

"This was just an accident, Rosha, but it could have been so much worse. There will be no more candles down here. That you know."

I wipe my eyes and look into Marta's face, which is rosier than I have ever seen. I am grateful for all her forgiveness, yet I don't know what to say.

Later, when it is quiet again and I am all alone, I return the pictures to the shelves above my cot. I am glad nothing else caught on fire, especially the pictures. I notice the man in suspenders who looks so much like Poppa. So much that I have to turn the picture around. On the back someone has written the words, *The Kane Family*.

What was wrong with Kaninsky, I wonder? Why would they ever change their name?

A Chance for Love

Jeanette prayed that Charlie would remain in the den with the card players long enough for her to make the phone call. She pulled the crumpled piece of paper from her trouser pocket and stared at the number. She had never ever telephoned a man before. That's what she had told him when he scribbled the digits on the back of a cocktail napkin. No way could she allow him to call her at home. Since the incident in the factory, the entire family hovered over her like a bunch of swooping hawks. They watched her much too closely, as though she were some rare species capable of extinction. All this made her extra claustrophobic, causing her to survey herself from the outside looking in. She would hear her own voice speak aloud and then immediately some inner critic intruded, wanting to revise what she had said. This nagging tentativeness invaded almost all her actions. But not that night—the night when she first met him.

She and Rena had not had a getaway for nearly two years, and the Catskills had always been a family favorite. Originally a bunga-low colony and small farm since the 1930's, Grossingers had rapidly become a luxurious resort hotel, frequented by the rich, famous, and hard-working Manhattan singles, most hoping to find a mate. For their Christmas bonus Charlie had insisted on paying for his sisters' vacation. Usually, they would decline, telling him a Broadway show would suffice, but this time they were terribly anxious to get away from their myopic existence in the house.

On the very first night of the holiday weekend, Jeanette was having difficulty sleeping. She felt like a wound up coil ready to spring across the room, and Rena's snoring in the next bed made matters worse. In the distance she could hear the orchestra coming from the hotel's nightclub as they played, "You, and the Night, and the Music."

Jeanette parted the lacy curtains and peeked out of her hotel window, and saw a young man and woman cup their hands to light up cigarettes before entering the nightclub doors. She lifted the alarm clock next to her bed. It was still early, she thought, only eleven o'clock, and she had taken a very long nap that afternoon after watching Rena win the ping pong tournament. No wonder Rena was out like a light. She had badly beaten three teenage boys and an old rabbi from the Bronx. The prize was a free tango lesson with Juan, the resident dance instructor and lady's man, and a bottle of Chardonnay, which Rena finished off by herself that night at dinner. She had offered the tango lesson to Jeanette, but she declined.

Slipping out from under the warm covers onto the cold pine floor, Jeanette tiptoed and took her dress, heels, and coat into the small bathroom in the hallway. After she dressed, she looked into the gold oval mirror above the sink and tested her smile. Her brother was right. It felt good to be away. After just one day in the country, she looked better than she had in months. Her hair still had its tight permanent wave and needed just a little patting down. She tucked her lipstick and room key in her pocket and snuck quietly out of the room into the darkened hall.

A blast of cold air surprised her the instant she stepped outside the bungalow, and she raised her coat collar to shield her neck and cheeks. There was a very slippery path that led to the nightclub. She chided herself for not wearing her rubber galoshes, but they were so bulky and unglamorous; besides she had only about 50 feet to go. Methodically, she counted her steps, which kept her from falling down on the heavily packed snow. A twig from a buried evergreen bush snagged her coat. She was glad to see so many people still up and about, walking across the grounds. Some nodded at her, but most moved quickly, appearing anxious to enter the warmth of the club or the nearby coffee shop for a snack before bed. The art of eating was the most popular pastime at the resort. She knew if she wasn't careful, she might easily gain a pound a day. She'd have to pace herself for the weekend ahead of overabundant choices of edibles.

For a second she thought about turning into the path that lead to the *Nochery* for one of their enormous hot fudge sundaes, but instead she pushed through the large brass double doors that led to the night-club, a place known as Harry's Starlight Room. Inside, the spacious room was lavishly decorated in shades of deep purple and royal blue. Votive candles flickered on the tables giving off a warm rosy glow, and the scent of gardenias wafted from crystal centerpieces. A young male soloist was singing, "I'm forever blowing bubbles . . ." and the room filled with iridescent soap bubbles. They multiplied before Jeanette's eyes, and like a child she reached out to grab one before it collided with the tip of her nose. She slipped off her coat and fidgeted with her gloves while standing and watching some couples dance, their arms entwined around each other's necks. She thought about turn-ing around and leaving when a boyish looking waiter escorted her to a table next to two women; they looked like mother and daughter. They nodded hello to one another, having made eye contact earlier in the evening during show time. Earlier, Georgie Jessel, the comedian and storyteller, wearing full army regalia had performed to a packed house. He had gotten quite serious at the end of his act talking about the war and wishing all the young soldiers and their families well. Jessel had mentioned that he was beginning a bond tour with many other famous performers. One of them was Carole Lombard. Many in the audience broke down in tears, giving him a standing ovation.

Jeanette was relieved to see the mother and daughter putting on their coats to leave. She really wasn't in the mood for conversation. She raised her hand to say goodnight, but they had already turned their backs and headed out of the club. Jeanette hoped she hadn't snubbed them. She sat back and took a deep breath. Why did she always feel she was being watched?

The waiter came back with a wooden bowl containing peanuts. "Ma'am, what can I get for you?" squeaked out of his adolescent mouth. Obviously, he was a local kid trying to make extra money for the holidays.

"I'll have a peppermint schnapps over the rocks, please."

The kid looked anxious to please and fetched Jeanette the drink in less than a minute.

She took a tiny sip, loving the way it slid down her throat, thick like syrup, instantly warming her. Liquor always traveled first to her groin and limbs, then to her fingertips, and finally her face, making her feel flushed and slightly feverish. It was precisely when she raised her hand to touch her forehead that he walked over, pulled out a chair opposite her, and sat himself down.

"Here let me," he said. "I'm a doctor . . . the name's Joe Lazaar."

He smiled warmly revealing a mouth of perfectly straight, white teeth. He wore his hair parted down the middle, and Jeanette noticed fine traces of gray threaded throughout. She guessed his age about forty-five though she was too inexperienced to be sure. Before she knew what was happening, he leaned over the table and placed his lips on her forehead. Startled, her head jerked backwards. It took only a few seconds, but for a long time she would remember every detail of that moment. His skin had smelled lemony, as if scrubbed clean, and his lips reminded her of chilled berries. The hairs on the back of her neck stood at attention waiting for a signal from her heart.

"You're absolutely fine," he said, and he sat back down to face her. "It's probably the dry heat in this room, and whatever you're drinking." He cocked his head sideways looking at her drink. "What is that thing anyway? It smells like cotton candy."

Jeanette found her voice. "Ah, it's peppermint, peppermint schnapps," she heard herself answer.

"Never touch the stuff," he grinned. "I see you're alone," he said. "Would you like to dance, Miss. . . ?"

"Jeanette Kane," she said. And like a curled delicate feather, she floated off the banquette putting her trembling hand in his. She didn't remember saying yes, but somehow she found herself pressed to this handsome stranger, their bodies soon entwined like a Rodin sculpture. They danced like this, not speaking more than a few meaningless words, until the band leader finally walked off the stage, all his noisy musicians following. Jeanette heard someone in the back of the room vacuuming. She realized they'd danced like this for over an hour.

Not wanting the evening to end, it was Dr. Lazaar who suggested they go for some tea or coffee. Sitting together in the tall leather booth at the Noshery, he held her hand while he began asking her so many questions. He was making her a bit dizzy with his fast talk: When had she come to this country? Where did she live? Where did she work? Why wasn't a pretty woman like herself already married?

Why was this stranger so insistent on trying to crack her open? Why, she wondered, had he picked her? She didn't have the courage to ask. Then he told her she had such sad eyes. What had those eyes seen, he wanted to know, to make them so sad? Though she looked away from him, she didn't want him to stop prying into her clamshell demeanor.

He walked her up the path into the hallway of her cottage. She turned away from him and whispered goodnight, when he grabbed her arm and spun her around, pulling her body once more to his. His strong arms encircled her waist, and he reached under her unbuttoned coat. His hands were so large that his thumbs grazed the bottoms of her breasts sending chills throughout her entire body. He kissed her hard pinning her against the icy door. She attempted to push him away, but then let his strength overcome her.

"I promise I'll never hurt you Jeanette, please believe me, he murmured in her ear." And soon her body folded limply under his. She loved when he recited her name. His voice sounded so calm, and the tone so deep. She felt the tip of his tongue sweep against her teeth, and she relaxed her jaw, letting his tongue meet hers. She had never kissed anyone with such feeling.

They nearly fell into the hallway as the front door quickly opened. It was Rena, peeking out from the dimly lit hall, her bathrobe thrown around her shoulders. She squinted, shielding her eyes from the lamplight. In a flash, Dr. Lazaar had already slipped away, leaving Jeanette's body heaving.

"Sis, is that you? Jeanette?"

"Yes, yes, it's me, go back in the room, I'm coming."

Like a frantic mother, Rena scolded her. "My God, do you know how worried I've been? I was just about to get dressed and find security."

Jeanette dreamily drifted past her into their room and undressed to the romantic melody swirling around in her brain. Rena was still ranting when Jeanette returned from the bathroom clad in her silk nightshirt, her face crimson. She got under the covers ready for more of Rena's inquiries. Rena turned on a small candlestick lamp holding it up to Jeanette's face.

"So, are you or are you not going to tell me?" she asked, calming down a bit.

"I couldn't sleep and you were out like a light, so I thought I'd go for a little snack. You know that the Noshery stays open late. Well, I met this very nice man who asked if he could join me for a cup of tea. I didn't mind, and besides he's a doctor."

"Really, a doctor, but it's already past one o'clock. What kind of snack? You could have had an entire smorgasbord during that time."

"We just started talking, and he was very nice and interested in books and travel, and before we knew it they were closing the coffee shop. I'm sorry if I worried you, go back to sleep."

She had no intention of telling her sister that she walked into the nightclub by herself and danced with this complete stranger like a pair of old lovers, both in perfect step, cheek to cheek, hip to hip. She was already planning on meeting him again tomorrow night. But this time she'd have to first introduce him to Rena.

The next night Dr. Lazaar joined them for dinner, and Jeanette saw that Rena hung on his every word. He talked about his practice mostly, how the field was rapidly expanding. He was a radiologist with a hospital in Westchester. He shared candidly that he was going through an amicable divorce.

"Oh, you mean you're still married?" Rena asked, causing Jeanette to kick her under the table.

"Not for long," he said, his head pointed down at the white table-cloth. "My wife, well, she just lost her tolerance with my long hours away and all the travel and conferences."

He said she had taken their five-year-old son and moved back to Boston to be closer to her parents. When he told this story his eyes filled and the table got very quiet. Rena just shook her head, and

Jeanette hoped she was feeling sad for his loss. This was his first vacation in years. He said he needed to relieve some of the pressure he was feeling. Then he lifted up his glass of red wine to toast them. "I'm so happy to have you two beautiful women join me," he said. "Last night the maître's sat me with the three merry widows from New Jersey. They literally piled food on my plate. I think they would have fed me if I let them."

Jeanette and Rena lifted their glasses and smiled. Joe leaned forward, as if he was about to tell them a secret. "They also shared some very interesting stories regarding their husbands' recent deaths."

"Really?" asked Rena.

"You understand, it's strictly confidential information," Joe said.

"Of course," Jeanette mumbled, disappointed that she wouldn't be hearing the gory details.

"Frankly, I think they were seeking my medical opinion. However, after watching them eat, I had a better understanding of the three heart attacks they talked about."

"What do you think happened?" Rena asked.

"I think their wives did them in with the salt and chicken fat."

Rena quickly placed the crystal shaker back on the table. Joe was probably right. Jeanette looked around and saw a room full of extremely overweight people gorging themselves on the huge portions of fattening cuisine. The room actually smelled of oil and butter.

After dinner, when they were fixing their lipstick in the ladies room, Jeanette mentioned casually that she would be meeting Dr. Lazaar in the lobby later that evening and that Rena shouldn't worry if she were late. It was movie night, and they'd probably go to the canteen room to watch *A Farewell to Arms* starring Gary Cooper. Rena said she'd already made arrangements with some women to play canasta and would also be out later than usual.

Dr. Lazaar's room was located in the main building. Jeanette was nervous that she might run smack into her sister and her card buddies. But the lobby was unusually empty, just a few bloated men, too full to move, smoking cigars, and staring at the dying embers in the fireplace. On the trip to his room, she kept reminding herself that it was okay. He was interesting to talk to and after all, he was a doctor.

He said he would never hurt her, and she believed him. She believed him while his lips kissed the nape of her neck. She believed him while he undressed her, carefully folding her clothes on a nearby chair, and when he covered her shivering body with the warm down quilt. Her eyes soon adjusted to the darkness, and she saw his tall, lean body cast a shadow over hers, as he slipped out of his trousers and lay down beside her. He stayed on top of the quilt for what seemed like a long time, talking softly to her, until her eyes, eyes she herself would probably not recognize, invited him underneath.

Afterward, she dozed off in his arms, but she awakened disturbed and confused. A hoarse muffled cry escaped her throat. Was that her voice, she wondered the instant she heard it?

"Shh Shh," he said, stroking her hair. "You were dreaming, that's all. It's okay."

He began kissing her shoulders, moving his mouth to her breasts. She was aware of the music coming from the nightclub, our accompaniment she thought, as he climbed on top of her. He carefully guided himself into her again rocking gently, his large shadow moving with him across the ivory walls of his room. She let him lead her as they had danced the night before, slowly, prudently wishing that she could make it last. Where was she, she wondered, floating above this couple on the bed, somewhere out of herself, like a cherub in a Rubens painting. And then that wonderful new feeling enveloped her again, took over and spread through every part of her body.

She watched him light a cigarette, and before blowing out the match, he held it just inches from her face. She never felt more beautiful in her entire life. Afterward, he walked her back to her cottage and they stood kissing in the doorway until Jeanette's cheeks were rubbed raw from his beard. She promised she would call in a couple of days. She didn't mention that she felt her family was watching her all the time. There'd be plenty of time to tell him all that and much more later on.

So, this night, as her family sat in the den playing cards, she excused herself and made the call from the upstairs landing. She used the phone perched on top of a small cherry wood stand. She heard Charlie humming in the living room and smelled his cigar, which made her terribly nervous. Any second, he might call out her name beckoning her to join him downstairs. She dialed the phone number quickly, impatient that it took so long between digits.

Joe answered on the third ring, just when she was about to hang up. "Hello . . . hello, anyone?"

She could hardly unglue her tongue from its thick dry saliva. "Joe, it's me Jeanette, Jeanette Kane."

There was a slight pause, enough to send a tremor of fear through her.

"Jeanette, I'm so glad you called, what took you so long? Are you okay?"

Her fear melted with his words. "I'm fine, really. It's been hectic since we got home. My niece, Mira, eloped over the holidays."

"Mira, the designer?" he asked.

"Yes, you have a good memory Joe."

"I remember everything you told me Jeanette, especially our time together, don't you?"

She looked around, beginning to squirm; her breathing was so heavy she could no longer hear Charlie's incessant chanting in the background.

"Yes, I remember Joe." She liked saying his name, how it made her feel instantly connected to him.

"I'll be out of town at a convention next week, but let's have dinner when I get back, promise?"

"I promise," she answered. "When would be good?" Jeanette had always felt better with specifics. Dangling threads made her nervous. She heard another slight hesitation, and then he picked the date.

"How's next Wednesday? Is the city okay?"

"Fine, yes, the city is perfect."

"Okay, then great, great, let's meet in the lobby of the Algonquin Hotel."

When they hung up, she was already worrying what she'd tell everyone. She figured she'd leave it up to Rena to find a good alibi. She always did. Not a twinge of guilt was evident in her sister's behavior. Sometimes she envied that.

Jeanette was still holding the receiver listening to a dial tone, when Charlie called for her to come downstairs.

"Sister, let's have some tea," he yelled from the living room. She heard Roy and Mira in the background.

"Damn you, Roy, you knew I needed that card, what did you do, sit on it?" Ina hushed them to no avail. Hattie had left for a church meeting, so Jeanette put up the tea kettle for Charlie and cut up some fresh melon for the others. She returned to the kitchen and pulled out a chair opposite her brother.

She watched him dip the sugar cube into his tea before biting it in half. Now the temperature was just right for sipping and slurping. Charlie never once looked up at her as he picked at his melon and finished his tea. Her mind kept wandering back to Joe. And then she wiped her eyes, suddenly overcome with deep feeling for her older brother, even as he sat opposite her, silent and detached. Maybe he had saved her after all.

The following Wednesday Jeanette rummaged through her closet and selected a simple gray knit dress trimmed with a mink collar. She had bought it on sale at Best and Company and was secretly glad it was too big on Rena. Unlike her boxy work suits, this showed off her small waist and full bust. As expected, Rena announced at dinner the night before that she and Jeanette were going to a movie after work. Rena said she'd pick her up in the hotel lobby. There was really no alternative, so she agreed, warning Rena not to show up a minute before eleven. Jeanette wanted as much time alone with Joe as possible. "How much time do you need for dinner?" Rena had asked over and over again. But Jeanette could not and would not tell her sister that she had slept with this man. As close as they were, she knew there were limits to what she could share. After all, she was still her baby sister and there were things you had the right to keep private. She imagined Rena's eyes widening in their sockets after hearing her confession. Most likely, she would think horrible things about her. Maybe she'd be motivated to tell the entire family, blaming her indiscretion on the medication she was taking. Or worse, perhaps they'd think her Dr. Lazaar had drugged her before dragging her off to his room to take complete advantage of her weakness and condition. *Her condition.* What exactly was her condition anyway? She continued to work although with a lot less enthusiasm; she cleaned, cooked, and listened. Couldn't she still feel love? And wouldn't they want her to be happy? For weeks, she had listened to Mira tell her of her deep feelings for Nathan. All at once there was romance flourishing throughout the Kane house, as if roses had bloomed in the middle of winter. What a welcome diversion from all the talk about business, and powerful medicine for healing the pain of having lost Mordecai and his family. Though she felt Mira's love and joy without jealousy, she could not deny that it had also stirred in her deep longing. She never continued with her classes at N.Y.U., but she still protected her favorite books under her bed. Two thin volumes of poetry: the works of Browning and Dickinson.

On this particular day she found herself filled with excitement, strangely euphoric. The women at the factory smiled at her constantly, peeking up from their towering piles of piece goods. The humming of their machinery, usually intrusive, all at once seemed comforting. She touched her face tracing her own huge grin. Soon she would see Joe, if only for a few hours. He had said he'd missed her, but she didn't have the courage to tell him that all she could think about was their time together. How every night, while lying in bed, she wished him in her arms.

The cab dropped her off at the busy corner of Sixth Avenue. She shivered both from the cold and from her nerves. It was a crisp, clear night, and she walked briskly into the lobby of the Algonquin Hotel. The bell captain showed her the way to the cocktail lounge. He looked around, seemingly surprised that she was alone. Jeanette's eyes scanned the room, and she looked at her watch. When she realized she was early, she thought of going outside and walking around the block, but she was just beginning to warm up. The piano player nodded to her as she sat down in a blue velvet banquette and removed her gloves. The large red carpeted and mahogany room had an uncanny resemblance to her home. She was startled for a second, seeing a swirl of cigar smoke rise up from an overstuffed chair. She sank back in her chair relieved when an old man stood and reached for his cane.

The piano player began his rendition of "Smoke Gets in Your

Eyes," and Jeanette tried humming along with the tune thinking this might relax her. The waiter brought her a rye and ginger ale, and she sipped at it while shredding the cocktail napkin, which left lint on the front of her dress. The room was beginning to fill up. She saw the bell captain look over toward her then whisper something to a man she thought might be a manager. How she wished Joe would arrive. He was already fifteen minutes late. She tried comforting herself with the thought that he was probably with a patient, or had traffic traveling in from Westchester. When the piano player took his break, she decided to visit the ladies room right off the lobby's entrance. She stood up quickly and felt slightly woozy. She hadn't eaten anything since noon. In the ladies lounge, a rosy checked matron about sixty wearing a ruffled black pinafore greeted her. Jeanette felt relieved to accept her warm greeting.

"Getting pretty cold out there, ain't it luv?" she asked. She sounded Irish or Scottish, Jeanette wasn't sure.

"Well, we can't forget that it's winter time, whether we like it or not," Jeanette answered.

"Those are lovely shoes you've got on darlin'. My feet were always much too wide for those fancy heels."

"Thank you," Jeanette smiled, dropping a quarter into a small basket.

The matron watched intently while Jeanette fiddled with some stray hairs, and then powdered her nose. Her gaze was admiring, and Jeanette welcomed it.

"What time do you have ma'am," Jeanette asked, looking at her own watch hoping it was wrong.

"It's nearly eight, honey, you okay?"

"Yes, yes I'm fine. I'm meeting someone for dinner and she, well he, must be detained."

"Oh, don't you worry luv, no one would keep a pretty lady like you waiting long, and if they did, they wouldn't be worth a halfpence."

"Well, thank you." Jeanette half closed her eyes as she walked back into the lounge praying that when she opened them, she'd see Dr. Lazaar standing there looking worried, surveying the room. But instead, her eyes were forced to squint and scan the room for him. Maybe she had missed him while she went to the ladies room. She hated doing it, but she asked the bellman if a gentleman had come in looking for her. Without speaking, he shook his head no. Jeanette thought, he must think I'm crazy, he probably thinks I made the whole thing up. She turned from him and sat back down. She ordered another drink and scanned a menu for appetizers. She was so hungry. But it would be rude to order something. She would have to just wait.

A female singer dressed in a black and gold sequined gown now stood beside the piano player. She had flaming red hair just like the actress Rita Hayworth. She burst out in song. "All of me, why not take all of me, can't you see I'm no good without you?"

"God," mumbled Jeanette, where the hell was Joe?

On her next trip to the bathroom, the kind matron held her head as she vomited into the white and black commode. Then the woman took a small towel embroidered with the letter A, filled it with ice and held it to Jeanette's head. She was sprawled out on a red velvet lounge, her shoes off, a bib of paper stuck in and around the mink trimmed collar of her soiled dress. She mumbled a weak, "Thank you."

"Darlin' is there anyone you'd like to call? You're in no condition to go home like this."

Jeanette looked at her through a haze, her tongue felt thick and she thought the lounge was swaying. "Not such a pretty picture am I?" she said, slurring.

"Oh, don't you fret, we all gotta tie one on sometimes. Besides, I bet you haven't eaten a thing, and it's nearly eleven. Are you sure I can't call someone?"

"Thanks, you've been so nice, but my sister is meeting me here in a few minutes."

"Honey, I hope you don't mind my saying so, but if I were you, I'd drop the bastard like a hot potato."

All Jeanette could do was nod in agreement. She felt too ill to even focus on Joe. She just wanted to go home, take off her itchy clothes and get under the covers.

There was a knock on the door to the ladies lounge. Jeanette recognized the voice of the bellman as he whispered something to the matron. She heard her shush him, saying that she'd stay later if she had to. She told him to look for a woman in a dark gray coat who'd be arriving shortly and to direct her to the ladies lounge. Jeanette turned in the direction of the door in time to see the bellman peeking in, a smug look on his face. I bet he thinks I'm one of those prostitutes who hang out in Times Square, she thought to herself. She laughed out loud which made the matron smile. "Good dear, don't let anything get you down. Life's too damn short to waste pining over a man." She handed Jeanette a paper cup filled with cool water.

Her kindness was so overwhelming Jeanette began to weep. She cried harder than when she had left her homeland, Riga, and said a final farewell to her parents, harder than she would have ever allowed herself to cry within the walls of the house on Avenue T. Strange, but as she sobbed into the damp white towel, she began to feel a lightness in her chest. Her head still throbbed and her stomach was queasy, but she felt more relaxed than she had in months. She had loved her time with Joe and desperately wanted more, but she had felt far from relaxed. She had given him control over her from the moment they met. She didn't know any other way.

She looked at the stranger caring for her, her burly cheeks flushed from the burden of her own weight and remembered what it was like to be mothered and nurtured. And then the door to the lounge flew open. Rena barged in startling them both. She stood over her sister, snowflakes melting on her dark hair. All at once the room felt colder. "What in God's name happened, JJ?" Jeanette motioned her younger sister to sit down. The matron tried making herself busy and started mopping up the tiled floor.

"Joe didn't come, Rena. Maybe I screwed up the dates or maybe something awful happened to him. I know he would have tried to reach me somehow."

"Something better have had happened to him, God look at you, JJ. Did you have anything to eat? No, no, but you drank, didn't you? Oh great, and I bet you took your pills today after lunch and haven't eaten since?"

"I guess I lost track of time. I didn't want to sit and eat by myself."

"Why didn't you call him or just leave for that matter?"

"I thought he'd come, even if a bit late, and besides, what would you have thought if you showed up here and you didn't see me? You'd probably be lying on this lounge right now in the same condition."

"Come, let's go home," Rena said, shaking her head.

Jeanette stood up feeling slightly off balance. She reached in her purse and handed the matron a few dollars.

"Please, it's not necessary, really," she said.

"Yes, it is," said Jeanette, and she crumpled the bills and stuffed them into the woman's apron.

"God bless you, dear. Please take good care," she said, squeezing Jeanette's hand.

The brisk night air felt good as they left the stuffy hotel lobby. It was still snowing, though not hard. Jeanette ignored the bellman's offer to get them a cab. Instead they walked arm-in-arm to a coffee shop on the corner, all the time Jeanette taking deep breaths, freezing her lungs. They took a booth in the back. The place was filled with theatre goers, and the atmosphere was much cheerier than the stuffy lobby of the Algonquin. Jeanette suddenly was starving, but she ordered some dry toast and tea. Rena wanted waffles with coffee ice cream.

"So let's get this story straight," Jeanette said. "What movie did we actually see tonight?"

Rena ignored her question. "Sis, I really think you should call the bastard."

"I will, I will, tomorrow I promise. Enough about him now, please."

"Okay, okay the movie," Rena said. "I couldn't decide, and then I saw this long line for *Suspicion*. The movie was great, although I'm not sure it would be a good idea for you to go see it."

"Why?" asked Jeanette.

"It's so scary that I practically fell off my seat. Joan Fontaine plays this shy British wife of Cary Grant who thinks maybe he's out to murder her."

"Well, does he?" Jeanette asked.

"I won't spoil it for you. I'll go again with you next week."

"But you already know the outcome, how could you enjoy it?"

"This time I'll sit back and just swoon over Cary," Rena said.

189

Swoon, an intriguing word, thought Jeanette. Hadn't she done just that, allowing herself to crumble and nearly collapse over a man?

It took nearly an entire week for Jeanette to call him. Rena asked her all day long. "Did you do it? No . . . when? Do it, or I will."

Finally, during her lunch break on a freezing day, she stood in a phone booth outside the factory, shivering for five minutes before getting up the courage to tell the operator the number. It was a Wednesday, and he said that was the best day to reach him home. Jeanette's breathing was so hard and fast; it fogged up every glass panel in the booth. While waiting to be connected, her finger automatically outlined the letter J, then she looped another J, and yet another, enclosing the initials in a large watery heart. The phone rang several times, and strangely she felt some relief. But then a young woman answered startling Jeanette, sending a rush of heat to her brain.

"Hello, hello, is anyone there?" the soft, sultry voice asked.

"Ah, Dr. Lazaar, please."

"Oh, I'm sorry, I'm afraid you've reached his home by mistake. I'm Mrs. Lazaar, just a second, please."

Jeanette heard her speaking to someone in the background, and then the loud indignant "No!" from a young child echoed in Jeanette's ears.

"Would you like his private office number at the hospital?" the voice asked. "Miss, can you hear me?"

Her heart racing, Jeanette slowly replaced the receiver. She was no longer shivering. She felt warm, so warm that she quickly unbuttoned her coat and threw it down onto the wet muddy floor of the phone booth. Then she unbuttoned her blouse and unzipped her long skirt. With her gloved hand, she erased the letters she had drawn. She rubbed furiously at the suffocating gray fog, clearing each small square of glass, breathing only when she saw the daylight filter in. She grabbed the wooden handle of the phone booth, and stumbling over her coat and a pile of clothing, she fell down on her knees, out onto the noisy street.

A Broken JJ

~

Mira made one of her infrequent trips downtown to check on the production of the bouclé suits— soon to be Kane Knitting's Chanel knock-offs. She realized that she would have to figure out a way to make these garments a hell of a lot cheaper. Her biggest accounts were canceling orders of many of the higher priced items. It was a sign of the times that women suddenly found themselves donning casual wear. So many young women were now alone or living with relatives, trying to keep up some semblance of a normal life. Some, out of pure necessity, had gone to work in the plants where strong young men recently toiled. Slacks and casual sweaters were definitely the fashion statement of the moment. Of course, there would always be women like Mira and her mother needing a more extensive wardrobe to function in daily life. But they were in the minority. Not many were running off to luncheons and charity benefits.

Mira closed her eyes and tried to imagine what Nathan might be doing at that same moment. One thing she knew for sure. He was probably basking in the warmth of the Florida sun. She pictured him dressed in his tight fitting Navy blues, minuscule beads of sweat above his lip, hoisting a frayed rope, his once smooth hands chafed and calloused from his labor. She'd kiss those hands right now if she could. Her body shivered as she sat alone in the coffee shop waiting for her Lipton tea and toast. She had to stop and eat before visiting JJ and Rena at the place or they'd insist on feeding her. She wanted to check the sketches, any new samples, and get home before the evening rush. With Nathan gone she was less enthusiastic about everything.

She looked through the streaked glass window still covered with fake snow left-over from the holidays. There were several people rushing and pointing in the direction just past the coffee shop. She pressed her nose hard to the window, looking to her left. Some men had formed a tight circle while others jumped up like sports spectators to get a better look. At what she wondered? An eerie feeling shot through her leaving a strange lightness inside her belly. Something in her head and heart connected her to the action on the street, and without telling her waitress, she grabbed her coat and ran outside. Mira moved quickly toward the throng of people stopping abruptly a few yards from the entrance to the factory. Her height allowed her a clear view, and the spectators seemed already bored with the scene. Some turned away and laughed. Others whispered and huddled together talking on the street. When she first saw JJ, Mira thought what an uncanny resemblance to her aunt, and then within seconds reality slapped her like the stinging wind. Someone had thrown JJ's coat over her bare shoulders. She stood there void of expression—barefoot in her ecru satin slip.

Mira viciously elbowed through the thinning crowd and stood blocking her aunt with outstretched arms. A young Negro woman handed Mira a damp pile of clothing. Mira fumbled with the buttons on JJ's coat and yelled for someone to please get her a cab. She looped her arm under JJ's, practically sweeping her up off the ground. Within seconds, somebody opened the door to a checker cab. Mira pushed her aunt into the back seat ignoring the curious faces that pressed close to the cab's window.

"Take me to Brooklyn," she shouted at a bewildered driver. His eyes waited for the rest of the information. But Mira had to catch her breath. She held onto JJ's hand, surprised that it wasn't a block of ice like her own. She knew not to speak. She must get her home first, then call Aunt Rena who'd probably be out searching the streets.

She hoped Momma would be out, but then realized it was Wednesday. Damn, she looked at her watch. Momma's canasta game would still be on. She'd try to sneak up the front steps quickly, to save everyone embarrassment. What did it matter anyway? She was tired of hiding all these secrets: her marriage to Nathan, Jeanette's illness, and Poppa's incessant worrying about business.

"He said Wednesday was a good day to call," JJ mumbled softly.

"Who?" Mira asked.

"Joe, my beau Joe."

Another secret, Mira guessed. She was afraid to pry. She had seen this delicate condition before and thought it better to just get her aunt home. Among the pile of clothing tied together by JJ's blouse, she found her pumps. She forced the shoes over the shredded soles of JJ's stockings onto her limp feet.

"Almost home," Mira said. The driver looked through his rear view mirror and met Mira's eyes.

"No, she's not drunk. She's sick, if you must know," she blurted out and strangely her voice cracked and she began to cry. She squeezed her aunt's hand and JJ's body slumped against her, eyes tightly closed like she was making a birthday wish, her head resting on Mira's arm.

Two chauffeured Cadillacs sat in the Kane driveway. It was only 1:30. Mira paid the driver, and he rushed around to open the cab door. The driveway was still slippery from last week's snowfall and Mira struggled, holding on to JJ and the bundle of clothing. Mira tossed the clothes into the metal milk box by the front door. She opened the door and pushed JJ in front of her. Her aunt looked at her with a stunned expression, as if she had just realized that she was indeed home. Mira placed her finger over her lips to motion quiet, and they moved through the vast hallway across to the landing. They might have been heard if the women had set up to play in the den, but it was probably too cold in there today. Instead they had chosen the smaller of the two dining rooms for their weekly card game. Mira smelled the freshly brewed coffee and remembered she hadn't eaten a thing.

The very first thing was to get Aunt JJ under the covers. She looked for her medication but couldn't find the pills. That would have to wait until Aunt Rena came home. Aunt Rena, she'd almost forgotten. She called from the upstairs phone and had her paged at the factory, not surprised that she answered the phone out of breath, probably expecting to hear the worst.

"She's really okay," Mira said. "She might be coming down with a virus or something. When I ran into her on the street she was shivering, so I decided to take her home. You can't talk to her now, she's sleeping. Really, why would I lie?"

Aunt Rena didn't sound convinced. She probably had one foot out the door, heading home. But it was the very best Mira could do. God, what was happening to this family? Please, she begged, don't let anything happen to Nathan. He was all she could focus on that was good and what made her happy.

While changing and freshening up, she thought of Faye. It had been weeks since they had written to one another. Mira wondered if Faye was at all homesick. She could use a little dose of Faye now, a little of her wacky humor and free spirit. When Faye left, some of Mira's dreams left with her. Now she focused on Nathan. She felt a new sense of responsibility, after all she was his wife—his absentee wife.

Her parents, however, had just last week announced to the immediate world that Mira was engaged to a successful fabric man whose career was on hold due to his desperate need to fight for his country. The wedding was to be held sometime in late April. Nathan would be home on a week's leave. She didn't doubt Poppa's ability to arrange that. Besides, she didn't care any more about how he managed to pull his myriad of strings.

His latest coup was to get Roy stationed in an Army administration office in Iowa. Ungrateful Roy whined that he wanted to be in a warm climate, where there would be at least pretty girls at canteen time. Poppa shut him up by promising a transfer if the war continued past spring.

Now with Roy gone, the house was quieter than ever. Bickering was at a minimal. Momma still sat wringing her hands, worried to death no matter how many times you told her the enemy wasn't going to invade Cedar Rapids, Iowa. She simply liked all her birds in the nest; without them she was lost, distracted, and lacking purposefulness. At least she had her card games and social functions to keep her going.

"Daughter, you're home. I didn't hear you come in."

Mira leaned over and kissed her mother's cheek. Ina beamed with pride while Mira went around the card table, first taking Mrs. Levinski's hand, then Mrs. Goldberger's, who had just stuffed her cheeks with two chocolate macaroons. Lastly, she greeted Mrs. Morris, who immediately threw her cards down and squeezed Mira's hand so hard, Mira thought she drew blood.

"*Nu*, so let's see. Oooh! Lovely . . . isn't the ring lovely, Esther?" she said to Mrs. Goldberger while stretching Mira's arm across the table.

"Lovely," they all chanted. Mira couldn't help but notice the enormous crystal candy rock on Mrs. Morris's right hand.

"Someday, when you're an old dame like me, you'll maybe have this." Mrs. Morris waved her chubby hand in the air.

"Your *Mazel* should be huge, Mira, that's what I wish you," said Mrs. Levinski. The women mumbled and shook their heads vigorously. Momma winked at Mira.

"Thank you, thank you, ladies," Mira answered. She felt hot and stuffy, a little lightheaded from the suffocating blends of powdery perfumes. She could easily identify Chanel on Mrs. Morris, and the more floral and subtle scent of Shalimar on Momma.

Hungry, Mira fixed herself a cup of coffee and prepared a plate of sardines and crackers from the buffet table.

Momma was adding up the score while Mrs. Morris shuffled the decks.

"You're home early today, darling, you okay?" Momma looked up over her marquisette lunettes at Mira.

Mira tried to sound as casual as possible while she cut a chunk of cheddar from a huge block. "I ran into Aunt JJ and she looked as though she was getting a cold, so we decided to come home together."

"Jeanette? So, where is she?"

"In bed, sleeping. She'll be fine," said Mira. She purposely avoided eye contact with Momma. Soon all the yentas would leave, and then there'd be plenty of time to discuss what had happened. Mira took her plate into the kitchen. She was afraid that this time JJ might have gone deeper and deeper into herself. Who knew when she might snap out of this? She remembered JJ's clothing. Before eating, she fetched the dress out of the milk box and threw it together in the laundry chute along with her own pile of clothes that Hattie said she would hand wash. Maybe she'd never have to tell anyone about how she had found JJ standing outside that bright red phone booth: barefoot, wearing only a sheer slip. Mira wanted to save her that humiliation. Perhaps no one had noticed them as they pulled away in the cab.

At first, she had almost not recognized her own relative. JJ's soft gray eyes had appeared tight with fear; and her lashes fluttered as if she had trouble focusing.

Mira thought that Rena picked the wrong time to press her sister about Dr. Lazaar. Aunt JJ had just awakened from a long nap groggy and disoriented. Mira decided to make light of the incident, sticking with the story she had told Rena over the phone. Mira's mistake was to question Rena almost the second she walked in the door asking who Joe was, and why Aunt JJ would refer to him as her beau. This sent Rena flying straight up the stairs to her bedroom. Mira followed her in, shut the bedroom door, and leaned against it. Rena, too upset to notice Mira standing there, sat down at the foot of Jeanette's bed.

"So sister, how do you feel?"

"Ah, not so good, Ren," Jeanette said, wearing a sheepish grin.

"Hmm, you think you caught a bug or something?"

"Bug? No, no bug." Jeanette sighed deeply, and her eyes sprung with tears.

"So I guess you called him like you said?" Rena asked.

"Oh, yes, I remember that now, I called Joe."

"I just knew something bad would happen. I was afraid you'd get hurt with that one. Boy, did he love himself, some doctor!"

"Not as much as I loved him."

"Jen, you hardly knew him."

"I knew that he made me feel happier than I've ever felt in my life, my small miserable life."

Mira wished she had exited the room earlier, but now she was afraid to breathe or move. She was stunned that there seemed to be so much she didn't know. She struggled between anger over being left out and downright pity for the scene she had just witnessed.

She watched Rena take JJ's trembling hand. "What happened? Tell me."

"Well, I finally found the courage to phone him, and guess what? His wife answered. She sounded lovely, Rena, really lovely."

"His wife? That lying coward." Rena said.

Mira guessed there was much more that Rena needed to ask JJ. She, too, wanted to hear everything. But there was that division that always jumped into the picture smacking her in the face. It always did. There, on that small bed, sat the indelible privacy of those two sisters. It's how they were able to survive all those years, in that house. But Mira would never know how Rena worried about JJ from the start when she had watched her wide-eyed with Dr. Lazaar. Rena had watched the heat radiating from her sister, noticed the ruby marks on her neck that she tried to conceal with pancake makeup. But Rena wouldn't say a word, not to JJ, and certainly never to Mira.

Mira understood by the look Rena shot her that she was no longer welcome in the room. Slowly, she opened and closed the door, and waited a few seconds outside in the darkened hallway, long enough to hear mumbled questions and the quiet answers JJ shared between her whimpers.

It was difficult for Mira to picture her Aunt JJ intimate with a man, not as difficult as it was to picture Aunt Rena, but nonetheless difficult. How did she ever get herself mixed up with a married man? Wasn't JJ much too smart for that? This could never have happened if Momma and Poppa had gone along with them to Grossingers. Mira was curious about this Joe, and she wondered if JJ was still a virgin. She would wait a few days and ask Rena to tell her everything she knew. After all, Mira wasn't a child. She was an engaged, no, she was a married woman. They knew her secrets, well, most of them anyway. And she had helped Aunt JJ, had always said her little special prayer for her because they were family. But mostly because she truly loved her.

Mira took it upon herself to tell her mother that JJ had had a small relapse saving Rena from the chore. After all, it would be Momma who would stay home with JJ for the next few weeks, helping her to get strong again, checking to see if she took her pills, and spoon feeding her when she refused to eat like the last time. Momma was good at this nurturing. Hopefully, it would help her stop worrying about Roy so much.

Poppa would be distracted anyhow, concerned about the sudden slump in business, and he'd leave it up to the women to get his sister back on her feet again. He needed her in the factory. She could fix some of the small knitting machines when they went down, which saved him the task of hiring some expensive engineer on the outside. Poppa trusted nobody. Everyone who visited the factory was a potential crook looking for ways to steal ideas, designs, even his workers. Poppa was constantly sniffing for spies. Mira remembered a story he once told about a young man, supposedly a buyer for S. Klein's. Uncle Louie had shown the man the entire fall line during market week. The buyer seemed very excited, leaving a three-page order, but one week later he had someone call and cancel. At first Poppa thought maybe the goods were a bit pricy for Klein's, known as a major discounter. So he called the main office of Klein's, willing to come down some in price. The buyer did not exist.

"Another Nazi spy," Poppa shouted throughout the place, scaring the hell out of Margaret, the bookkeeper. He was certain the buyer was some bastard's young son out to do the dirty work of checking up on the competition.

Mira knew she needed to concentrate more on her work. If she focused, really focused, she might deal better with Poppa and his demands. She made a promise to herself to make the bouclé suits Kane Knitting's biggest seller, even though they were a knock-off. Even though, the country was at war.

Avram Must Choose

~

He could hardly venture outdoors anymore without having to hand over his papers to a pack of men, boys really, only a few years older than his son. And lately, upon any interrogation by the Germans, Avram's hands trembled as though they had minds of their own.

Whenever he showed his papers, a soldier always grew impatient. Next, he would have to endure the forced "he-hawing" and snide remarks:

"*Ya, Ya*, the Judenrat. So, not too many of you people around these days, eh?" And then came more obnoxious snickering. Someone *always* spit on the ground, *always* just missing Avram's foot.

It was early afternoon, and he could smell the vapors of the stolen vodka as the men huddled together in the brisk, March air.

"Carpenter," it says right here. My, my, pretty risky with those shaky hands, old man. Maybe it's time to give it up before you cut yourself."

"Yes, you may be right, officer, I will definitely consider that."

"Perhaps, I can be of help to you in making this decision."

The air around Avram's face became colder. A chill traveled down the length of his body until he barely felt his toes.

He searched his mind for an option, but there were three of them and him. He thought himself a fool to have gone out when nothing terribly important was needed of him. It was true. The Jewish Council members had vastly diminished in number, while Avram waited for orders, any small job to perform, but there were none, other than delivering bad news to all the scattered families. Marta had warned him, of course, when he said he needed to go into town to purchase a new carpenter's file. The smallest one that he used for fine detailing had a cracked handle. He knew it would be difficult to find a shop-keeper brave enough to still keep regular hours.

Standing here now, he tucked the papers into a back pocket. His fingers grazed the sharpness of the file hidden by the heavy wool vest he wore instead of a coat. He thought of grabbing the file and pouncing on two of them at once; he could, he was that large a man. But the third soldier would surely shoot him in the back, the head or worse— maim his hands, then torture him while he begged for mercy with his bloodied fingers.

"Wait here!" the one with the carrot-colored mustache ordered.

They are only trying to unnerve me, Avram thought, as he glanced over to the tribunal. And seeing the soldier point in the direction of the woods, he began sweating profusely under his layers of clothing. He pulled his shirt collar closer to his neck. Hands clasped, he felt his pulse whimpering under his fingers. His loved ones faces danced past his eyes like long satin ribbons leading the way. Marta's ribbon was the darkest shade of blue, full of fear and regret. Sophie's appeared red and fiery, while Victor's ribbon dissolved into the air, ghostlike and vengeful. Victor had not been happy about Rosha, the child they'd hidden in the cellar. He taunted her at every chance he got. How could he ever forgive himself for putting all of them at risk?

He felt the cold slap against his cheek and woke from his daydream to find himself corralled by all three officers, the sour remnants of vodka lingered on their breath.

"If you do what we say, we will not tie your hands."

Avram knew arguing would do no good, and yet, part of him wanted to be done with this agonizing charade. He longed for his family, the warmth of their embrace but, above all, he craved his dignity. He knew he'd be a fool to disobey, and much sooner, a dead fool.

The sky had slowly turned to a squirrel gray. It was so cold Avram could no longer feel any sensation in his toes. His hands were tucked into his pockets, and without them for leverage, he had stumbled twice. As he struggled to get on his feet, he heard the belching laughter behind him.

Avram guessed they'd been walking for nearly two hours, stopping only for the soldiers to relieve themselves against a tree trunk, then more chugging from a flask. He was commanded to walk no more than six footsteps in front of them, forcing him to turn around several times, nearly losing his footing. The broken carpenter's file that pressed in his pocket kept him focused.

Dumb bastards, he thought. They'd never once searched him. By now, they were so drunk that he guessed his fate lay in the power of the drink and how it would affect their temperament. He had certainly taken other risks, ones yet undiscovered. Underneath each and every table or chair he had been told to make for a mere pittance for the Germans, he had etched a perfect Jewish star rubbed in a henna stain next to the family name *Juraska.*

As an early dusk set in, snowflakes began to fall. They were large, strangely misshapen; they reminded Avram of curls made of shaved wood, beautiful and weightless. The lumpy ground covered rapidly, and Avram began to stumble more frequently. This only outraged the youngest soldier, who shouted: "Look at the stupid Jew. Perhaps he can't see past his huge *schnozel.*"

Fuck you, Avram mumbled to himself, and then a vast sadness enveloped him. It clung like a shroud made of rough burlap.

There was a commotion, about fifty yards ahead, that sounded like prayers followed by urgent begging. Two distinct dialects rose up through the chilled air, the sound echoing through the tops of tall pines. Avram recognized the guttural commands in German, and the mournful cries of a woman speaking in Russian. As they got closer, he could see that the soldiers had rounded up a family. Most likely they had been hiding deep in the woods. A woman was on her knees facing an open pit, large enough to build a small barn. Her husband, a small, fragile man was clutching the hands of a little boy. Avram guessed he was the couple's son. He interpreted the scene immediately while his captors tripped and laughed behind him, until a tall, bulldog of an officer on the site screamed for them to halt.

"I want to go home, Poppa," the child cried out. His features were small and angelic, bright red, his delicate skin badly chafed.

Avram swallowed down a surge of vomit. He wished he were home, asleep, having one of his terrible dreams.

While the family stood shivering in the failing light, the soldiers met near a clump of pines. The bulldog stomped out his cigarette against a tree trunk, another passed the flask around, and they each took a sip, as if part of an ancient ritual—one that precedes sacrifice.

The father of the child was sobbing now, which Avram thought was not much help to the little boy. He couldn't bear to look at him. When the wife's eyes met Avram's, he could see that she had let go of something. There was a haze over her sunken eyes, as if she had suddenly gone blind. The boy broke loose from his father's grip and came running toward Avram.

"No," the father yelled, and within seconds, they were surrounded by soldiers.

Avram was lifted off his feet and placed directly behind the boy's mother. There was a loud shot, one single sound, that Avram could swear ceased the snowfall. He turned his head slightly and saw blood pouring from an aperture in the man's head. The father was slumped against a tree trunk; his blood soaking into the bark turning it a gruesome shade of purple.

Someone had tossed the boy into his mother's lap. And with what seemed to be her last ounce of strength, she pushed him off onto the ground.

"No!" she howled, and then, "Help!" into the frigid air.

Avram wished he could remember a childhood prayer, but he had given up praying a long time ago, before this war, when as a small child he was to witness the pogroms that wiped away complete villages, taking away many beloved family members.

"Take this, and face straightaway," the red-headed officer spat out. The pistol felt warm against Avram's arctic fingers. He had to actually see the revolver to realize what he was clutching in his hands.

The soldier lifted the boy and his mother so they were a small table's length in front of him. Avram smelled the young mother's filthy hair and odors from weeks of hiding out in these woods.

"Count to three, and fire. Do you hear me?"

Avram lifted his arm. The pistol felt like a ton of lumber. Enough lumber to build a sanctuary.

"Shoot!" the soldier said, after some seconds lapped.

Avram felt the carpenter's file press once more into his lower back. He thought of all the beautiful cabinets he had made over the last thirty years, the dining room tables and chairs that had stood witness to so many dinners and holidays where families had once gathered in the name of enduring love.

There was the hot breath of the insistent soldier on his neck, the vapors of the alcohol—his last aroma on earth. Avram's knees buckled to the ground. He looked once at the sky then bowed his head, right before he placed the pistol in his mouth—right before he fired.

The Wedding

~

Mr. and Mrs. Charles H. Kane
Mrs. Gertrude Berk
Invite you to share in the joy
Of the marriage of their children

Mira Elizabeth

and

Nathan Julius Berk

Saturday, the twenty-first of April
Nineteen hundred and forty-two
At half past seven
Ocean Parkway Synagogue
Brooklyn, New York
Black Tie Reception to Follow

Today, a frigid Saturday morning, the thermometer that pressed against the kitchen window read five degrees. No one ventured out. And because there was so much to do and yet no where they could go in this weather, the women paced back and forth, upstairs and downstairs, like prisoners in their pastel bathrobes and matching slippers. Uncle Louie struggled through the *Daily News* then switched to his favorite: *The Jewish Record*. He kept sucking his teeth and sighing, while reading what he would keep to himself for another time.

Hattie baked two trays of chocolate chip cookies making the kitchen the warmest room of the house, and the aroma of piping hot cocoa floated over everyone, keeping the mood mild and pleasant. There was a sweet calm in their chatter this morning as Ina, Mira, and Rena sipped their cocoa and dipped small pieces of the cookies. Across the room from them, JJ crouched on the cold floor lost in the chore of rearranging the entire pantry. She had decided to stack all the cans by alphabetical order, then changed her mind, and started over having decided that the small cans should go on the top two shelves, the largest ones on the bottom. She hummed some repetitive child-like melody to herself, and constantly scratched her head as if trying to remove an annoying bug.

The doorbell chimed its four familiar notes causing everyone but JJ to look up. *No company expected* was what everyone seemed to say with a shrug of the shoulders. Hattie wiped her greasy hands on her apron and ran to answer the door. She returned quickly avoiding all eyes and handed a flat yellow envelope to Charlie who sat deep in thought in the kitchen chewing on a toothpick. Noticing that this was a telegram stamped with the seal of the United States Navy, Charlie leaped from his chair and tore it open immediately, while Ina, hand on her heart, braced herself for bad news. Within seconds, Charlie waved his own hand in a calming gesture. "It's all fine, fine," he said. The smile that formed on his lips allowed them to exhale loudly, in one collective breath, like the wind on the back porch. Mira hovered over him trying to read the short message, but he pulled the telegram away and tucked it into his vest pocket.

"What, what? Tell us," everyone, but JJ, cried. They could no longer take his stalling.

He first handed the telegram to Ina. Mira could see her mother's chest heaving through the thickness of her robe. But then a soft smile sprung to Ina's mouth and she sighed deeply obviously relieved. Mira grabbed the paper next. The message did not register at once, so she read it again aloud.

In less than two sentences, it said that Charles Kane's request had been accepted. Ensign Nathan Jules Berk would be allowed an eight-day leave of duty in April so that he could return home to marry Mira Elizabeth Kane.

Mira threw her arms around her father nearly knocking him off balance.

"I can't believe you did it, Poppa. You really did it!"

His bald head barely reached her shoulders. Mira stiffened, realizing that since she began working for him, there was almost no physical affection exchanged between the two of them. Maybe it was because she had tried so hard to maintain a professional atmosphere at work, but no, in truth, she had not fully forgiven him for taking her out of school.

Charlie beamed, having pulled off another one of his maneuvers, and Hattie passed around a fresh tray of the steaming cookies while Rena poured milk into a large pitcher. She busied herself filling glasses with cold milk, while Mira and her mother grabbed a small calendar from the drawer, compliments of the Brooklyn Union Gas Company.

"April, that's just around the corner. How can you plan a wedding in just a few months?" Rena asked.

"That problem I will leave up to my wife and daughter," Charlie answered.

"Look," Momma said, pointing to the calendar. We can try for the Saturday night the week after Passover."

"But I will gain ten pounds during the holidays. Promise you won't let me eat any of your special Matzoh Brei."

"You'll be a gorgeous bride, won't she, Rena?"

Rena forced a crooked smile while Hattie belted out, "Hallelujah!"

Uncle Louie walked over and knelt beside JJ. "Sister, did you hear the good news, there's going to be a *veddin*?"

JJ looked up from her organizing and clapped her hands clumsily, like a toddler. A worried expression flashed across her flushed face. "But what about your dress, Mira?" JJ asked, pulling herself up from the floor.

"My dress, yes, my dress. Well, I don't know. I'd always dreamed that I would design my own. I mean, how could I not? JJ, would you like to help me?"

JJ nodded enthusiastically while a look of pride spread across her face.

"Well, if I were you two, I'd start this very minute," Rena said. "You know how much work we must produce to keep up with all our *real* orders."

Mira took a deep breath and counted to three. Nothing, no nothing, would ruin this moment for her. "You're so right, Rena," she said, "But it's not like I have tons to keep me busy in the evenings. The business comes first though, as always."

Charlie and Louie used this opportunity to move toward the den where they listened to the radio. They preferred doing that alone anyway, without having to answer any anxious questions after another grim report about the latest in American casualties.

The wedding would give them all something positive to focus on. Their minds would be occupied, and time would move faster for them all. Realizing he'd have to shell out big for the upcoming affair, Charlie figured it was about time he collected on some of his loans to his cronies. He thumbed through his little black book. He'd have to make some calls first thing Monday.

"First things first," Ina said, sipping a tall glass of tea. "Tomorrow we will confirm the date with the rabbi, and we will order the invitations the same afternoon. People will need, at most, six weeks' notice. Yet, where would they be going? Few are off traveling, especially now, while there's a war going on. Next to a moil performing a circumcision, a wedding is a most joyous occasion for all. And these days, who isn't looking for a reason to celebrate?"

A thought must have suddenly struck Ina's mind, because as soon as she finished talking, she jumped up and pressed both her temples as she went running through the living room toward the den. Her voice belted throughout the house with the force of a contralto. "Charl, Charl," she shouted, "what about our Roy?"

Other Voices and Concerns

~

March 10, 1942

Dear Dr. Lazaar,

I have nothing much to say to you except this: If you ever try to see my sister Jeanette again, I'll make sure that the only thing you'll ever practice is the piano. You took a beautiful person, twisted all her hopes and broke her heart. How can you look at your wife and son knowing how you deceived them? And, how do you look in the mirror? I wonder how many other vulnerable women have fallen for your Casanova routine. Stay the hell away!

Rena Kane

March 23, 1942

Dear Mira,

I was both thrilled and disappointed to get your beautiful wedding invitation. I'm so happy that you and Nathan will be celebrating your marriage in such a grand way. (You're not pregnant are you?) Just kidding! Mir, it will be impossible for me to return to New York in April. I just got the news that I've been hired as an assistant designer for the shooting of the film Song of Bernadette. The star is the gorgeous actress Jennifer Jones. Nice name, huh? Mira, they're actually paying me. I can hardly believe it. *The job is an entry to Century Fox and who knows where that might lead? I sure do miss you a lot. The people out here are pretty darn snooty. I'll be getting my own place soon and I'd love for you to visit. The best to you both.*

Love,

Faye

March 11, 1942

Dear Pop,

I was thinking wouldn't it be better if I could be home a week or two before Mira's wedding? I could help out with some of the details. Maybe this would be a good time for you to see about my transfer. I wouldn't mind Florida. Mira says Nathan has fallen in love with the south. It is cold as hell here Pop, and the food is hardly recognizable. Everything is covered with brown gravy. Some of the guys in my unit said not to go near the mashed potatoes. They put something in it to control your sex drive. Don't tell Momma it'll upset her.

I have some exciting news. I need you to send an extra train ticket. I met a really terrific girl. Her name is Bobbi Ann. She's from Iowa and a real knockout. She wants to stay in New York permanently. Maybe you can give her a job in the showroom. Anyhow, I'm bringing her home for the wedding. You'll love her.

Your frozen son,

Roy

P.S. Listen Pop, please don't get angry. But just got to tell you. We got married last weekend. Bobbi Ann says she's definitely pregnant and it's definitely mine. The baby's due in November. I'll tell Momma after the wedding.

March 8, 1942
Dear Momma,
I'm homesick as hell. Can you believe I really miss going to the place everyday with Uncle Louie and Pop? I've lost over six pounds since I'm here. The food is very trayf, meatloaf, ham, something called liverwurst. They put some chemicals in the potatoes that's supposed to quiet you down at night. Instead, it just makes my heart pound. Well, it's a small price to pay for being here in Iowa instead of some ship in the South Pacific. I could really use a warm pair of gloves and a new wool cap. It's very drafty in our barracks especially at night. I think I might be getting a cold. I look forward to seeing everybody at Mira's wedding. I'm bringing you a surprise.
Love,
Roy

March 25, 1942
Dear Joe,
I'm feeling much better now, and I've gone back to work, although things have slowed down a bit. Charlie is worried, what with the wedding coming up, but I'm sure business will pick up. I appreciate you making arrangements for me with your friend Dr. Evans. He was kind to me and very gentle. He gave me something that put me to sleep, so I didn't feel much pain. He said you had taken care of everything and he wouldn't take my money. I had to tell Rena because I was already into the third month and I needed her help. Joe, I wished this had never happened. I could almost feel the baby growing inside of me, and I wanted it so badly. But don't worry. I won't make trouble for you. I've always hated being a burden. But it's best that you don't try to reach me again. I forgive you but I will never, never forget you.
Always,
Jeanette

April 1, 1942
Darling Natie,
(This is what I've decided to call you), guess what? I'm pregnant. Ha! Ha! April Fools. Wouldn't that be a kick? Poppa would probably have the caterer dim the lights so low that people would be tripping over one another. Imagine me a pregnant bride being lifted up on the chair while the guests dance the Hora.

Just three more weeks and we'll finally have our honeymoon. I heard Atlantic City is lots of fun and close by so we don't have to spend all that time driving. Don't worry honey, I've taken your car in for the oil change like you asked, and I gave a sweet kid in the neighborhood five bucks to wax it. Uncle Louie ordered your tuxedo from his friend Mr. Zeller. They measured your gray suit for the fit. My gown is almost finished. I can't wait for you to see me in it. Aunt JJ has helped me a lot, almost hand sewing the whole garment. She can sit sewing for hours with the limited motion of a mime. Sometimes she scares me; she's so withdrawn. I'm disappointed that Faye can't come, but I'm happy that she's finally getting work. I doubt they're paying her much. God only knows how she survives out there. She's asked me to visit her after you go back down, but I don't think I can go until business picks up. I've got this new design idea swirling around in my brain. I've enclosed a sketch of it. What do you think? Bet you like the way it fits my rendition of Betty Grable. Okay, you can pin it up for the guys. Anyhow, I'll start on it right after the honeymoon. That's if I'm not too tired. I can't wait to hold you in my arms. I'm already sad to have to say goodbye again. I pray every night for this war to be over.
Forever yours,
Mira Kane Berk

Without a Father

Today when Marta carries my breakfast, I notice she is dressed all in black. Usually, she is quick to speak to me, to smile, but not today. She looks as though she's locked inside a dream.

Her eyes are red and puffy, and I wonder if she is feeling ill. The very thought of this causes a kick in my belly because I have grown so fond of her. I look forward to the nights when she comes down to visit, bringing her large box of candle making supplies and sometimes letting me watch her work. She knows how much I love the candles.

"Are you going somewhere today?" I ask, but Marta busies herself putting fresh linens on the brand new sleigh bed Avram made for me on my birthday. Marta mumbles some words in Polish that I don't understand. She takes a crumbled handkerchief from her pocket and blows her nose.

"Are you sick?"

"No, Rosha, not sick in the way you mean, child."

"Then how? Can you tell me?"

"My Avram was sent far, far away, and well, the children and I miss him terribly."

She stands by the casement window and opens the shutters, then closes them half-way so that I may enjoy the daylight without the fear of being discovered by a neighbor or their barking dog.

"Perhaps he will return sooner than you think," I say. I sit squatting on the cold metal vat in the corner of the room. My pee splashes on my leg as I stand up too quickly. I am worried about Marta and Sophie and myself. It felt so much safer to have a *Poppa* in the house, even if he wasn't my Poppa, even if I don't really live in the house at all.

Marta opens the trap door under the floor boards, then pulls open the metal plank, and the awful smell rises into the cellar. I hold my nose and Marta looks like she is about to smile, but then a tear trickles down her cheek. I think it is because of the awful smells or because of all the extra work she has to do since she brought me here.

"I'm big enough to do that myself," I say. I stand and take one end of the bucket as Marta pours the liquid into the ground. She slides the metal sheet and already it begins to smell better. She lights a wooden match stick and twirls it around until it is about to burn her fingers.

"No, no, Rosha, it is hard enough for you to live down here by yourself. You are much more than a guest, you are part of our family now, but you are not free to roam about. That, child, has been for your own safety."

"Will you still come down every day to visit me?"

My hands are shaking, and suddenly I am very afraid. Something awful has happened, I can tell. It is too quiet upstairs. There are no footsteps, no one playing tag throughout the rooms, no laughter between a brother and sister.

"Yes, of course. As a matter of fact, I have a nice surprise for you."

Marta sits down on my bed and folds her hands. She thinks for a few seconds and then speaks.

"Now, with Avram away, Sophie has been sleeping with me in my bed. So, late at night, after everyone is tucked away in their room, and no one is wandering about, I will bring you upstairs to sleep in Sophie's room. You will be able to bathe in the kitchen where you won't shiver from cold, and yes, Rosha, I promise to show you how to make your own candles, your own beautiful candles."

I crouch on the floor and hug Marta's feet. She pats my head and runs her fingers through the sticky strands.

"We will start with a good, hard shampooing," she says, and I am happy to see Marta smile.

Then the very next day, Victor places the tray on top of my new bed, something his mother never would do. He turns from me, his mouth one mean horizontal line and walks over to the big supply of burlap bags. He takes out his pocket knife from his jacket and slices an X into one of the bags. I back up against the cold wall. Dozens of dark skinned potatoes burst from the opening and roll across the floor. Some land by my bed.

"Now, look what you've done," he says to me, "Mother will be furious."

"But I didn't do it, Victor. Why would you say such a thing?"

"Because everything is your fault, you skinny little runt. If it weren't for you, my father wouldn't be dead. He was a really good man who helped a lot of people, but he died because of you! Oh, don't give me those big crocodile tears. We no longer have a father. Do you understand? Are you just another stupid girl?"

Victor reaches down and scoops up some of the potatoes. He throws one against the wall, right behind my head, and I am so afraid that I pull the blanket over my body hoping he can't see.

I wish I could stop crying, but I am afraid Victor wants to kill me. He looks that angry. I didn't know Mr. Juraska was dead. Dead? Nobody told me. It is not my fault. No. He has to be wrong.

Marta yells from the top of the stairs: "Victor? What are you doing down there?"

I have never seen Marta move so quickly. Her feet pound on each step and before long she is holding Victor by his shirt collar. Because he is so tall, like Avram, she has to jump up and down to hold her grip on him. It is a funny sight, but because I feel that Victor said it was my fault, I can't help feeling sad.

Marta pulls a wooden spoon from her apron and swats Victor three times on his shoulder. He laughs and points his finger at me once more. He mouths "hey, you, just wait," and then his mother lifts her leg backwards and brings it forward with so much force that Victor lands flat on all fours. The blow was to his behind, what Poppa called the "*tuchus.*"

"Get up this minute and tell Rosha you are sorry for your God awful behavior. This is how you honor the memory of your poor father who worked hard so many years, who wanted, above all, to raise you up to practice decency and respect?"

"But if she wasn't here, father wouldn't have been shot, and you wouldn't have a bag of his bloody clothes in the corner of the shed outside. I've seen them, Mother, don't think I haven't."

My whole body is shaking. Victor is still on his knees and soon he begins to cry. He cries loudly, as if he has stored his sobs in a hidden corner of his body for the longest time. He has more tears than there are potatoes in all the sacks. I put my head under my pillow, embarrassed for Victor but secretly hoping he will treat me more kindly.

Marta pulls her tall son up from the floor.

"You are a man now," she says in her softest voice. This is how she spoke to me the night she and Avram told me about Mama, Poppa, and Bubba, when they said they were all . . . what was that word she used, hard to remember, don't want to, no, not now, not ever. Gone.

"Come on, Rosha, eat your breakfast. I know you are hiding under the blankets. I can see your pretty hair sticking out from your pillow."

She lifts the pillow off my head, but I don't move. "I've wet my pajamas," I whisper. She bends over me and her heavy bosom presses into my back squashing me.

"That's all right. We will give you a pair of Sophie's to wear until I can do the wash. I'm sorry that Victor scared you, Rosha. It has been hard for all of the children. They loved their father very much, and now they miss him terribly."

This is exactly how I feel every second of every day I spend in this house.

As if she has read my thoughts, Marta scoops me up and holds me against her chest. Her body is rocking slightly, and she begins humming a melody that sounds familiar. She strokes her busy fingers through my hair, then takes my hands and brings them up to her lips. Marta's eyes fill with tears. For the first time in a long while I stop thinking about myself.

Victor comes down the folding stairs carrying a mop and bucket. Head down he begins picking up the potatoes that spilled out of the bag.

"Victor is there something you want to tell *our* Rosha?"

He stands with the mop and bucket staring at the dark spot behind my bed. His voice is thin, missing all the sparks of anger.

"Sorry," he says. "I was wrong to try and scare you."

"And?" Marta asks.

"And I promise it will never happen again."

Mira

Tulle

~

The gown was kept under wraps in the factory while they shipped out all current Kane Knitting orders. It had been a blustery March, and Mira imagined herself in the creation, made of several layers of tulle, billowing like a parachute, and landing in the midst of downtown traffic.

She had searched the markets like a scavenger finding several yards of imported French lace, practically nonexistent since the war. Instead of Austrian crystals for trim, she settled on tiny, freshwater pearls that would be interspersed with minuscule clear rhinestones. She knew the effect would be dazzling, but not overdone, just a sprinkling of beading on the bodice and kabuki sleeves. The rest of the gown would be antique ivory tulle. Yards and yards of tulle. She had gone back to her textbooks and found some sketches by the famous designer, Jo Copeland, which gave her the inspiration for the wedding dress. She could almost hear the praise of her teacher, Mr. Forte, back at the Rockefeller School. By all standards, the dress was indeed couture.

Pay attention, she reminded herself as she nearly collided with two tall Negro men pushing a wobbly rack of summer frocks. Summer. Would it ever arrive? And would she be alone this summer, without Nathan? Smile, she commanded herself. Damn you, smile.

Nathan would be home in just three weeks. Her body tingled at the memory of his scent. He always smelled so fresh, like a pine forest mysteriously growing in Brooklyn. She had started taking long walks downtown instead of cab rides in preparation for her annual Passover weight gain. Hopefully, this would be her last fitting.

Today, she pushed herself faster, clutching her black portfolio that held her newest design. It wasn't exactly a work of genius, but it was extremely marketable. Mira often caught herself thinking like her father. Was it some contagious sense of responsibility or the need to beat the competition?

JJ crouched on a small satin pillow. She wore a red felt pin cushion in the shape of a tomato on her wrist. She motioned for Mira to turn toward the mirror while she placed the last pin into the hem. The reflection they saw startled them both. Mira balanced on a step stool looking almost regal in all that lace, perfect and filmy in the slightly dusty mirror that hung on the sample closet door. Below her, literally at her feet, was JJ, the dutiful servant, working hard to push away her own pain. She smiled up at Mira permitting her to revel in the moment.

"Oh, JJ, we did it," Mira said, her throat tightening.

"No, it's all you, Mira. Your genius down to the very last pearl."

JJ swayed as she stood up. The pills she took, all the time now, were probably responsible. Mira reached for JJ's hand and stepped down from the stool. She turned around slowly, the long lace train following her like a bow on a huge gift box. Shuffling around Mira, JJ scooped up the delicate fabric before it became twisted.

There was a startling knock at the door, and then in walked Rena. She gasped, covering her mouth, embarrassed, as if she had intruded upon naked lovers. Mira wasn't sure she heard Rena correctly because the sewing machines buzzed loudly in the background and outside cars and taxis honked furiously. But she knew she could not ask her to repeat herself. That would be too hard for the uncomplimentary Rena. Mira hoped she had heard the words she would never forget:

"Look at you, niece. You are as lovely as a princess."

Mira fell silent while her aunts prattled on as her backdrop. She giggled aloud while she turned and turned, first away, then toward the mirror sending a crystal rainbow of dust particles dancing in the air.

Victor

He had not visited his father's work shed for weeks. The last time, he was asked to fetch the carpenter's file that Avram always used when creating special etchings along the edges of chairs or tables. But that day, in March, when his father had asked him to bring him the special tool, Victor had dawdled in the overly cramped and spider-webbed space looking for something to steal. He didn't understand why this sudden urge came over him, but he knew lots of other boys who carried their own knives, and well, he just wanted a weapon for his own protection. A friend of his had bragged about being in a fight with a young German soldier, though Avram didn't believe a word of it. He doubted his friend would have survived to retell the story.

In his clumsiness and because of the problem he had with balance, Victor had stumbled into a saw-horse that fell over and into a crate. This crate also contained many of Avram's most dependable tools. The carpenter's file was one of them, and when Victor examined it, he noticed that the curved handle was now split beyond repair.

For an instant, Victor thought about lying. He wanted to say he found the tool exactly that way, but Avram would stare him down until his face nearly exploded from having to conceal the lie. So, he had decided to spend time cleaning up to buffer the mishap. His tardiness, however, was hardly appreciated. Growing more and more impatient, Avram had finally decided to go get the tool himself. He had practically yanked off the door to the shed wondering what could have taken Victor that long to fetch one lousy tool and nothing more. When Avram barged in, Victor was busy lining up a slew of cans containing nails and screws in an array of sizes. The furious father had leaped toward his son practically choking him; he yelled telling him to get the hell off his workbench. To make matters worse, Victor had to show Avram the favorite, most used, and now unusable tool he'd asked him to go find. His father's eyes had filled with bloody rage, his hand went up, and when Victor ducked, Avram smacked his head on the bench.

Victor hated remembering that *that* was the last day. And worse, that the very last time he had been with his father, he had disappointed him. Yet, more than the reality of those final moments was the hideous feeling Victor has harbored—he had wished his father dead, having no idea then of the power of those wishes.

Standing in the shed now, looking for the vat of beeswax his mother needs brought inside, Victor's eyes spot the largest of containers holding the bolts and nails. Weren't his hands on that exact same one that he was about to lift before his father's raging entrance? It was so heavy that Victor had to climb up on the table in order to gain leverage. He took two smaller cans thinking he would divide the contents of the larger making his job easier. Frustrated, Victor pummeled it with a mallet and split through its metallic seams. Screws, nails, and bolts poured all over, stinging the skin on his legs. At first he was fearful of his father's wrath, and then remembered that he was dead. Wouldn't he rather be scolded now than have things like this? Yes, he admitted to himself as tears streamed down his face.

The corner of a dirty white envelope stuck out from the debris. Victor thought it might contain special fasteners that were costly and hard to come by. The envelope had been opened and sealed again with a patch of yellow adhesive. Victor's heart beat faster and faster. He felt closer to something, but had lost all his patience. He ripped open the envelope only to tear some bills. There was so much money falling around him, he gasped aloud. "Fuck," he said, once and then again, fuck... the forbidden word and thus most satisfying. He jumped from the table and put a chair in front of the door blocking entry. Sitting on the floor he began counting out bills, much of the value of which he was unsure. A letter was written in an unfamiliar hand. He could barely make out the signature but only the letters KAN at the end. He saw the name *Rosha* written many times, and he realized this money was meant for *her*, the girl. The amount was scribbled on the back of the envelope. But it also appeared as if another folder had already been emptied.

Inside a note in Avram's handwriting stated: *Taken on January, 3rd, 1942. Will pay back on February 3rd after sale of two oak chairs made for Commander Schlinglaucht.*

Victor closed his eyes trying to imagine his father removing the money that did not belong to him. And when had he mentioned that he was making furniture for the enemy? He took the note and tore it into pieces. This, he did not want his mother to know. His lips curled into a smirk as he realized Avram was not the perfect man he had thought him to be. That he, too, had lied. Then, suddenly, he was captured in a net of pure jealousy and wrath once more for Rosha. He envied the affection and tenderness displayed in the note and knew that this money, with all its prayers, wishes, and hopes was meant for the care of the stranger who had been living in his family's dank and dusty cellar.

He noticed that many of the bills had been removed from a metal clip. He wondered how it was used by his father, but knew he would never really learn the truth. He could do so much with this money that slid through his fingers like sawdust. Victor's thoughts of running away grew stronger, but he did not wish to suffer the same fate of his father, nor was he ready to hand over this new discovery to his mother. He wondered if she even knew about this money and whether she was depending on it for their survival.

He stuffed the envelope into a smaller can and covered it with bolts and nails, and for good measure a piece of sandpaper on the top. He reminded himself the jar said: Coffee Beans, though it had been emptied of beans for well over a year. He finally remembered the vat of bees wax and grabbing it, he took one look back to the shelf. He felt safer now and in control. Victor had choices to make, things he would have to think about a great deal. He hated this business of thinking.

"What in God's name took you so long? I was beginning to worry." His mother had been waiting for him at the back door of their house. She startled him so that he leapt in the air like a giant cricket.

"I needed to search for a vat that was full. Most are half-empty. The wax supply is running low."

"That can't be. Are you sure you looked carefully?"

"Yes, I'm sure, mother."

"I'll have myself a good look tomorrow," she said, sending shivers up Victor's spine.

VOWS

~

Umbrellas the size of tents leaped from the limousines parked along the curb of the Ocean Parkway Synagogue. Torrential rain pounded the sidewalk. They should have expected it. After all, it was April. Mira threatened to murder Roy if he didn't can his Al Jolsen imitation of "April Showers." He had started singing the tune the day before the wedding when you could tell just by looking at the sky that the sun was buried far beneath the stream of nimbus clouds.

"It is very good luck, my angel," Momma had said at least a hundred times that morning, and kept on repeating it as she and Aunt Jeanette threw cellophane drop cloths over Mira's headpiece and gown. She was fully dressed underneath the smelly drop cloths.

The temple had called to say there was a leak in the bridal suite, and it was better that the family dress at home.

"With what I'm paying these people, they can't afford a resident handyman? God dammit!" Charlie shouted, rummaging through his drawers looking for his lapis cufflinks.

"Charl, please, not now, she's nervous enough," Ina pleaded.

"Nervous, why now, she's already married, remember?"

"Shush, go, take Roy and what's her name, Betty Sue. . . ."

"Bobbi Ann," Charlie corrected her, laughing now, containing the knowledge that could make him lose his mind if he let it. But he wouldn't. He couldn't afford to. Why aggravate himself over his new daughter-in-law, even if she happened to be a shiksa? A pretty and

227

pregnant shiksa as well. Thank God the girl wasn't showing. Charlie thought, sure, I send my only son off to defend our country and he can't keep his pants zipped. But there were worse things. Oh, how he knew that. And a baby! A wife would perhaps serve to anchor Roy, hopefully giving him a real sense of responsibility. Charlie still hadn't told a soul what had occurred some weeks ago. One of his old pals, a contract knitter, owed Charlie a few grand for almost five years. It turned out this same guy had a brother who happened to be a doctor in the Bronx. After Charlie received Roy's letter, he visited his friend and decided to apply a little pressure for the dough that was owed. They got to talking about the families and one thing led to another. Within a week Charlie gets a letter from the doctor, including an updated version of Roy's medical record. And sure enough, just what Charlie had always expected, Roy was almost totally deaf in his left ear. Seemed he must have had a bad cold, and fluid had built up to cause an infection. Charlie got lost in the medical details. All he knew was this sounded real good to him, this diagnosis of deafness. What mattered most was that Roy would soon return home from his service to his country for good. Hopefully Ina might sleep a little better.

JJ, Rena, and Hattie kept company with Mira in a dingy classroom used to give adolescent boys Hebrew lessons. The air was heavy with an oily pubescent smell that nearly made Mira gag. "I can't breathe," she whined. Hattie tried to pry open one of the windows. When she did, her shiny black hair got soaking wet. Mira kept herself calm by watching Hattie's straight hair turn into tight little ringlet curls before her eyes.

The only place to prop up the bride was the large oak desk used by the rabbi. Right before the ceremony, it was where Mira and Nathan would solemnly sign the *Ketuba*, making everything legal in God's eyes, with Mrs. Berk, Charlie, and Ina as witnesses. Meanwhile, just down the hall, extravagantly dressed guests mingled in the elegant foyer, eyeing each other while sipping seltzer in tall champagne glasses. Underneath their expensively tailored frocks, their bellies growled like lions. All were anxious for sundown, the ceremony, and the rewards of what they knew would be a grand display of epicurean food.

Charlie and Ina greeted their guests with royal aplomb. Charlie draped Ina's arm through his as they chatted briefly with the Morris's and Goldberger's. Ina wore a long navy taffeta dress, which complimented her auburn hair. Over the large chignon she had placed a fine circle of navy mesh. She wore a round-cut diamond around her neck, making Mrs. Morris's eyes nearly leap from their sockets. Charlie looked stiffer than usual in his old tux. He had refused to buy a new one for the occasion.

"You can bury me in a new one if you like," he had said. He pulled at the collar trying to free his Adam's apple. He was dying for a cigar, but promised he wouldn't smoke until after the ceremony. There was enough smoke filling the room already, smothering the lavish aromas of Chanel, Shalimar, and Joy. Not to mention destroying the natural fragrance of nearly twenty dozen long stemmed red roses.

Mira had to look away from Momma while they stood under the ivy and lily flowered *Chupah*. If she didn't look away, she would surely be swept into her mother's tears. Like an unrelenting undertow, she'd be tugged back through all the years of loving one another and cherishing each other's companionship. It might be too hard to leave at all. Instead, she locked eyes with Nathan taking him as she would a stranger. Everything she had first seen in his face was here, only, this time, larger and glossier, like the eight-by-tens that adorned the walls of Pearly's Soda Shop where she had first laid eyes on him.

Rabbi Glick stood at the *bimah* chanting words Mira barely heard. Suddenly she was jarred back to the present. The rabbi grinned and waited. He whispered, "In sickness and in health, so help me God."

Mira recited, "In sickness and in health, so help me *DEAR* God." Nathan pushed the thin gold band over her knuckle. She winced slightly at the pain; it felt snug.

Yet, another prayer, followed by another sip of wine and then the sound of Nathan's foot, not a random shattering like the broken glass the ritual represented, but a firm hard stomp, the affirmation of their bond. Blessings of *Mazel Tov* chorused throughout the chapel. The couple kissed for the eighteen seconds they had practiced. Eighteen, being *Chai*, and therefore, good luck.

The doors to the chapel opened into the ballroom and starving guests lost all demeanor nearly trampling one another as they rushed to the several smorgasbord tables. Many were topped with ice sculptures in the shapes of mermaids or fish. Within the confines of this room, it was hard to believe there was a war raging. That men and women serving the country were dying. The only real hint was the food stations serviced by either young attractive waitresses or very old men looking a bit crumpled in their white jackets.

While Mira and Nathan shook hands, politely retrieved envelopes and accepted congratulations, Charlie began his mental inventory. He was intent on finding the *Chateaubriand*. After all, he had paid extra for it. And where the hell were the baby rib lamb chops? From across the room, he spotted Roy standing with a plate piled high. Bobbie Ann sat at the cocktail table next to him looking bored. Charlie blinked. What was it she gulped down like there was no tomorrow and from the bottle no less? Probably a Rheingold. He should have told the caterer not to serve that German crap. Roy was too busy munching on the chops to notice. Charlie had no choice but to intervene. He dragged Bobbi Ann onto the dance floor where circles and circles of laughing guests danced the first dance of the evening, the traditional *Hora* around the bride and groom. The couple looked down from their bouncing red velvet chairs to all the laughing and tear-streaked faces who wished them well. Mira tossed her hankie into the air, and Nathan grabbed one end. She screamed, gripping the sides of her chair while Nathan, imitating a bronco rider, spun the hankie around as if lassoing his bride. In a small inner circle, Mrs. Berk looped arms with Rena, Ina, and Jeanette. They paired off swinging each other around while the others clapped louder and louder, stomping their feet. The room shook with genuine gaiety. The sisters pulled Charlie into the circle. And he took turns swinging each of the women, his women, wildly. Mira and Nathan, down on the floor again, joined in for the finale. The trumpet sounded its final notes and everyone stood clapping and congratulating one another, wiping sweat from their necks and brows, as if they had just swam the English Channel.

Charlie and Ina made their rounds from table to table during the sumptuous six-course dinner to be sure everyone was having a good time. Rena was engrossed in conversation with a handsome man

about ten years her senior. His name was Fritzy, a German Jew from
Wiesbaden, who had moved to the States after visiting a cousin in '38,
and had fortunately decided not to return to Europe. That cousin was
one of Charlie's best engineers, and as a favor Charlie helped Fritzy
get a job as a pattern maker with a company in Queens. Fritzy, or
Fritz as he preferred being called, had a thick, watery accent. He was
so animated when he spoke that his arms flailed recklessly in front of
him. Now watching them speak, Charlie wasn't sure whether Fritzy
was about to hit Rena or kiss her. Yet, he could clearly see his sister was
having a terrific time. When had she smiled so freely?

Next to Rena sat Louie and his surprise guest, Gloria, a sometimes
showroom model for Kane, and about twenty years younger than
Louie, and a half-foot taller. She wore a skin-tight gold lamé sheath,
and her body resembled one of the mermaid ice sculptures from the
cocktail hour. Charlie tried to deflect his glance, but he noticed when
his brother spoke to Gloria, it looked as if he were talking directly
into her cleavage. Charlie finally understood why Louie had so vigorously campaigned a few weeks earlier for Gloria's raise.

"She's terrific, don't you think?" Louie had said several times.

"What terrific?" Charlie answered, "Lou, pardon me if I say so,
but most of the time she sits in the dressing room polishing her fingernails. For this we should give the girl a raise? Better you shouldn't
get a heart attack." Louie had looked flustered and stormed out of the
room.

There was a thunderous drum roll, and the popular band leader,
Lester Lanin, summoned Charlie over the microphone to escort Mira
to the center of the floor. Though he had been to lots of weddings over
the years, and none as extravagant as this, Charlie had never focused
on this particular dance. Even with the few shots of scotch he had
already consumed, he was nervous. He smiled a tight little smile as
he took Mira's hand and lead her to the dance floor. The guests were
already standing at their respective tables to get a good look. A beautiful tenor voice began crooning, "My Little Girl," and blinding flash-
bulbs bounced off their faces when Charlie and Mira danced, then
stopped to pose and danced again. People began singing along with
the band; some formed a circle at the fringe of the dance floor. Charlie

bit the fleshiness of his inner cheeks so not to cry, but his heart felt as if it would burst. When Mira reached her arm tightly around his neck he finally glanced up at her.

"Have you always been this tall?" he said to her.

She laughed, looking down at her father who seemed shy all of a sudden with little to say.

Through the blurriness of the photographer's incessant snapping, and the rhythmic swaying of his guests, he remembered a little girl, maybe four or five, who used to love to dance while standing on his wingtip, laced-up shoes. Her skinny little body would reach up and cling to his like a caterpillar twirled on a branch, while he hummed a tune from the old country—the country that had never once left his soul.

Nathan and Mira made their fast getaway at 1 A.M. while a few guests, mostly family, waved them off. Mira had changed into a powder blue suit with a matching pillbox hat, and Nathan wore his uniform. Charlie insisted on hiring a limousine. He made sure to ask for Maxi the Taxi for their late night honeymoon ride.

At 2:30 in the morning they arrived at the Atlantic Towers hotel in Atlantic City where Nathan had made arrangements for the honeymoon suite. As soon as the bellboy left, Mira made Nathan come out with her into the quiet hallway to carry her over the threshold.

"Isn't one threshold enough?" he said, laughing as he hoisted her up in his arms.

"No, Natie, this time it really feels as though we're married, don't you agree?"

"I've always felt like we were, Mira. It's what's kept me from getting too homesick."

"Oh, Nathan, I guess sleeping in my old bed, alone, in that big house, kept me from feeling like a real wife."

"And what exactly is a real wife supposed to feel like?" He put his arms on her shoulders, and when he said that it sent a new tingling sensation up her spine. That desperate way he looked at her. She noticed a hunger in him she had never seen before. She knew instantly she wanted him and answered by quickly unbuttoning her suit jacket and blouse. She took his cool hands that still held the room keys and placed them lower on her perfumed chest. The bustier she wore had pushed up her flesh to reveal the deeper tone of her nipples, and Nathan's tongue began hungrily searching for more of her. Finally, he tugged at her skirt while she helped, her long fingers fumbling with his buckle, opening the metal clasp and undoing the several buttons on his fly. Clumsily hopping on one foot, Nathan pulled off his tight, bell-bottom trousers. Then he scooped her up, nearly tripping over the heap made of their clothing as he headed for the bedroom. He carried his new bride to a large circular bed aptly placed in the middle of the room. Both of them looked puzzled, yet excited, by the bed's lack of edges and corners; it was as though they were now captured in one continuous web of love-making.

Sunday morning they lay exhausted, naked, and giggling like teenagers. Mira's hair fanned out around her shoulders, and Nathan twirled pieces of it in his fingers. They realized that if their bed was a clock, by the end of their five-day honeymoon they probably would've made love at every hour on the hour. A way of making up for lost time.

"I think we're at six o'clock," she laughed.

"Nah, it's probably three," he answered. "Didn't we start here?" He threw his body across hers catching some of her hair with his forearm.

"Ouch, that hurt, you big brute."

"Uh oh, here it is . . . our first real fight."

"Don't say that," Mira said, rubbing her scalp. "This is our honeymoon and in a few days you'll be gone again and. . . ." She began to cry.

"Don't," he whispered. "It'll all be over soon you'll see, and I'll have my old job back. Then we'll be able to get our own place just like we planned."

"I know, I know. It's just that now Roy is going to be back, and he and Bobbi Ann are getting their own place."

"Mira, it could be a great deal worse. There are a lot of guys out there in PT boats getting blown to smithereens."

She put her fingers to his lips. "Hush. I can't stand to think about that."

Mira jumped out of bed and soon returned with two apples. She tossed one to Nathan. She looked behind the large velvet curtain, squinting while dragging them open.

"Nathan, it's the most glorious day. Just look at that sun." From the window she saw the boardwalk bustling with people. Some sat on benches looking out at the calm ocean. There were food vendors on bicycles, and jugglers and mimes entertaining passersby. "Let's get dressed and go outside."

"But what about traveling a bit longer around this clock?" Nathan asked, shielding his eyes with a pillow.

"We've got all night. No, actually, the rest of our lives."

Once outside, they squeezed together on one of the sun bleached wooden benches. Mira lifted her face to the sun. She smelled the salt-water air and sighed. She made a silent wish to always feel just like this. It didn't hurt to wish, she thought. She knew things changed, understood that bad things could always happen. "Please, please, God," she mumbled under her breath. "I promise to try and be a good person." It had been a long time since she'd done that—talked to God and too long a time since she felt happy.

"What did you say?" Nathan asked.

"Oh, nothing." She put her head on his shoulder, and noticed he was shivering.

"Natie, what's wrong?"

"I'm trying to adjust to this northerly weather." He blew into his hands trying to warm them.

"Why don't we take a walk, it'll do us both good," Mira said.

They headed for the boardwalk café with a huge striped awning and bold red sign that read, *Checkmate.* They strolled by several people, mostly much older than them. There were a few young men in Navy uniforms. As they passed, they saluted Nathan, and Mira thought they looked like new recruits. She was shocked by how young these men appeared. Too young. She held Nathan's arm tighter as the cool wind slapped against their faces. Nathan's head tucked inside his shoulders like a turtle. Mira was now sorry she'd suggested they leave their cozy room. As they walked through the swinging saloon type door, that's when she spotted him. She wasn't a hundred percent sure, but she'd be willing to bet on it. But then who could she tell, certainly not Nathan, and who would ever, ever believe her? Her father showing up to spy on her while she honeymooned? His incredible *Chutzpah*! She watched, holding her breath, as Charlie tipped his grey flannel hat to a tall, balding waiter who handed him what looked like change. Then, like *The Great Houdini*, this man, who looked exactly like Charlie Kane, slipped out the exit door, which led to an adjacent hotel lobby. When she blinked and opened her eyes again, he was gone.

Rosha

Me, a Candle Maker

❦

This morning, for the first time in a long time, I awakened completely joyful. A tiny sparrow chirped wildly against the casement window as if announcing himself to the world. I lay completely still, fighting the urge to lift up the shade. But I could see myself actually doing it—knocking on the glass, then the bird hopping over to get a better view of me, but right then, all at once, the chirping ceased. I felt awfully sad then, as if the entire world had made a decision to go somewhere and leave me behind. My heart thumped loudly inside my chest. To calm myself, I pictured Bubbe, sweaty and breathless, trudging down the staircase of our building, carrying her glass jug of sliced lemons and water. That's when I remembered what she said about "the sweetness," the lesson Bubbe taught me the exact moment everything had seemed so hopeless.

Since I've been here, every day, without realizing, I have tried to find something that makes me happy, no matter how small a thing that might be. Today it was the little speckled bird chirping outside that reminded me that it is nearly spring.

Sometime after sundown, Marta lowered the staircase in the cellar to take me to my new bedroom, which is really Sophie's room. The house upstairs was very dimly lit; and Marta held my hand so I didn't trip or bang into the furniture. There were beautifully carved wooden chairs, a desk, a pine pedestal, and bookcases—all crammed into corners or pushed against pale green walls. The first thing I noticed was the smell. Strange, but the smell was lemony. The house felt dry and warm, so warm that I couldn't wait to take off both my sweaters. Though they are quite snug on me, I like wearing them, mostly because they were a gift from my family in America. I wish I could remember all of their names, but I can't. I recall only the name of my first cousin, Mira. She is a lot older than me, a teenager, who Bubbe had said was tall and beautiful.

On top of Sophie's patchwork quilt, Marta prepared freshly laundered pajamas for me, a toothbrush made of wood and bristles, and a pair of fluffy slippers. She said they were an early birthday present since my real birthday is soon, at the end of March.

"Go ahead," Marta said, watching me as I studied every square inch of the room, "why not try out the bed." Using the step stool I climbed upon the puffy mattress. I lay sprawled across the bed feeling as if I had fallen up and landed in heaven. I didn't say it aloud, but I wondered how I'd manage to spend my days back in the cellar now that I had been spoiled by the comforts of this perfectly neat little room. Though there was much more space downstairs, this space truly reminded me of home.

"Where are Sophie and Victor?" I asked. There was such a noticeable silence. I could hear the ticking of the mahogany clock out in the hallway.

"They're asleep, Rosha. It's late, already past ten."

"Oh, I forgot." At that moment, I realized that my visits upstairs would not include much play time with Sophie. I was a bit disappointed and then felt bad for being so ungrateful.

"Why don't we see how things go? Perhaps all will settle down soon, and life will return to normal."

Marta looked away from me for a moment as if she were slapped by a cold wind. She wrapped both arms against her chest and stood perfectly still. Though her eyes didn't move, I could almost see a film playing inside her head. I bet it was a film about long ago. Some happier time when she, Avram, and her children were together enjoying a picnic in the forest, like the home movie Poppa showed me of him and his brothers swimming in a lake near Riga. Not a day passes when I don't see my own film. Mostly, they are times with Mama and Bubbe in the kitchen preparing meals, or Poppa helping me with my arithmetic about which I was always confused.

In the kitchen, I washed my face and hands and dried them on a fluffy towel. It was so soft I counted to ten while drying my neck. The pajamas were too tight on me so Marta cut the waistband with a knife and tied a ribbon through a button hole to keep them from falling down.

"Are you sure you're not too tired?" Marta asked.

"No, not at all, I took a long nap this afternoon after I finished my letters and numbers drill."

"Well, I for one, think that a good home student like you should be rewarded. How would you like your first lesson in candle-making?"

"Now? Really? Are you sure it's not too late?" I was hoping she wouldn't quickly change her mind. Mothers did that sometimes, faster than a jack rabbit in the field.

"I'm sure, child. How about you? Perhaps, you'd like to climb into Sophie's bed instead to enjoy the next seven hours of sleep. You know that before long, I'll have to send you back down?"

"No, no. I am ready, 100 percent." I had just been studying percentages that morning and the number popped right into my head."

"Well, first, making candles is not the same as saving the melted wax and forming little figurines. The candles are needed for their function, and now with beeswax so scarce, we must be careful not to waste any."

"But there are always so many bees, especially at picnics during the summertime." I realized that it had been so long since I'd gone on a picnic with Mama and Poppa. Once, when I was turning six, on a very hot day, we had to fold up our blankets and move inside. Mama's cousin, Yakov, had gotten stung on the tip of his nose. Initially, Poppa had laughed, but Mama shushed him, giving him one of her tight-lipped looks. Later that night though, behind their bedroom door I heard them both laughing and talking about Yakov and how he sat eating his lunch with wet mud packed all over his face. Marta laughed when I told her this story.

"Yes, there are plenty of bees, but now there is problem. Avram once explained to me that beeswax is used to coat certain types of machinery that is needed by the armies, especially in wartime so they won't rust. Luckily, Avram kept a large supply in his shed. He used cans and cans of beeswax to polish all the new furniture he made and often gave some away to customers. And, of course, to me for the candles that I sold in the marketplace. But now everything has changed. There are only two aisles of merchants still selling their wares, and the hours are very restricted." Marta's voice got heavy and she cleared her throat, "well, now, let's begin."

"What about the chicken man? Mama was a really good customer. I had to turn my head away every time he killed our shabbos dinner."

"I'm sorry to say, dear, no one knows of his whereabouts. Now come, we are wasting precious time."

I wondered if the chicken man was lost or hurt somewhere deep in the woods like Poppa. I pictured him with chickens tied on a rope around his waist, a large knife in his hand.

Marta waved her hand across my eyes. She could see me daydreaming even though it was night.

"First lesson and most important rule. Roll up your pajama sleeves and fetch me the wooden spoons in that drawer. There is no time for anything fancy tonight. Just a basic white candle that you can use on Friday nights, and depending on how quickly you work—that will decide the size of our candles."

Marta scooped the sticky beeswax into a pot that looked a hundred years old. She placed that pot into a larger pot that was filled to the brim with boiling water. I sat at a small table to do my job, which was cutting the cotton wicks into foot long strips. Marta showed me how to tie and double knot on the handle of each spoon. For this first lesson, she suggested I tie two cotton wicks on each spoon leaving enough space between them.

"Good, girl," she kept saying, and I felt myself smiling so big, as if my face had grown into a melon.

"Here comes the fun part," Marta said. "Slowly, but surely, Rosha Kaninsky will make her first candles."

Marta checked my sleeves again, pushing the already tight pajamas up past my elbows. With one foot, she slid a stool over to the stove upon which the pot boiled furiously.

"Take the spoon like this, see? Now dip into the inner pan—the one with the wax; dip once or twice then rest the spoon on that door-knob for a few seconds while you do the same exact thing with the other two spoons. This will make you . . . "

"Six," I said.

"That was much too easy for you, Rosha," Marta smiled.

And so my work began: me upon the stool, dipping one spoon, watching the clear fragrant liquid as it turned whiter and whiter, coating the long cotton wick, dressing it in a summer shawl. Then I was off the stool, while that one dried just slightly. I did this over and over until it became a dance—a happy candle maker's dance and a celebration of me—Rosha Kaninsky, who would soon turn nine in a house that was not hers but where she had become part of something good—a family who had kept all their promises to protect me.

Part Two

A Year of Changes
1945–1946

~

It felt as though they had driven for days, but it was only two hours earlier when Mira and Nathan had piled into the car with the twins, a straw picnic basket containing lunch, and a pee-pee jar for Mickey in case of an emergency. Mira turned toward the back seat to scold two and a half-year-old Mickey who was standing on his head with his legs flailing so that he kicked his sister, Sari, squarely in the face. When Sari pinched him, he shrieked so loudly that Nathan was forced to bring the car to a screeching halt, nearly causing a pileup on the heavily trafficked Sunrise Highway.

"Once more and no pony rides," he said, restarting the stalled Packard. Within seconds Nathan's elevated tone had curbed the children's behavior, bringing a welcomed veil of silence to their car trip.

"Natie," Mira whispered above the temporary quiet, "we should find a spot for lunch and get some fresh air. Besides, it's time we ate those salami sandwiches. The smell is making all of us hungry and cranky."

Without answering, Nathan reached over and held Mira's hand. Instinctively, she placed his on her protruding belly. There was one faint kick and then another, much stronger. Nathan's mood softened, and they both laughed. Without a doubt they agreed this pregnancy was the hardest. The twins were a constant drain on Mira's energy even with the help of Ina and her aunts. She realized that if they moved, she would not have the same aid and assistance they had always offered so

245

lovingly. And then there was the problem of Nathan's traveling. But it was time. Their apartment, across the street from her parents had only one bedroom, and the twins slept in daybeds on either side of Mira and Nathan's double bed like bookends.

From the time she arrived, ten minutes after her brother, Sari had been a very feisty child requiring a great deal of attention. Now with another sibling on the way, she would have to share the stage even more. A natural at theatrics, she had earned the nickname of "Sarah Heartburn." Mira remembered how Roy used to call her Sarah, referring to the *prima donna* actress of the twenties, whose last name was Bernhardt.

And their little boy was no slouch. Mickey was a ball of energy, constantly challenging everyone's nerves. Just a month ago, while Mira sat reading on a bench and the children played on the stoop, he had thrown a rock at a scraggly, barking dog. The angry dog charged at Mickey causing him to climb the wrought iron fence that surrounded their apartment building. Just as he was about to jump over and onto the grass, his pants got caught on a rusty spike. The spike tore first into the fabric and then punctured the skin next to his groin. An older neighborhood boy quickly lifted him off, but there was already blood everywhere. When Mira saw him lying on the ground soaked with blood, she felt her stomach muscles spasm. She was afraid she might lose the baby already five months inside of her. With every ounce of strength, Mira scooped Mickey up, put him in the stroller and with Sari by her side, and a dozen neighborhood children following, she rushed to the pediatrician's office two blocks away.

She had prayed the entire way, making deals with her reliable pal, God, to spare her child. The doctor announced the wound had missed the main artery by just half an inch. After twenty stitches, two nurses holding him down, and three lollipops, Mickey was bandaged up and they were driven home by the doctor himself. Glancing over at Mickey in the back seat, Mira thought it proof of a miracle that the boy had healed so quickly.

Mira spotted a sign that read, "Fishing Dock Half a Mile South."

"Turn here," she said. "The boats will be a great distraction for the children, and I'm sure there's parking." Nathan slowed down, made a quick turn, and found himself in a caravan of cars. It seemed everyone had the same idea; boat-watching would be a nice break on this toasty Sunday afternoon.

They pulled into a lot designated for Nick's customers. Nathan got out and stretched his legs. Two seagulls perched on the top of a boat slip, and Nathan led the children out of the car to see. Mira got out carefully, one leg at a time. She lifted her face toward the glaring white sun and closed her eyes. The sounds of the seagulls and the rhythmic splash of the water against the wooden pier were so peaceful. While Nathan took the children, being potty trained, into a public restroom, Mira unwrapped the sandwiches and placed them on big checkered napkins on the hood of the car. She knew that it would be Sari's and Mickey's favorite place to eat, while she and Nathan sat in the car, doors opened, having some quiet moments together.

Nathan came back holding a large map. "You won't believe this, we are only minutes east of your brother's new house."

"Well, maybe since this is a bit further away from the city, the houses might be a little less money. I do like this area, Nathan, don't you?"

"I like seeing the water, that's what I like," he said. "I spoke to Nick, this guy inside, and he said there are new developments sprouting up all around here.

"Did you ask about the schools?"

"Nick said there's one, just completed, surrounded by a duck pond right down the road, though I think we have a few years to start thinking about that."

"Nathan, I don't know why, but I think I am actually excited. Also, if we lived near Roy and Bobbie Ann, it would be so much easier for Momma and Poppa when they drive out to visit us."

He couldn't tell her then that the idea of bringing Roy and his father-in-law together on weekends, after the work week, was not what he had in mind.

"Mickey, get down from the roof, I said you could sit on the hood, not on the roof. And what are you throwing at the seagulls, Mick?"

"*Bwead cwust*, Daddy, that's all."

A carved wooden archway invited them into the properties of three model homes for *Meroke Shores.* They parked their car in a pebbled lot, and Nathan took Mira's arm to make sure she wouldn't fall. Sari and Mickey held on to the hem of Mira's billowy, chiffon dress as if it were a wedding gown. But before they entered one of the models, Nathan emptied Mickey's fists of enough pebbles to fill a small aquarium. He shook his head, not quite sure how his son was able to move so quickly. "You kids better be good," Nathan warned. He saw doors that led to a gated patio area where other children were playing while they waited for their parents. While Mira used the restroom, Nathan walked the children outside. There was a white wooden fence surrounding the less than half-acre property and two circular sprinklers watering part of a lush green lawn. The children sat down together on a large metal rocker and held hands. When face to face with other children, they always clung to one another, and Nathan felt confident that Sari would watch out for Mickey, especially since the dog incident. He kissed them both on their warm heads and went inside.

Nathan was not in the habit of making snap decisions. Usually he took weeks, even months analyzing each and every move. During card games, more than once, the family had displayed their smoking exasperation while he discarded from his gin hand, but this was a house, a house for his soon-to-be family of five.

Since time was an issue, they looked at the smallest of the Meroke Shores models, the only one they could afford. Nathan would never think of borrowing money from Mira's father; he was just too proud. Called the Cape Cod, it offered three small bedrooms, 1 1/2 baths, and a tiny sitting room which Mira could easily turn into a nursery for the new baby. The house had a full basement that the sales agent said many other couples had finished into a recreation room. Nathan guessed that might be quite a project knowing he'd have to do most of the work himself. The two bedrooms upstairs would be more than suitable for Sari and Mickey. He would put in an intercom to hear their every move. One of the bedrooms in the model had been decorated in a cowboy motif, and the other was perfect for Sari with its ballet slipper prints and rose-patterned paper on the sloping walls. There was also a bathroom, no tub, just a stall shower. Nathan pictured himself bathing his children in the downstairs tub each Sunday night, a ritual he'd been enjoying since the twins were able to sit up on their own.

After about ten minutes, they heard the raised voices of children coming from the patio, what sounded like a boisterous blend of laughter and squeals. The sales agent turned to Nathan and Mira and asked if their son was, by any chance, a redhead. She had peeked out through the kitchen window, "it's a window, perfect for watching your children playing in the yard," the agent had emphasized earlier. Now Nathan banged on the window to get Mickey's attention, but the child didn't hear him. While other children stood in a circle, Mickey tossed a frog up in the air, trying to catch it before it hit the ground. Sari had found an older friend who was braiding her hair while the two sat on the patio.

"It's okay," the agent assured them. All the children are drawn to the frogs, especially the city kids."

"It's not a way to treat animals," Nathan said. He didn't feel the need to stress amphibians.

"Yes, but it's so much safer than playing stickball, don't you agree?"

Nathan nodded, excused himself and went out back to scold Mickey.

Outside, he took note of the proposed lots, what would be small backyards, square to square with one another. He did what he rarely did anymore; he smoked a cigarette, taking in the many children dressed in their Sunday best, all red in the face from chasing each other in tag. Some were already caked with mud from exploring the dug-out basement windows the frogs seemed to inhabit. Nathan realized that this was the suburbs, specifically the south shore. Millions were flocking here, a new migration seeking nature, wide open spaces, and what many called the other Promised Land.

He gave Mickey his third final warning of the day, then stood up from the damp ground and put down a very small deposit on the house.

Mira had said little during their tour, but Nathan noticed how she walked through the house with one hand on her rounded belly, as if it were the ledge of a table. Her skin looked radiant, and she had recently stopped wearing much make-up. A brand new home was what his wife needed, Nathan thought. He had smiled at her lovingly at the end of the short tour. Widening his eyes, he silently asked for her opinion. Well? Well? And in the nearly four years the couple had been married, it was a gesture easily interpreted.

"Timing is everything," Mira had said while the agent pretended she needed to make a call. But Nathan, the salesman, understood this classic sales routine called the stall.

After the promised pony rides, and stopping by the pond to feed some rather aggressive swans, they returned to Brooklyn in time for Sunday night dinner at Ina and Charlie's house. The children were tired and filthy and stood nearly dozing in the hallway while Aunt Rena, her lips pinched, stripped them of their soiled socks and shoes.

"We went faraway Aunt Rena to Long Island," Sari said. "Daddy bought us a brand new house, and now I have my own room."

"It's true, Rena, we were going to announce it at dinner but some people can't keep a secret." Mira leaned down and straightened Sari's skirt.

"Not too far, I hope," Rena said. Mira was surprised by her aunt's reaction. "JJ looks forward to seeing the children every day. You know how they make her smile, especially that one." Rena gestured toward Sari, who had already placed herself at the baby grand in the living room, where she was about to conduct one of her imaginary concerts. Sari could sit on that needlepoint piano bench for hours, her little hands scaling the keys, creating chords and tones that were shockingly pleasant. Mira had done the same as a child; often, she'd go into a trance pretending she was someone else, a princess living in a huge castle surrounded by all the people she loved. Now that was about to change. For the first time there would be real distance between her and her parents. It occurred to Mira that except for her very short honeymoon, and her parents' trips, she'd seen them almost every week of her life. She laughed to herself, remembering that even on her honeymoon she was not spared their overbearing presence.

"It is time," Nathan reminded her when she began shredding tissues as they pulled up in front of the house tonight.

"I know," she'd answered, but her parents' home had never looked more beautiful to her, and never more spacious. The house at Meroke Shores was more like a cabin than the opulence of her parents' home—what had been her only childhood home. Had they made their decision too impulsively? Now, with a new baby arriving, there'd be no room to spare. Their generation could not follow the tradition of having adult brothers living among sisters; adult children residing under their parents' roof until marriage. Oh, but of course that might happen with Sari and Mickey and the new baby. Like Mira, they might live with her and Nathan for a long, long time. At least she hoped so. And it was their first house, perhaps not their last.

Hattie carried a large platter of sturgeon to the dining room table. Ina, slicing the last of the bagels, stopped mid-air to give her daughter a kiss on the lips.

"So, why so late today? It's nearly six. Poppa's stomach has been roaring for the last hour."

"Sorry, but you'll find out soon."

"*Nu?* What now?"

"Don't worry, it is good news, really."

Ina glanced at Mira's torpedo belly. "Well, you've already got a bundle ready to drop, so what else, what else is good news?"

"I'll take that, Momma. Go round up your Sari and Mickey. Be forewarned, they're slightly disheveled from their day."

"Since when did that bother me? Children should play, get dirty, and drop into bed without a care in the world."

"You're right, Momma, but I think Poppa prefers cleaning their fingernails with his toothpick."

"Between you and me, it's his way of getting them to sit still."

As if on cue, Sari came racing through the hot kitchen, Mickey chasing her with one of his dirty socks.

Mira grabbed both of them by their shoulders and warned them they'd better behave. Ina held out her arms and they ran to her, each pressing against one bosom, each locked in the flesh of their grandmother's arms. Ina sniffed the tops of their heads.

"Like two wet puppies," she said, kissing them. "Come, let's sit down to eat so you can get home at a decent hour."

"But we want to play *hide and seek* at your house, Nana. Please, Mommy, please," cried Sari.

"That depends on the two of you, doesn't it?" Mira was definitely the stricter parent. Although Nathan scared them more with his penetrating stare. Mira marveled at how quiet the children became the instant Nathan walked in the house at night. He'd accused Mira of exaggerating many times—that she'd found them opening the apartment windows and throwing pennies outside, that they'd thrown the slippers left on Mrs. Henry's doormat into the incinerator, and that they already knew how to lie.

JJ sat at the table meticulously folding the dinner napkins. The children ran to her and Sari clasped her cool hands over JJ's eyes. Like always, their great aunt played along.

"Oh my, who's there?"

"Guess," Sari squealed, disguising her voice into something that was a cross between a wicked witch and a hyena.

Mira walked in with Nathan and Charles and counted the place settings. Uncle Louie was away with his new wife on a buying trip in California, and Roy hadn't been visiting much since he and Bobbie Ann had moved to the Island. Mira wondered how long it would be before she and Nathan would start doing the same.

"JJ," Mira said, "I think there's one place setting too many."

"I thought you might have heard. Max is coming for dinner. Remember Max?" JJ said, looking down, appearing a little nervous and shy.

"Max? Max? Oh, yes, the nice man from Fourteenth Street who imported the sewing machines. Mira glanced at her father to test his reaction, but he was too busy piling slices of the oily sturgeon on his plate.

"Charl, let's wait a few more minutes for Max. It's not right."

"Thank you, Ina," JJ said, tucking a napkin around Mickey's shirt.

Mira noticed how gently her aunt handled the children. She felt sad that JJ had never had the chance to have her own babies to care for, to love them naturally. Mira gulped hard hoping JJ would not suffer another setback once they moved away to the suburbs. Since the war had ended, JJ had seemed less afraid of things. She worked only three days a week, and had finally decided to return to New York University for a college degree. Sometimes, this made Mira terribly envious, and then she was overcome by a stronger longing—some unfinished business she didn't fully understand. She'd be catapulted back to her design classes with Mr. Forté, and she'd have a difficult time recognizing the young woman she saw in her fantasies—the person filled with untapped talent and flamboyant ideas.

"I'll get it," Mira said, as the door chime played out a chord of Chopin notes. She needed a break from the table, the clatter, the faces imprinted on her brain like the familiar, daily labels of her life: Breck shampoo, Boraxo 20 Mule Team, Borden's Milk, and Tip-Top Bread. How easy it was to get lost among the snappy logos of everyday objects and completely disappear.

She opened the door and greeted a pair of crystalline eyes belonging to Max Panzer. In his short, breathless string of apologies, Mira could discern his thick accent, much thicker than her parents,' more Polish than Russian, but not as liquid as Louie's. Louie would have to live in America a hundred years before he'd lose his accent.

"So sorry I am late. Someone opened a fire hydrant and the water filled my entire street," Max said introducing himself. He followed Mira through the hallway into the dining room where at least a dozen eyes X-rayed him.

Mickey broke the tension when he stood up on his chair and outstretched his hand. "I'm Mickey. So who are you?"

Mira was relieved that's all Mickey said. Anything could come out of that child's mouth.

JJ's face sparkled while Max leaned over to kiss her hand. He made polite murmurs showing respect to Ina and Charlie, thanking them for having him in their "elegant" home. Poppa grunted, his mouth gulping down a glassful of fresh ruby borsht. How did her father manage to get away with such rude behavior? Mira prayed Mickey would not take after him.

"*Es, es*, everyone," Ina announced.

JJ sliced fresh bagels while Max continued to beam. The light from the chandelier bounced off his balding head. Mira guessed it was the only time he'd seen her aunt in the presence of young children, and he seemed to marvel at it—the tenderness so authentic and consistently her.

Hattie came in to say goodbye to everyone. She had to leave early as she was taking a train down south to visit her cousins who she hadn't seen since the war ended. With the jerky gestures of a mime, Rena motioned for Mira to help her in the kitchen. The noodle pudding and blintzes had not yet been served.

"Please don't tell her your family is moving away. She is happy for a change, can't you see?" Rena said, her lips inches from Mira's face. The smell of onions crawled from Rena's tongue.

"I'd never do anything to hurt JJ, don't you know that? We'll wait, if that's what you want, but sooner or later, she's going to notice we no longer live across the street."

"Make it later, then!" Rena said, and scooped her hands into two calico mitts to fetch the pudding.

Mira called for Nathan to come into the kitchen.

"No announcement tonight, honey. Rena said JJ—well, let's wait awhile."

"Sure, I understand. He seems nice, doesn't he? Older, but you know he's been through a lot. Your father filled me in, actually while Max was pulling in his chair and tucking his napkin."

"Tell me, quick, before we go back inside."

"That man survived Bergen-Belsen," Nathan said.

"Oh my. Wait. I bet he had a family, a wife, maybe a child."

"I don't know, but he must have lots of stories."

"I'm not sure how good that would be for JJ. You know how sensitive she is, and how sick she got after losing her brother."

"We'll have to wait and see. No one would have guessed she'd come this far."

"You're right. I guess you're always right, you." Mira kissed Nathan on his cheek and handed him a steaming platter of cheese blintzes. She took a small cut crystal bowl and filled it with Borden's sour cream. There it was that label again. But when she entered the dining room, she found everyone on their feet skulking behind their chairs. Everyone but Nathan. He was flushed, as if he'd run the four-minute mile. Mira put down the bowl, then jumped back at the sight that she thought she had to be imagining. Sprawled across one of Ina's lace embroidered dinner napkins was a leaf-green shriveled up toad, emaciated and stuck to one of Mickey's candy wrappers that he'd stuffed in his shorts' pocket. The dead amphibian looked bizarre against the backdrop of such fine cutlery and sumptuous platters.

Like a magician pulling a rabbit from a hat, Nathan lifted Mickey by his red-rimmed ear. Hattie would have loved this, Mira thought. It would have reminded her of home in North Carolina when kids emptied their pockets of anything they might have fetched while playing outdoors. With Hattie headed on vacation Aunt Rena was the only one who sprang into action. She wrapped the dead toad into the cloth napkin, tucking the edges just as she'd prepared her famous cheese blintzes earlier that morning. Then she excused herself and soon everyone heard the toilet flush in the small adjacent bathroom.

A few weeks later, after Nathan had sent his second payment on the new house, he got a surprising call. It came from the sales agent saying she had an exciting offer for him. Skeptical and priding himself on rapidly becoming a man who had a good head for business, Nathan listened, quietly, while the woman chatted on, nearly exhausting herself. But there was no denying this was a great offer. Nathan and Mira, if they so desired, would be able to buy one of the completely furnished models for *only* a thousand dollars more. And, the best part was that they would be able to move in right after Christmas, giving the children at least half the year in their brand new school.

Nathan brought the news home that night to Mira, but she stood staring wide-eyed, looking slightly disappointed. "What's wrong? I thought you loved the model with the little pink flamingos everywhere, and the salmon-colored bathroom with black checkerboard tiles. That's all you talked about for days."

"Yes, but the model's exterior is a dark, bluish gray. I've always dreamed of a pink house." She knew she was stalling, suddenly afraid of leaving her Brooklyn roots.

"If that's all, I'm sure they'll repaint it, but there'll be a charge, of course. The agent said I have to get back to her tomorrow. This deal won't last."

"Of course, you're right, Nathan, and I do like the idea of moving in early spring. By then the baby will be sitting up, and it'll be so much easier."

"You're nervous about moving away? That's it, isn't it?"

Mira rubbed her belly, moving her fingers over her belly button that protruded like a tiny penis. "I think we're having another boy," she said, changing the subject. The kids were at the cramped dinner table in their apartment spitting out their applesauce. This was a time of fleeting calm when it was necessary for Mira and Nathan to report all important information. Even in their own bed, late at night, they did not share much privacy, since the children's daybeds were propped against the longest wall. It was embarrassing to think that she had conceived this third child with her other two asleep in the same room.

"I guess it's all the changes lately affecting my moods."

Nathan put his arm around her. "Change is good, kiddo, you'll see. You need some distance, Mira. We all do. Things will change, even if you don't. Do you imagine your parents staying in that house for the rest of their lives?"

"Shhh, yes, I can't imagine them anywhere else, certainly not Florida."

"Okay, okay, let them stay if that's what makes you happy, but we have to think about ourselves and *our* family. We are the next generation."

Mira liked the way he said that. His words made her feel proud and protected. At least she was sure of him and his devotion to her and their children. Sometimes, though, she wondered if she was a good enough wife. Nathan was so smart and independent, able to do so many things well that, at times, she felt as if he didn't really need her. She wished that he'd said those words, just once. *I need you.*

The children, of course, needed her. Although, more often than not, she had an extra pair of hands. Even though they indulged Sari and Mickey, these mother substitutes offered the children something Mira no longer had—focus and energy. This third pregnancy had already taken its toll, and she was more than happy to allow herself to be catered to. She had never been this lazy, and yet, had become comfortably accustomed to it. To keep from feeling guilty, she simply told herself, over and over again, that she was not needed. Somewhere within the fissures of her surrender crawled tiny ants of self-doubt. Slowly, she learned to convince herself that everything could go on without her—that Nathan and the children would be absolutely fine. These ruminations were all she needed to have her run across the street to fetch the children before Nathan came home from work. On these occasions she'd serve one of Nathan's favorite meals—sautéed chicken livers and onions (which took no more than twenty minutes to prepare). The children, gagging at the sight of the slimy livers frying in the skillet would have scrambled eggs or French toast. Nathan would eat quietly, and she'd watch him, proudly, feeling momentarily intact.

Now, as she listened while he told her that they had a chance to move months earlier than planned, she felt overwhelmed by the reality of so much transition. Again, he said, "It's time we take control over our own lives."

She worried if he was angry with her for being so attached to her family. She hoped he knew that she believed in him, and was proud of all he'd already accomplished.

"Okay, Nathan, let's do it. We can keep the baby in our room for the first couple of months. Lord knows, we've done it a lot longer here."

"I'll call the broker right now. Then I'll call the family," Nathan said, beaming, "and tell them they'll be taking a little trip out east for the holidays."

They stood in the hallway of the apartment hugging while Sari and Mickey ran around them, as if they were an oak tree planted firmly in the ground. Mira's belly pushed like a caboose into Nathan. He pulled back, giving her more room, but the children, seeing an opening between their parents' bodies, squeezed themselves through. Each grabbed onto a kneecap, gazing at them as if they needed the reassurance that they'd always be there, that a new baby would never steal away their love.

A Boy Named Rosh

On Halloween, right around dusk, Mira gave birth to her third child—a boy. She named him Rosh, after her cousin, Rosha, the little girl who had perished during the war, killed in the Ponary woods near Vilna. Sari had been named after Nathan's father, Solomon, who died when Nathan was barely two years old, and Mickey was named after Uncle Mordecai, Rosha's father, who had perished alongside her.

When Mira and Nathan announced the baby's name, the family's reaction was bittersweet. Yes, they were grateful and appreciated the gesture, considering Mira had only heard about her relatives in Europe and never got the chance to meet them. But the memory of the shock of the event, now nearly four years ago, conjured up fresh grief, especially in JJ. Although she seemed more connected and less prone to her deep purple moods, she worked hard at avoiding all organized visits to herald in the new baby.

Mira rationalized that since she met Max, JJ was probably torn between spending time with the family and time alone with him. At 45, she would never have the chance of birthing her own children, and on some level that had to fill her heart with melancholy. So Mira was delighted that Max seemed to genuinely care for JJ in a way no one had ever exhibited—maybe he needed her because he was truly fond of her, perhaps a fondness not born out of want.

At Rosh's *bris*, Charlie made a toast welcoming his new grandson and then surprised the family with the announcement that JJ and Max would be getting married right before Thanksgiving in a simple ceremony with just immediate family. Of course, he would be honored to give away his younger sister, and would host a dinner reception in a popular restaurant in the city. The news was met with vigorous applause. A warm communal buzz traveled around the room while Mira held her newborn, recovering from what she felt was the archaic assault of his circumcision. She lifted her tearful eyes from Rosh's flushed face and noticed that JJ's skin tone matched his exactly.

With Rosh snuggled in her arms, Mira couldn't applaud, but she hooted loudly, making everyone laugh aloud, especially Sari and Mickey, who were already sprawled on JJ's and Max's laps.

Rena had quietly faded into the background. Her elation was nowhere to be found as she stood, arms folded tightly, her back against the front door of Mira's new home. Rena looked as though she'd like to bolt from the room. Please, someone say something, Mira thought. The laughter quickly evaporated, and a weighty silence filled its space.

"To Jeanette and Max," Nathan said in the nick of time, downing *schnapps*. Poor Nathan, Mira thought, he was already wobbly from the toast for the baby. She was secretly glad he didn't enjoy his liquor like her father and Roy. Roy, who now lived less than ten minutes away, became pie-eyed at every family get-together and usually had to sleep it off before getting in the car with her sister-in-law, who was now neck and neck in the children department with Mira—expecting her third in the spring.

Mira motioned for Rena to come take the baby from her arms.

"What is wrong with you?" Mira whispered. "You look like someone just committed a murder. This is supposed to be a happy day, remember?"

It struck Mira that perhaps Rena was feeling a bit jealous and couldn't contain herself. She'd had many suitors, but her guard was always up. After a few months most relationships with men turned into a friendship where Rena became an advisor on many subjects: career moves, problem relatives. At no time did she exhibit romantic intentions no matter how handsome, rich, or genuine the catch. She guessed Rena would always be stuck in her role as sister, and with

JJ's engagement, she'd be losing part of the invaluable bond she had depended on all her life.

Mira thought about her own baby sister who had died so many years ago. How had Momma survived such a devastating loss? At that moment, she made a silent promise to never, ever take for granted the fragility of life and all the gifts she'd been given. Just then, Rosh began to scream, the effects of the red wine the moil had wiped on his gums had obviously worn off and now he was feeling the blunt pain of having been cut.

"Let me take him," JJ asked, remembering to kiss Mickey as she lowered him off her lap. Amazing how sensitive she was of her other niece and nephew's frantic need for attention now that there were three.

Rena, her scowl softening, placed the infant in JJ's arms and miraculously the baby ceased crying. Mira was moved deeply to witness her infant son resting so peacefully in JJ's care. It was something beautiful to behold. Like staring out at your garden all winter long, not expecting anything, and then one day, there it is—a perfect yellow rose peeking through a cluster of twigs, and thorns, and blades of grass, reminding you that change is inevitable.

Mira
Alone and Lonely

~

Nathan's road trips became longer and longer. Sometimes he'd be down south seeing customers for as long as two weeks, and Mira spent the nights in her new home lonely, listening to the strange sounds made of thermostatic heat or the oil burner rumbling, interrupted only by one of Rosh's midnight crying sessions that left her exhausted for days.

Often, she found it difficult to fall back to sleep, and would stay up all night, working on projects for the house: painting a pink vanity for Sari's room, sketching an enormous giraffe on a wall of the nursery. She kept Rosh in a wicker white bassinet at the foot of her bed while painting the giraffe because the fumes from the oil-based paint were toxic. Sometimes forgetting to breathe, she felt light-headed and queasy. Tonight, as she painted some flowers at the bottom of the wall mural, Mira laughed out loud, realizing how far she'd migrated from her short-lived career as a fashion designer. Working for one's parent, she thought, was not exactly the ideal "entrepreneur." She'd heard the term used to describe one of the neighbors on her block—a woman who owned a framing shop in town—a woman who was never home when her children came home at the end of the school day—a woman whose husband supposedly had a serious drinking problem. Mira had bought some Degas prints for Sari's bedroom. She'd make it her business to bring them into town next week. She'd introduce herself as a newcomer to Meroke Shores—as a woman whose husband traveled a great deal—as somebody who once had huge dreams of her own.

A wave of guilt crashed around her. Here slept three perfectly healthy children right under her roof. Her parents were seemingly well and still very much a part of her life. And Nathan. Look how hard he worked and never complained. For this alone, how could she ever stop loving him?

Mira wiped her paint-stained fingertips on a rag soaked in turpentine; she watched as the solvent dried them out, turning them gray. She checked on Rosh; he was sound asleep, and as it was her custom, she leaned over and kissed his forehead, making the seven-week-old stir just slightly—enough to fill her with enormous relief. She had not admitted this to a soul, nor would she, but Rosh had become the new love of her life. She'd been ready for him, for whatever had been extracted from her to really nurture this child. Secretly, she was ashamed because she hadn't felt the pangs of maternal instinct with either of the twins. She'd been happy to lay off the children on Ina and her aunts at each and every opportunity. She hoped that God would one day forgive her.

Mira walked around the house making mental notes of what projects she might do next while Nathan was away. Roy and Bobbi Ann had given her a paint-by-number serving tray as a house gift. *I don't need the numbers, you idiots,* she'd thought of screaming at Roy, but of course, Bobbi Ann had probably selected the gift, and knew nothing of Mira's talents.

Her thoughts turned automatically to Faye. Faye would have accepted the black tray graciously and painted a design completely of her own invention. Mira giggled to herself envisioning something risqué to be hidden from all parents and children.

In her top dresser drawer there was a small sewing box, once a cookie tin, where she kept thread, safety pins, and needles, but mostly old photos and phone numbers. Some of the thin frayed phone books Mira had saved since the sixth grade. She found the latest and opened it to the last number she had for Faye at her West Hollywood address. Mira looked at the Timex on the night stand. Three hours earlier would make it only eight o'clock in California. She picked up the phone and put it down again. She realized she had no idea how much a long distance call to the West Coast would cost. Nathan would certainly never miss such a call on their phone bill. He'd be alerted by an increase more than the norm. This part of Nathan, although always predictable, she found irritating.

Nevertheless, Mira picked up the phone and dialed the operator. It had been almost two years since they'd last spoken. Mira had never informed Faye that she was expecting a third child. She lived with the belief that Faye had always wanted marriage and a family. Even though they lived so far apart, Mira still wished Faye's admiration for her to be based on her talents and not the number of babies she'd carried to full term.

The phone rang three times filling Mira with a rare girlish merriment, and then another operator answered, saying the phone number was no longer in service. "There is no further information." The only good news being there would be no charge for the call.

Placing the receiver back in the cradle, Mira realized Faye must have been hired for several big movies. Maybe she was on location somewhere in Africa or Morocco.

"I'm glad for her," Mira whispered aloud. And that was true; why shouldn't she want success and all the joys that came with it for Faye? Faye had talent, but more than that, unlike Mira, she'd never straddled the fence. Faye saw an opportunity and immediately seized it. What made them different was what had attracted the two in the first place.

Mira turned off the outside lights as Nathan had instructed. The kitchen stove light was enough wattage to burn through the night. An owl hooted in the distance. At least, that's what she told herself as she checked Rosh's breathing one more time. Soon it would be time to feed him again, and Mira would, once more, feel important.

Victor and Sophie

~

His mother would never know that in the days before Sophie had become terribly ill with pneumonia, Victor had been planning his escape. Weeks before, he had carefully divided the money he found stashed in the tool shed into "his" money, and money designated for his mother and younger sister. He still couldn't bring himself to think about taking care of *her*, Rosha, even though he knew the money was from her parents. Victor read Mordecai Kaninsky's letter over and over again, each time feeling pain deep inside his belly, as if he'd ran into a sword.

Marta would also never know about the gun. The one he had bought from a nearby farmer who was frantically in need of cash. When asked why he needed a weapon, of all things, when food had become so scarce, Victor convinced the nearly deaf old man the gun was purely for his family's protection. He told him that his father had been shot in the woods, but really there was no way of knowing. Two days after Avram had failed to return home, Victor discovered a small box left on the dirt road leading to their house. In it he and his mother discovered Avram's blood-soaked clothing. When Marta emptied the pockets, she found the remnants of his broken file.

There would not be a body. Nothing to bury and how difficult it was to mourn because it was impossible to believe Avram was gone—this father that Victor often feared, but mostly loved.

Victor's meager sack of supplies had been gathering dust under his bed. He decided to travel light now that the worst of the winter was over. He had no real plan other than the one called *revenge*. He could not imagine or visualize his victims; all he knew was that the pine forest was surely the place for opportunity. He was not frightened because he did not expect to return, or survive for that matter. In his mind the journey was purely to avenge his father's murder.

He had noticed that Sophie had been pale and thinner than usual, but he too had lost so much weight that he could not keep a pair of pants up. Supplies had dwindled in the last few weeks, and he secretly hoarded the envelope that held the money for his escape in a hefty can that was too heavy for his mother to budge. To get to it, someone would have to climb up on the work bench and balance on one leg while dipping in the jar to remove its contents.

Years from now, when he was an old man, a cabinet maker in Vermont, he would think about how his sister Sophie's high fever had ultimately saved his life. He would sometimes get the feeling that his father was watching over him as he fastened the bolt to a table's leg, or when he rubbed the sweet-smelling orange stain into a desk's surface. But, as proud as he imagined Avram's look, he equally envisioned his father's scorn for thinking about taking what did not belong to him.

That morning, the morning of Sophie's high fever, Marta's cries of fear had reached deep into his chest. For the first time in his life, although he was afraid, he felt needed. If only he could have success-fully completed the small mission his mother had requested of him. But when he got to the doctor's house, he saw that all the windows had been broken, the front door pulled off the hinges. Victor walked through two stories of wreckage. It was hard to imagine that the place had once been inhabited by a big loving family: Dr. Steinhagen, his wife, and four children, the eldest, a pretty girl named Rifka with long black hair, who Victor had more than once noticed when they were in class together. He was angered by his own naiveté thinking the Steinhagens might not have been transported to one of the work camps he had heard so much about. He felt frustrated that he returned with nothing more than a jar of honey he'd nearly tripped on in what he imagined had been a well-stocked pantry.

Later that day, Marta carried Sophie outside into the cold, just for a few minutes hoping to bring down her raging fever, but the frail girl lay limp in her arms, her blue eyes staring into Marta's with quiet resignation—a sweet, innocent wish to be taken back inside so she could fall asleep in her mother's warm bed. Victor sat quietly beside his mother for hours as she rocked Sophie in her arms, first reciting a prayer in her native Polish, then stumbling through one in Hebrew. It was a prayer Victor had heard his father recite many times when remembering his Jewish grandparents, but Victor had never needed to learn it.

He stood beside his mother as she lit the special candle, one that would burn for an entire week. Then together, while Rosha slept, unaware, they buried Sophie in a small pine box that Victor had constructed working late the night before, shivering outside, not wanting to return to the house where he felt so much shame. Together, mother and son lowered the box into the dark red earth, what had been a large patch of green grass just beginning to poke through the last remnants of snow—a promise of spring.

Jeanette

On a blustery winter morning, Rena paced the factory, rubbing her hands together for warmth. Charlie had refused a salesman peddling electric heaters, mostly because his crony Moe Moskowitz's ribbon factory in Queens had burned down to the ground, supposedly after the night watchman snuck out for a beer with the cleaning woman. Luckily, no one was injured, and Moe had collected enough money from the insurance company to return to Palm Beach. Business was in such a slump that Rena wondered if her brother's refusal to purchase heaters hinted at his own mistrust for what he might do as a last ditch effort to save Kane Knitting.

Chanukah and Christmas decorations dangled from the sooty factory windows. Some of the sewing machine operators were told not to return to their jobs after New Year's, even though they had been employed by Kane for over twenty years. Many took the news with an overwhelming bitterness, storming out without stopping to gathering any little mementos that had propped their work stations, making their place of business like a second home.

Two hours had passed and now Rena's fingers ached from dialing JJ's number. A wave of nausea took her by surprise, and she rushed to the water fountain for a drink. In the past few weeks since JJ married, Rena noticed that her sister appeared to have slipped back into what Rena called: "that quiet place," talking very little, refraining from making direct eye contact, and rarely eating so that she'd already looked as if she dropped a few pounds.

Rena reminded herself that Max was very loving, and attentive to Jeanette, but the couple hadn't known each other that long. Before Max, there had only been Joe, who had crushed JJ's spirit and hopes with his reckless deceit. Men! Rena felt the steel knot of her belt gripping her belly. She would never let herself fall in love. Never.

She dialed her sister's number one last time, and when there was no answer, Rena grabbed her coat and headed for the elevator. Outside, she was surprised by the sprinkling of wet flurries melting into nothingness as they hit the windshields of cars and cabs. Squinting, she looked up to the grey sky and stuck out her tongue. She could not remember the last time she'd done that. It had to be when she and JJ were girls playing in the countryside in Riga. When had she gotten this old?

A checker cab pulled close to the curb, and with her coat flapping open, Rena jumped inside and gave the driver the address. She could have called Max at his place of business, but why worry him for no reason? Rena was trying to get used to her new role of sister-in-law. The last thing she wanted was to be labeled a meddler or give JJ additional pressure.

The cab dropped her off, and Rena thought about having him wait, but an expectant young mother was already maneuvering herself and backing into the seat with great difficulty. The flushed woman looked as if she were about to pop any second. Rena held the door for her and then slammed it shut. A tiny piece of the woman's camel coat hung out the car door. Rena felt a twinge of guilt that she hadn't been more careful in sending her off.

Once in the mustard-colored lobby, she scanned the directory for JJ's apartment listed under her new name—Panzer. She pressed the black button over and over again waiting to be buzzed in but no one answered. She figured there might have been trouble with the lines. While riding the elevator to the seventh floor, Rena searched through her handbag for the key Jeanette had given her for safe-keeping and to allow her to water the house plants when Jeanette and Max went to Philadelphia for their brief two-night honeymoon.

Rena stood stiffly in front of apartment 7 G tapping lightly on the door. To do so any louder would have brought a nosey neighbor peeking out over their threshold. Perhaps, she should go to the corner and try calling once more she thought. It would be just her luck to have missed her sister by just a few minutes. Exhaling loudly, Rena took the long metal key and inserted it in the lock. Two hard turns to the right and the door opened creakingly into a dark foyer. The apartment appeared especially dark because of the bleakness of the day, the kind of day when anyone in their right mind would choose to stay home in their pajamas.

As Rena's eyes searched the foyer, she noticed the antique brass hat rack mounted to the wall. The hat rack had been a wedding gift from Rena. Unlike her, JJ never left the house without wearing a hat. Her favorite was a curved Dutch girl style in black velvet with a short veil that barely covered her eyes. Rena was surprised to see that exact hat placed neatly on the hat rack, perfectly balanced on a brass hook.

Walking into the kitchenette, she could smell sulfur and burned metal. A white porcelain pot was simmering on the burner, the flame barely visible. Inside the scorched pot was one blackened egg cracked throughout. Rena reached out and turned off the gas. Her hands shook as she reached for the pot with a terry towel and threw it in the sink. She poured cold water over the pot and steam flew up and wet her face and glasses.

"Jeanette?" She heard herself scream as she turned on the kitchen lights, left the kitchen, and walked down the hallway to the only bedroom. "Sis, are you home? Jeanette? Max, anyone?" The bed had been neatly made; the satin pillows were propped in place, but on the vanity table lay Jeanette's pink gold watch and her thin platinum wedding band. Rena's mind began playing a rough game of ping pong in her head. She felt relieved that there hadn't been a robbery. But then the images of the bluish flames, the black egg and her darling sister's favorite hat swirled into an eerie puzzle.

With both fists Rena banged on the bathroom door. Why was she crying? She knew the door was unlocked, but she could not open it. Her hands could not turn the crystal doorknob. They were shaking too hard. Finally, she threw herself into the room, her eyes sealed tightly shut. At eye level, she could see her sister's pale, pale feet, the hem of her new chenille robe. She wanted to look up, truthfully, she wished she could, but she could not bear to see JJ's face. Instead, she stood next to her, as close as she could get without touching her. The faucet was dripping, the sound nearly maddening. Rena turned the faucets on full blast. She leaned her face into the coldness and washed the vomit from her chin and the collar of her coat. Rena's heart beat galloped while her body stood frozen in the musty bathroom.Once more she dared herself to look up, to see what she wanted so badly to see for one last time, but something saved her from herself and the desire to destroy the rest of her own small insignificant life.

Rena turned toward the door, avoiding the mirror that hung from it, avoiding the towel racks, the light switches, anything that carried with it an essence of life. Walking faster now, she stopped in the foyer and stuffed JJ's velvet hat under her coat. She ran down the seven flights to the moving traffic and into the cold. A few doors away she found a candy store and pushed through the glass phone booth ignoring the stares from people sipping coffee. Her head throbbed at the temples, and she tasted bile on her tongue. She looked through her handbag hoping to find her address book for Max's place of business, but she had left it home. She couldn't even remember the name of his company, and found herself dialing Kane Knitting instead. Margaret answered in her professional switchboard voice. She put Rena on hold for what seemed like hours.

"Jeanette, dear is that you?" Margaret finally asked. She was always confusing the sisters' voices. Their accents made it difficult to tell them apart, and Margaret had shown signs of hearing loss in recent months.

"Where's Roy? I need Roy," Rena said.

"I believe he's in a meeting with his father. Would you like me to interrupt?" Normally, Margaret wouldn't think of suggesting this. Slightly deaf or not, she'd obviously picked up the urgency in Rena's tone.

"Yes, Margaret, but please call him outside the room first. I'd like it if my brother didn't hear our conversation."

"I'll do my best, certainly. Hold on." Rena's fingers were chalky white. Her veins lifted as she switched the receiver to her left hand, squeezing it as though it were a rubber ball.

"Hi Auntie," Roy said, startling her. He sounded unusually chipper for having been in conference with Charlie.

"It's JJ," Rena breathed into the receiver. Her voice gave in to her emotion, rising and falling like bellows; it opened and closed, started and stopped. "There's been an accident. You must call . . . call an ambulance and get over to her apartment. I left her key under the door mat."

"What do you mean?" Roy asked, "Where the hell are you?"

"I found her, Roy. My poor sister. She's gone, I know she's gone. I knew it this morning when she was late, when her phone kept ringing. I'm going home Roy. I want to go home. Please, take care of it, so Charlie doesn't see . . . doesn't see . . . her."

"You can't be alone, let me call Mira. She'll want to be with you."

"Go to JJ, Roy you must go now." Rena hung up the phone and pulled the accordion doors of the phone booth open. A man in a plain overcoat took her by the elbow. She didn't even realize she had tripped. Rena wiped gray dust off the bottom of her coat hem, and pulled away from the gentleman.

"Ma'am," he called after her. "I believe you dropped your hat."

Rena mumbled a thank you, and as if she'd done it a thousand times before, she pulled the cultured pearl hat pin out of her sister's hat and fastened the hat and pin securely to the crown of her head.

In the weeks and months to come, no one would ask the question. Did you look at her, Rena? Did you touch her hands, her feet? Was she still warm? How could they, and what difference would it make now? Jeanette Kane's suffering, nearly a lifetime of suffering, had ceased forever. And just like the times and incidents she'd had in the past, this incident—her apparent suicide was now locked away, shrouded like an antique they kept in storage and because of its fragility never put on display. This is how the Kanes would handle this death, the tragic loss of one of their own.

Each mourned JJ in their own private way. Some, like Mira, more vigilantly. But Mira had her own family now, and she and Nathan had made the decision to keep Jeanette's death hidden from the next generation. They concocted a story that would seem reasonable when questions were asked. Hadn't the aunt recently married? Well then, perhaps, she was very far away residing in Palestine or South Africa, where many Jews had fled before and after the war. When their beloved JJ would return was anyone's guess.

The Best Letter

~

The men huddled in front of 1400 Broadway talking their shop talk, but this day there was an unusual lilt to their voices. The conversation seemed hyper at times, as keyed up as a barber shop quartet, each voice taking a turn at some revelation.

Younger men had again joined their fathers, father in-laws, and uncles in their respective businesses, yet some looked frail and hardly prepared for the task of rebuilding their lives. But there was really no choice. That's what men did, had always done, since the battles fought on America's soil over two centuries ago.

Someone patted Charlie's shoulder, and he winced at the gesture. He was lost in the most melancholy of thoughts. This had nothing to do with the fact that he was now nearly broke due to the settlement he had to pay out to the bastards representing Chanel for him knocking off the bouclé jacket—their biggest seller. Julia Crane, the ever-stunning buyer from Dillard's had made him purr like a kitten when she suggested he make the fringed suit garment exclusively for Dillard's. Mira did warn him he might be sued, but he thought she was reacting like any young designer—not at all impressed by the status of a designer, but the actual line and construction of the design. Louie went along as usual and had coughed up a hefty sum of money that surprised Charlie and rendered him suspicious. He no longer trusted anyone; trust had become much too risky. His paranoia began soon after JJ's death. That is what they called it, not a suicide, but a death—brought on by an illness that had caused her to fade away, first slowly, and then swiftly like a burst of snow showers in spring.

After a quick lunch with Louie, Charlie sat at his dusty desk opening a towering pile of mail. He had been going to the office only a few days a week, and now he and Louie were planning a huge pre-season sample sale to which they would invite the entire fashion district. Hopefully, he'd be able to recoup some of his losses with cash. Ina had offered to sell all her jewelry, but Charlie warned her not to venture anywhere near 47th Street. He had not yet mentioned that he already hocked his own star sapphire ring, a gift from Ina, for a very pretty sum.

He reached into the pile of mail randomly and picked up a pamphlet that advertised a new retirement community in Miami Beach. It was one of those high-rise towers painted in cool shades of coral and aqua. A kick-line of gorgeous blonde models stood in the front entrance beckoning takers. These gals were at least forty years away from retirement, Charlie thought. He sighed, remembering when a picture like this could give him a shot of hope, or jolt the remnants of his sleepy masculinity. But not today. Today, even his mail depressed him. He purposely left the bills from Con Ed and Bell in a dusty pile. The only bill Charlie paid diligently and on time was the rent. He cringed at the thought of not keeping a showroom for his loyal customers, though he had no idea that soon accounts like J.C. Penney and W.T. Grant would turn to importers for most of their merchandise. If you had told him that Henry Meyers, owner of Meyers Yarns, who'd lost two sons overseas would be buying from the "Japs" he would have thought you were spouting a malicious lie.

To accommodate these loyal customers in past months Charlie used synthetic blends for many of his stock items to bring prices down, but the garments lacked the fine finishing that had been a signature feature of Kane Knitting for nearly thirty years. Charlie picked up the brochure of Miami's real estate once more then firmly tore it in half and tossed it in the pail under his desk. He nearly threw away the last letter on his desk, an ivory colored envelope, tissue thin and stamped with a stamp from Vilnius, Lithuania, what had been *Vilna* prior to the Nazi regime. Before nearly all the Jewish population had been exterminated by a plan put into action by one psychotically evil man.

As he began opening this letter, he saw that his hands were shaking and his throat became parched. He slipped a single piece of paper from the envelope, bracing himself for some new pain—this, he realized, he'd become proficient at; this was his forté.

His eyes skipped through the letter and then reversed its focus until finally he read the words aloud. He reached in his desk drawer and fumbled for a peppermint Life Saver. Charlie stood up then sat back down. He had the sensation of wanting to call everyone he knew while he was still reading words he found unbelievable. He had to fight disbelief, and the evil intrusion of ghosts, and face the deaths and atrocities that pervaded the message within the piece of paper that quivered between his fingers.

Words jumped like pebbles from the page. Could it be possible? Wake up, he told himself over and over again. *Rosha was still alive.* His niece, the only child of Mordecai, had survived the war thanks to the generosity of a Polish woman whose name he would utter in his synagogue for years and years to come. *Marta Juraska.* She had been married to a Jew, a hard-working and talented carpenter. She had recently lost a child—her own little girl, and still had been looking for a way to send Rosha back to her family in America. There had been a small satin label sewn in the child's sweater that had ultimately helped her with the search. And now that search was over. Through the hard work of a group of surviving families, an organization had recently begun seeking out relatives of lone survivors. Marta Juraska had spent months searching for the link that would promise Rosha her real family.

Although the widowed Polish woman had grown to love the child as if she was her own, she knew Rosha belonged among her family. When all efforts to find the Kaninsky's had hit a dead end, Marta did not give up. She looked for other connections. Her only regret was that she would not be able to bring the child to America herself—that she would send the girl across the sea on a ship full of lost and frightened strangers. It was just she and her only boy, Victor, heading into an unknown future.

Survivors. Yes, that was what they were, whether Jews, Christians, adults, or small children. Everyone now faced the identical hardships and challenges that came with each new beginning. And as he had done before, more than three years earlier, Charlie tucked this letter in his suit pocket. Was it coincidental that he was wearing the same pin-striped tie he'd worn the day he learned of the death of Mordecai? He shuddered, remembering that day and the grief that had permeated his home, as if reflected in the crystal lighting, bouncing on every surface.

Had he forgotten the simple sensation of joy? Had too many losses, over too short a time made him hard and cold? It was never his business setbacks or his loss of status among his peers. It was this—the unmooring of his family that rendered him so powerless.

Sitting in the cab on the way home, for the first time in many years, he realized he was getting another chance at something he couldn't quite put his finger on. What he was good at, he knew, was keeping secrets, but what he loved most was being the maestro of surprise. He shut his eyes and ears, blocking out the gibberish of his driver. He leaned back and let the tears spill onto his cheeks. My brother's child, he thought, as his body quaked with the strange sensation of joy—a Godsend.

A Gift from Marta
April 1946

When she opened her eyes on the last morning she would spend in the Juraska's home, Rosha realized she had been dreaming of Bubbe. She shut her eyes again hoping to continue the soothing fantasy not knowing where it might lead. Trying desperately to pay attention to each tiny detail like Bubbe's jovial smile, her hand waving like a butterfly, she felt cheated when her grandmother's features faded into an aura of hazy dust circling around the room. It was a room in which she had spent the last months of the war because of someone else's misfortune.

She was upstairs lying upon Sophie's bed, her entire torso nearly sliding off the edge. Rosha was trying to make room, as if Sophie were lying right there beside her. Nothing had felt as normal as when Sophie was alive. Even though their time together had been limited, the two had gotten along so well. Sophie's visits, although brief, had given Rosha something to look forward to.

For safety reasons, and as painful as it was to do, Marta had removed all photos of Sophie and hidden them away. In their place, just days after Sophie was buried, there was a photo of Rosha. It had been taken reluctantly by Victor using Avram's beat up Kodak, a camera once used to photograph chairs and tables. In every shot Victor snapped, Rosha looked on the verge of tears.

Prior to her moving upstairs, Marta had restyled Rosha's wavy hair into long, tight braids, the way Sophie always wore her hair. She had gone so far as mixing a concoction of household bleach, lemons, and baking soda to lighten Rosha's hair to the palest blonde.

Although she continued to take precautions, Marta, more than worn down by her losses, also took several uncharacteristic risks. Some days, she had gone as far as allowing Rosha to help with chores outside, hanging out the laundry to dry in the sunshine. Until that day, last summer, when two soldiers in an open jeep had stopped short at the sight of the frail and beautiful child, wearing of all things, boy's boots.

Through the dust storm made by the jeep's screeching brakes, they backed up to investigate, while Rosha stood, reciting her parents' names and praying, under the dangling ropes of laundry. It was a scorching day, and her braids where pinned on top of her head, exactly the way Sophie had often worn hers. Exactly as they appeared in the government papers buried in a kitchen drawer.

"Remember, your name is *Sophie*," Marta had warned, if anyone should ever question her or stop by the house. "You look so much like my baby girl, my precious Sophie. So, be her! It might save our lives."

As the men jumped from the jeep, Rosha's hands began shaking violently. She grabbed some towels from the clothes line to hide them.

"Hey, little birdie, go fetch us some apples," one of them shouted. "Hurry, now!"

Rosha went flying across the damp grass, slipping into a side door that led to the kitchen. She could barely speak, and when Marta saw her pale face and owl-like eyes, she sent her immediately to her room. She told her, no matter what happened, not to move. Victor had left only an hour before to find supplies for a storage chest he was making. Soon after his sister died, he began spending a lot more time in the work shed. Something about the atmosphere of that cool dark place had seemed to calm him. Thank God, Marta thought, when realizing he was not around, because her son had been itching for a fight for so long, he surely would have instigated something that could have ended them all. Caput! Marta pictured them lined up like dominos and shot execution style. There were too many stories like this one, and especially the one she would never hear, how Avram had sacrificed his own life, rather than harming another human being.

Marta had just finished baking some apples, a small miracle that she would never, ever forget—a sign that somehow signaled that everything would be all right. On the stove was a large pot of melted wax for the candles Rosha would be making later on. There was enough wax if she needed it, if those two men dared to step foot in her house. Marta could easily imagine herself tossing the bubbling wax straight into their cold eyes. Then they would run and keep running. But where and to whom?

Lifting the still steaming dish of baked apples, Marta hurried outside and headed bravely to the jeep. Forcing a smile, she invited the soldiers to drink water from the spigot next to the tool shed, then turned and went inside while her heart pummeled through the cotton of her garment. Within seconds, she heard the wheels of the jeep as it crunched against the gravelly road and sped away.

Victor had walked in the house just five minutes later; no, she would never tell her son what he had missed.

Now on this last day, Rosha looked across the room and noticed that Marta had already packed up all her things. Still she wanted to check that all her favorite books and photographs were wrapped up inside. The duffle was nearly as big as her, and yet she was able to grab one end and hoist it on her shoulder, something she had practiced for days.

Marta came in carrying a pot of sweet tea and a small piece of bread and then made an about face saying she forgot something. Rosha could only nibble on the bread. She felt much too nervous to eat. This voyage awaiting her would be long and lonely and while she was excited to be meeting her father's relatives in America, she was scared they might change their minds the second they laid eyes on her. She did not want to be a burden to anyone ever again. It had taken so long for Victor to warm to her, to forgive her for changing so many things in their lives. What if all her aunts, uncles, and cousins felt the same way?

She dressed herself in a navy flannel skirt that Marta had sewn from one of Avram's old jackets. Marta had also crocheted a little pink sweater, all the time wondering what the Kaninskys would say when they saw the poor, sallow, undernourished child. Surely, she had done her best to care for her and loved her as if she'd given birth to her. In the small and frightening world they had inhabited together, devotion had become the most important remedy for survival.

Marta walked into the room this time, her face flushed, her eyes brimming with tears.

"They're here for you, Rosha. The Kleinholtzes are very kind people. There is nothing to worry about; they will see that you get to your family."

"What's inside that package?" Rosha asked.

Marta looked down at her hands and laughed. "I must be getting old—I nearly forgot. Here, Rosha Kaninsky is a belated birthday present for you."

"But you already made me this pretty sweater."

"That you will grow out of once you get a liking for American food."

Rosha ripped open the single layer of brown wrapping. Inside the package was a wooden box about the size of one of her old story books. In the center of the box Rosha saw the picture of all her cousins, the one that Avram had found when he went to Sadowa Street. Marta had used wax drippings in an array of pastel colors to create a wavy frame around the photo, which also sealed it to the box. Rosha brushed her finger lightly over the little flower bud drippings. Tiny butterfly shapes adorned all four corners.

"This is so beautiful. I will keep this forever."

"Look inside. There's more."

When she lifted the lid, Rosha saw all the pictures she had kept with her in the root cellar. They were the photos that Avram had placed on the shelves he'd so carefully built, so the child would never forget her people or the place from where she came. Underneath the layer of pictures and wrapped in tissue paper were several bills, more money than Rosha had seen in all of her thirteen years.

She stared at the cut on Marta's arm, which had formed a strange V-shaped scab. Weeks ago, Marta had said she had gotten the cut when reaching for a heavy can in the tool shed, nearly falling off a ladder. She found something that had obviously been forgotten, or perhaps misplaced. Smiling, Marta told the child that her minor accident was worth every bit of the pain.

Finding Faye

~

Mira's favorite new neighbor was a kind and jovial, sixty-year-old woman named Teresa Tierney. Mrs. Tierney's husband died of a heart attack in his late forties, and the stout, talkative, Irish born widow had told Mira she had no interest in remarrying. Childless, she kept herself busy by babysitting in her own home for many of the neighborhood children, attracting them with her eclectic collection of pets, which including two hamsters, four parakeets, a dog named FDR.

The first time Mira left Sara and Mickey with Mrs. Tierney, she felt guilty all afternoon and swore to herself she would not tell a soul. But whenever Nathan was away for more than a week, she could hardly bear it. She hated herself for arguing with him when he called to say he'd be gone for the weekend, but since they'd moved to Meroke Shores, she saw her family less and less. Sometimes she would pile the kids in the car and drive to Brooklyn but ever since JJ died, the house on Avenue T was steeped in a dreary sadness that permeated the walls, the furniture, even the interior lighting, which now somehow appeared dimmer. Aunt Rena hardly glanced at the children anymore, and Momma and Poppa often acted annoyed at the invasion of Mira's growing noisy brood or maybe this was all in her mind. Her loneliness caused her to doubt what she once took for granted. She felt more vulnerable, and her emotions were like the parachute jump at Coney Island—either up, up, up or spiraling way, way down.

Sometimes she wondered whether or not she was a good mother. Just the other night, she had let the baby cry for nearly fifteen minutes before pulling herself out of bed to warm a bottle. Finally, when she went to him, she kissed his soaking wet face until she felt out of breath. Mira tried to convince herself it would be good for the twins to spend some time with Mrs. Tierney. Perhaps, they, too, needed a change of pace. And, as if sensing Mira's vulnerability, they always acted up whenever Nathan was on the road.

So, one afternoon, without thinking much about it beforehand, she dropped off the children, warning them to behave, and she and the baby headed for a neighboring town, Centerville, about twenty minutes away. Supposedly this was the ideal place for shopping and she needed to buy a dress for Uncle Louie's wedding with the tall and slinky model, Gloria.

She had searched all the local newspapers and found an ad for a fashion boutique: L'Elegance. She was drawn to the ad, a woman's curvy torso that reminded her of the old days back at the Rockefeller Institute, the days when dreams were so big and colorful they kept her up all night. Something tugged at her heart now, a feeling she'd noticed often since giving birth again, made more intense by JJ's death. She realized that although Nathan had finished his tour of duty early, cut short by his mother's failing health and Poppa's few remaining strings with draft boards, she felt the same heavy loneliness since he returned home and the war ended. But not really home she told herself. Home, but not here. She had enough to keep herself busy, three children under the age of three, a new home, a weary husband, but keeping busy wasn't enough. She didn't want to spend each and every day robotized; she craved the unexpected, but only, of course, if everyone remained well and thriving. And then like an electric jolt, came a new surge of guilt and the "how dare you, Mira" she imposed upon herself for even imagining a less conventional existence.

As if on cue, Rosh let out a cat-like howl from his car bed that Mira had tied carefully to a window handle. She would feed him in the car before her shopping, that way she knew he'd be a satisfied little Buddha, if only for an hour or two.

This town seemed a lot more bustling than sleepy Meroke Shores.

Everywhere Mira looked there was new construction in progress, signs that forecasted a new French bakery, a hair salon, and a toy store. Nathan had told Mira that the further from the city they were, the cheaper the real estate. She hoped one day her little town would have its own library where she could take the children on Saturdays, and a movie theatre for special dates with Nathan. It wasn't that long ago that the two of them had parked along the water's edge near Coney Island looking at the Steeplechase in the distance. She remembered how the car windows had fogged from their kissing, and the only remaining light was Nathan's cigarette shrinking in the ashtray.

Now, almost four years later, Mira glanced at herself in the visor. She turned off the ignition and applied a fresh coat of Revlon's Cherries in the Snow—Momma's favorite lipstick and now hers. Parked just a few doors from L'Elegance, she noticed a pink plaster façade and intricate white fencing with ivy leading into the store. Very theatrical, Mira thought for a Long Island suburb, but why not? Her days of running around Best and Co. or Macy's were definitely on hold. After feeding and diapering the baby in the backseat, Mira wrapped him in a warm woolen blanket and put him back in the car bed that converted into a carriage—one of her favorite and most expensive baby gifts from Momma's Mah Jong friends.

As expected, Rosh squinted at the bright sunlight then quickly fell into a satisfied trance alongside his furry, toy monkey.

Mira pushed through the double glass doors setting off a cacophony of chimes. The boutique smelled of a light floral fragrance, something springy and young. Had she worn this once? Had one of her Aunts? She would ask the saleswoman as soon as she saw her. The shop was quiet now, the chimes fading behind her baby's breathing.

"I'll be with you in a moment," someone yelled out from behind a lacy white curtain. "I'm just finishing with the UPS man. Ha, oh my, I hope you know what I mean."

Mira moved closer so that her body skimmed the sheer fabric of the curtain. "Could it be?" she asked aloud, and then answered herself in the negative. Embarrassed that perhaps there might have been more going on behind the curtain, Mira began looking through a rack of cocktail dresses. They were all strikingly beautiful, very unique and well-priced for the obvious quality. As Mira glanced back toward the curtain, Faye, a pair of tortoise spectacles perched on her nose, her red hair loose and curly flowing behind her shoulders, made an exuberant entrance that Mira would remember for the rest of her life.

As the sun dipped behind the lace curtains, and the sky took on a texture of crushed velvet, the two friends chatted as if they'd never been apart. Mira called Mrs. Tierney to say she'd be later than expected, and asked if she would mind giving the twin's their dinner. Gracious, as always, her neighbor told her not to worry, almost insisting that Mira have a good time.

Did it show, Mira wondered after hanging up, did everyone surmise that she was starving for something much more than motherhood and domestic bliss?

Faye sat forward in an overstuffed Bergére chair with Mira's Rosh, who gurgled happily in her lap. She waved her colorful scarf in the baby's face, and he looked mesmerized by the stranger with the infectious laugh and searching eyes.

"Did you ever consider calling me? You know I wouldn't have judged you. You took a big risk by going out there in the first place." Mira took a sip of the tea Faye had poured for them after officially closing the shop precisely at 5 PM.

"I thought of contacting you, really Mira, but there were other things that were too embarrassing. Once I waited and six months had passed, well, I started a whole new life, and it became easier to put everything behind me."

"You did send me a few letters from the coast; you sounded happy and very busy. Truthfully, I became awfully envious at times."

"Believe me, you would not have envied what it was really like to work in one of those Hollywood studios. You know I was never great following conventional ideas . . . "

"Oh, do I ever."

"Well, when the prima donnas got one look at me, they complained to the head designers to try and tone me down. Honestly, I don't know how I lasted as long as I did."

"And L'Elegance? Please don't mind my asking, but it couldn't have been easy going into retail, especially with a war raging?"

Faye held Rosh against her shoulder and patted his little back. Tears brimmed in her eyes.

"I did have a life for a very short while. There was this really nice guy, sweet as hell, from Seattle. We were married in '43 while he was on leave. Six months later, there was that dreaded knock at the door. He was declared MIA."

Mira leaned in closer and stroked Faye's arm.

"I'm terribly sorry, Faye. I wish I'd been there for you. No one should have to go through that kind of loss alone."

"Well, you asked about the store, and Jimmy, that was his name, had put away every penny he earned for our future—our baby, as he said."

Rosh sneezed and the initial tension dispersed into warm smiles. The two made plans to see each other again, and later when she walked her to the car, Faye wrapped her arm around Mira's waist and said, "now that we've found each other, we have to move forward together. I believe it was meant to be. How do you say it? *Berchert*?"

"Yes, that's it, fate. Well, of course, I want you to come visit us, have dinner. I know Nathan will be thrilled."

"Mira, that's not what I mean," Faye said. She held the car door for Mira as she placed Rosh safely in his car bed before sliding behind the wheel. "I want us to work together like we'd always planned. Screw Hollywood, who needs them? Towns like this are popping up all over the place, and that means women, and that means business. I need a partner and that partner has to be you!"

"But Faye, do you realize I have *three* small children?"

"Oh, that, well, we can figure something out. Isn't that what we creative types are supposed to do?"

"You know what I've always loved about you Faye?"

"Go ahead, I'm all ears."

"You make what feels nearly impossible seem like cake."

Mira kept the radio off the entire way home. Instead, she listened to the music inside her head, an intrusive beat that just wouldn't stop—a jazz quartet shaking her up and telling her: yes, yes, yes, in a variety of chords and rhythms. She knew what she had to do. First, she had to truly believe she deserved this, and then give herself the permission to go forward, to go as far as she wanted to go.

A Sunday in May

~

Charlie called the family together on the pretense he had an important announcement to make. And, it was only after hearing the words flow from his own lips that he would actually begin to think about selling the house on Avenue T and moving to Miami. He pictured the brochures he'd received advertising a relaxed, yet active, lifestyle, and now circumstances made the once fleeting projection seem more than feasible.

Ina pleaded with him not to tell the children about her illness, and he agreed that talking about her declining health might deter any chances for improvement. She was constantly in pain because of her arthritic spine, which the doctor said was worsened by the frigid weather of the northeast. So, Charlie began implementing a six-month plan. Within this time slot, he would find a buyer for the house, investigate the real estate market in Florida, and make sure everyone else was settled in their lives. Mira and Nathan had certainly made a wise choice in buying a home in the suburbs, although the budding tension between the young couple worried him. And of course, this worried Ina even more.

Charlie was convinced that Mira's going back to work would make things worse for the two, not better. Nathan had more than hinted that he thought Mira had made a hasty and thoughtless decision. With him traveling so much, he believed their children should have at least one parent available at all times. Charlie, himself, had shunned the idea of his wife ever working, and would have felt it a personal embarrassment among his friends. He automatically sympathized with his son-in-law's sometimes cool, almost punishing detachment. But Charlie could not deny the fact of his daughter's exceptional talent, how she had sacrificed her childhood dream because of his desire for familial cohesiveness.

With all his lamenting, kvetching, and stubborn indignation, inside him was a core stronger than steel—indestructible and evidence of all the struggles that had come before.

Charlie understood that retirement meant letting go, giving up the role he loved, the one that fit him better than any Hart, Shaffner, and Marx he had ever worn on his stubborn old back. But it was the circumstances surrounding his sister's sad departure that had finally chipped away at his strength and robbed him of his will to fight. No more "dukes up" for Charlie Kaninsky. Even an old bastard like him was capable of a reluctant, yet necessary, transformation.

*

Charlie stood on the porch watching as Mira and Nathan pulled into the driveway, followed, seconds later, by Roy and his unruly brood. Ina breathed a raspy sigh trying to stand from the metal rocker. Charlie knew Ina was rarely thrilled when the "kids" were coming to visit them. She was afraid to show any joy, in case, God forbid, something happened to them during the two hour trek, which on Sundays became this steady migration of grandparents driving to see children and vice versa, causing major traffic jams on poorly paved roads. He took Ina's hand and helped her down the steps where both cars were now parked a little too close to his precious Caddy. He pointed this out to Roy the instant his son stepped from his Ford.

"What, you wanted maybe to sleep in my backseat? Move that jalopy a foot or two, please."

"Sure, Pop. Hold your water."

After a quick wave of his hand, Nathan opened the back door for Mickey and Sari, who ran, as if racing, to greet their grandparents. Mira had dressed her twins in matching navy cardigans and white shorts, even though there was a chill in the air on this Sunday afternoon in early May—Mother's Day.

Mira stepped from the car, cautiously, cradling Rosh in her arms. As usual the baby had fallen asleep the second Nathan turned the key in the ignition. She and Nathan had thought it amazing how this little one could sleep through anything, the twins being warned or scolded, someone always crying. It was Rosh's demeanor that had made it easier for Mira to leave the children a few days a week, and Mrs. Tierney had made it more comfortable by babysitting in Mira's home. The entire adventure was all very new, and Mira had said she was determined to give designing another real try. The opportunity had risen purely out of fate, and she was much too superstitious to turn away the chance to follow her childhood fantasy. Faye's generous offer had included enough money to cover child care, and for now that was all Mira needed. She was not abandoning her children, nor had she caused any financial strain on Nathan, issues that would have made her quickly decline.

So today, Mira would celebrate *her* Mother's day dressed in her very first design for L'Elegance: an aqua knit skirt and matching sweater with white lace trim. The yarns were all synthetic and inexpensive, and she was delighted to have the opportunity to buy the piece goods from her father, someone who now needed her business. Mira's folks had not yet seen this finished garment, only sketches, and after pecking his daughter on the cheek, Charlie spun her around while Ina applauded.

Then, as her eyes scanned the surroundings, Mira was struck with the nagging feeling that something was missing. She tried stuffing the feeling down, but it wagged in her face like the long branches of a weeping willow. All around were the signs of JJ's talents and love of this house: the crisp chintz fabrics welcoming the warmer weather, the sheer, lacey curtains framing the rows of windows behind them. Mira swallowed hard, missing JJ, missing what she had once promised to never take for granted.

It was almost lunchtime, and once everyone had settled on the array of rockers and chaises, it was Charlie who went in to check on how Rena and Hattie were progressing. This Mother's Day spread, like many, consisted of a smorgasbord of smoked fish, salmon, and pickled herring. Cool borscht brimmed the tops of two glass pitchers—tiny islands of sour cream afloat in each. Rolls and assorted bagels were arranged in a basket, and condiments of butter and cheeses sat in an ice chilled bowl. Yet, today, Charlie's mouth did not water at the anticipation of feasting on lunch; instead it had gone completely dry. All at once, he doubted his decision—this decision of surprise. Hadn't there been enough surprises in the last few years? Yet, when he looked out the kitchen windows and saw his grandchildren enjoying the see-saw he had gotten them, he hoped that only joy might infuse the years that lay ahead. Changes would come, losses too, but something else was about to step through the heavy velvet curtain of darkness to enter their unsuspecting lives.

Charlie gulped down seltzer, then belched out his nervousness. Rena shot him the expected sisterly frown. He noticed how Rena, quieter than usual, was able to thoroughly lose herself in the food preparation, as though they were expecting the President, or first lady, Eleanor, who they liked a great deal more. Rena handed Charlie the basket of bagels and asked him to find some portable trays for their front porch luncheon. He guessed she was trying to stop him from loitering in the kitchen. In recent weeks he'd listened to his sister complain way more than usual. Rena had said she felt smothered by, not just him, but by the entire family. And then, one night, in the middle of dinner, she announced she was moving into her own apartment. She told her brothers she thought that once she was living on her own, Fritzi, who she'd seen steadily since Mira's wedding, would finally find the courage and confess his true feelings. Charlie was afraid to tell her he believed the real problem lay with Fritzi's mother with whom the bachelor had resided for the last twenty years.

"The trays are nowhere to be found," Charlie said.

"Well then, look harder," Rena answered. "Here, first try one of these," and she handed Charlie a sampling fresh out of the oven, from a batch of JJ's recipe for apricot-walnut rugelach. He tasted one and shook his head, *No*. It was obvious. Rena had forgotten to add the walnuts—something JJ would never have done because she always laid out the ingredients into small glass bowls beforehand.

Charlie moved in and gave his sister a loving squeeze on her shoulder. It was as though they were both locked in the same thoughts. There were too many memories in this house. They had taken their places like the cobwebs hidden beneath the sconces, the alcoves, the Spanish tiled-ceilings, each brick and mortar. Every square foot seemed to reverberate with the laughter and tears of such a complicated past. It was time for a change. But first, lunch.

*

There was no one else Charlie could entrust with this job. This would not be the usual three-hour schlep to the Catskills, plus the necessary nosh and toilet stop at the Red Apple Rest. Maxie's number one client, Charles Kane, had something else in mind for his favorite driver of nearly ten years. Something neither man would ever forget. Since the trip was to be only one way, from Ellis Island to Brooklyn, Maxi asked if he might pick up a few regular customers later that same day. But Charlie made a fast deal with Maxi. There was no way to predict how long it might take to get through immigration. Like it was yesterday, he remembered when he had first stepped onto U.S. soil, nauseous from the endlessly choppy voyage; his body rubbery under soiled clothing. He was a "Kaninsky" then. Young, hopeful, and very much afraid, yet, with Louie at his side, everything seemed easier. He recalled that while he stood in the snaking line of downtrodden travelers, he realized he might never see his mother and father again. Although the thought lasted a few seconds, it made him shudder. He would see them again, but nearly two decades later when he visited Mordecai and urged him to join him in America.

Now, again, he thinks he should have tried harder. Why hadn't he insisted? Not that his brother could have been swayed. Once their child was born, like so many families, his brother had found a way to rationalize his existence in what too soon became a war ravaged country—a place where, week by week, Jews disappeared by thousands. By then, no amount of urging could have altered the course of events. One day, he would tell the child how he had begged her father to come to America. No, instead, he would tell this girl, Rosha

Kaninsky, how proud her father and mother were of their country and all they had built together. Their time in Vilna had indeed counted for something, and she was the legacy of that time, all their hopes, and especially their love.

Standing behind a white pillar and sipping his tea, Charlie now spied on Mira and Nathan, who leaned into one another whispering. Mira used Nathan's hankie to dab tears from her eyes. It was no secret that Nathan wasn't thrilled about his wife going back to work. The Kanes had gotten to know him well in the past five years. He was now one of them, someone who didn't let go of his principles easily. Certainly not as stubborn as Charlie, but still, a man's man, who wore his pride and disapproval in the way he carried himself, how he folded his arms tightly to his chest, which was how he sat now listening to Mira. Slowly though, Nathan's shoulders seemed to sink and soften, and his face moved in toward hers for a light kiss. Mira threw her arms around his neck, concealing a new rush of tears. Those who knew her best would guess she had refused to beg, stating that her returning to work would be better for all of them. She lifted herself from Nathan's embrace, and checked on her baby who was still fast asleep in his carriage. Mickey and Sari guarded the porch steps, each perched on one of the weathered, lion figures at the front entrance.

"Hold on tight," she told Mickey, who yelled giddy-yap with a dizzying abandon. Sari leaned into the lion's etched mane and whispered into the statue's ears. "Are you hungry, Mr. Lion?" Mira laughed—something no one asked a lion, especially while riding side-saddle as her daughter did now, without a care in the world.

A long, black limo pulled directly in front of the house. Mira recognized the car immediately. It was Maxie the taxi, Momma and Poppa's trusty driver to the Catskills. Had they planned a getaway right after Mother's Day? That was doubtful considering her father's laments over money.

The children had never seen a car that long, a car that stretched along the length of the entire sidewalk. Mira took their hands and led them down the steps to get a closer view. She didn't know why her heart was beating so fast, like on those mornings when she used to run frantically across Ocean Parkway to catch her bus.

Standing beside her now, Charlie broke out a fresh cigar, but quickly put it back in his pocket with trembling hands. A new sense of responsibility pressed against his chest and shoulders, but not as if he was facing another burden. Instead, he hoped he would have the chance to make things right, to somehow alter the past. He, too, found himself standing on the sidewalk. A darkened window lowered just inches so that he could see Maxie's eyes, his quick smile, and what might have been a wink. Charlie took the liberty and opened the back door.

Mrs. Kleinholtz, her hair slightly disheveled, dressed in a plain grey housedress, crawled out of her seat with the aid of Charlie's outstretched hand.

"Thank you, thank you," Charlie repeated having not yet laid eyes on the girl.

"My poor husband, I'm afraid, was detained at immigration with an eye infection. But, I didn't want to send the girl alone. Rosha darling, are you ready?"

There was no answer from inside the car, and the name, Rosha, had not traveled up the steps to the porch where the entire family stared with a slightly detached curiosity. Perhaps, this was someone Charlie had known in business or why would one of his workers show up to his house on Mother's Day looking like she hadn't slept in weeks?

It was the child's scrawny legs they spotted first. Were those boy's boots she wore, laced up to her shins? Her scraped knees peeked below a short navy skirt, paired with a pink crocheted sweater. Then came her face, a face so familiar that for a few seconds the slight afternoon breeze ceased. It was as if they were watching the same movie, and now a frame was stuck, stuck on the face and body and feet of a character that had lived in their dreams for nearly five years.

Charlie, not overly affectionate with his own grandchildren, lifted the child off her feet and pressed his lips to the side of her small angular face. He didn't seem to mind that her long braid bopped him in the nose. He studied her, smelled her, and when sensing the slightest trepidation, he let her slide down his body to the sidewalk where he stood holding her hand.

It was the children who ran to her first. All they could know was that, like them, she was a child, and so she must be terribly important. She must be loved. Everyone spoke their questions to the fragrant springtime air. In slow motion, and like a dream, the film continued. Hands swept up to ruddy cheeks in a stunning recognition, while tears spilled down the front of silk, of wool, and cotton. Tears became their Mother's Day dessert.

"This is Rosha," Charlie said, hoarsely. "There is much to tell, but for now let us rejoice."

Charlie begged Mrs. Kleinholtz and Maxie to stay and have something to eat but Mrs. Kleinholtz declined, saying she did not want to be separated from her husband. Instead, the driver and his passenger took some pastries and fruit for the ride back to the city. Mrs. Kleinholtz hugged Rosha promising she would visit in a few days. Charlie handed Maxi a hundred dollar bill. The man was so grateful he kissed Charlie smack on the mouth.

All this time, Rena had been making multiple trips back and forth from the kitchen, carrying the food. Fastidious, as always, she was most likely avoiding the onslaught of giant ants that had already coated the Peonies out back. She and JJ had always hated bugs. On her last trip, Rena broke out of her daydreaming, and joined the entire family linked like a chain fence on the sidewalk. The black limo had already pulled away.

Rena suddenly dropped the tray she was holding. Cake and cookies flew everywhere and ants of all shapes and sizes crawled in for the feast. Those on the sidewalk turned to gaze at her. She looked as though she was counting the heads of her nieces and nephews, Roy's two, and Mira's three. And now there was this taller girl, so pale, with a cherubic face she could not place.

The neighbor's children were all dark, the Syrians that Charlie had hardly spoken to in all the years they lived next door. The flash of a dream filled her head. For a second, she looked frightened, as if she had seen a ghost—some apparition of her sister. In the dream they are walking toward one another from across a field filled with wild flowers. They are playing their favorite game. It is a staring contest in which they must keep from making the slightest sound. As they get closer and closer to one another, they struggle not to laugh out loud.

The first one who does, loses. As always, it is JJ who breaks into a hearty giggle. So it is Rena who wins the game.

Hattie kneeled to pick up the pieces of the broken tray. She mumbled words reminiscent of a sacred prayer, while the child wearing boy's boots moved easily into Rena's open arms. Their recognition was swift and mutual. And for the first time, in such a very long time, Rena Kaninsky allowed herself to cry.

Questions for Discussion

1. In the first chapter of The Sweetness we are introduced to young Rosha who sees signs of impending doom. What were some of the early hints things were about to change for her family? How does the child display her fears?

2. When we meet Mira for the first time, she, too, exhibits a sense of anxiety and yet she is focused on her fashion designs and career. Is this how she deals with her concerns?

3. Charlie Kane's survivor guilt is an ongoing theme in The Sweetness. How would you describe his character, and what, besides his guilt, do you think drove him to make many of his decisions?

4. How would you compare Avram Juraska to Charlie Kane? As fathers and husbands, how are they alike and dissimilar?

5. There's a quote from the Talmud that says: when you save one life, it is as though you have saved the entire world. What do you think creates that the kind of selflessness as shown by Marta, the candle maker? Do you believe there are people like her in the world today? Does she remind you of other literary characters?

6. Each immigrant experience is uniquely different and yet when it comes to the younger generation and first generation Americans, often the struggles are similar. Do you think this is a problem in families today, and where do you see this most prevalent?

7. Practically all of the women in The Sweetness go through tremendous upheaval and change. Who was your favorite female character and why?

8. Discuss the culmination of Mira's and Rosha's journey. What do you envision for their future? What would you like to see happen?

Acknowledgments

There were always stories, whispers and tears, and though I didn't understand the funny language they spoke, I leaned into doorways to learn more. And so, to those I once cherished, who no longer speak in hushed tones, I am forever grateful to you for sharing the richness of your heritage, even what was never intended for little ears. I love you and miss you every day.

Special thanks to my mentors and encouraging teachers who made me believe I actually had something interesting to say, urging me to focus on those particular tales most dear to me. I can still recall the inspiring words of my college professor, the late Harry Bloom, who read my short story aloud, and years later, the warm generosity of Frank McCourt. Thank you to a most inspiring faculty and student body at Stony Brook Southampton College's M.F.A. program, especially writer/editor/professor, Lou Ann Walker whose encouragement and support made this book possible. My deep gratitude to Robert Reeves for creating a stellar writing program and unique setting to write, learn, and thrive, so close to home. And to the talented writers who became each summer like a family... Meg, Matt, Melissa, and Roger. Thank you for your warm humor and true inspiration. And I am so grateful to author Hilma Wolitzer for her willingness to read and offer encouragement.

To those special few whose love, friendship, and wisdom showed no boundaries when advising me with this story: writers Beth Schorr

Jaffe and Elizabeth McCourt; I could not have done this without your incredible support. Thank you also to Carole Gaunt and Bridget Casey, members of a much cherished writing group in Manhattan, and to the brilliant poet and editor, David Groff, for allowing me to kvetch at all hours.

To my immensely dedicated publisher, Brooke Warner, and the grand team at She Writes Press, thank you for all your hard work, patience, and belief in this book. And to an incredible editor, Krista Lyons, who looked through the same glass window and took special care of my characters, a huge thank you.

Gratitude always to my amazing daughters, Bari Siegel and Jennifer Goodman, who bear witness to my love of writing, and have always been terrific supporters. And last, but always first, my husband, Steve—my first reader, whose pride and belief in me has made everything possible.

About the Author

©Richard Lewin

After nearly two decades as a scriptwriter and video producer for Fortune 500 companies, Sande Boritz Berger returned to her first passion: writing fiction and non-fiction full time. She completed an MFA in Writing and Literature at Stony Brook Southampton College where she was awarded The Deborah Hecht Memorial prize for fiction. Essays and short stories have appeared in over 20 anthologies including Aunties: "Thirty-Five Writers Celebrate Their Other Mother" by Ballantine, and "Ophelia's Mom" by Crown. Her novel, *The Sweetness*, was a semi-finalist in Amazon's yearly Breakthrough Novel Awards. Sande lives in Manhattan with her husband and has two daughters.

Please visit her blog and website at www.sandeboritzberger.com

Selected Titles from She Writes Press

She Writes Press is an independent publishing company
founded to serve women writers everywhere.
Visit us at www.shewritespress.com.

All the Light There Was by Nancy Kricorian
$16.95, 978-1-63152-905-4
A lyrical, finely wrought tale of loyalty, love, and the many faces of resistance, told from the perspective of an Armenian girl living in Paris during the Nazi occupation of the 1940s.

The Belief in Angels by J. Dylan Yates
$16.95, 978-1-938314-64-3
From the Majdonek death camp to a volatile hippie household on the East Coast, this narrative of tragedy, survival, and hope spans more than fifty years, from the 1920s to the 1970s.

Portrait of a Woman in White by Susan Winkler
$16.95, 978-1-938314-83-4
When the Nazis steal a Matisse portrait from the eccentric, art-loving Rosenswigs, the Parisian family is thrust into the tumult of war and separation, their fates intertwined with that of their beloved portrait.

Faint Promise of Rain by Anjali Mitter Duva
$16.95, 978-1-938314-97-1
Adhira, a young girl born to a family of Hindu temple dancers, is raised to be dutiful—but ultimately, as the world around her changes, it is her own bold choice that will determine the fate of her family and of their tradition.

Bittersweet Manor by Tory McCagg
$16.95, 978-1-938314-56-8
A chronicle of three generations of love, manipulation, entitlement, and disappointed expectations in an upper-middle class New England family.

A Cup of Redemption by Carole Bumpus
$16.95, 978-1-938314-90-2
Three women, each with their own secrets and shames, seek to make peace with their pasts and carve out new identities for themselves.

CPSIA information can be obtained at www.ICGtesting.com
Printed in the USA
BVOW02s1344260115

385006BV00001B/1/P